P9-ARS-028

VIDEO PALACE
IN SEARCH OF THE EYELESS MAN

VIDEO PALACE

IN SEARCH OF THE EYELESS MAN

collected stories

SOURCE ▶ DR. MAYNARD WILLS

EDITED BY NICK BRACCIA AND MICHAEL MONELLO

TILLER PRESS

New York   London   Toronto   Sydney   New Delhi

TILLER PRESS

An Imprint of Simon & Schuster, Inc.
1230 Avenue of the Americas
New York, NY 10020

Copyright © 2020 by Menace & Woe, LLC
Courtesy of Digital Store LLC

All rights reserved, including the right to reproduce this book or portions thereof in any form whatsoever. For information, address Simon & Schuster Subsidiary Rights Department, 1230 Avenue of the Americas, New York, NY 10020.

First Tiller Press hardcover edition October 2020.

This book is a work of fiction. Any references to historical events, real people, or real places are used fictitiously. Other names, characters, places, and events are products of the authors' imagination, and any resemblance to actual events or places or persons, living or dead, is entirely coincidental.

TILLER PRESS and colophon are trademarks of Simon & Schuster, Inc.

For information about special discounts for bulk purchases, please contact Simon & Schuster Special Sales at 1-866-506-1949 or business@simonandschuster.com.

The Simon & Schuster Speakers Bureau can bring authors to your live event. For more information or to book an event, contact the Simon & Schuster Speakers Bureau at 1-866-248-3049 or visit our website at www.simonspeakers.com.

Interior design by Davina Mock-Maniscalco
White Noise Texture by pashabo/Shutterstock

Manufactured in the United States of America

1   3   5   7   9   10   8   6   4   2

Library of Congress Cataloging-in-Publication Data has been applied for.

ISBN 978-1-9821-5644-2
ISBN 978-1-9821-5649-7 (ebook)

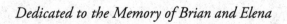

Dedicated to the Memory of Brian and Elena

CONTENTS

CONTENTS

PREFACE

My name is Daniel Carter. I'm a graduate student at the New School in New York City, where I have studied folklore and mythology under my mentor, Professor Maynard Wills. I have been employed as his teaching assistant since 2016. Some readers, especially those who have an affinity for urban legends (and the more remote corners of the Internet), may know his name; you'd most certainly recognize his various online pseudonyms. If you've come across a surprisingly erudite post about Ogopogo's influence on British Columbia's economy or correlations between chupacabra sightings and livestock pandemics, it's probably Maynard undercover, tapping away at the witching hour, a frosty mug of A&W and his cat, Baba Yaga, his only companions.

I only wish he were still able to enjoy these indulgences.

Professor Wills became a near-mythic figure himself, at least in the field of folklore and urban legend. Yes, plenty of tenured academics hold up their nose at Maynard and belittle his niche arena of expertise. To a fellow folklorist and obsessive like me, though, he's a hero. He taught me that by tracking our monsters we can learn so much more about our own nature. I'm proud to say that my association with Professor Wills remains my most gratifying academic and professional accomplishment. You can only imagine my horror when I, his most faithful pupil, set him down the path that has cost him his sanity at best and, perhaps, his life.

This book and Professor Wills's tragedy share an impetus, and I alone shoulder the blame for it. You see, I introduced Maynard to *Video Palace*, a podcast I heard on the streaming platform Shudder. *Video Palace* is hosted by a young man named Mark Cambria, who became obsessed with a series of white VHS tapes filled with inscrutable avant-garde footage. Cambria's inquiry into their peculiar features and enigmatic origin led him and his girlfriend, Tamra Wulff, on a harrowing journey from New York City to New England and back. Their experience was disconcerting, filled with threats, injury and worse. A mythic figure loomed at the center of this story. A figure Maynard has tracked for years: the Eyeless Man. This book, likely Maynard's last work, is dedicated to this phantom's place in culture, folklore and now our lives. I want to clearly establish that I wish I'd never shared *Video Palace* with Professor Wills. That I did so with such enthusiasm only adds to my guilt and my grief. If you choose to listen to *Video Palace*, it might help contextualize aspects of this book, but I cannot promise that you won't have an adverse reaction. Its story has a way of burrowing into the skin before moving on to corrupt the heart and infect the brain.

I have done my best to assemble this volume based on the professor's notes. His vision was to juxtapose his quest for the cultural origin of the Eyeless Man with fascinating stories, either experienced by the author, acquired secondhand or heard around the campfire. He wanted to show the pervasiveness of the Eyeless Man figure across cultures, and I believe the contributors he's enlisted soundly prove his point. I'm grateful for the helpful emails and the chats I've had with the talented writers who shared these personal stories. For all the hours he spends in his library, Professor Wills is, like most champion storytellers, quite an extrovert. And so, he made friends across the movie and publishing industries. When he put out the call, many answered. Despite my sadness, I am grateful for that.

It's my responsibility to represent this collection as I believe Professor Wills would have wanted it. I chose to embrace this burden, no matter the cost. As I write this preface, I pray that the book's publication brings us answers. I'm just not sure where exactly to direct these prayers.

For you, dear reader, I hope the stories and interludes within these pages deliver wisdom and inspire insights. Perhaps they will open your eyes as they did mine. Though I feel obligated to warn you: you may not like what you see.

Please note that, periodically, I interject with my own observations, discoveries and hypotheses, all composed as Professor Wills began to slip away.

—Daniel Carter

DR. MAYNARD WILLS: AN ORIGIN STORY

I grew up in a tiny Maine community tucked into Marsh Island's eastern edge. It's called Old Town, and old it is, at least by America's standards. It was settled a couple of years before Hancock dipped the quill that birthed an idiom, and it became a township well before the Southern secession.

Old Town in the 1950s was a nice enough place for a child, but among the Eisenhower normalcy (excepting the duck-and-cover drills), I longed for a taste of the extraordinary. Not so unusual, I know, but my ears pricked up at the mention of anything, well, *strange*, especially in our little corner of the world. The Monster of Pocomoonshine Lake just two hours' drive! The Lost Settlers of Norumbega buried right under our feet! I'd loiter around the pharmacy—whether I had the pocket change for a Coke float or not—waiting for the older boys to quit their chatter about girls and pester the soda jerk for twice- and thrice-told folktales, both weird and woeful.

My grandfather, who taught classes a short bike ride away at the University of Maine, recognized this fire inside me and decided to fan the flames. We saw many Saturday monster movie matinees, but he supplemented low culture with high and gifted me Edith Hamilton's *Mythology* (superior to that crusty old prig, Bulfinch). My world expanded—exploded!—beyond the parochial scope of soda fountain banter. I became lost in boundless stories that transcended space and time, Heaven and Earth.

I was fascinated by the gods and their dramas. Love! Scorn! Revenge! Death! (It's no wonder that soap operas and the fine art of professional wrestling later became part of my media diet. Laugh all you want, but they teach this stuff at MIT!)

But my absolute favorite episode concerned mortals: the tragedy of Orpheus and Eurydice. You know the story: Orpheus braves the Underworld to rescue his love, Eurydice, only to turn back and look at her at the last moment, condemning her for eternity. It's been told by Virgil, Ovid and Boethius. Countless others. Adapted by Cocteau. Hell, I think Guillermo del Toro even alludes to it in *Blade II*. While I love the bones of the myth, all these tellers have their own twists, their own subtext. Each molded the myth as the story exchanged hands and evolved over epochs. Myths live in a thousand forms; they are organisms of multiplicity.

I sit today at my—extremely—cluttered desk in a shared adjunct office in Manhattan, unsure if I should splurge on a sandwich at Lenny's but exceedingly grateful that I found my purpose at such a young age. The streets of Greenwich Village certainly are a far cry from Old Town, where I'd spent countless hours wandering the vast, verdant expanse glimpsing (or so I thought) trolls, goblins and fairies wandering the same woods, peeking behind branches and sneering from inside rotted trees.

You can probably already sense that I don't really fancy myself an "academic." I don't have much patience for literary theory and get tied in knots trying to grok the postmodernists. Instead, I think of myself as a story detective. Or maybe a narrative archaeologist? Choose whichever metaphor you like. Both suggest I get a cool-looking hat, so I'm good either way.

It was in the mid-sixties—during my high school years—that my professional identity began to form. *The Epic of Gilgamesh* was on our syllabus and, as you probably remember, the poem includes a great Mesopotamian flood that's caused by wrathful gods. My teacher, a wise and patient man named Harlowe, asked the class: Is there another ancient text where we hear about a massive flood? I raised my hand and gasped as I gave the correct answer, the Bible. It was a eureka moment for me—the realization that two separate works of the Old World mentioned a great flood and the implication that perhaps the flood, in some sense, was a historical event in our world's ancient past that had birthed a multitude of stories.

As much as I loved old man Harlowe, I skipped quite a bit of school so I could hoof (or bike) over to the University of Maine and sneak into the library, where I'd grab a pile of dusty tomes and trace myths and legends across cultures. Then I'd go home and plot their origins and influences on my corkboard like some crazed FBI pro-filer. (It's worth noting that at exactly this time Maine's favorite son, a young Steve King, was studying at U of M. If we ever crossed paths in the library, I didn't notice. I was too busy hunting monsters, though I like to think we probably cursed each other over borrowed volumes.) Harlowe caught me in there once, on a Saturday, and smiled. I think he understood my absences. I detected a sense of pride.

Now that you know who I am and, well, *my* origin story, we can discuss my nemesis: the Eyeless Man.

For decades, I have pursued myriad pet projects. Most bring me immense joy, but the Eyeless Man is a source of torment. I have tracked and traced his presence across continents and cultures from the birth of the Atomic Age through today's digital deluge. He is a shadow, an elusive bogeyman. His story fragments don't fit patterns as neatly as I'd like and whispers of his name seem to evaporate before I can form any hypothesis with solid footing. I've discussed him with like-minded friends—some who have contributed to this volume—but I was ultimately confounded. He was too slippery a phantom, and I was prepared to stuff the bastard in a drawer and be done with him.

And then my teaching assistant, Daniel Carter, told me about *Video Palace*.

I believe that Mark Cambria and Tamra Wulff lived a version of the myth. What's true and untrue, I don't know. Where Mark Cambria is, I have no idea. But I'd like to find out as this legend is birthed in real time.

This book has two tracts. I have extended an invitation to my fellow folklore and urban legend enthusiasts. There are writers, filmmakers and academics among them. And they have either heard campfire tales of the Eyeless Man or know someone who has felt his presence. In some cases, the connection is quite personal. They share their stories in these pages. As they do, you will learn more and more about the Eyeless Man, just as I have.

Between these stories, I will provide interludes that chronicle my search for the origin of this legend, an entity that breeds terror. I'm not afraid, for every story has its beginning, and once I find it, we, my friends, will control its power.

Let us begin.

DOORWAYS OF
THE SOUL

Owl Goingback

5

I don't like talking about the Eyeless Man. Just saying his name out loud gives me the willies, makes me lock the doors and spend the night looking over my shoulder. And I've been writing horror novels for over twenty years, researching all kinds of spooky stuff to put into my stories. I should be immune to fear and superstitions, but there are some things that give me the creeps and blow icy kisses up and down my spine.

My longtime friend Emma Yellow Hand, a Lakota elder, told me that just saying his name gives the Eyeless Man power, makes him stronger. She also warned me that speaking his name causes him to notice you, makes you stand out like a candle in the dark. I don't know if any of that is true, but it's definitely food for thought.

Many of the traditionals on the Pine Ridge Indian Reservation in South Dakota believe in the Eyeless Man. Stories about him have been passed down orally for decades, long before creepypasta and the Internet even existed. They call him Taku-he, and Walking Sam, a shadow person believed to be responsible for the deaths of many young people.

I guess they need to blame someone, or something, because in the past year over one hundred Lakota teenagers have attempted suicide. Nine of those were successful. Nine young lives cut short, never to experience all the joys, wonders and frustrations the world has to offer. Fucking tragic.

Oddly enough, quite a few young people living on the reservation also believe in the Eyeless Man. They talk about him on Facebook and in chat rooms, sharing stories and videos, voicing their fears, spreading gossip and rumors. Some of those who recently attempted suicide blame Walking Sam, saying he got into their heads via social media, convincing them they were unloved and worthless. Last year twenty Oglala Lakota teenagers answered his siren's call and attempted a mass hanging. They would have been successful if a local pastor hadn't been tipped off and stopped them.

I'm not sure I believe in a suicide god, an evil Pied Piper

that convinces people to end their lives. But Emma believes, and she's not the type to make up stories. She's old-school, a healer and a keeper of tribal knowledge.

Emma told me about what's been happening on Pine Ridge. She also told me about her grandson, the letter he wrote, and the things she found on his computer. She let me listen to what was on the digital recorder he always carried. I made a copy of his audio files, but I rarely listen to them because they scare the hell out of me. Not so much what her grandson says on the recordings but what he captured in the background.

Emma Yellow Hand doesn't want me to go public with what I know about the Eyeless Man; she wants me to keep the information close to heart. But I feel compelled to warn others, so I'm sharing her grandson's story. Like Emma says, there are things out there roaming that no one ever talks about. Doorways are opened all the time, and they are never closed.

—Owl Goingback

"JAIMIE WATERS DIED just two weeks shy of her fourteenth birthday. Her body was discovered along a narrow dirt road on the Pine Ridge Indian Reservation, near the town of Porcupine, a severed noose still tied around her bruised neck.

"No one knows who cut Jaimie down from the tree or why they left her body next to the road. They probably didn't want to get involved with BIA tribal police, or local authorities, but wanted to make sure someone found her body before the vultures and coyotes got to it. Official cause of death was listed as suicide, just another victim of the endless poverty, unemployment, depression and isolation plaguing the third-world environment of the reservation.

"Bullshit. No way Jaimie killed herself." Aaron Looks Twice turned off the tiny voice-activated digital recorder he held in his right hand. The recorder had been a gift from his late mother after he announced he wanted to be a reporter someday, working for *Indian Country Today* or one of the other Indigenous newspapers. He carried the recorder with him everywhere, uploading his monologues into the secondhand desktop computer his mother also bought for him.

He wasn't alone in his opinion about Jaimie's death. Many on the rez thought there was more to her story than a simple suicide. The young girl was the daughter of a tribal chairman, an honor roll student, a Junior Miss Oglala Nation Powwow Princess, and very popular among her peers. She had no reason to take her own life.

Aaron didn't think depression was the cause for Jaimie's suicide. He had experienced depression firsthand after his mother was killed by a drunk driver, had even attempted suicide by slicing his own wrists. Somebody, or something, had messed with Jaimie's head and corrupted her spirit, convincing the teenager to tie a noose around her neck and take a leap into empty space.

Nancy Waters also didn't believe the medical examiner's report about her younger cousin's death. The day after Jaimie's funeral, she showed up at the tiny mobile home Aaron shared with his grandmother. She brought along her cousin's laptop, wanting to search social media for possible clues to her death.

Aaron was more than happy to help Nancy. After all, she had been there for him when he was at his lowest, the two of them actually meeting for the first time in the lobby of the Pine Ridge Indian Health Services Hospital the same night he sliced his wrists. She knew his mother was white and had teased him that cutting his wrists would not rid him of his *wasicu* blood. Her comments made him laugh, despite his pain, and they had been close friends ever since.

Turning on the laptop, they looked through Jaimie's emails and instant messages, searching for evidence that she had been in trouble or had been cyberbullied by other kids. But they found nothing out of the ordinary, mostly just chatter with friends about school and daily life. She was excited about the upcoming powwow, looking forward to wearing her hand-beaded princess regalia. A person that happy does not kill themself.

They checked Facebook next, scrolling through Jaimie's timeline. There were several photos of her taken at school, laughing and goofing around with classmates when the teachers weren't watching. Other photos were taken during picnics, sporting events and when she was out riding horses. She was smiling in all the photos, nothing to indicate she was suffering from depression or having dark thoughts. There were also several links to music videos on her timeline, but the songs were all upbeat and not likely to send a thirteen-year-old spiraling downward into the depths of despair.

Continuing to scroll down the timeline, they came upon a grainy black-and-white photo of a large oak tree standing alone on a hilltop surrounded by endless prairie. Aaron thought it was an old photo from a history book, something taken on the reservation a long time ago. He started to scroll past it, but Nancy pointed at the screen.

"Wait. Stop," she said. "Go back to that picture."

"Why? Did you see something?"

"Maybe. Just go back."

Aaron backed up to the photo. At first, he didn't notice anything remarkable about it, but then he saw what had caught Nancy's attention. Standing at the base of the tree, barely visible in the shadows, was a man. He appeared to be very tall and thin, but it was hard to see him clearly because the photo was dark. He also wore black clothing, making it even harder to see him. The man's face was in profile, his features hidden in the shadows.

The man appeared to be looking up into the tree, at a smaller figure hanging from one of the lower limbs. Though it was also difficult to make out, the second figure appeared to be a girl. She wore a dress, her legs and feet bare, long dark hair hanging down and covering her face.

Nancy pointed at the screen, shocked. "Oh, my god. Is that Jaimie?"

"Can't be. It has to be photoshopped," Aaron replied. "Here. Let me zoom in." He moved the computer's mouse, enlarging the photo. The second figure did look like a young girl hanging from a noose. But if it was Jaimie, then who took the photo, and how had it appeared on her Facebook timeline?

"It's got to be some kind of sick joke," Aaron said, studying the image. "Someone's idea of a prank."

"It's not funny."

"Was Jaimie wearing a dress when they found her?"

"I don't know."

"What about shoes? Was she wearing shoes?"

"I'm not sure. Maybe."

Toward the top of the photo, in the sky just above the oak tree, was a light-colored rectangle about half the size of the tall man. It was probably just a flaw in the digital image, but it looked like a window or open doorway. The rectangle was filled with a random pattern of light and dark pixels, like static on a television screen.

"What's that shape?" Nancy asked, pointing at the rectangle.

"I'm not sure. Probably just a glitch in the image. But I want to make a copy of this photo for the police. It might be important. If it's legit, then maybe they can figure out who cut your cousin down and put her body by the side of the road."

"Maybe it's the same guy in the photo."

"It's possible. But I wonder who took a picture of him?"

Below the photo, Jaimie had typed the phrase *Ota Keta*.

Nancy said the words aloud. "Ota Keta. What does that mean?"

"I don't know," Aaron replied.

"Is it Lakota?"

He shrugged. "I'm not sure. Maybe."

Neither Aaron nor Nancy were fluent in the Lakota dialect. Many young people spoke very little of their Indigenous language, a result of their parents, and grandparents, spending years in government-run Indian boarding schools where they had been punished for speaking their native tongue. Those who survived the ordeal of boarding school life either forgot how to speak Lakota or refused to teach their children for fear they too would be punished.

"The phrase seems familiar; I think I've heard it before."

"Where?" Nancy asked.

He shook his head. "I can't remember. Maybe I heard one of Grandma Emma's friends say it. Her Bingo buddies from Kyle and Oglala rarely speak English when they come to the house."

Aaron left-clicked the computer's mouse, sending the photo of the oak tree and the two shadowy figures to a wireless printer across the room. As the printer powered up, it squeaked loudly. Nancy turned to look at the printer and didn't see the image on the computer screen flicker and suddenly enlarge, wasn't watching as the tall figure in the photo turned his head toward them. But Aaron was watching, shocked to see the man in the fluttering image move.

"He has no eyes," Aaron whispered under his breath, stunned by what he saw. The man in the photo appeared to be eyeless, or at least none could be seen in the grainy image, his face almost entirely featureless.

Moments later, the image distorted, seeming to melt and

burn like a filmstrip negative against a hot projector lamp. The image crumpled, turned brown, and disappeared from Jaimie's timeline as if it had never been there at all.

Aaron crossed the room, grabbing the paper off his printer. The wireless signal had been sent before the image disappeared, but the printout was different from what they had seen on the computer screen. The tree and the valley beyond it were still there, a length of rope hanging from a lower limb, but the Eyeless Man, Jaimie, and the odd rectangle of light were no longer in the image.

"What the hell?" Aaron stared at the photo. "They're gone."

"What do you mean, they're gone? Let me see." Nancy took the photo from him. "I don't understand. How could they just vanish? It doesn't make sense."

"Doesn't make sense to me either." He turned to look at Jaimie's computer, but the image was no longer there. Maybe the person who posted it on the timeline had decided to remove it.

Nancy looked down at the printed photo. "The rope is still in the picture. This could be the same tree where Jaimie hung herself. The rope could be important."

Aaron nodded. "We need to find that tree."

The following morning, Aaron and Nancy borrowed horses from a neighbor and set out to find the tree in the photo. They spent most of the day searching and were about to give it up as a lost cause; the Pine Ridge Indian Reservation covered over three thousand square miles on the southern tip of the badlands. They assumed the tree would be close to Jaimie's house, but the truth was it could be anywhere. They had just turned around to head back when Nancy spotted the tree in the distance, a severed piece of rope still hanging from a lower limb.

Galloping their horses across open grasslands and up a hill, they dismounted, and Aaron climbed the tree and retrieved the rope. Back on the ground, he and Nancy pondered the mystery of Jaimie's suicide. Why had she done it, and who had cut her down? Had the person who cut the rope, and left the teenager by the road, also assisted in the suicide? That would explain why they hadn't taken the body to the police. Maybe Jaimie's assistant had also taken the photograph.

"Do you think the police can get DNA off this rope?" Nancy asked innocently. "Maybe they can find out if this is the rope Jaimie used to hang herself, and who cut her down."

Aaron laughed, but his smile quickly disappeared when Nancy gave him a sharp look. "Let's hope they don't get any DNA off this rope, seeing how we both just handled it. But if it is the rope she used, they'll be able to match it to the piece found tied around her neck. I'd be willing to bet—"

He was interrupted by an ominous chittering in the tall grasses that surrounded the hill. The sound rose and fell, rose and fell, stopped, and then started again.

"What's that?" Nancy asked, looking around, trying to locate the source of the noise.

"It's nothing," Aaron replied. "Just the wind rustling dried grasses."

She looked up at the leaves of the oak tree above her head.

They were motionless, untouched by even the slightest hint of a breeze. "There's no wind."

"Then it's insects. Grasshoppers. Cicadas, maybe."

The noise grew louder, causing Nancy to take a step closer to him.

"Probably just a prairie dog," Aaron said, looking around.

"Doesn't sound like a prairie dog," she stated.

Nancy was right. It didn't sound like a prairie dog, at least none he had ever heard. They were both familiar with the wildlife that called Pine Ridge home, and this didn't resemble anything Aaron had ever heard before. It seemed menacing, alien.

The noise appeared to be coming from a grove of pine trees, in a valley to the west of the hill. Aaron tried to see if he could spot the source of the noise, but the sun was already starting to set, casting long shadows across the area.

In addition to the chittering, they suddenly heard an odd whistling. It wasn't the joyful harmony of an unseen bird. The recurrent three notes were shrill and grating, setting Aaron's teeth on edge, like fingernails on a chalkboard. He felt a headache quickly forming behind his eyes and knew he would be sick if the piercing noise persisted.

Thinking that the unremitting racket might have been made by a boisterous songbird, Nancy stepped back and looked up into the tree. As she stood there staring, she noticed the air directly above the oak tree begin to ripple like waves of heat over a cooking fire.

The shrill whistling abruptly stopped, leaving behind a strained silence. The sudden quiet was foreboding, causing the hairs on Aaron's arm to stand straight up. He rubbed his forearms and looked around nervously, almost expecting to see someone, or something, sneaking up on them, but all he saw was empty prairie.

"Aaron, look," she said, pointing at the wavering air. Aaron stepped beside her, focusing his attention to where she pointed.

As they watched, the rippling condensed and took on shape, forming into a luminous rectangle a few feet above the top of the tree. The shape was about four feet long and three feet wide, filled with a flickering static.

"It's like in the photo on Jaimie's computer," Nancy said, her voice laced with fear.

"Yeah." Aaron nodded. "But what the hell is it?"

"It looks like television static," she said.

"Maybe it's electrical; maybe somebody is testing something."

"Who?"

"Jesus, I don't know. Maybe the government," Aaron replied, shaking his head. He looked around again, suddenly feeling very vulnerable out in the open. "You know they're always doing things on Indian land without permission. Just look at the bombing range they made back in World War II; they still haven't given back all the land they stole for that. Maybe they're testing some kind of particle weapon."

"You read too much science fiction," Nancy said, mocking him.

"I'm serious. If they are testing something, then it might have an effect on people. That might explain why people's heads are messed up, why kids are killing themselves. Maybe the Eyeless Man stories are just a government cover-up for what is really going on."

"If it is a weapon, then we probably shouldn't be standing here."

They watched as the static within the rectangle slowly faded, replaced by blurry, wavery images of an unfamiliar landscape. The landscape looked dead, haunted, like a nuclear bomb had gone off.

"What is that?"

"It looks like someone is broadcasting a video signal from somewhere."

"But how is it appearing here?" Nancy asked.

"I don't know. Some kind of freak anomaly, I guess," Aaron replied.

"It really is a window to somewhere. Or a doorway."

"Yeah. But to where?"

And in that strange, dead landscape something stirred. Dark shapes could clearly be seen moving in the nuclear barren countryside, but Aaron and Nancy could not tell if they were people, animals or something else entirely. There was something terribly unnerving about the unknown shapes in that rectangle in the sky, and it caused the two teenagers to step closer together, their shoulders touching.

Aaron and Nancy were so captivated by what they saw, they didn't notice a silhouette separate itself from the darkness at the edge of the pine grove in the valley below. Tall and ethereal, the Eyeless Man looked like a being without body or form, fluid as India ink in water, moving freely in the spreading shadows of the approaching dusk, his clothing floating about his body like layers of night.

He looked upon the young people on the hill, seeing them

without the aid of binoculars, glasses, or even eyes, making a peculiar chittering sound that seemed to come from a hollow void deep within him.

Aaron heard the strange chittering and turned to look into the shallow valley beyond the hill. At first, he saw nothing but tall grasses, pine trees, and the lengthening darkness, but then he spotted the wraithlike figure moving their way. The Eyeless Man appeared to glitch in and out of the fading sunlight, like a bad video feed, using the shadows and the darkness for camouflage as he drew closer.

Oh, my god.

And from the spreading night an invisible force seemed to reach out and touch Aaron's mind, caressing his thoughts and subconscious like fluttering moth wings at a lighted window, seeking a way into his brain and maybe even into his soul.

Walking Sam.

Fear stabbed icy fingernails deep into his stomach. He wanted to cry out in terror but could not find his voice, wanted to run screaming in the opposite direction but felt his legs frozen to the ground.

The horses must have sensed approaching danger. Neighing loudly in fear, they tore their bridle reins free from the branches holding them and fled away at a gallop, leaving Aaron and Nancy momentarily dumbfounded.

"Run!" Aaron yelled, finally finding his voice and grabbing Nancy by the hand. "The Eyeless Man is coming!"

They ran for their lives, fleeing down the hill and across the flatland, pumping their arms and legs, too afraid to even look behind them, knowing Walking Sam might be snapping at their heels. They stumbled out of control, almost falling, onto a dirt road, oblivious to the pickup truck barreling their way.

There was the screech of brakes, followed by the deafening roar of a shotgun blast. Aaron halted and looked to his left, breathing heavy. Nancy also stopped running.

Grandma Emma stood beside her pickup's open door, a pump twelve-gauge pointed in the air. But she didn't get a second shot, the Eyeless Man dissolving back into the shadows. The doorway floating above the tree shimmered for another moment, and then it too disappeared from view.

"Where did he go?" Aaron looked around.

"I don't know." Nancy shook her head. "He's just gone."

"You kids get in the truck," Grandma Emma called out, lowering the shotgun. "Be quick about it."

Aaron and Nancy hurried across the road to the pickup truck. "Grandma, what did you see?"

"Just a shadow. Now, get in before it comes back. I'll help you catch the horses, then escort you back to the house. We'll talk as we ride."

Aaron told his grandmother everything as they went after the frightened horses. She was mad at first, thinking they might have been trying to follow in Jaimie's footsteps, but relieved to learn they weren't thinking of committing suicide. And now she had more evidence to prove to the tribal council that the stories about the Eyeless Man were true.

That night Aaron recited all his thoughts into his digital recorder, listening to what the voice-activated microphone had captured earlier in the day. The strange chittering heard at the oak tree was clear as a bell, as was the whistling. Creating a new audio file, he uploaded everything from the recorder onto his computer.

After that, Aaron logged on to Facebook and discovered that someone had posted a photograph on his timeline. The photo was of the same oak tree, only now there were two nooses hanging from it. The broken length of rope was also missing, meaning the picture had been taken after he removed the rope from the tree.

"What the hell?"

Numerous hateful comments were posted below the image, telling him that he was a worthless half-breed Indian, a *wasicu*, and nobody liked him—especially his mother and father—that he should take his own life to make everyone happy. Aaron doubted the comments were actually from people he knew, seeing how one of the remarks was credited to the late Jaimie Waters. His Facebook page must have been hacked.

More comments appeared as he watched, including one with a blurry photo of Walking Sam. He stared in stunned silence as the portrait grew in size until it took up the entire screen. As it enlarged, the now familiar chittering came from his computer's speakers. Aaron turned up the volume, listening carefully. It almost sounded like someone talking, but it was so alien he couldn't be sure. He was reminded of the old monster movies from the 1950s that featured giant insects, like the ones they showed late at night on satellite television.

The chittering grew louder, and as it did, the screen on his monitor rippled and pushed outward as if something on the inside was trying to escape.

"It really is insects!"

Aaron pushed back his chair and jumped up, backing away, fearful his computer was about to explode.

A loud knock sounded behind him, startling him. Aaron spun around and saw Nancy standing just outside his bedroom window. She knocked again, wanting in.

"You almost gave me a freaking heart attack," he said, opening the window and helping her climb into the room. "Why didn't you come to the front door?"

"I was afraid your grandmother was already sleeping."

He closed the window. Nancy straightened her clothing and smoothed her hair. She pulled her cell phone out of her pants pocket, turning it on. "I wanted to show you something."

"I think I already know what it is." He turned and looked at his desktop computer, but the monitor screen no longer bowed outward. The photograph of the Eyeless Man was also gone, making Aaron wonder if he had really seen the image or only imagined it.

"Think I'm losing my mind."

"What?" Nancy asked.

"Nothing," he replied. "Show me what you wanted me to see."

Nancy also had hateful comments on her Facebook timeline, along with a duplicate photo of the tree with two nooses. "It's the same tree we were at. I think those are meant for us."

Aaron nodded. "The Eyeless Man must have done it. Maybe Grandma Emma is right; maybe he really is an evil spirit. I wonder if any of our friends have seen him?"

"Let's look."

They searched through the social media pages of their friends and classmates, discovering many had been the recipients of Walking Sam's disturbing photos and verbal abuse. On a Facebook group page, they found another picture of the oak tree with eight nooses hanging from it. The image had been taken at night, a full moon shining in the background.

"Oh, my god," Nancy said, her voice barely a whisper. "Look at all the nooses."

As Aaron and Nancy stood there looking at the photo, they noticed that the nooses in the image swayed back and forth. It was not a photograph.

"It's a video," Nancy said.

Aaron looked closer. "Not a video. I think it's a live feed."

It took another minute or two before they noticed someone standing in the deep shadows at the base of the tree, tall and thin and dressed all in black, barely visible in the night. If it hadn't been for the light of the full moon, they wouldn't have seen him at all. They couldn't see the man's face, but they knew it would be devoid of eyes.

"He's waiting for them," Nancy said, her breath catching in her throat. "It's happening tonight."

"We've got to do something."

"Get your grandma and her shotgun."

"Can't. She went with a friend to Bingo at the church in Batesland."

"And her shotgun?"

"It's here, but she always keeps it locked. And I don't know where she keeps the key."

"Great. No weapons."

"I have a .22 rifle I use for target practice. It was my dad's, but he left it behind when he left me. Guess he forgot about it."

"It will have to do," Nancy said. "Get your gun, and make sure to bring extra ammo. We're going to need your grandmother's truck."

"I know where she keeps the key for that."

"Meet me outside. I'm going to see if I can get a cell phone signal and call the tribal police, tell them what's going on. Maybe they can get to that tree before us. I only hope we're not too late. Eight ropes. Jesus."

Aaron joined Nancy by the truck a few minutes later, carrying his .22 rifle and a box of ammo. "I left Grandma a note, telling her where we're going and why. Did you get ahold of the police?"

She shook her head. "Cheap phone. No signal."

Even if Nancy had gotten hold of the BIA tribal police, there was no guarantee they could make it in time. There were only thirty-two officers on the police force, covering a reservation the size of Rhode Island. The closest cop could be miles away.

Climbing in the truck, they pulled out of the driveway and headed for the hanging tree. They soon left all the houses in the town of Porcupine behind, driving across open countryside. Aaron gripped the steering wheel tightly, staring out the dust-streaked windshield into the heavy darkness in front of them.

Beside him, Nancy sat on the truck's bench seat, clutching herself and shivering. She too stared out the windshield, trying to see what lay ahead in the darkness. "Aaron, I'm scared. What are we going to do if we find the Eyeless Man?"

"I don't know. We'll have to figure that out when we find him."

He reached forward and turned on the stereo. "Here. Maybe this will help calm your nerves."

Aaron pushed the play button on the stereo's cassette player, the soothing harmony of Native American flute music filling the cab. But halfway through the third song, the flute music changed into an eerie three-note melody similar to the whistling heard at the hanging tree. They also heard a strange voice speaking in an unfamiliar dialect.

"Aaron, what's that?"

"I'm not sure. It sounds like someone chanting, but they're not speaking English or Lakota. Or any Indigenous language I'm familiar with. Do you recognize it?"

"No," she replied. "Is it part of the song?"

Aaron shook his head. "No. I've listened to this tape many times while riding with my grandmother. Strictly instrumental. No singing."

Nancy removed the cassette tape from the stereo, the sounds of country music from KILI-FM replacing the flute music. But the voice was still there, overtop the music being played, speaking in an unknown language. Mixed in with the voice was a strange chittering, making it even harder to hear what was being said.

"It's still there," Nancy said.

"But that's impossible."

As they listened, they began to pick out individual words: "No . . . pain . . . join. Ota Keta."

The voice was soothing, hypnotic and deadly. Aaron turned to look at Nancy. She had gone very quiet, staring motionless at the dash as if mesmerized. He quickly turned off the stereo. "Enough of that."

Nancy blinked several times, like she was waking from a dream. She stared at him for a few moments, wide-eyed, then turned to look out the windshield. "Watch out!"

Aaron slammed on the brakes, bringing the pickup to a screeching halt. Six teenagers had come out of the darkness, suddenly becoming visible as they stepped into the glow of his headlights. He turned off the engine and climbed out of the truck. Nancy followed him.

The teenagers crossed the road in a group, walking as if in a trance, heading for the oak tree where Jaimie hanged herself. Two bodies already hung from nooses in the tree, clearly visible in the moonlight.

"Oh, my god. Look!" Nancy pointed at the bodies. Above the tree floated two more of the rectangles, doorways to another world.

"Two bodies, two doorways," Aaron said, shocked, realizing what was happening. "The Eyeless Man is opening a doorway with each death."

Nancy looked around, quickly counting the kids moving toward the tree. "What happens when eight doorways open?"

"I don't know. Maybe a lot of things can come through from wherever the doorways lead. Or maybe Walking Sam can stack them all together and something really big can come through."

"We have to stop him."

Aaron glanced down at the rifle he held, which suddenly seemed very puny and insufficient. "I don't think this is going to do us much good, but maybe we can shut down his power source."

He ran forward, positioning himself between the tree and the hypnotized teenagers. "Stop. Don't do this!" he yelled. "Walking Sam is lying. You're not worthless. You are loved."

"Please stop," Nancy added, joining him. "This is not the way of our people. You are Oglala Lakota. Your ancestors did not give up when they were starved and driven onto the reservation. They did not quit when soldiers slaughtered their families at the Knee."

"That's right. Listen to her!" Aaron shouted. "Your grandparents did not give up when they were sent to Indian boarding schools, forbidden to speak their own language." He held up his wrists for emphasis. "I know it's not easy. I've been there, felt what you feel. But you have to fight him."

The gang of teenagers continued walking toward the oak tree. "They're not listening," he said.

"I've got an idea." Nancy stepped in front of a tall boy, blocking his way and kneeing him in the groin. The teenager dropped like a rock, clutching his testicles and moaning in pain.

Nancy pointed. "See? He's snapped out of it. Physical pain wins every time. I learned that in gym class, when a boy tried to get fresh with me."

"Oh, hell. You've got my vote." Aaron turned around, dropping the rifle and slapping a girl across the face. She fell to the ground, holding her face and crying. "Sorry, but you'll thank me in the morning."

They moved quickly among the other teenagers, slapping, punching and inflicting pain to snap them out of their trances.

They heard a cry of anger, and a tall shadow separated itself from the darkness at the base of the tree.

"He's coming!" Nancy shouted, terrified. "Walking Sam is coming."

"Don't look at him! Finish what we started." Aaron turned his back on Nancy and continued his work. He threw a slap, landed a punch, kicked a shin and kneed another groin. In a matter of seconds, all the teenagers were on the ground, crying and rolling around in pain. But they were no longer hypnotized. They would have bruises, welts and sore testicles in the morning, but they would be alive.

He had just slapped the last teenager when an unholy scream split the night. Aaron turned and looked around, but he saw no sign of Walking Sam. The Eyeless Man was gone, at least for now.

"We did it. We won. Hey, Nancy?"

Looking up, he was surprised to see three doorways floating in the night sky where there had only been two before.

"Three? But we stopped them. We—" His voice fell silent as he spotted a third person in the tree. "No. Oh, no."

Aaron ran forward, his eyes filling with tears. He stopped in front of the newest victim, hanging lifeless on a rope.

"Dear God. No. Not you, too," he cried out as he sank slowly to his knees.

He had momentarily turned his back on Nancy, and that was all the time it had taken for the Eyeless Man to claim her. Had the hypnotic voice of the suicide spirit filled her mind with sorrow and despair, causing her to give up all hope and take her own life? Or had he physically grabbed Nancy and hanged her in the tree?

Aaron would probably never learn the answer. All he knew was that he had lost his one true friend, the person who had given him hope when hope hadn't existed. Her positive ray of sunshine was forever gone from his life.

As Aaron climbed up into the oak tree, slipping a noose over his head, he hoped his spirit would be able to find the same doorway Nancy had gone through. Together they would face whatever waited on the other side.

"Ota Keta," he said, stepping off into space.

DR. MAYNARD WILLS:
THE SEED OF HORROR

I love horror movies. No surprise there, I'm sure. And this passion is sometimes to my detriment. What do I mean? Watch *Dead Ringers* on a first date and it's unlikely there'll be a second. I speak from experience.

Within the horror genre, I especially like monster movies and hauntings. And while I do enjoy Kaiju pictures (the original *Gojira* is definitely a horror movie) and Harryhausen's many-limbed menageries, I'm more interested in the entities that inspire terror rather than the ones that induce wonder.

Why? I am fascinated by the seed of horror; the conception of the beast, the wraith or demon. Let the guys and gals in the psych department bicker over what made Dahmer tick. I want to trace the Wendigo back to birth and Bloody Mary to her very first mirror so I can determine why these legends arise at specific times and within (or across) particular cultures. A wise friend in the movie business once told me that horror is the result we get when we procrastinate an existential question. Are urban legends born when we do this as a collective? As a culture?

I had an itch for answers even as a young moviegoer. I longed to follow every silver screen vampire back to their crypt and Frankenstein's monster to his birth, not in the laboratory but on that night near Lake Geneva, where Mary Shelley made her magic. And I saw every monstrosity the projectionist put up there. By the late forties and early fifties, Universal was near the end of their famous run and decided to introduce Abbott and Costello to their iconic monsters. That wasn't my cup of tea, so my grandfather and I eschewed the first-run fare in favor of drive-in double features and revival houses where the best thirties and forties Frankenstein, Wolf Man and Dracula movies ran. And when I was a bit older—just before he died—we fell into a Saturday-night ritual: we'd stock up on candy, fill the icebox with sugary drinks, then tune in for local legend Eddie Driscoll, who hosted *The Weird Show* on Bangor's WLBZ 2. God, how I miss Eddie's Uncle Gory character introducing the segments; some groovy horror and sci-fi schlock. But I digress.

Anyhow, I'd bounce between the cinemas and that aforementioned university library, where I traced the origin of every legendary creature. The werewolf, for example, through German paganism, Norse mythology and clinical lycanthropy. And I'd quickly discover how immigrants in our New World imported their own stories, which would be borrowed and evolved by neighboring ethnic groups, sometimes in fascinating ways, other times in tragic ones. It's not uncommon for xenophobes to absorb half-heard tales and distort them, applying a corrupted version of a folktale to the folks who told them. It's a particularly virulent form of racism. Just because our myths evolve doesn't mean they're always for the better. Wonder what can happen when folklore and the fear of a people converge? Consider the European witch craze and, later, the one in our own country. Put yourself in the shoes of an epileptic woman in 1690s Salem and you'll understand what happens when hysteria drowns out reason.

As we see with creepypasta today, myths still form freshly in

America and around the world. And they can still be dangerous (Google "Slender Man Stabbing" if you're incredulous). Some reside in niche subcultures within subcultures; others flourish and expand into the mainstream. I believe the Eyeless Man is a distinctly twentieth- and twenty-first-century myth and is on the verge of cross-cultural breakthrough. And while I have worked to uncover his mythic ancestry I'm (thus far!) largely unsuccessful; the only theme, the only string worth pulling, concerns media and, perhaps, behaviors around it. But which ones? I search for the signal and find only noise.

Let me provide a well-known example of the kind of connection I've longed to make. I'm sure many of you are familiar with the Japanese film *Ringu* and its excellent US remake, *The Ring*. Adapted from a novel by Koji Suzuki, *Ringu* is the story of a VHS tape that summons a vengeful spirit from a television seven days after it's watched. While this is a mass media–age story, the iconography of a young girl with long, stringy black hair has origins in ancient Japanese folklore, particularly the Yurei.

Yurei are essentially ghosts, often depicted as women with long, disheveled black hair, white clothing and pale, lifeless hands. The term *Yurei* is a bit of a catch-all to describe ghosts in general, but there are subsets called Onryo and Funayurei, which influence the type of spirit we see in *Ringu*'s ghost, Sadako Yamamura. Onryo are vengeful spirits, whereas Funayurei are the spirits of those who died at sea and appear as scaly, fish-like humanoids. In the original *Ringu*, it is hinted that Sadako is the product of a union between a human and a sea god. Part Onryo, part Funayurei, she's something of a mythological remix. My point is that we trace her DNA to the 1700s on scrolls and in records of Kabuki performance. The videotape is a nice contemporary wrinkle, and it did make me wonder if, maybe, the Eyeless Man is Sadako's American cousin. Sadly, I believe the similarities are superficial. The White Tapes are an aspect of the Eyeless Man's myth, but he—as the stories in this book suggest—contains a multitude of tools and, possibly, motives.

I suppose it's possible that Koji Suzuki had heard about the Eyeless Man when he wrote his novel in 1991, but I doubt it. It's more likely that cultures converged unknowingly.

Perhaps by virtue of procrastinating the same existential question.

THE REAL
SHARON
LOCKENBY

Graham Skipper

Professor Wills, thank you for reaching out. The following is the story I was telling you about via email. First, a little bit of back story for readers as to how I came to hear this in the first place. Also, if you are indeed able to track down Catrina (again, I'm sorry I don't remember her last name), please do let me know. I would love the opportunity to reconnect and would like to know that she's okay.

I've traveled to the UK frequently throughout my life, whether it be for film festivals, vacations with family (my mother has roots in Scotland) or on a few occasions to the Edinburgh Fringe Festival. I've performed there once and have gone a couple of times as a spectator, and it was on one of these trips where I met Catrina, a local actress. My wife and I met her waiting in line for a circus show and struck up a conversation, which eventually turned into meeting her and her castmates for drinks after their show. These things happen at the Edinburgh Fringe.

We became fast friends, and one night, as the sun was coming up, she asked if we wanted to hear a crazy story. Of course we said yes, because crazy stories are best told as the sun is coming up with about a dozen pints in you. This is the story she told me about her friend Sharon.

When she was finished, I asked if I could write it down, and she agreed. Sadly, after this night she seemed to withdraw a bit. I don't really know what happened to Catrina—she's not on Facebook or anything, so we haven't kept up since that night. I hope she's well. She certainly seemed shaken by just sharing this story with me, but I'm glad she did.

Also, just a quick note regarding what you're doing, and this Eyeless Man project. I have to admit, when you first told me about the myth, I didn't understand how it connected to my story. But thinking through it since our first correspondence, I'm pretty rattled. You've given me a lot to think about, Professor. Good luck with your research. I hope you find some answers.

—Graham Skipper

I T WAS THE summer of 2016 when a young woman by the name of Sharon Lockenby was at one of her monthly get-togethers with her group of friends. The ladies—all friends since elementary school—made it a point to get dinner on the last Saturday of every month, a tradition they'd kept for four years going. It was always a boisterous night out, with too much wine, a rotating series of stories they'd told one another thousands of times before and lots of laughs.

This time it was Sharon's turn to choose the restaurant, so she chose a small seaside spot in the town of Margate, 130 kilometers southeast of London. Her friends groaned and complained about having to travel so far for dinner, but it was Sharon's call and she lived in Margate, so fuck 'em. She was always having to take the train into London to see them, and then either crash on someone's couch or take the long, sobering ride back at two in the morning. She felt zero sympathy for any of them.

They had a lovely dinner in the tiny restaurant, packed with tourists on a clear summer night. Sharon's table was the loudest by far; they laughed and clinked glasses and at times shouted over one another, uncommon for reserved British locals and even more uncommon in a small café in Margate. Needless to say, they drew attention from the other patrons in the restaurant. Some were annoyed at their unruly neighbors, while others were bemused, the joviality of the ladies' table being somewhat infectious.

At some point during the evening, several bottles of wine in, Sharon was regaling the others with a story about some encounter she'd recently had with a lady in a supermarket, and the climax of her story was (in her words) a spot-on impression of the insufferable woman:

"Move your arse, you cunt, 'less I cunt-slap you in the arse!" she growled in the woman's toad-like squawk. She accompanied this with a contorted face, her brows creased, her eyes crossed and her lips curled like a cartoon pirate. She was always good at impressions, and this one felt like an instant classic—outlandish, gross and hilarious, all made better by a mouthful of wine-stained teeth. She even allowed a bit of the red to drip down her chin for added effect.

As she'd hoped, the impression brought the house down. The other ladies at the table laughed raucously, remarking how Sharon "always was the class clown," and how she "really should have been a stand-up comic," and that she's "just so crazy."

What none of them had noticed, or perhaps had but hadn't given another thought about, was that a flash had gone off during Sharon's climactic performance. Somewhere in the restaurant, a fellow patron had snapped a photo, catching Sharon at her most grotesque. Perhaps they enjoyed her performance and wanted to capture it to tell friends back home; perhaps they resented her interruption of their quiet meal and wanted to immortalize such an annoying person. Whatever the reason for snapping that picture, it would go on to change Sharon's life forever.

The next morning, Sharon woke to the blinding sun and a pounding wine headache. She was grateful it was a Sunday—this was a hangover for which she would have called in sick. She practically crawled into the kitchen to make some tea, guzzling water from the tap.

Bleary-eyed, she picked up her phone and began her compulsive morning ritual: scrolling through Facebook. There were the usual news posts, some pictures of friends' babies (*why were all her friends having babies?*) and political posts, mostly about the upcoming US election. But one blurred image, coasting past as she absentmindedly swiped up, caught her eye. She reversed and slowly scrolled back up her feed, until she found the offending photo.

It was her.

More specifically, it was a picture of her from the previous evening, her face contorted ridiculously, and it had been "meme-ified," emblazoned with the words "I'll cunt-slap you in the arse!"

She let out an audible laugh, covering her mouth incredulously. Who had posted this?! Who had taken this picture? It was posted via one of those clickbait websites, the kind whose "big newsbreak" were dumb memes like this. The kind of website she scrolled through on the loo.

She read the accompanying "article," which was little more than speculation on what the "crazy drunk woman" was doing, and laughed at her own idiotic expression (and red wine–stained teeth). She also thought it was hilarious that she'd been immortalized wearing the stupid dinosaur sweatshirt she'd worn. Her friend Catrina had gotten it for her as a gag gift for her birthday (because she was "as old as a dinosaur"), so she wore it to spite her. It got a good laugh out of everybody.

She was most relieved, however, that the article did not once mention her by name. Thank God.

She immediately saved the picture to her camera roll and went into the group chat she always had going with the dinner ladies. She attached the picture with the comment: "Which of you bitches took this picture?? WTF??? LMFAO."

Almost immediately the others started responding, every one of them denying having taken the photo but agreeing that it was "fucking hysterical."

"You're a legend!" Catrina commented. "#Immortal."

Sharon went about her morning, enjoying her three minutes of fame, and chuckled when she saw the image pop up on a couple of other places on her feed. One friend from university tagged her in it, with the comment, "Holy shit, Sharon, is this YOU?!? #ClassicSharon." Every comment was good-natured and kind, albeit with a little bit of well-deserved ribbing. Sharon's mother had always told her that her silliness would get her the "wrong kind of attention" someday, and so Sharon knew that if her mother ever saw this she'd never hear the end of it. But she didn't mind. It was funny.

As the day went on, more and more blogs and "news sites" (nothing legit, just more clickbait aggregators) picked up the photo and shared it. One site even had several variations—the original photo, but with different text accompanying it.

"Who wants a wee kiss???"

"Got Syphilis?"

"'Ello, ya cunts, welcome to Toad Hall!"

She laughed at that last one. She was amazed at how quickly it had traveled and transformed, how sudden and swift its rise had been. It was comforting to think that its fall would be just as swift. *That's how these things go*, she thought to herself. *Instantly famous, instantly unfamous.*

But as the week went on, she came to realize that her becoming *unfamous* was not coming quickly at all. The meme spread, popping up on a few local late-night talk shows around the UK and Ireland. One of them featured twenty different variations of the meme! Twenty different captions to her same stupid face. Blogs wondered if she had a drinking problem. A nonprofit benefiting those with mental handicaps urged people not to share the meme, as it "mocked the mentally challenged."

Strangers on the street began to recognize her and asked for selfies, always begging her to "make that face." She obliged at first but then stopped altogether. People called her "rude" for refusing a picture. "You're famous, you should be grateful," they'd say.

But she wasn't grateful. After two weeks of the meme's continuous spread—like the world's most annoying virus—her boss called her into his office. He told her that the company was concerned at the negative attention the picture was bringing to her and that prospective clients, when they came across her picture on the company's website, were hesitating to come in because they thought she was a crazy drunk. Or, conversely, people were contacting them purely to see if they could get a meeting with "the cunt-slap lady."

She was fired. She was devastated and immediately filed a complaint with Human Resources, but she didn't hold out much hope that she would be reinstated. And really, did she want that? *Fuck them*, she thought. *I'm famous now, I can do whatever I want.*

Good timing, then, that a book publisher called her within the week, offering her a staggering advance to write a book about her "rise to Internet stardom." Apparently, she learned during the phone call, hers was one of the most swiftly shared and duplicated memes in history. On par with Ermagherd Girl, Grumpy Cat, and Harambe. "It's a miracle," the lady on the other end of the line told her. "You're sitting on a gold mine."

Sharon took the deal without even thinking. Fuck yes, she'd write a book! The publisher even told her they would hire a ghostwriter and that she wouldn't have to type a single word. She could just share her thoughts and the writer would do the rest, and then she could sit back and collect a check—sounded pretty good to her. She started to become more comfortable with taking selfies with people. She started to own her newfound stardom, even going so far as to get the original meme framed and hung on her wall.

A month passed, and it was time for her dinner with the ladies—what stories she'd have to tell this time! She'd kept mostly in touch with Catrina throughout all of this; she was the friend she was closest to, and they spoke on the phone regularly. Catrina, of course, thought all of this was bizarre but hilarious. Sharon couldn't help but notice, however, that Catrina seemed distant lately. She'd asked her about it, but Catrina insisted it was nothing. Sharon doubted this but let it go. *Oh well, we all go through weird stretches from time to time.*

The restaurant was chosen—some place in Soho, in London. She didn't mind taking the train in this time; she needed to get out of Margate for an evening, become anonymous again.

Dinner started fine . . . but her friends were all acting differently around her. Even Catrina. *Especially* Catrina. She couldn't quite put her finger on it, but there was something stilted about their interactions, and she swore that Catrina seemed nervous. At first they tried to act as if nothing were different, which she appreciated but which also seemed ridiculous. She'd already texted them about her book deal, and her face was literally everywhere, so she naturally assumed they'd at least discuss all this craziness. The conversation was also not as lively as it normally was—less wine was drunk, the stories were quieter, the laughter more subdued.

Eventually, Sharon wanted to talk about the elephant in the room. "Are you all mad at me or something?" she asked the group.

She was met with silence. Eventually Catrina spoke up.

"It's just awkward, love. All of us keep getting asked about you, and what's wrong with you, and were you drunk that night, and are you on drugs . . . all this horrible stuff. And it's made things hard for us. Sorry, but it's the truth."

Sharon had to take a second to fully understand what her friend had said. Did she really just claim that *their* struggles were at all comparable to hers? That just being associated with her was too difficult for them?

"We're just saying, dear, that we don't like being in the spotlight."

Sharon erupted at them. How dare they? she growled. They had no idea what she'd been through, how this had affected her life. Had *they* been fired over this? No. Were their pictures plastered all over God's green earth proclaiming them to be idiots, or psychopaths, or drunks, or drug addicts? No. How dare they say it was hard on *them*? She told them all they could go fuck themselves and stood, enraged.

Then the flashes started.

Cameras, all over the restaurant. Snapping photos, filming, Instagramming . . .

#CrazyCuntLadyIsBack.

Sharon didn't care. She stormed out of the restaurant into the London night and made a beeline to the nearest pub, where she ordered a shot of tequila. No, two. Pint of lager, please.

I feel it's important to note that when Catrina told me this, she seemed devastated by what had happened. She said the group had all spoken privately beforehand and that their intention was to have a conversation about it, and maybe see if Sharon could stop leaning into her newfound fame quite so hard. They thought that maybe if she stopped this book deal they could all go back to being anonymous regular people. Catrina insisted she had had the best of intentions but had bungled the whole thing. She was really depressed about how it all went down.

The rest of the night was a haze—Sharon drank more, bummed several cigarettes from a nice-looking gentleman outside the pub, got his number, grabbed a tall can of Heineken from the corner store and drank it on the train ride home.

On these late-night train rides, there's always a creeping feeling of anxiousness, the possibility of danger hanging in the air. Sharon always kept her guard up, keeping half an eye on her fellow train passengers. That night there was one old woman slumped in a rear-facing seat, sleeping soundly. A couple of rowdy teen boys drank from a flask of whiskey and were playing some dumb game where they kept punching one another in the arm and giggling. And she had a vague memory of another man, hunched in the corner. Or it might have been a reflection in the window—she had been pretty drunk, after all. But this was something she specifically remembered: a man who was there, but who also was not there. She wondered if she'd dreamed him.

After a bit, one of the teen boys was glancing at his phone when he did a comically large double take, looking directly at Sharon.

"Oy!" he said, pointing. "That's the lady! The meme lady!"

His friend laughed and affirmed this.

"Hey, lady! Do the thing for us, eh?"

"Not in the mood, boys," Sharon said into her too-quickly-dwindling can of Heineken.

"Aw, c'mon, don't be a bitch about it. Just do the thing! I wanna Snap it!"

Sharon sank into her seat and buried her face in her beer again.

The teen boys—filled with testosterone and fearlessness—stood up and walked over in her direction, beginning to shout obscenities and insults her way. How dare she refuse them what they wanted? Little punks had always gotten what they demanded. They were getting so loud that the old lady in the corner stirred and grimaced.

But something strange happened. As the boys approached, they seemed to see the man in the corner—the hunched-over, maybe-is-a-reflection man. Or maybe they didn't, and just had a change of heart. They stopped and rubbed their eyes, as if they had a sudden headache. Both boys teetered there for a moment, confused and in pain.

"Fuck this," one of the boys said eventually. "Bitch ain't worth our time."

Then they walked away, using the door to go to the next car. Sharon's blurry memory of the encounter would haunt her. Especially that man in the corner, hunched over, almost-but-not-quite-there, the man who existed only in the reflection in the window. She sent a text to Catrina, a force of habit a decade old, to let the others know she'd made it home safe. She forgot for a moment how mad she was at her friends and drunkenly typed about the strange man she'd seen and about the asshole kids.

She ended the text with "I love you, C. Sorry about earlier."

Sharon was grateful for the morning. Her head was pounding (she swore her hangovers got worse as she got older), and her memory of getting home was even fuzzier than her memory of the train ride itself. She checked her text messages and was thankful she'd texted Catrina. She saw that Catrina had texted back a heart emoji— simple but comforting. She hadn't wrecked *all* her friendships, it seemed.

She turned on the TV and plopped down with her tea, hoping for something mindless to soothe her aching mind . . . but was so shocked by what she saw that she dropped her mug to the floor:

The two teen boys who had accosted her were found murdered only a few blocks from the train station. Not just shot or stabbed, like one might see from a mugging—they'd been torn apart. Disemboweled, throats ripped open, eyes gouged out, real medieval stuff. Police were looking for information regarding the crime, and Sharon knew she'd have to call in and tell them what happened. She was not looking forward to being back in the spotlight, but she knew what she had to do . . .

. . . Until the newscast put up her picture next. What the reporter said seemed to come out in slow motion, Sharon's mouth tingling and going dry, her vision narrowing on the images in front of her. They were looking for her in connection with the murders, because CCTV had captured her *following* the boys down the darkened alley, shortly before the murder had happened. There were no cameras to see the actual murder take place, but they showed a clip from the security footage, and yes, sure as hell it was *her*.

How was this possible? First, why would she follow them? Second, where their bodies were found was way out of the way from her house. She would have had to take a significant detour to go that way. It just didn't make any sense. Had she been that drunk? She admitted that she didn't really remember leaving the train, but she always did a decent job of being able to think like Drunk Sharon would have thought, and no way would Drunk Sharon have ever been a) that brave as to follow those two shits, or b) so out of it as to walk the complete opposite direction of her house.

But there she was, on camera. She couldn't explain it. Granted, the footage was grainy and in black-and-white, so she thought perhaps it could have been someone who just looked a lot like her. The weirdest thing, though, was that it looked like the woman in the video wore her same stupid dinosaur sweatshirt. But maybe she was just seeing things in the grain that weren't really there. . . .

She met with the police, who questioned her for hours. She texted Catrina during her brief breaks, almost as if to document the craziness that was going on. It was nice to know her friend was there with her, even if only digitally. Catrina offered to come down to sit with her, but Sharon insisted she'd be fine. She told the police the complete truth of what happened and swore that she was as flummoxed as they were as to why she was on that camera. It had to be a woman who looked like her. (*But how was she wearing that sweatshirt?*)

She also described—or tried to describe—the man she'd seen on the train. Perhaps if they found him, he might provide some answers as well. Her efforts at a description were largely fruitless, sadly, and all she managed to get out was that she believed there had been a man on the train, and she believed the boys had seen him. One line of questioning bothered her more than the others, though: *Did you see his face? Any details at all? What color were his eyes?*

She hadn't seen his eyes. She didn't recall seeing any eyes at all.

Then she had a thought: Why don't they check any of the cameras installed on her normal walk home? Surely that would show them that she was elsewhere at the time of the murder. Or at least she hoped it would.

Lo and behold, it worked. A CCTV camera picked her up walking about ten blocks in the opposite direction at exactly the time she—or whoever it was—was recorded following the boys. She couldn't be in two places at the same time, obviously, and so the police apologized and decided it "must just be someone that looks a lot like you." One of them joked that maybe she had an identical twin she didn't know about. Sharon didn't find that funny.

But, of course, she was all over the news (at least it felt like she was—it was mainly local news stories and blogs), and it didn't matter that the police released a statement saying that it wasn't her in the video and that she'd been cleared of all suspicion. The Internet took the story and ran with it, and all of a sudden the memes were back, but this time captioned with things like, "Me Murderer, derp!," "I like ta eat young boys in alleys!" or "I'm gonna cunt-slap ya to death!"

The book publisher was thrilled—this would surely spike interest. How quickly could the book be written? She'd kept putting off reading and approving the first couple of chapters that the ghostwriter had churned out, and she knew she needed to do that. But not today. Maybe not this week. Her brain was a mess, trying to figure out how she could be in two places at once. Not that she actually believed she had been, but damn, that woman did in fact look a lot like her. Exactly like her. *And that dumb sweatshirt.*

Later that week, a tabloid ran a story: "Margate Meme Murderer Spotted in California," with an accompanying photo that showed a woman who looked tremendously like her on a beach in Los Angeles. But the photo was somewhat grainy and obviously wasn't her because she was still on the English coast.

Over the course of the next month, more stories ran: "Globe-

Trotting Meme Murder Suspect in Paris," "Meme Murderer Spotted on the Same Day in Prague and Montreal," "Is the Acquitted Meme Murderer Our New Bigfoot?" She appreciated the last one for at least adding the word "acquitted" and for the creativity of photoshopping Bigfoot fur all over the original photo.

Over the next several months, the popularity of the meme seemed to slow down a little bit. The publisher was in a rush to finish the book so that they could get it onto bookshelves before interest in the meme waned. Sharon continued to get recognized in the street, but that started to become less and less common. Another meme was popular now—some baby eating an ice-cream cone.

And with the slowing of her meme's popularity, so too did the sightings of her around the world become less and less frequent. Once in a while her Google alert would ping that she'd been spotted in some fantastic location—once it was as far away as Madagascar! But the truth was she never left Margate. She didn't even go into London anymore to have her monthly friend dinners. She hadn't spoken to any of them except Catrina (and even she only via the occasional text) since that horrible night.

Then one day she received a phone call from her mother.

Her mother called her about once a week, sometimes less, but it was always a pleasant conversation. She picked up and could immediately tell her mother was in tears.

"Mum, what's wrong?" she asked. She was convinced she was about to find out her father had died.

"How could you?" her mother replied, sadness and venom in her voice.

"What are you talking about?"

"The things you said, how hurtful you were. Your poor father, he's still in shock...."

Sharon was beyond confused. "Mum, what did I say? When was this? I don't know what you're talking about."

"Last night, Sharon! What you said last night!"

Sharon had no clue what her mother was talking about. They hadn't spoken on the phone. She hadn't done any kind of an interview; hell, she wasn't even on Facebook anymore, so this couldn't even be in reference to some unkind post she'd made.

"Mum, we didn't speak last night—"

"Don't try to get out of this, Sharon. We spoke, all right. You walked right in this door, and—"

"What did you say?" Sharon couldn't have heard what she had just heard.

"I said, you walked right in this door, and you started spouting such hateful—"

"I'm in Margate. I was here last night," Sharon protested.

"Then who was it that walked in through my front door and called me such horrible things? It was like you were on a rampage—"

"Mum, I don't know who you talked to last night, but it wasn't me. I haven't left Margate. You live in Scotland, for Christ's sake, I'd have had to be on a train all day yesterday—"

Her mother obviously didn't believe her. "You're a hateful young woman. You drink too much; I could smell the booze on you. It was like you were a completely different person than the lovely young woman I raised. And your father ... he is just devastated...."

"Mum, it wasn't me! I'm telling you!"

"And you're a liar now, too. Or maybe you're schizophrenic. Either way, you need to get help. And until you do, don't bother talking to us."

Her mother hung up. Sharon's mouth fell open in dumb shock. She had been in Margate all night, there was no doubt of that. She'd spent the evening on her sofa, had one glass of wine and went to bed early. Why would her mother think she'd been at her house in Scotland? Had she dreamed it? Had some crazy woman come to her house and berated her mother and father, and in the dark of night she'd looked like Sharon? That didn't make any sense. No matter how dark, you'd know your own daughter if she was staring you in the face.

She tried to call her mother back several times, but to no avail. She wouldn't answer. Nor would her father. She would have emailed them, but they didn't have email. So she decided she would simply go up north and see them herself.

She got on the train that afternoon and took the overnight up to their small suburb outside of Edinburgh. She arrived early in the morning, about 6:00 a.m., but knew that they'd be awake and so went straight to their home. And, of course, she texted Catrina that she'd made it safely. She was more grateful for their friendship now than ever. Catrina's texts felt like a lifeline to the real world, while she stumbled around beyond the looking glass.

She knocked on the door and called their phone from the front porch—she could hear it ringing inside, going unanswered. She shouted for her mother that she was outside, but she wasn't coming to the door. After about fifteen minutes, certainly long enough for her parents to have woken up if they weren't already, she felt behind that weird ceramic toad on the ground to find the spare key and grabbed it, opening the door.

The house was cold and quiet. She called out for her parents but got no reply. Even if they hadn't wanted her to come in, now that she was inside the house she at least expected them to confront her. What were they going to do, hide in the pantry?

She went from room to room, calling out for them. She wondered if they'd suddenly gone on a holiday? Their car was in the driveway, but perhaps they'd gotten a friend to take them to the train station. Maybe they'd gone up to Aberdeen as they sometimes did?

But then she arrived at their upstairs bedroom and was horrified to open the door and see . . .

It was too ghastly to even describe. Her poor parents, their bodies totally ravaged by what could have been a bear or a tiger. It was beyond a nightmare.

She called the police, of course, and answered hundreds of questions. She told them the whole truth, about the phone call and why she'd gone up there to begin with. At the end of it all, she told the police she'd stay in town to help however she could, and they responded with what she felt was almost a chuckle: "Of course you're staying in town. You're staying at the station."

"You're arresting me?" she asked, incredulous.

"Ma'am, your mother called the police last night, saying that you had barged into their home and were threatening their lives."

"It wouldn't have been last night, it would have been the night before, and it wasn't me, she just thought it was me."

"No, ma'am. Your mother called then, too. But she called

back *again* last night. Saying you had returned and were threatening them."

"But I was on a train last night, coming up here. I didn't get here 'til six this morning."

"Ma'am, we came to the house. We spoke with your mother and father . . . and we spoke with you. Everything seemed to have calmed down, and you agreed to leave."

"Who spoke with me?"

"I did, ma'am. As did Sergeant Dean over there."

"But it wasn't me. . . ."

"It was you, as sure as I'm sitting here. Now please, turn around."

Bewildered, Sharon allowed the officer to place her in handcuffs and led her to the police car. She told them from the back seat, "Check the cameras! I was in the train station in Margate yesterday afternoon; there's no way I could have made it up here! Check the tapes!"

They assured her they would, in a very nonreassuring voice.

News spread quickly that she'd been arrested, that the Margate Meme Murderer had struck again and that she wouldn't get away this time. The meme circulated like wildfire, such awful, hateful things being captioned to that idiotic photo of her telling that stupid story.

But the police kept their word and did, indeed, check the tapes. And just as she'd said, there she was, on the train exactly when she said she'd been, four hundred miles from the scene when the police had been interviewing . . . her. It was bewildering, especially to Sharon, who couldn't understand why not only the police but her own mother had been so convinced by this imposter. Of course, the other problem was that she looked so similar to the imposter that the police now weren't sure if she was the actual Sharon, or the imposter who just happened to know where the real Sharon had been. So they held her in custody until they could "sort through it a bit more."

Over the next several days, Sharon was able to provide more evidence of where she had been over the past couple of weeks. Just to prove that she hadn't somehow flown back and forth between her nearest airport, Southend, and Edinburgh in an attempt to create alibis. She'd had a video doorbell installed at her house in Margate when her popularity began to rise, so she had a fairly consistent document of when she came and went from her house. It proved without doubt that she could not have committed those murders.

So they released her, but asked that she stay up north for further questioning. She rented a hotel room and looked forward to a shower and a good night's sleep and some time alone.

She couldn't resist logging on and seeing if her meme had had any kind of a resurgence in popularity. It had become a bit of an addiction of hers: looking at herself in that horrible pose and seeing what people were saying about her. "Never read the comments," so many people said, but she couldn't resist. Sometimes she'd log into social media channels as an anonymous profile and argue with people who were being negative (most were negative).

After the news had broken that she was back in jail, suspected of another murder, the vast majority of the memes now had captions along the lines of "What you look like when you first get to Hell," "The personification of Karma," "DIE BITCH DIE" and "This is your brain on I KILLED MY PARENTS ON METH DURRRRR."

She tried texting her group of friends, but none of them responded these days. None of them except Catrina seemed interested in patching things up. Catrina encouraged her to "give it time," but Sharon wasn't optimistic that things would ever get back to normal.

She looked back online: her meme really was ramping up, it was all over her various feeds and more and more the captions called for her death or for much more horrible things to happen to her. It was really distressing.

Then she received a phone call, which she assumed was the police since they were the only ones who knew what hotel she was staying at. But the voice on the other line was definitely not a police officer. . . .

"Hello?" Sharon asked, a bit annoyed and a lot tired.

A woman's voice responded on the other end of the line. There was a sharpness to her, something vaguely malevolent.

"Hello, Sharon. It's me."

"Who is this?" Sharon responded, frustrated and with no patience for games.

"You know. The people want what they want, Sharon. Your head on a pike."

Sharon had an uncanny feeling that this was the person who'd murdered her parents. And who killed those two teen boys. She shuddered at the thought of this person knowing where she was.

"What do you want?" Sharon asked, her voice cracking.

"You. You. You. You. . . ."

The woman on the other end then started laughing. It was horrible. Just as suddenly, she stopped.

"Meet me in the graveyard across the street from your hotel. Five minutes. No police."

Then she abruptly hung up.

Sharon, of course, immediately called the police, telling them everything and that she was going to meet this woman in the graveyard (an appropriate place for a murderer's meet-up) and they better be there, ready to catch the real murderer. The police said they would be there, not to worry.

Sharon worried.

She also texted Catrina briefly what had happened and what she was about to do. She ended the text with, "Love you, C. Thanks for sticking by me."

It would be the last contact Catrina ever had with her friend.

So this is where Catrina's story intersects with hard reality. After hearing about this whole thing, I decided to do a little digging, and I found that pretty much everything I was told is backed up by police and news records, if you look hard enough. I've attached one news story here. I read this, and my heart felt like it dropped like an anchor through the floor. No wonder Catrina became so withdrawn after sharing this with me. What a painful, horrible, insane memory this must be for her.

BREAKING NEWS

Police arrived at Morningside Cemetery on the outskirts of Edinburgh after celebrity murder suspect Sharon Lockenby claimed the real murderer would soon be meeting her for a clandestine rendezvous. Police arrived at the scene to find Ms. Lockenby standing with an identical twin sister—still unnamed—in the cemetery. They appeared to be arguing, and when police made their presence known, both began claiming that they were the "real" Sharon. One officer commented, "It was like something out of a movie."

Soon, one of the women attacked the other with a hidden knife, and police opened fire. The attacking woman was shot dead, while the surviving woman was taken into custody with grave wounds. The surviving woman claims she is the "real" Sharon Lockenby, but police were able to determine after viewing CCTV footage from the hotel that Ms. Lockenby's clothes as she left the hotel were consistent with the deceased. The other as-yet-unnamed assailant is currently in custody.

And here's a couple of other interesting bits of information. The Sharon double has yet to reveal a name or to be identified through DNA testing. Her DNA is an EXACT match to Sharon Lockenby, which means they have to be identical twin siblings, although there is zero record of Sharon having been a twin. In addition, when the imposter was arrested, she was wearing a sweatshirt covered in dinosaurs. An identical match to the one Sharon is wearing in the meme.

But here's the kicker: In the days and weeks following this news story breaking, the meme became super popular again, this time with captions talking about "More twins yet to be announced," and "Will the real Sharon Lockenby please stand up?" And in that time, THREE MORE MURDERS occurred, in different countries around the world, while the Sharon lookalike was still in custody. And in every single case, the description of the assailant, whether caught on camera or from an eyewitness, was identical. They looked exactly like Sharon Lockenby. The official theory is that these are the actions of copycat killers or perhaps just a kind of mass delusion—we see what we want to see, and people want to see Sharon Lockenby.

I'm not sure what I believe, to be honest. Or maybe I do, but I don't want to admit what I think is the real truth.

One final thing I found very interesting. There's a clip from the BBC's coverage of the cemetery incident, taken immediately after the shooting and arrest of the Sharon double. In the background, as the camera moves to try to catch a shot of the gurney being wheeled toward the ambulance, you can see a bystander in the background.

It's a man, blurry and part static, almost there but not quite. In the same instant when you think you can see him, another part of you wonders if he's there at all, or if it is just a trick of the recording. I had a buddy of mine who works in film restoration take a look at it, and he was baffled. He said even if you isolate a single frame, the image of that man still appears to skip.

"Must be something wrong with the data itself," he said. "Could just be a ghost in the tape."

DR. MAYNARD WILLS:
MY DARK BIDDING

With several friends and colleagues engaged and working on this project, I turned my attention back to my own investigation. As I scoured reddit threads and decade-old message boards dedicated to urban legends, I received a chat message from a stranger, username VI00pniR (a reference to the mythic Nordic bird Víðópnir). The message was simple: just a link to an eBay listing. The item for bid was an old, broken television with an image burned onto the screen. This itself is not a phenomenon. These phantom images were a frequent occurrence with older cathode-ray tube (CRT) TVs. The phosphor compounds used to emit light and produce the images would lose their luminance over time. In cases where a screen would show a single, static image for a long time, that image could get permanently "burned" onto the TV. This effect would essentially render the TV unwatchable. So what's interesting about this particular TV set? The lister purports that the image burned onto its screen depicts *the Eyeless Man*. A Shroud of Turin for the media age. The lister refused to share pictures. And they had no other listings or previous sales. Was it a hoax? The seller's username evoked the young man lost at the end of the podcast: Come2Cambria. A plea? A taunt? It didn't matter to me. I had to gamble. To bid and win, whatever the cost.

My home is packed with books and curiosities. Yeti track casts, alloys collected from Roswell, ambergris-scented plague masks. Even if I hadn't embarked on this book project, I'd still be in the mix for this television. It's simply my nature. The auction process started out quite well. For days, I was the only bidder. But events escalated quickly. A user called Z challenged me for the TV, and we bid back and forth day and night. After forty-eight hours, I won the auction and bought the television for $3,500. A price I suppose Z was unwilling to meet and that precipitated a terribly awkward conversation with my landlord about the month's rent.

I listed my contact information and sent the money, and Come-2Cambria sent the package, which I was able to confirm via UPS tracking. I had one nagging thought, one question I could not shake: Who was Z, and why were they so intent on outbidding me? A *Video Palace* podcast fanatic? A fellow disheveled adjunct? Someone with more knowledge than I had? And if so, were they benevolent in their pursuit?

To my surprise, Z contacted me via email. I've no idea how this fellow bidder procured my address. We exchanged a number of correspondences, and I want to share them with you here:

From: Z
To: ProfWills

Subject: TV

Dear ProfWills,

Congratulations on your bidding victory. A well-played auction. But I wanted to reach out to you and inquire as to your interest in this item? Do you know *what* this is? Do you know *why* it's so important? This is too serious an artifact to go to a nonbeliever or, worse, an enemy. Tell me, who are you and why did you buy this television?

From: ProfWills
To: Z

Dear Z,

I'm glad you contacted me, and I have questions for you as well. I'm sensitive to your frustration. I've lost my share of auctions! My name is Maynard Wills, and I am a professor of folklore in New York City. I've been studying the Eyeless Man for some time now, and with *Video Palace* prompting curiosity across myriad subcultures, I'm embarking on a large-scale project devoted to this myth. You don't need to worry. It will remain respected, protected and in my good care.

Now, I would ask you the same question: Who are you? And it is clear that you know what this is, but what is *your* interest in it?

My best,
Maynard

From: Z
To: ProfWills

I'm glad to hear that you bought this with knowledge of its importance. But I have to say I bristle at the thought of some academic having it when others have devoted their lives to the

EM. This item has power. Describing him as a myth is unwise.
I cannot afford the $3,500 you paid, but I must have this. It is
more important to me—to us—than you can imagine. Please,
let us pay you. I can give you $3,000, that is all we can pool, as
our goals have other requirements, other expenses. If you care
about the EM as much as we do, then you likely care about us,
too. Please. Take this deal. We beg you.

———————

From: ProfWills
To: Z

Dear Z,

I am sorry to say that I cannot sell this television to you and your
cohorts. It is important to me as well, and I won the auction, as
they say, "fair and square."

However, I repeat my initial question: Who are you? Why are
this TV and the Eyeless Man so important to you? Perhaps you
could share more with me.

Best,
M

———————

From: Z
To: ProfWills

We believe in the EM. I have seen one of the tapes. Yes, the
White Tapes. And I can tell you that this is all very real. We know
the truth, we wish to worship and you—a nonbeliever—have

taken hold of our altar. Unacceptable. You must share it. I will find the rest of the money. You have to give it to me.

From: ProfWills
To: Z

Dear Z,

You've indicated that you are part of a group? Is this true? Where do you meet? I would genuinely like to meet you or speak on the phone. Even a digital chat, if you'd like to remain fully anonymous.

Perhaps if you were more forthcoming and could share information of value, I would be more inclined to sell you the television. I am very interested in learning more about you and your beliefs. And maybe I could help enlighten you a bit, too.

Please let me know if you would be amenable to meeting, whether in person, via phone or online?

Best,
M

From: Z
To: ProfWills

Don't patronize me. You don't negotiate with us. I will have that TV. We must have that TV. You will not put us under your microscope or prod at us with insolent questions. I am not your lab rat. And now, you will give me the artifact.

From: ProfWills
To: Z

Dear Z,

I didn't mean to offend you, and I'm sorry if my negotiation tactic was perceived as an insult. As a gesture of good faith, I've attached a document to this email that includes all my notes on the Eyeless Man and his influence throughout world culture this last half century. It seems that you believe him to be a real entity, and I am fascinated to learn more. Again, in a very respectful way. Tell me what I've got wrong. Teach me what there is to learn.

Well, I do meet some eccentrics (reddit is, as the kids say, a dumpster fire), but even by the standards of monster chasers and conspiracy theorists, the correspondence with Z was unsettling.

Maybe I *was* patronizing. Frankly, I'd never encountered such fanatical devotion to a folk character or urban legend in modern-day America.

Z stopped emailing me after that last message, much to my disappointment.

And worse, when the TV arrived, the screen was smashed in. Whether it was the result of poor packaging or something more nefarious, I'll never know. Money lost. And worse, a potential lead destroyed.

A TEXAS
TEEN STORY

Brea Grant

I'm telling this story because I have become a person I no longer recognize. I am obsessed. I can no longer leave my home. I can't think about anything else. I don't know what's real. The only thing I know is that the Eyeless Man exists. He is torturing me, and he has tortured people I knew. He preys on your weaknesses—your obsessions—and he uses them to take control. If he targets you, I don't know if there is anything you can do to stop him. I'm writing this in hopes that someone else can prove that wrong.

—Brea Grant

S OMETIMES I FEEL like I grew up on another planet.

Not just because it was East Texas, home to a strange mix of football fans, cowboys and adult women who liked to decorate their kitchens with cutesy signs and Precious Moments figurines. It's that technology has changed so much that my teenage years feel obsolete. It was a small town, so we were always about ten years behind anyway. I didn't have a personal email address until I got to college, and my family shared a computer with dial-up so slow that I couldn't have downloaded porn even if I wanted.

So, binging media was an impossibility for the most part. At least in the way we do now with Netflix and Instagram. I mean, I'm at the point where I have to set a timer on my social media accounts so I don't scroll all day. But back then, we had our own way of binging media, and it all centered around music.

My attempts to grow beyond my small town were deeply set in discovering music that no one else listened to—punk, goth, hardcore. You name it, and as long as the jocks weren't listening to it, I was into it. And surprisingly, I had a group of comrades interested in this music, too. A set of fellow outcasts. We wore dark lipstick, cut our hair short and talked about liking Green Day before they were popular. I'd take my measly allowance from my surprisingly good grades and, after poring over music catalogs full of records I had never heard of, I'd just choose the ones with girl singers. I can't say this always produced great records arriving in the mail, but I felt cutting edge nonetheless. And mostly it was about the rebellion of it all and the acknowledgment that there was something outside my small town—a world to be discovered and explored that was interesting. Maybe even dangerous.

Well, definitely dangerous. I just didn't know that yet.

Music was my life and I crafted my world around it. We all did. If you live in a town where identity is usually formed based on your place within the hierarchy of a cheerleader versus nerd crowd, to choose *neither* is a statement. One we embraced whole-heartedly.

My friends and I watched MTV obsessively. It was like a window into an outside world. Sure, it had boy bands with their bleached tips and the nineties music tropes we all laugh at now, but it also had *120 Minutes* and bands like Nirvana and Weezer, who were mainstream but, in our opinion, very cool.

The most important part of this story, however, is understanding the friend group itself. Our friendship was based on our outsider status and our love of music. We'd trade CDs as quick as we'd trade tampons. We'd drive three hours to Dallas for shows, only to drive back that same night to get home in time for school in the morning. I mean, come on. If you wanted to see the Descendents live, what other choice did you have? (Apparently we could've waited twenty years for all their reunion shows, but how was I to know that then?) We talked about bands constantly, in addition to the normal things like boys and how much our town sucked. Graduation seemed like it was on the horizon but always a little too far away.

I loved those girls. We spent every moment together we could. Afternoons lying in each other's beds plucking one another's eyebrows. Hours and hours on the phone every night. I walked to and from school every day, and they'd often join me in the afternoons, as there is nothing quite as great as a teenage latchkey kid's house and a big TV. On my way home, there was an abandoned shack we'd often stop inside to tell spooky stories while eating bags of chips on the dirty floor. It was the beauty of being a teenager.

Teen-girl friendships run deep, and there is a pecking order innate to all of them. Not to brag, but since that time in my life, I have been in many situations with powerful people—actors, some of the most famous directors in the world, even a few famous politicians—and I will say that not one of them can hold a candle to the power of a teenage girl who is the head of her clique. The head of the clique is the most powerful girl in the world.

Ours was Melody.

Dyed jet-black hair and the ability to wear stovepipe jeans that didn't make her look sloppy and three feet tall. She could even skateboard, which was miraculous to my scrawny, indoor-kid body. She had that alternative style that was hard to achieve because it involved looking effortless while wearing the most demanding wing-tipped eyeliner. Melody had the ability to change your life by loving or hating you. And she often took the time to prove it to you.

She carried around a notebook. It was just like a normal one you'd buy at Walmart in a pack of three, but hers may as well have been plated in gold. She referred to it as her "secret dossier." I'm sure she got this from an *X-Files* episode or something, but she said she used it to keep tabs on everything that happened in our small town. Most importantly, she kept tabs on *us*.

We could never see inside it, and even if she had left the secret dossier alone, it was too powerful for us to take a peek. I felt it would have blinded us with what I only imagined were the harshest truths that could ever be written. Once a week or so, she would notice something—a new way we wore our hair, a comment, anything. She would smile a strange smile, open the secret dossier and write a note. A personal note that none of us would be privy to. Something that could take us all down. It was the peak of teen-girl cruelty.

Combine the secret dossier, her aesthetic and her general confidence, and you had the coolest, most powerful girl in the world.

Unlike me, Melody was a rule breaker. She would cut class, and she smoked cigarettes. I had no idea how to do those things without feeling monumentally guilty. The one time we got caught going to Burger King during lunch, I cried to my parents for days. They didn't even ground me because they knew I already felt bad enough. Looking back, I think my good-girl mentality got under Melody's skin, but every leader needs a herd of sheep to follow them, so she kept me around.

It wasn't her rebelliousness that led to her downfall, though. I think it was her obsession. She would become obsessed with one band or one boy or one T-shirt, and that would be the only thing she could talk about for days. I think he used that. The Eyeless Man. That's what I call him, because that's what she called him. He might have used her cruelty as well. That teen-girl meanness made her both a leader and an outsider, and that's something he could use to his advantage.

I think about it a lot because something had to make her an easy target. Otherwise it could have easily been me. It could still be me.

The intensity of a teenage female friendship cannot be over-stated. These girls are your best friends, your confidantes, the people you learn from and the only reason to get up in the morning. What they think about you *matters*.

And at the time this happened, they couldn't stand me. Or at least Melody couldn't, and the rest of them fell in line. Female infighting is about as easy to explain as the passive-aggressive shit that happens to a couple after ten years of marriage. Why is there tension about the dish towels? The answer cannot be found without exploring every intricacy of a long-term relationship. But teen female friendships don't need ten years of marriage for them to become complicated.

In this situation, there had been a long buildup. It was hard to get cigarettes at that age, and Melody had secured a pack. After all her effort, which I'm sure involved hard-core flirting with the entirely too old convenience-store worker, I wasn't interested in partaking, and that burned her. She picked up her secret dossier, glanced my way and made a note. The next day, the entire group wanted to skip fourth period to go to the mall food court and get corn dogs. Again, I said no. I had a test, and I didn't want to face the possibility of getting caught. Yes, I was lame. I've always been a rule follower, and breaking even the dumbest high school rules seemed like the end of the world. An insight into me is that I get my taxes done months early. I was the same person then but with the added pressure of knowing I had to make good grades to get into a college and get me the hell out of that small town. I wasn't about to skip a test. This got me a second note in her secret dossier. Two over the span of two days. That was a lot.

While they were at the food court without me, they decided to have a sleepover at Melody's. They conveniently forgot to tell me until they all arrived at school the next day with their overnight backpacks ready to go.

I was destroyed. I went from thinking those girls were the only reason to be alive to wishing they would all die in a fiery car crash. I had such awful feelings of anger toward them, and I regret that. I wished the worst would happen.

And then it did.

My anger toward them is not what I regret most. Trust me. It gets way worse than that. But I guess regret is part of why I'm writing all of this. That and the guilt. Did I bring it on her? Was my anger toward her a part of why it happened? Did I want her gone so badly that I manifested it? I don't believe in that manifestation bullshit, but sometimes it is an easy explanation. It doesn't matter. I kept this all a secret for too long, and I have to get it out there. Just in case there are other girls like Melody.

Because I wasn't invited to the slumber party, this part of the story is secondhand from several of the girls. The entire group went over to Melody's. Her parents were never around, so slumber parties at her house meant you could stay up as late as you wanted and occasionally sneak out to go run around the golf course nearby. I don't know why we wanted to do that, but the rebellion of running around the empty green hills in the moonlight seemed so infectious at the time.

This night, though, it was raining hard, as it tends to do in East Texas, and the clique was forced to watch TV using Melody's dad's old rabbit ears. Remember, it was the nineties in a small town. Certain people there probably still don't have cable. But you could find some stations if you would just work those rabbit ears back and forth to find the right spot. That's exactly what the group did. They found the various channels you'd expect—local shit, the networks, but then . . . something weird. Something they had never seen before.

On that little TV, there was a random channel, and it had music on it that they'd never heard. Something similar to what you'd see on late-night MTV at that time, when they played videos. There were a lot of live performances in front of small crowds, but nothing any of the girls could identify. Some of the recordings looked like they were shot on camcorders. They were hard to hear. Definitely not stuff that would draw enough attention to be on television. It was more like cable access or bootleg videotapes. This was pre-YouTube and smartphones, so it wasn't like someone could just record these things as easily as we do today, when every stupid person at every show is Insta-streaming their horrible view from the crowd. These videos had to be done on an actual camera, then approved and put on television. That was a big deal. So, it was weird to see something this shitty on TV. But in spite of the poor quality, or maybe because of it, the girls were stoked.

Remember, I prided myself on being the musical one in the group. I mean, we all were, but I wanted to be the most knowledgeable. I wasn't good at sports. I wasn't rebellious. I was nerdy. Music was my thing. So, when they told me this story, I thought it was just to get under my skin. I'm telling you—teenage girls are fucking mean. They would do that. Just make something up to bother me. But over the years, I've realized it all had to be true. What other explanation is there?

The channel was the height of what they wanted—they had a direct feed that could make them the indiest, punkest listeners because no one had heard of this shit. They sat in front of the TV for hours, absorbing all that came on; they couldn't believe their good fortune.

But as the night progressed, some of the other girls confessed to me that they felt as though the songs started to repeat, or at least sound as though they were repeating. The shitty quality of the videos started to get to them, and at some point, they grew bored. The bands were singing about the same thing. Some man. Not that he was the central figure in every song, but he was a part of it. That was the first time I heard about him— *the Eyeless Man.* They couldn't tell me the exact lyrics, but they knew the songs mentioned him. They also knew that the singers sang about the Stack and something else called the Transfer. But the stories always seemed muddied. They couldn't remember anything exactly.

So that was it. They didn't know what the Eyeless Man looked like or even what the bands were talking about. The Stack. What could that even be? And trust me. I tried to get more information out of them. I wanted to know everything. They would try to conjure up the names of the bands when I asked, but mostly they would pronounce a weird Cthulhu-sounding combination of vowels and consonants that didn't belong together. I presumed that meant black metal and went into a deep dive, but they responded to anything I found with a shoulder shrug. It was like they didn't *want* to remember. There was something that they understood even then about those videos. You didn't say the bands' names because it felt . . . bad.

But not Melody.

Unlike the other girls, Melody did not get bored of the secret channel. As each girl gradually peeled away from the TV to get snacks, call boys or go to sleep, Melody stayed next to it, trying to take in every moment she could. She was addicted. I think this is when their allegiance to her started to wane. Her normal confidence and take-charge attitude went out the window.

Imagine you're at dinner with someone, and they take out their phone to start scrolling Instagram. At first, you feel like maybe it's you. Like maybe *you're* boring. I mean, they are scrolling instead of talking to you. But pretty quickly, you realize—*no. This person is boring.* The person who starts scrolling at dinner instead of talking to you is just addicted to Instagram (and also kind of an asshole). There is nothing more boring than being addicted to Instagram.

This was the start of Melody's downfall. She was becoming *boring.*

Post–slumber party, I spent some time trying to get back into Melody's good graces. The group regaled me with stories about the evening, mentioning the channel, but for Melody, it was all she could talk about. I took that and ran with it, asking about these new bands she loved. I wanted to be the indiest of indie listeners too, just like her. More importantly, I wanted to be Melody's friend again. I wanted her approval. Two birds with one stone. Learn about the bands and I would be back in, right? But she always said she couldn't really remember. Again, I thought it was just an excuse. In Melody's case, I was sure she just wanted to keep excluding me. But now I think she really couldn't remember. There was something about the songs or the music that made you forget. Or made you be quiet about what you did remember.

The only thing she'd tell me was her favorite lyric: *The Eyeless Man has his ways.*

(It's honestly not a very clever lyric. But she always was a little more goth than me, so at the time, I figured it was just a weird goth thing.)

I wrote down the song lyric. Over and over. I would write it on all my notebooks and papers as an attempt to get on Melody's good side again. I could show her how cool I could be.

It turns out I didn't have to prove anything to her. Because like the person who just scrolls Instagram at dinner, Melody was dull now. Whatever power she held over us started to disappear. And quickly.

The whole group dynamic changed. Melody wasn't present and ready to take us all down a peg. She didn't smile her weird smile and write in her secret dossier. I saw her writing in it occasionally, but it never seemed to be about us. She was in her own world. She was absent-minded and uninteresting, which is sort of the worst thing a queen bee can be. I didn't have to be a needy follower anymore.

More importantly, there was a new opening—the group had lost its leader.

This is where my anger toward her for ousting me, not just from that slumber party but from so many times before, played out. I had so much built-up resentment. I was tired of begging for her to acknowledge my coolness, and the moment I realized I didn't have to anymore, I felt free. And I knew how to never be subjugated again. I could use all of Melody's tactics against her.

Would this have worked if she hadn't been so blinded by her obsession with these bands? I don't know. Probably not. But there is no scorn like that of a rejected teen girl. It was my chance. I wanted her power.

As everyone started to feel like Melody was getting weirder and weirder, I began to plant seeds. Now it was *me* who thought *her* eyeliner looked crooked. It was *me* who thought *she* spent too much time worrying about what the jocks thought. It was *me* who said that I saw *her* stuffing her bra.

Awful shit. I know. The kind of stuff that I just knew worked. You plant seeds. You make the other girls question her godlike influence. At the same time, compliment their shoes. Let them borrow your records. Invite them all over and accidentally forget to invite Melody. Just like she did to me. True mean-girl stuff. The stuff you aren't taught but you pick up as you watch other girls do it. And you don't even know you know how to do it until you are actually the one not inviting the other girl to your slumber party. Deep down, though, I knew I could be the queen bee. I could outsmart them.

Just like the Eyeless Man, I had my ways.

So when Melody actually quit showing up to school, it took a while for it to click with us. I had spent so much time trying to get them to forget about her that I was surprised when I didn't have to anymore. She wasn't there for them to forget about. She was always cutting class anyway, we reasoned. We were better off not having to hear her obsess about trying to have everyone over to find that silly channel again.

Rumor was she wouldn't leave the TV and her parents were worried. I only used this to fan the flames of my personal vendetta. I took the words that the cool kids always used against us and used them against her. *Weirdo. Freak. What the hell is wrong with her?*

I don't think I need to say it again, but teenage girls are *fucking mean.* That included me.

I wanted her gone. And then she was. And that's my fault, too. I'm going to lay it out for you and let you judge me how you see fit.

Writing this down has me thinking about the supernatural in general. Maybe all supernatural things are just our guilt manifested. We are able to justify the heaviness we carry with us by blaming it on ghosts or demons. Or maybe that's what I want to think because the other possibility is too scary. It's too insane to think that all this shit is real. I don't know. This is the kind of stuff that takes years to sort out, but there aren't enough therapy hours in the world to deal with what I did next.

Melody actually disappeared. She was gone. Not at her house. Not at school. No one could find her. At the time, I couldn't give two shits. I was the leader of our little group of outcasts. The clique was mine now. I dictated every move, and the only reason Melody's disappearance affected me was because I had no foil to pick on. I had no one to make me look good.

The whole town shut down. Sure, no one liked her family, but you don't just lose a teen girl in a small town and *not* send the whole town out to look for her. So, everyone gathered. We divided the town into sections and joined search parties. We looked everywhere. We put up posters. It felt like it was all anyone could talk about. Just like the stuff you'd see on TV. We were all out to help. School was canceled. They *talked* about canceling some of the football games, but small Texas towns don't cancel football games. Not even for a lost girl.

But remember, it was the nineties, a time when a black trench coat was a reminder to keep your distance (and soon would become something much worse). And Melody, she dressed *weird*. She cut class. She had bad grades. So as much as the town rallied, interest died off quickly when rumors went flying about where she could be hiding. Most people thought she ran away with an older guy who got her pregnant. Or killed herself. Both equally bad in an uber-Christian town.

We weren't all sure. Or at least, that's what we said. But I think we girls all kind of thought the same thing. It was about those bands and that channel. Maybe she left town to find the bands. Maybe she went to go find the source of the channel. But since we didn't know the bands' names, we couldn't figure out how to follow her or even where to begin. Even when questioned by the police, we couldn't help. What would we say? She watched a bunch of music videos and then decided to skip town? It was useless. Our group gave premature eulogies, held séances and did all the things teen girls know to do.

But nothing. No one found her. Not a trace. And I was okay with that at the time. Good riddance to a girl who had made my life hell.

I mean, sure, I had some sweet moments with her. She once bought me a pregnancy test when I was sure I was pregnant even though I had only had a heavy make-out session with a guy in a stairwell. (The nineties were not a great time for information on sex.) And she hadn't even made fun of me. In fact, she said she would drive me to get an abortion if I needed one. And what else can you ask for from a friendship besides someone who would drive you to get an abortion?

I just thought she'd eventually show back up.

And then she did.

This is the part no one knows. *No one.* It's hard to even write down, and it makes me feel things and have thoughts that I've spent years trying to suppress. I've pushed this shit down deep.

But here goes.

After Melody's disappearance, my parents didn't like that I was still walking home from school. They were scared of abductors or attackers or whoever took Melody. They weren't wrong, but we also didn't have much of a choice. I didn't have a car, and the school was less than a mile away.

Plus, I liked walking. I still do. You notice more, and sometimes you find things along the way.

And that day, I found Melody. *I fucking found her.*

Goddamnit.

I was passing that abandoned shack that my friends and I sometimes frequented. It was that crazy time of year where it seems to get dark at 4:00 p.m. I had stayed at school late tutoring, and as I was walking home, I saw a glow from inside the house.

Now, I did not consider myself brave, but I was curious and, honestly, determined to embrace my new self. Going into the house was something the leader of a group did to tell her followers later. It wasn't something a sheep did. And I had made the decision that I was the leader. Besides, we had all been in there before to sneak around. Just not after dark. So I went in.

As I approached the house, there was a staticky crackle from inside. I already knew what it was. I had this feeling.

I went inside, and there she was. *Melody.* In front of that little TV with the rabbit ears from her house. It was on, but the screen was just snow, and she was staring straight at it.

I remember being so shocked that I didn't know if I should say her name.

"Melody."

Her posture told me that she would never hear my voice, no matter how loudly I spoke.

She didn't turn. She didn't move. She looked like . . . I can't describe it. Like she hadn't bathed in days but worse than that. Like she hadn't closed her eyes in days. Like she *couldn't* close her red-rimmed eyes.

And with her was her notebook. The secret dossier.

I inched forward, trying not to breathe in her very human smell. I thought of calling her name again but didn't. She was miles away anyway. She was there, but she wasn't. She was already a ghost.

I don't know why I didn't run home, get an adult, call the police, do anything. . . .

I did nothing.

No. Not nothing. I had one instinct, and it was to save my own ass. This girl who had terrorized me was right in front of me, and she needed me for the first time. But my gut said not to help her. She was already gone, and if I did help her, I'd go down, too.

Or maybe that's what I say to myself to justify what I did.

There was only one thing that still had power to me about

Melody. The fucking secret dossier. Her notebook. I could still be in power. I could know all her secrets. I could make her feel like she made me feel.

I grabbed the secret dossier. And I left her there. Just like that.

And no one ever found her again.

It's my fault. That's the heart of the story. The truth. I can feel bad for ousting her, for talking shit or for making people forget her, but what they don't know is that I could've saved her. I could've even been a hero. I could've made her parents happy. I could've kept her alive. But that anger in me burned so deep that I thought maybe that was what she deserved.

When I walked by the house the next morning, there was no glow, no TV and no Melody. No one ever saw her again. I was the last.

But I had the secret dossier. It took me days to open it. I was going to say I found it on the side of the road. I still had a path to heroism. I could still give a clue that could lead to Melody. It had to have information on where she was and what she was doing. She wrote everything in there, right?

And I could look at it before I gave it over and read all the shit she had written about me. I could prove that I was right to dispel her from my universe. I just knew it would be full of bullshit that would justify my actions.

But days later, when I finally decided to open it, there was nothing like that inside. It was just filled with the same line over and over again: *The Eyeless Man has his ways.*

Over and over. Covering every single page.

The Eyeless Man has his ways. The Eyeless Man has his ways. The Eyeless Man has his ways. . . .

That should be impossible. She had that stupid notebook for years. It had band stickers on the cover from shows three years before (a lifetime as a teen). But every page was covered with those same words. Like she had never written down anything about us when she smiled. Like we never existed. Like, somehow, she had been writing about this man years before she had seen that channel.

Every. Single. Line. *The Eyeless Man has his ways.*

I guess he does. For Melody, it was addiction and binging. For me, it was power.

I was just a kid. A hurt kid who had just lost her friend. Not even her friend. More like her idol and her torturer. The girl who gave me a purpose. I made a huge mistake, and I knew it. I threw away Melody's notebook and never talked to anyone about what happened. I was ashamed. I was an asshole. I was the worst friend.

And I spent a lot of years trying to pretend it never happened. Trying to just forget.

But then something happened recently that made me realize I *hadn't* forgotten about it.

When I'm traveling for work, I love my Saturday downtime. I like to go to museums and new restaurants, but my favorite, *favorite* thing to do is to binge shows. I'll go deep into an Amazon Prime or YouTube dive. Sit back and see where the next weird British baking show or true crime series leads me. I'll let them play while scrolling my phone, and it feels like the most luxurious thing of all time. Screens. What did we do before them? Put something on the TV, scroll through Twitter and open the iPad with writing ideas. Insane, right? That amazing Venn diagram where addictive technology meets meaningless distraction.

This all happened when I was alone in Kansas City. And I was feeling *alone*. That kind of deep loneliness where you don't know anyone and you wish a stranger would just start talking to you so you can be reminded that you exist. It's the weird loneliness that comes with constant travel, starting new projects and, to an extent, success. I'm happy that I'm constantly onto something new. I'm my own boss and a lot of other people's bosses. It's a scary thing. After all this time, I have to say I still don't feel as all-powerful as Melody was in high school, but I have the power I was craving all those years ago. Yet there's nothing as powerful as a teen girl in high school. I stand by that.

On this particular Saturday, the loneliness and the bad weather in Kansas City had trapped me in my hotel room, and I started the binge process. Pajamas on, screens on, ready to be mindless.

I was down a truly great rabbit hole—some mix of nineties bands from my childhood alongside those skateboarding videos where guys hurt themselves in some serious way to be funny. Those videos should probably be illegal. After hours of watching, I was falling asleep when it came on. A song by a band—I couldn't tell you the name—and it had *the lyrics*. The ones I had thought about for so long but then managed to just . . . forget. Until that very moment.

The Eyeless Man has his ways.

I sat up straight and stared at my laptop. I knew those lyrics. And what was more important was that I knew that singer.

Goddamnit if it wasn't fucking Melody singing at me through the YouTube video. It had to be her. Aged a little, yes. But same eyeliner. Same hair. Same perfectly symmetrical face. And she was singing *at* me. Even though I knew . . . I fucking knew she was dead. I had left her for dead. She couldn't be alive. Not after the way I saw her . . . one foot in the grave . . . when I abandoned her.

And what could I do but watch her? Listen to her. Listen in the way I refused to listen before when she was trying to tell me about those bands on that weirdo channel or when I left her all alone in that stupid house. Now I had to. I couldn't look away.

She was singing. And she was power personified. She was sexy and interesting, and she commanded the screen. She was the woman I wanted to be.

She always had been. Nothing had changed.

That's all I could tell you about the video. I don't know where she was or what else was in the song. And then it ended just like that. Some other song started, but my mind couldn't comprehend it. I was fucking haunted.

I tried to replay the video, but no luck. I started looking on the Internet for the things I had forgotten about for so many years. The lyrics. The bands. The channel. Melody's disappearance. Only the last one turned up anything, and there had been no updates on it in twenty years. Time just slipped away. Mindless binging turned into obsessive watching. Searching for her. Searching for something. *Anything.* I had to find her. I had to make things right.

I was obsessed. I called in sick to work and canceled my flight home because I knew that if I moved out of that hotel, I would never be able to find that song again. I had to find her. I owed it to her. I took everything from her. I was responsible for all of it.

I stayed there for days. I ordered room service when I was hungry, but honestly, I wasn't ever that hungry. I didn't sleep. I didn't shower. I didn't move.

We switched places. Now I was the woman in the shack, staring at the TV, refusing to be found. I felt like if I just read enough pages about her disappearance or threads on weird message boards, someone somewhere would tell me what happened to her. Someone would know these lyrics. Someone would be as punk and as indie as we had been, and they would have found this channel, too. I started my own posts, website, Facebook threads about the Eyeless Man and Melody, but nothing turned up.

Then I found this podcast called *Video Palace*. It connected it all for me. The Eyeless Man and the way he creeps in. The way he might have used Melody's weakness. The way he used her obsessions. That was me, and I knew it. I knew he had found me. I know it sounds insane, but then you hear something like that and it makes you ... grounded. Connected. It made me at least understand that I wasn't the only person going through this.

In the end, that's all I found, though. I found Mark Cambria, and I learned his story and that's something, at least. I found an explanation of sorts.

I wish that was the end of the story, that somehow I felt satisfied, but it didn't go away. *This obsession.* It's hers. The same as hers. I know it. Her obsession transferred over to me. Whereas once I only wanted power, now I want to know what happened to her. I want to know where she is. And, weirdly, deep down, I want to know whatever she found, because I want to be obsessed with it, too. *I want him.* He must mean something. Something incredible. Which, I think, is exactly what Melody wanted. It's what they both wanted. They wanted me to fail. They wanted me to become obsessed.

Until I decided to write this, I never felt I could reveal what really happened. There was too much to lose. But after I found that video, I had to talk about it. Just for my own sanity. And for Melody. And what I did to her. Hopefully, it'll keep someone else from making the same mistakes.

Now it's me who can't stop talking about these bands or these lyrics. I'm the one writing it all down. I can't stop talking about *him.* I'm Melody. I'm lost and obsessed.

At the end of all this, Melody kind of won. I think about her now more than I did then. I want her approval. I want her power. I want her to be okay. She has power over me. After all these years. Whether it's through guilt or addiction, she found a way to get me in the end. Or maybe he did. Or maybe they did together. They have their ways.

DR. MAYNARD WILLS: THE FAMILY AFFAIR

The eBay debacle was a point of frustration, and it haunted me for several weeks. But late one lonesome Saturday night, I had a break. As 3:00 a.m. approached, I toiled in an endless subreddit where amateur sleuths swapped Mark Cambria theories and lied about finding their own White Tapes. There, amid the trolls and tall-tale tellers, I discovered a story that had the distinct ring of truth. A few cursory Google searches later, I had more than a hunch—I'd found hope.

One of the more mature members of the community—a redditor, in fact—shared a story he'd heard from a friend. A friend who has since passed. Suicide, he said. I found the man's obituary, which seemed to confirm this grim fact, as it contained the sort of vague language that sometimes masks a cruel end.

The redditor recounted the outline of his friend's story, which involves a Boston-area man named Casper Johnson, who's lived as a guest of the state at a psychiatric prison for the last twenty-five years. In 1995, this Johnson worked as a video-store clerk who dealt in bootlegs on the side; nothing as sordid as snuff, but he did peddle grainy porno dubs to high school boys and difficult-to-find domestic and foreign titles to the film buffs. These he'd usually acquire as second- and thirdhand VHS copies. The redditor's deceased friend claimed to have purchased Todd Haynes's *Superstar:The Karen Carpenter Story* from Johnson, for example. That film, as most cineastes know, was removed from circulation following a lawsuit brought by Richard Carpenter.

Casper Johnson's black-market dealings brought him into contact with another tape, though, one that possibly triggered the events that led to his current and unfortunate address. I don't think I need to tell you the color of its plastic.

In 1995, Johnson was married with two daughters: Vivian, who was twelve, and Emma, nine. Today, I was able to speak with Vivian. I'll let you hear the story as she shared it with me.

To be honest, I was hesitant to call her. The police report and articles I'd found online were quite graphic. I didn't know how she'd respond to my call or react to my questions. She and her sister are, after all, the victims of a terrible trauma.

I was lucky. Vivian was gracious and open. We shared a long phone call, though she confessed that, had I called her sister, I would have been met with a much more caustic response. Vivian, however, chuckled and explained that she's "spent tens of thousands of dollars on therapy so that I can function like a fucking human" and "telling the story for free sometimes makes me feel like I'm getting something for nothing."

My lucky day, I guess.

Vivian explained:

December 12, 1995, Dad came home around 11:00 p.m. from the video store, as was usual. I woke up when he walked into my room—he sometimes did this. He'd come in and give me a kiss and say goodnight and, if I was awake, he'd say goodnight to whichever stuffed animals I had with me. Ida, Blah-Blah, Forsooth. It was an adorable little ritual, actually. But this time. This time was different. He just stood in my doorway and stared at me. It was like he didn't even know who I was. Worse, it was like he didn't know what I was. He was looking at me, I don't know ... the way some- one stares at a strange insect they're seeing for the very first time. It was chilling. Still is. I called to him, "Daddy?" But he didn't answer. He just kind of grimaced, like the sound of my voice was a surprise to him. Not just a surprise. Painful. I put my head under the covers. I'd never felt that kind of rejection from him. He'd always been such a loving father. He closed the door and walked back out into the hallway. Emma doesn't remember waking up, but I thought I heard him enter her room.

After that, he went downstairs where my mother, Sarah, was. She'd fallen asleep on the couch, which wasn't un- common for her when he worked late. She greeted him when she saw him coming down the stairs. She'd assumed he would follow her to bed, but he just ignored her. Also uncharacteristic. He took this white videotape out of his satchel and made for the basement, which was kind of a TV rec room–type place.

At the trial, my mom testified that after waiting about an hour she went down into the basement and found him star- ing into the TV, sitting inches from the screen. He wasn't really watching anything, just static and maybe some ab- stract shapes. There was an unbearable, piercing hum, too. She felt as though the sound and images made her sick. She felt nauseous. She didn't know what was happen- ing. Dad wasn't responding to her at all. She was fright- ened he'd had an aneurysm or a stroke. Was there carbon monoxide poisoning? She didn't know. But she tried to pry him from the television.

That's when he attacked her. Viciously. He unsheathed his knife from his waistband—he'd carried it after the video store got held up a couple of times—and stabbed her. First in the arm. Then, right in the chest. He was definitely trying to kill her.

I hadn't fallen back to sleep, and I could hear, even two floors down, that something was really, really wrong. Dad walked back into my room. He had the knife. Instinctively, I grabbed my clock radio. Battery powered, so no cord. It was shaped like Hello Kitty. I threw it at him as hard as I could. It hit him above the eye, and the radio switched on. I'll never forget this. It was blasting Sheryl Crow's "All I Wanna Do."

Yeah, I'm no longer a fan.

Anyway, the second the radio turned on, he stopped. He dropped the knife and stared at the radio on the floor. He listened intently—as intently as I've ever seen anyone listen to anything, and he asked me, "Do you hear him? He's in there, too. And he's calling me."

I ran and woke up my sister. We found Mom and called 911. The paramedics saved her life and Dad was arrested.

He only spoke a few words at the trial, all against the advice of his lawyer. He said, "The Eyeless Man. I was finally able to see him. So clear was my path, but she pulled me away. That's where I should be. I belong to him, I belong in the Stack."

I was delicate when I asked Vivian if she would grant me permission to interview her father. She agreed. Her mother had passed in 2007, and Vivian now holds the power of attorney. I remain extremely grateful for Vivian Johnson's help. She added one more detail: the police took the tape and she never saw it again, though she does know that it was played for the jury.

I drove to Massachusetts a few days later, on a Friday morning. I arrived at the hospital and was led to a sterile waiting area—for horror fans it reminded me of the mental hospital in *The Exorcist III*. Brad Dourif was nowhere to be found, though. Instead, I was introduced to Mr. Johnson. The man who tried to murder his wife because a white tape spoke to him.

It's odd, but what struck me about him first was that he has kind eyes. Light blue, big and soft. They looked like the sort of eyes to which tears come easily. And he has wild white hair and deep wrinkles on his face.

He smiled when we met, but it was the kind of placid, medication-induced smile you see on a lot of faces in a place like that. I told him I'd spoken to his daughter Vivian, and he lit up when I said her name. I admit I had difficulty imagining this man trying to hurt anybody, let alone his own family. It seemed unfathomable, but I knew it to be true.

We made some small talk, and I bought him a can of Country Time Lemonade from the vending machine. I summoned the courage to mention the Eyeless Man, and his eyes lit up with real fire. Excitement. He was thrilled that I wanted to ask him about it, and when he spoke, it was clear that his experience with the Eyeless Man and the White Tapes was the most important thing to have happened to him in his life. As he became more animated, the orderlies took notice. I tempered my tone of voice, and he followed my cue.

We chatted for an hour, and I'm comfortable sharing a portion of our conversation, the part most pertinent to this book. I asked him to describe to me who or what the Eyeless Man is or was. And how he came to know about him.

This is what he said:

I saw him in the tapes. He lives inside the tapes, you see? But he also lives in the screens. They're linked, the tapes and the screens, two halves of the same being, energy moving back and forth between the two, and then back and forth between the three, into and out of my eyes, and your eyes, and all our eyes, you know? That's why he doesn't need any, because he has ours. All of ours. And I had seen him before, after I'd watched the first tape the first time, I'd seen only static, but in my dreams, I saw him, but not clear, because he never appears clear. I felt him. He floats. He is, and he isn't. But in my dreams, I knew it was him. And I watched the tape more when I was awake, and I could see more clearly, him into me into him into the tape into the screen into that other realm. That place where he wants us to be, that place where he wants us to feed. And I'm willing, damn it, because who the fuck wouldn't be? 'Cause the beauty is when you finally con- nect, there's this link, this direct line, and it feels so good. You don't understand. It feels so good. And I learned how to see while I was awake. I didn't need to dream; I could sit at the screen and, with my own eyes, my now open eyes, I could see him. And feel him. Because that's the thing, you know, so many people think he's nasty nasty nasty, but he just wants to welcome us. Welcome me, welcome you. Welcome us to his world.

The conversation haunted me. The Eyeless Man seems to have such power over people. For the first time I felt fear. I was afraid that I'd rung a bell I couldn't unring. And through Johnson's rambling, I became convinced that the Eyeless Man is not the legend of a creature that comes after you, like a Mothman or a Wendigo, but instead this myth is a more original concept—a nebulous spirit or demon. A pervasive and pernicious energy. What scared me most, though, much more than the story of Johnson's violence, was that deep in my soul I knew that I wanted to take a closer look.

RANGER RONIN PRESENTS . . .

Gordon B. White

As a writer, I admit I'm a thief. If you've ever seen a heist movie, though, you'll know that sometimes thieves can steal a prize worth far more than they'd expected, so here you go.

I'd been publishing horror stories for a couple of years without much of a ripple in the larger world, but at home it was different. I was one of the few who had stayed away—North Carolina to New York to the Pacific Northwest. Published author. I still couldn't get invited to a panel at my local cons, but back home my family members passed around printouts of my stories. In part it was pride, I'd wager, but they were probably also looking for themselves.

Anyway, my cousin's husband did his basic training at Fort Bragg with more than a few Carolina boys, including Kerry Wilson. That, of all the dumb things, is how I came to hear this story, even before I knew what it might mean.

I was at a family reunion that happened to coincide with a family funeral down in Saratoga, and my cousin-in-law cornered me while I was getting another helping of pecan pie in the Family Center. He told me he had a story I'd want to hear. Normally I'd have told him I don't take ideas from other people—"Bless your heart" is what I say when I'm polite; "Write it your damn self" when I'm not—but I was in a church, and so I nestled deep into my unsweetened tea to hear him out.

When he was done relaying to me the secondhand horror show I'm about to relay to you, my cousin's husband grinned. "That's messed up, right? And I bet you remember those videos too, don't you?"

I realize now that he was looking for a different kind of validation, but at the time I just nodded. I remember the videos, of course, from the Army-Navy surplus stores and flea markets. Actually, I remember the covers and the names, but I'd never watched one of them. My mind was reeling, though, already trying to write down everything without a pen.

"I told you you'd want to hear it, Mr. Writer Man," he said, and clapped me on the shoulder. "Just be sure you mention my name if you use it, okay?"

I told him I would, but, well, look above. That's what happens when you trust a thief.

He'd been right, though. Kerry Wilson's story was one I'd wanted to hear. In fact, on my drive back to Raleigh and then later on the flight back home, I couldn't shake it. I wrote it out and filled in the blanks with artistic license, but then once I heard about Professor Wills and his project, well, I tried to really dig in. Honest.

Believe me, thief though I am, that I've tried to do this justice. I've tried my best to untangle what I could between fact and fiction, but while there were certain bones of information I was able to confirm—people, places, Ranger Ronin—there's no one left to ask about the sticky bits connecting them. My cousin-in-law hadn't known at the time, but Kerry never came back from Afghanistan. As for the others, well, I'll tell you just as I'm pretty sure it happened.

—Gordon B. White

T HE FIRST TIME Kerry Wilson saw a Ranger Ronin film was with his older brother Ben at Timmy Moule's house. It was early June 1992 and already unmistakably summer in Jefferson Oaks, North Carolina, but with Mr. Wilson at the packing plant all day, Ben was saddled with dragging Kerry around the neighborhood like a plow. Timmy Moule was the third least popular kid in town despite having a Nintendo, but for Kerry and Ben—eleven and fourteen and still the "new" boys—there seemed shit else to do.

The Moules' house was a few blocks from where Kerry and Ben lived with their widower father in what might be considered the little heart of Jefferson Oaks—houses close to one another, an easy drive to Main Street, a Sunoco service station, two schools, and the First Baptist Church. Farther out, the town dissipated into crop fields and eventually the unincorporated county, but Jefferson Oaks was one of those medium towns that dot the eastern stretches where the state sleepwalks between the Blue Ridge and the Outer Banks. It wasn't a small town, where everybody infests one another's business like weevils. It wasn't a large city either, where like congregates to like and communities grow up like kudzu. Jefferson Oaks was just a medium place, one where the losers and the loners—the most medium of people— just got lost.

That day, the boys had retreated to the basement rec room to escape the heat and Gramma Moule. A wood-paneled affair, it retained a damp cellar smell and housed a mangy couch with fewer springs left than Gramma Moule had teeth. They were playing Mega Man 3, and surprisingly, Kerry was given the controller first while the two older boys talked in the corner. In the past, he'd been left to wait for turns that never came. "Just one more life" became "Just another" became "Game Over."

Gemini Man had just blown Mega Man to atoms again when Ben pulled the controller from Kerry's hands. Before he could protest, however, Ben shushed him. "We're going to show you something, but you have to promise not to get freaked out, okay?" Ben was holding something behind his back. "Can you do that?"

Kerry nodded, but mostly out of habitual appeasement.

Timmy stood to the side, his arms crossed. "He's too little."

Kerry's ears burned. "I am not!" Timmy was a runt and still about Kerry's size despite the age difference, so Kerry pointed at him. "*You're* too little!"

Ben cackled, and Timmy fumed, pouting in silence. "Listen," Ben said to Kerry, "you're not a baby, are you?"

Kerry shook his head.

"Because I'm not. Timmy's not. We're something else." He looked over to Timmy but got only a shrug. "We're adventurers. If I have to look after you, then the sooner you grow up, the sooner you can be like us. Got it?"

Kerry nodded and Timmy sighed, but Ben seemed satisfied. He pulled out a VHS tape from behind his back and held it out for Kerry to see. Big block letters in a faux-distressed font read: *RANGER RONIN PRESENTS: Surviving Blades.* The logo in the upper corner showed a face with a question mark over the features and the name "Ranger Ronin Press®" below.

"It's a training video," Timmy said as he took it from Ben and put it in the VCR. "Captain Jason is preparing us for an adventure, and he gave us these tapes from Ranger Ronin so we can train. They're very educational." Both older boys nodded solemnly. "But you can't tell anybody."

"About the Captain?" Kerry asked. "Can I meet him?"

"Maybe one day, if you're good," Ben said. "But until then you can't tell anyone about the Captain or the tapes, okay?"

"Not even Dad?"

Ben shook his head. "You have to give your word of honor to protect it. An Argonaut never breaks his word."

"A what?" Kerry asked.

Timmy sighed as he switched over the television input. "One thing at a time." He turned off the lights.

Scan lines flickered, and the question mark face quivered onto the screen. "Ranger Ronin," the text read in a crawl from the void below, "Training for the Modern Adventurer." Then it flashed white and black like a strobe, accompanied by a distorted grinding that might once have been music. Then it went black.

The video proper opened in a room with mats on the wall. A man wearing a camouflage karate gi tied with a fluorescent orange belt beneath his small potbelly and wraparound mirror shades stood with his arms crossed. His pale chest—grainy with unkempt hair—peeked through his spread lapels. The light balance in the low-quality image was blown out by too much glare from his pallid skin and the hunter orange sash. He looked more like a gas station attendant than a martial arts master, but the older boys were rapt, and so Kerry stayed silent.

The man could have been any one of a certain kind of person who populates those medium places. His only distinguishable features were his rattail and the manicured goatee that shaped his neck wattle. Both bobbed as he executed a brief, grunting series of punches and a single stiff front kick before landing in a wide-legged stance and bowing, fist in hand before him.

"Oh-tah, key-tah, adventurers." His drawled voice warbled in time with the streaks on the tape.

"Oh-tah, key-tah," Timmy and Ben responded.

"Who's that?" Kerry whispered, but a glare from Timmy shut him up.

The man continued: "Welcome to Ranger Ronin's guide to Surviving Blades. As you know, it's dangerous to go alone out there." A butterfly knife slipped from the sleeve of his gi and fluttered its wings to become a gleaming silver point. "Let's take this together."

Next came close-ups of a hundred types of blades: thin stilettos, fat cleavers, balisong butterflies, sharpened keys, thick bowies, a toothbrush filed into an awl, switchblades, tantos, machetes. All sharp enough to pierce the Veil, as the man in the sunglasses and gi repeated.

The Veil. Over and over again.

Close-ups of a hundred stab wounds of just one kind: deadly. Crime-scene photos with pools of blood. Shaky reels of victims stretched into ambulances, crimson in the flashers. Corpses in the morgue, thin black modesty bars over their eyes but not their dicks, and a dozen washed wounds like thin-lipped mouths across their chests, forever just about to whisper the secret of what lies beyond.

The man in the camouflage gi, hands moving like a magician, faster than the degraded tape could track, demonstrated lethal blows against the empty air. "Bam, you're dead," he said. "Bam. That's the other guy, gone." Another flick and spin. "Bam. That's how Ranger Ronin does it." He turned to the camera and bowed.

Timmy and Ben both bowed back. The video cut to black, then the strobe from the beginning burst once more and Kerry vomited all over the Moules' couch.

"You goddamn puke baby!" Timmy screamed as he ripped pillows away from the spreading sick.

"Calm down," Ben said. He was wiping up chunks with a throw blanket, but that only made Timmy apoplectic.

"Get out!" Upstairs, Gramma Moule was stirring, the floorboards creaking under her ponderous shuffle. "I should never have showed that to either of you."

"Shut up," Ben said. He dragged Kerry, now crying, from the couch and toward the stairs. "It's not just yours."

When Mr. Wilson returned after a long day packing meat to find Kerry still crying, Ben got the belt. Such punishment wasn't new—whenever Mr. Wilson felt Ben was shirking his brotherly duties, corrections followed. The distance Ben kept from Kerry afterward, however, was different. Instead of making up as usual, whenever Kerry brought up the video or the Captain or the Argonauts, he got silence at best and a fist at worst. Not even two days later, Ben began abandoning Kerry as soon as their father left for work, returning only in time to threaten him into silence before Mr. Wilson returned.

It's a mistake, of course, to imagine that younger brothers don't know when they're being excluded. And so, one morning, Kerry made a big production of having the trots—brandishing a comic book, moaning about his stomach, all of it. Once in the bathroom, he turned on the fan and scrambled up on the toilet to open the bathroom window, then fell out ass over heels onto the grass below. He hid in the rhododendron for less than a minute before Ben crept out, easing the screen closed behind him. When Ben took off down Loblolly Drive, Kerry gave chase.

Slinking behind fences, weaving around trees, Kerry followed Ben to where the four-lane highway separated the last residential lawns from the first crop fields. Kerry ducked into a storm ditch to watch as Ben waited silently beside the road. Eventually, a car pulled up beside him.

It was a dusky gold Oldsmobile, the kind of two-door battleship a little blue-haired lady might drive once a week to church and back. Through the open passenger window, Kerry recognized Timmy Moule, but there were other boys Ben's age or thereabouts in the back—Luis Cranton from down the way; Billy Hermann, who was a year older but had been held back; Henry somebody or other. The driver leaned across Timmy and greeted Ben with a grin.

"Adventurer," the man said.

"Captain." Ben saluted, fingers to brow.

For a captain, there was nothing immediately commanding about the man. He was resolutely average for Jefferson Oaks—

maybe late twenties, close-cropped brown hair and a trimmed beard that framed his mouth like a muzzle. Stocky and a bit soft around the jaw, as he leaned over a ring of pale skin flashed beneath the neck of his shirt. He was a medium person from a medium place whom Kerry had either never seen before or had seen a hundred times.

The man reached over Timmy's lap and popped the passenger door. He jerked a thumb to the full rear bench. "In the back, Tim."

"He's the newest," Timmy whined. "He should—"

"That's an order," the man barked, and even Kerry trembled in his hiding place.

Cowed, Timmy unbuckled his seat belt. As he wriggled through the seatbacks, the man gave his rump a resounding thwack, the intensity somewhere between a teammate and a disciplinarian. A rustle of nervous snickers from the back seat answered Timmy's yelp.

"Hop in," he said to Ben. "You get the mate's seat today."

Even as Ben climbed into the Oldsmobile, Kerry scrabbled out from the ditch. Maybe it was that gnawing loneliness that drove him. Maybe he felt it was his turn to look after Ben. Maybe it was simple jealousy, although whether for the attention the man showed his brother or his brother showed the man, who could say?

"What the heck?" Timmy shouted from the back. "Why'd you bring the baby?"

Ben paused in the seat, his mouth briefly open, but then his face boiled red. "Go home," he growled.

Kerry froze beside the car. The man looked puzzled. "Who's this?"

"I'll call Dad," Kerry blurted out. He surprised himself with that outburst, but he was now irreversibly committed to its momentum. "I'll tell him where you've been going. I'll tell him what you and Timmy were watching."

"Don't listen," Ben said. "He's lying."

Kerry struggled to dig up something he could say to prove that it was true. "Oh-tah," he mumbled, "uh, keytar?"

The Captain frowned but then composed himself. Ben struggled to undo his seat belt, but the man laid his arm across the boy's chest in restraint. "You actually showed him the videos?" the man asked.

"Just one," Ben said, shrinking beneath the pressure. "But he's too scared to see any others."

Kerry shook his head. "I'm not scared."

"Yes you are," Timmy called from the back. "You're just a puke baby. A big—"

The man snapped his fingers, and Timmy fell silent. "You were all scared once." He glanced at the mirror, and the boys mumbled in subdued agreement. He turned back to Kerry. "But they learned, because where we're going, we're going to do some scary things. Could you handle that, little man?"

Ben clearly wanted to speak but instead faintly shook his head, signaling Kerry to leave and keep quiet.

Kerry ignored him. "I can handle it."

The man laughed and elbowed Ben in the ribs hard enough to draw a wince. "Scoot over, brother." He offered Kerry his hand and pulled the boy in. "Welcome aboard. I'm Captain Jason, and these"—he tilted his head to the boys—"are my brave Argonauts."

The Argonauts rode mute from the edge of Jefferson Oaks out into the unincorporated county. The Captain, however, kept up a running commentary down the rough roads through lush ears of tobacco and low clusters of soy.

"We are preparing, of course, for the great adventure. You know what an Argonaut is?" The Captain jostled Ben next to him, pushing him into Kerry and Kerry against the scorched vinyl lining the door. "It's from a movie. *Jason and the Argonauts.* Jason is the captain and the Argonauts are his crew, and they go looking for a golden fleece. We're a band of brothers, but I'm in charge." The boys grunted their agreement from behind.

Kerry had flashes of a familiar Saturday-afternoon movie—sailors fighting herky-jerky skeletons and plastic beasts. He shuddered, though, as those memories conjured up the wound-mouths and clay-like flesh from *Surviving Blades.* Nausea rose up alongside the green taste of bile as they left the paved road for dirt, but Kerry fixed his eyes on the horizon to quell his discomfort. He wouldn't embarrass himself in front of the Captain.

"That's why Ranger Ronin made the tapes," the Captain was saying. He'd been going on about voids and veils, but Kerry had lost the thread in his fight not to be a puke baby. "They do God's work, making these skills available to the modern man in the convenience of his own home." He glanced over at Kerry and Ben. "You know how to fight?"

Ben nodded, but Kerry shook his head.

"I got a tape'll teach you. You want to be an adventurer like your brother, don't you?" Kerry nodded, so the Captain went on. "Want to move like a ninja? What about make napalm with deer blood and gasoline? Build a bunker? Choke an enemy? Bandage a bullet hole? Use psychic powers and leave your body?"

Ben stared ahead, his chin set in that stubborn Wilson way. Kerry, though, couldn't help mooning over the Captain. "Can you really do all that?" Kerry asked.

"Fuck yes, he can," Luis said from the back.

"Language," the Captain snapped. "But, yeah." He smiled wide enough to reveal a missing molar. "Fuck yes, I can."

They passed by fields left to sit a cycle fallow, then followed a lonely power line slung post to post down a gravel driveway to the low ramshackle house tucked into the tree line. When the Oldsmobile stopped, the boys tumbled out like monkeys from a barrel—stretching, scratching and shoving one another. The Captain exited slowly, hiking up his jeans and spitting on the parched grass.

"Assignment time, adventurers," he said. "Timmy and Luis, hand to hand. Watch *Clubbed Weapons*, and there's a new jujitsu one in the player. Henry, you're ready for *Improvised Munitions*. Ben, just take care of your brother. Show him around."

"No," Ben said.

"No?" The Captain looked puzzled again.

"I don't want him here." The other boys had backed away, leaving Ben alone before the Captain. Despite his rejection, Kerry felt an instinctual draw to his brother's side, but then Ben said, "That puke baby can go to Hell," and Kerry's sympathy evaporated.

The Captain's smile curdled. "But I want him here, big man. Luis, Tim, help Ben get ready for the Ghost Tape." He hissed the words, drawing the sibilance into sharp plosives.

Like a snake striking, Luis corkscrewed Ben's arm up behind. Ben tried to kick backward, but Luis cranked down and Ben sank to his knees in the dirt.

"Come on," Timmy said, a butterfly knife in his hand, its wings clicking open to reveal its sting. "Just follow the Captain's orders, okay?"

Grimacing, Ben rose, his arm still locked in Luis's grip. The two other boys ushered him out and around the house's far side. Kerry turned to the Captain, his mouth open in mute protest.

"He'll survive." The Captain grinned and winked. "Maybe he'll even treat you better."

From the sagging porch, the front door entered into a former living room the Argonauts now called "The Library." Shelves of videocassettes stuffed past overflowing attested to an organization long since abandoned for piles that grew like anthills and sprawled across the mildewed furniture like houseguests. A framed poster of the man in the camouflage gi occupied pride of place on the center wall. Despite the low print quality, Kerry recognized the goatee and aviator shades of the Ranger Ronin man.

The Captain struck a fist-in-hand pose and bowed to the poster. He glanced sidelong at Kerry until the boy followed suit.

"That's the *sensei*," the Captain said. "It means teacher."

"He's from the tape," Kerry said. He wondered if *Surviving*

Blades hid somewhere in the plastic mounds, its corruption seeping out.

"He's from all the tapes," the Captain corrected him. "He's Ranger Ronin's founder. He's the one who made these." The Captain held out his hands to the precarious largesse around the room.

Kerry looked at them all—some still had their jackets, most were naked, but all bore the same big block letters and Ranger Ronin logo. He saw *Hiding in Plain Sight, Shortwave Radio, Surviving Fallout, The Forager's Guide,* and *Krav Maga Revealed!,* among dozens more.

"Are all these real?" Kerry asked.

"These aren't home movies, son," the Captain said. "You can't just make up a bunch of hooey and sell it. That'd be crazy."

Kerry nodded. It made sense, he supposed. "What's his name? The sensei?"

It slipped from the Captain's lips with hushed reverence: "Master Kim."

"Like a girl?" Kerry asked.

"No! He trained with the Grand . . . under Master. . . . Oh, never mind. That'll be part of your homework." The Captain took a water-stained Ranger Ronin pamphlet from a pile and tore away the back page order form before handing it to Kerry. "Learn to respect your elders."

The rest of the house was a warren of misshapen rooms that stunk of mold and unwashed male bodies. Cordoned off by unfinished drywall, paneling with no studs beneath or merely curtains staple-gunned to the ceiling, the Captain named each one: the Dojo, the Refectory, the Sanctum, the Captain's Lodge. The heavy air quivered with the whine of hidden televisions and the hiss of tapes as Ranger Ronin's strobe and snatches of Master Kim's mechanicalized drawl leached into the hall. Despite the Oldsmobile holding a mere handful of boys, the house felt as though it was almost bursting.

Head spinning, stomach gurgling, Kerry stopped abruptly. "Where's the bathroom?" he asked quietly.

The Captain paused his tour. "Oh. Septic's broken, but just go outside. Nature is your toilet."

Kerry nodded and walked quickly back the way he came. Past the Sanctum, where a deep "oh-tah-key-tah" hum rattled the floor. Past the Captain's Lodge, where a Sunoco uniform hung from a hook, "Jason" embroidered on the breast. Past the Dojo, where Master Kim's tinny "Bam! Bam! Bam!" popped over the grunts of a scuffle. The fug of heat and sound and sweat and strobes was overwhelming, so he ran before the sickness took him.

When Kerry burst out from the Library's teetering archives and into the yard, the muggy blanket of summer air was no relief. Whimpering, he reeled into the woods, but even the tree bark thrummed with voltage and the leaves trembled with hidden signals like satellite dishes. Kerry stumbled farther out, the sizzling current of Ranger Ronin videos all around boiling the tears he tried to hold back until finally they exploded in a great steamy, wracking sob.

When he finally buckled over to catch his breath, Kerry noticed an orange extension cord slithering across the ground. It was buried a little but, once seen, glowed like Master Kim's neon sash across his camouflage gi. It hissed with current like a venomous snake, and Kerry, beguiled, couldn't help but follow.

Winding away from the house, over roots, under a log, it

finally wrapped like a snare around a sapling and disappeared into the ground. Even up close, it took Kerry a moment to realize he was looking at a camouflage netting over a kind of trapdoor. Beneath it, something was moving. No, not moving. Talking.

The sound of two voices grew clearer as Kerry kneeled down. He peeled up an edge of the netting to reveal a plywood lattice over the top of a rough-hewn hole. The cord ran down to a television set and a VCR nestled on a mound of red clay soil, a naked child squatting before them. For a moment, it was too dark to make out the boy's face, but then the Ranger Ronin strobe flashed and Kerry recognized his brother.

As the strobe played across Ben's glass-eyed gaze, he flickered skull face to no face, skull face to no face. It finally settled into a cold blue glow, turning the red walls purple.

"Greetings, adventurer," a tinny voice spoke, but it wasn't Master Kim. "By now you are prepared for what is out there. You are prepared to see what the Eyeless Man sees."

A different voice, just as warped, replied: "I am prepared." At that moment, Kerry realized both garbled voices were coming from Ben's open mouth as if he was channeling them from different, distant shores. "I am ready. Oh-tah—"

"Hey!" the Captain shouted from just down the path. "What are you doing?"

Startled, Kerry tripped backward, yanking the cord from the sockets below. In the pit, Ben turned upward in the dying cathode tube, his face cold blue, his eyes wide and white. Before the darkness swallowed him, he opened his mouth as if to scream, but what erupted was the feedback squall from a dead station.

All thoughts of loyalty and fraternal duty vaporized. Kerry

sprinted from the woods, past the house and up the driveway, hauling ass to the road.

"Puke baby!" Timmy yelled, materializing seemingly from thin air. Other boys too seemed to pour from the house—more than Kerry had thought were there, their faces blurred and distorted through his tears as if quivering out of tune, their laughter like static. As he ran, the Oldsmobile grumbled up the gravel behind him, but Kerry didn't stop until it rolled past and cut him off.

"Get in," the Captain said, leaning out with a weary air. Kerry shook his head, but the Captain sighed. "What do you think is going to happen here?"

"I'm going home?" Kerry didn't honestly know.

"Assuming I let you," the Captain said, shrugging, "what's there for you?"

"My dad? My brother?"

"Your dad's at work, your brother's here," the Captain said, as if reading Kerry's mind. "They don't have time for you, but I do. I'll show you if you hop in."

Kerry resisted. The blacktop stretched out just beyond the Oldsmobile, but Kerry now felt the emptiness expanding out forever in all directions.

"Loneliness can be valuable," the Captain whispered, barely audible over the engine's sputter. "I want you." He gestured to the empty seat. "I want you to see the Argo."

"I was like you once, so I get it," the Captain lectured as he drove. His eyes covered by a damp bandana, Kerry had lost track of the twists and turns of the road and the Captain's logic. "But, see, everything you learn at school—everything your parents tell you—that's all bullshit. You've heard Master Kim talk about the Veil, right? It's what separates this side—with all the 'be good, get a job, go to church' garbage—from the other side." He let out a low whistle. "That other side's where things get real."

They left the paved roads, then returned, then left again before finally stopping. The Captain, still talking, climbed out and walked around. "I'm preparing you boys because it's not safe out there. I know that; Master Kim knows that; and now you know, too." He opened Kerry's car door and leaned in close enough that Kerry could smell the menthol on his breath. "Are you scared of what's out there?"

The yawning space beyond the car door was silent—no road sounds, no traffic, not even birds in a forest. Kerry nodded.

"I know," the Captain said. "Which is why I'm going to carry you." He wrapped his arms around the terrified boy—something tighter than a hug—and lifted him from the car.

The Captain held Kerry against his chest. He didn't speak as he walked, but his breath whistled through his nose against Kerry's shoulder. With his arms around the Captain's neck, Kerry felt the damp heat welling up between them. Beads of sweat tickled as they ran down to Kerry's elbows and pooled there before dripping off. There was a deep tremor as their hearts beat one against the other.

They finally stopped, and the Captain lowered Kerry to his feet. Locks clicked open, a chain slithered out and then, with a creak, cool air yawned against them. The Captain put a hand on Kerry's back and pushed him forward as he pulled the blindfold away.

"Welcome to the Argo," the Captain said as Kerry's pupils shrank from the sudden dazzling brightness. "This is what's going to take us beyond."

Once Kerry could see, however, it could have been the Moules' rec room. All except for the television screens—of every size, on every surface—which fixated on Kerry and the Captain like a single creature with five hundred sleeping eyes, all ready to blink open. The burst of static, Kerry knew, would blast his skin off.

"The Argo will get us beyond the Veil, then we'll help others follow. See?" The Captain gestured to a single circular lens at the center of the square screens, a camcorder positioned to record the room. A VHS cassette, the color of worn ivory keys, protruded just from its grasp, ready to be plunged down and consume the scene. "But when we get there, of course, the Argonauts need to be ready for anything. The others are training for one set of challenges, but I've got something just for you, okay? If you master this, you'll be stronger than anyone else, but you can't come back until you're done."

In the myriad dark reflections, the Captain produced a tape from behind him as if by magic, then passed it over Kerry's shoulder. The label read: *RANGER RONIN PRESENTS: THE TOUCH OF DEATH!*

Although both were Ranger Ronin productions, where *Surviving Blades* had been about flesh—blood, bodies, the gasping mouths of wounds puckering skin—*The Touch of Death* was about spirit.

Master Kim—no longer in a camouflage gi but a white linen Kung Fu suit with his wraparound shades—still talked of the Veil and the beyond, but this time he also talked about links and energy. Instead of focusing on crime scenes, the screen flashed with charts of qi lines and energy meridians, vibrant chakras that blew out the white balance and paintings of silver cords stretching off into midnight starscapes beyond neon pink wireframe pyramids. This was life, Master Kim's reverb-washed voice told Kerry, the flow and connection.

To sever these, then, was death. It was the last resort when there was nothing left.

The rest of the video was Master Kim demonstrating the Touch of Death on a sexless store mannequin, its smooth body painted with a highway map of energy channels. "Zap!" the Master yelled, hitting the nerve cluster on the dummy's right shoulder with fingers crimped into the shape of a bird's beak. "Zap! Zap!" The words crackled in Kerry's ears, firing through his brain as the Master hit two more meridians on the solar plexus and the left side of the rib cage.

"Zap! Zap! Zap!" Kerry yelled the words and moved in time to the Master's call. He practiced in front of the television, picturing an invisible foe.

"Sever the ties! Zap!" the Master called from the other room as Kerry's fingers pecked against his own reflection in the bathroom's floor-length mirror.

"Zap! Zap! Zap!" Kerry screamed, hitting the couch cushions again and again until the fabric started to fray and the stuffing was broken.

Day after day after day—zap, zap, zap—Kerry practiced when Ben left him behind. He pictured severing ties, disrupting channels, breaking the flow. His eyes closed, he was alone; the bodies fell before him, their energy forms spinning off into the Void. Timmy Moule. Luis. Henry. Even the Captain. The Master. Dad.

Ben's guffaw snapped Kerry back from the world of energy channels and into the living room, caught in mid-zap on the upended seat cushion. The tape continued to play, Master Kim now discussing the power of breathing.

"It's the Touch of Death," Kerry explained, panting. Being back in the late-afternoon light was strange.

"It's bullshit," Ben said with a laugh.

"The Captain gave it to me," Kerry said.

Ben sneered. "He gave you this to keep you busy. It's not real."

"Then how do you know the other tapes are real?"

Caught off guard, Ben frowned like a catfish. "They're— Just shut up, okay?"

"I'm ready to go back," Kerry said. "I want to see the Captain."

"No way." Ben tossed the cushion back on the couch and flopped onto it. "You embarrassed me last time. Things are getting serious there. The Captain's completed his collection and we're—" He paused. "Never mind. It doesn't concern you."

"Take me," Kerry said. "Please? I'm ready."

"Nah." Ben switched over to the television, letting the tape play on without an audience. "It's not for babies."

Kerry took a deep breath. Zap. "Then I'll tell Dad."

The tattling gambit worked again, but the Captain had changed during the weeks of Kerry's hermitage. From the back of the gold Oldsmobile, Kerry noticed his beard was patchier. His eyes were red and watery, and the pouch beneath his neck had deflated to a loose flap of skin. Still, his attention—distracted though it was— lit a glow that Kerry was desperate to kindle.

The Argonauts' stronghold too had changed. The outside walls seemed thinner and hummed with magnetic waves that tingled through the brittle grass. Tree branches over the tin roof were baked as bare as finger bones. When the boys tumbled out of the car, Timmy Moule walked to the house's side and began to piss on it, not even seeking the modesty of the wizened trees.

"Septic tank still broken?" Kerry asked, but the Argonauts paid no heed as they followed the Captain inside.

In the Library, Master Kim in his camouflage gi still hung on the wall, but the hillocks of VHS tapes he had previously sur- veyed had erupted into a full Appalachia. Dozens more, maybe over a hundred, had congregated like flies on the mounds. They weren't standard Ranger Ronin tapes either. Instead, their home- made labels bore a hand-drawn attempt at the logo and names scrawled in fat, dull Sharpie.

Kerry was so taken by the titles—*Assassin Skills, Gun Stuff, Brain Safety (Waves), Sleep Experiment*—that he didn't notice Timmy Moule stripping until the bird-chested boy was hop- ping on one leg, wriggling out of his pants. The Captain entered, now dressed in red silk pajamas with a tiger embroidered down the side. He threw a shimmering blue bundle to Timmy, who snatched it from the air and slid into the complementary costume. His bore an iron-on snake patch with enormous cartoon eyes.

"C'mon, Tim," the Captain said. "We gotta finish this one." Timmy's silk costume billowed as he skipped barefoot around the piled videocassettes and back toward the Dojo.

Kerry looked to Ben, but the envy and anger burning behind his brother's eyes roiled like a filmstrip cranked to the point of disintegration.

"Can I come, too?" Ben shouted at the Captain's back, his voice rising to a squeak before cracking.

The Captain stopped at the Dojo's threshold. As Timmy disappeared beyond the hanging sheet divider, Kerry saw mattresses against the walls and stiff crash pads duct-taped across the floor. A tripod-mounted camera gazed hungrily at the center of the room.

"You just"—the Captain waved vaguely—"just take care of him, all right?" The Dojo's curtain swished closed behind him, hiding everything.

Around the brothers, the house shuddered with Argonauts toiling away in their cells. Grunts and flashes of light leaked from doors, and music blared as tapes began or ended. Master Kim's wilted portrait stared down as the constant drone of his voice from beyond the house's veils filled the space between the boys. Nausea overwhelmed Kerry again.

"You've ruined it," Ben said, snapping the tension like a band. "You can't let me have anything."

Kerry's jaw dropped. "What? I didn't do anything."

"'I didn't do anything,'" Ben repeated in a mocking whine.

Unsure of what to say, Kerry stammered. "You l-left me alone."

"I just wanted my own friends, my own things," Ben snapped. "This was supposed to be mine."

"But there are a bunch of you here. And the tapes, the order forms, there must be—"

"I just wanted something that's not yours too, okay?"

"You're an asshole." Kerry shoved Ben, but it barely moved him. He reared back to try again, but Ben caught Kerry's wrist and spun it backward. Kerry bent under the unexpected pain.

"I'm a better-trained asshole than you." Ben twisted again, and when Kerry looked up, Ben smacked him across the head. He was drawing back again when the Captain stormed out from the Dojo, setting the thin walls trembling.

The Captain was frazzled, his face flushed. Vicious marks scored the side of his neck, and he ground at his eyes with his palm.

"Who here watched *Combat Medicine*?" he hollered. The noises in the other rooms ceased. "Who watched *Combat Medicine*?" he bellowed again.

Ben slowly raised his hand. Kerry felt the urge to press it down and pull him away, but other boys were coming out of the rooms and in from outside. Kerry felt a presence far beyond the other five boys who had been in the car, but he didn't dare turn away to count. Rejuvenated by his audience, the Captain puffed out his chest.

"You come with me." The Captain grabbed Ben by the wrist. "Argonauts," he said, facing the others, "I've received the signal. Prepare to disembark." As he dragged Ben toward the Dojo, the other boys began to scurry like sugar ants. Luis and Billy were raking big scoops of VHS tapes into shirts held out like aprons, then running them outside. Henry, the tallest, pulled down the picture of Master Kim. The bustle as the hive disassembled itself was astonishing, but Kerry was purposeless there, having been left alone to practice the Touch of Death on the couch all summer.

Kerry moved against the current, down the hall and toward the Dojo. The quilt nailed above the doorframe had bunched together, and through one gap Kerry saw the camera again as it stared impassively at the floor. Through the other side, Kerry saw two tiny white feet, soles up, like hermit crabs retreating into the wide cuffs of blue silk.

"Is he okay?" the Captain asked, still hidden but his voice high, almost plaintive.

"I . . . I don't think so," Ben stammered. Closer now, Kerry saw his brother facing toward the Captain but staring down.

"Help him," the Captain ordered. "This is what the tape taught you, isn't it?"

Now just outside, Kerry saw the little pile of blue silk and the back of Timmy Moule's head, his hair matted on the crown as if licked once by a stupendous cow. Ben, still looking down, shook his head, and the first of his tears fell.

For a moment, Kerry thought his brother was the only one sobbing, but when the Captain spoke, his voice was choked. "It's not my fault," he said. "We were just practicing. I can't . . ." He trailed off, the words rattling in his throat like voices on a television tuned too low.

The Captain's wheeze was all Kerry could hear, swelling into an ocean of static. Bodies, blades and wounds like mouths engorged Kerry, and the need to see what Timmy Moule had become swelled his brain. He flung aside the quilt.

"Get the fuck out of here!" the Captain snarled, and grabbed Kerry by his shirtfront. The little boy flew up, too startled by the sudden fury to even scream.

A charging bull, the Captain rushed Kerry down the hall to the Library and threw him into the piles of cassettes. The corners bit Kerry as he toppled back, the impact shuddering the plastic and setting the ribbons inside to hiss with magnetic energy.

Dazed, Kerry saw Ben standing beside the Captain, though he was dwarfed by the grown man. The Captain looked comparatively ancient. He pointed to Kerry. "Take care of your brother."

Although tears ran down his cheeks, Ben nodded. A butterfly knife appeared, waved its wings and glistened cruelly in his hand.

"I told you not to come." Ben stepped forward and slashed through the air. "But you kept threatening to tell on us."

"I promise I won't." Kerry clambered to his knees and raised a hand. Ben swung the blade again, but while his aim was wild and only grazed the flesh beneath Kerry's thumb, it made wicked work of it.

Kerry stared dumbly at the cut as the blood began to flow. *Surviving Blades* raced back—knives, bodies, clean and tight-lipped mouths of wounds. This mouth, however, was open and red, and it swallowed Kerry down a long, dark throat until the rest of the world was just a tiny speck of light above.

"I don't want to," Ben was saying, but it was far away and boxed in, like a television playing across an empty room. "He's my brother."

The Captain was shaking his head. "The Argo only has room for one of you," he said. "The one whose loyalty is to his brother Argonauts and his Captain."

"Please?" Ben whispered.

"Think of your training." As the Captain placed a hand on Ben's shoulder, Kerry zoomed in on that spark—flashing like a sun dog—and watched in slow motion as Ben's resistance crumbled. "It's just like a video."

Ben left the Captain's steering grip with the blade outstretched. Kerry was alone now—the last bonds of brotherhood severed with the wisp of static as Ben's knife cut the air. He had nothing left but his loneliness. A loneliness he had been trained to spread.

"Oh-tah, key-tah!" someone, somewhere, screamed.

Regurgitated from the throat of darkness, fingers pressed like a hawk's bill, Kerry shot past the knife's arc and hit the first nerve cluster in Ben's advancing arm. The pop of energy exploded like a bulb, and Ben's knife fell from numb fingers. His surprise only barely registered, however, as Kerry's practiced movements arced like lightning. Zap—the solar plexus. Zap—the left ribs. Zap. Zap. Zap. Energy channels disrupted, bonds broken, bodies hurled out into space, Kerry sent Ben to the darkness and made him just as alone as Ben had made him.

With an enormous crackle and burst, Ben crumpled, as if boneless, without a further sound. Kerry knew his brother was dead even before the odor of burned flesh could rise.

"Shit," the Captain whispered. For a moment, Kerry saw fear in his eyes—perhaps for what he'd created, or perhaps what he'd left to be formed in the Void. Then, however, there was a wave of revulsion, although whether aimed at Kerry or at the Captain himself, Kerry could never say.

The Captain swung and punched Kerry square in the face. Everything broke, and Kerry fell into pieces to the floor. He felt the Captain lift him but was too broken to struggle. The arms and chest that were once strong and comforting were now wiry and hollow. Their hearts beat fast and ragged, the rapid pulses blurring into static.

Here's where I intrude again, instead of slinking around behind the narrative. Here's where Gordon B. White tells you that I remember Ranger Ronin—and that my brother Elliot and our friend Sergey from down the block and my cousin's husband, Mr. Bless-Your-Heart-Write-It-Yourself all do, too. But also that none of us has one of the tapes in our collections. Internet sites that obsess over forgotten videos have a few traces and reconstructed titles, but there isn't a Ranger Ronin website on the Wayback Machine or an Amazon page. There aren't electronic records of the company with the North Carolina Secretary of State.

Here's where I tell you too that while plenty of us remember Ranger Ronin videos, nobody agrees on what they were. Some people claim Ranger Ronin was government psy-ops designed to root out backyard anarchists and stay-at-home militias. Others think it was just a homegrown cash grab during that middle period after VHS democratized information sharing and profiteering and before the web made transparency unavoidable. A few people, who I promised not to name, swear it was actual, factual information disseminated in goodwill in preparation for the new millennium. Others, of course, believe it was something more sinister.

I'll tell you, though—honor among thieves—I just don't know.

In a credit to the fine members of law enforcement serving Jefferson Oaks, it took less than a day to piece things together. After Mr. Wilson reported the boys missing, one of the deputies recognized Kerry's *Touch of Death* tape from the circle rack at the Sunoco where Captain Jason worked. They'd gone out to question him but found the house empty and a smoldering burn pile of black plastic in the yard. Timmy Moule was still facedown in the Dojo, but any tape from the camera there must have been destroyed with the others.

Jason's Oldsmobile was still in the driveway, though, the battery running and the radio tuned to the very right of the dial. The sheriff popped the trunk, and bam, there were the Wilson boys. One of them was even still alive.

In the hospital, Kerry tried to tell them most everything as best he could, but it was blurry, disjointed—like a tape that had a magnet run over it and then played too long. He told them about the training and the videocassettes. About the Argo and Master Kim. What Kerry didn't tell them, though, was how, as he lay there in the darkness with his brother's body, he heard the static coming from the corpse's open mouth. How it had gradually tapered off from *oh-tah-key-tah*, into a chittering static, then finally silence. He didn't tell them how, before the voices vanished, he heard the chorus from behind Ben's slack lips whispering about the Void and the Veil. Begging him to reach beyond.

And that was that, it seemed. Despite an APB and a trawl of the woods, neither hide nor hair of Captain Jason and the four missing Argonauts was found.

Not until ten years later, that is, when the lot was bought and the new owner dug up the busted septic system. That's when they found the Argo, which had been built as well as one could build a DIY bunker guided by videos, which is to say not very. The crew was all there too, although the single camera trained on the room was empty, the white cassette Kerry had seen poised in its grasp having either vanished or never been recorded to begin with.

I dug as far as I could, but the official position, for what it's worth, is that the Argo's ventilation system failed almost immediately, leaving them to suffocate there, bathed in the static of dozens of televisions running on an endless loop. Eventually, though, the batteries died, the screens went black and the Carolina summers baked the Argonauts into leather and withered out their eyes.

DR. MAYNARD WILLS: MUSINGS FROM THE QUANTUM REALM

When the *Video Palace* podcast begins, Mark Cambria is asleep. In his slumber he speaks a cryptic phrase. I've seen it phoneticized in different ways, even by the contributors inside this book. Not an unexpected quirk for a written component of a cross-cultural myth. Here, we'll depict that phrase as "O Ta Keta." Mark's somniloquy is the impetus for his quest—one that's maybe taken his life. Remember, Mark tells us that he doesn't usually remember his dreams. And then he contemplates, "Maybe that's why this one interests me so much. If that [dream] was the cause, then what was I dreaming about?" Mark didn't know who—or what—visited his mind's eye when he spoke those words, but when Casper Johnson suggested the Eyeless Man appeared to him in dreams (and elsewhere), I began to wonder. Could a manifestation foster in the collective subconscious of a culture? Of many cultures? I'm confident that the Eyeless Man phenomenon isn't exclusively a representation of dreamwalker myth. He's not Freddy Krueger. There's too much evidence and interaction in the daylight hours. But this doesn't mean that dreamtime plays no role. I wanted to explore further.

But please understand, I am certainly not the first to investigate the link between dreams and mythmaking. The Aboriginals of Australia have long held the belief that all of creation is the result of Dreamtime (or the Dreaming), in which the universe dreamed itself into existence. All Aboriginal spirits and ancestors exist in the Dreaming and are responsible for creating the world around us through the use of songs. Of course, throughout human history songs have been an intrinsic part of storytelling for various cultures. I wondered, though, were we on the cusp of a breakthrough in the relationship between the dream world and the physical one? One steeped in science that might help explain how the idea of the Eyeless Man was born and, perhaps, spread? I needed to access a greater mind than my own to pursue this line of inquiry.

I greatly admire the author, physicist and retired Stanford professor Dr. Peter Gilliam. His work centers on the study of quantum physics as it relates to dreams. He's published some fascinating essays on the topic. While they're academic-level, I recommend looking them up at your local university library. I reached out to him utilizing the New School's network of university contacts and emailed him a few of my, well, let's call them "starter thoughts," explaining my work and inquiring if he might have insights or could at least point me in the right direction. I worried he'd dismiss me as a nutcase. He wouldn't have been the first.

But, to my delight, he responded very quickly:

From: Gilliam, Peter, PhD
To: Wills, Maynard T.

Dear Professor Wills,

It was a surprise to receive your email—in my post-retirement years I have found myself relegated to the academy's musty

130

bookshelf. Seems there's always a newer and more slender tome from a freshly minted PhD with an Instagram account, so thanks for reaching out. What a fascinating course of study. An ambitious proposal, linking the worlds mythic and scientific. And through dreams, no less. Ambitious indeed!

My immediate thought is that yes, there is some relationship between the quantum realm and the dream world. In fact, there's a relationship between the quantum realm and everything. Apologies if this sounds flip, but it's true. The real question is: To what degree does the quantum realm directly inform our dreamscapes?

Dreams are interesting because one could consider them a factor of the "macro"—e.g., the large, three-dimensional world that we inhabit. Gravity, for instance, is a factor of the macro, for we are directly affected by it in our everyday lives. We are not, however, directly affected by whether or not light is in the form of a particle or a wave. To us, it is still just "light."

We *experience* dreams as though we're in the macro world, but as they happen inside our heads, some theorists consider them to be more like holograms: the work of neurons firing and electrical signals, much closer to the function of the quantum than macro scale.

Of course, dreams are thought to be our brains defragging; it works through bits of information while we sleep so that we may process complex thoughts while unconscious. The brain is a terribly efficient machine.

There are some researchers who believe that when we dream, the electrons that exist in our brains—which cause all the neurons to fire and render the dreams themselves—are briefly jumping into another dimension. And when they do, they take us with them—or our thoughts, at least—and therefore give us interdimensional experiences that we believe to be real. This is still largely conjecture, yes, but it is interesting. If you are interested in pursuing this theory, I highly recommend a book on the subject: *The Dreaming Universe*, by Dr. Fred Alan Wolf. An incredible thinker and one of the foremost leaders on the subject.

The basis of this theory is that quantum particles behave, frankly, magically. They can affect one another over long distances through a kind of telepathy. They can freeze and even move backward in time and, most relevant to this discussion, subatomic particles will perform every conceivable action. They will travel back in time to the age of the dinosaurs, circle Alpha Centauri and sink into the core of the earth—all before finally arriving at the result with the highest probability, which might be, say, causing a neuron in our brain to fire.

It's difficult to wrap one's head around, but let me put it this way: these minuscule pieces of us really do travel to the ends of the universe and perhaps beyond, into dimensions we couldn't possibly understand. And the only thing that finally places it back in this most likely of scenarios is that we observe that to be the case.

Our dreams: Could they be postcards from the edge of existence? And what if we were able to bring back a souvenir? Or, more troubling, pick up a hitchhiker?

I hope this late-night email provides some new context for your studies. I beg you to be cautious, though, as we really cannot conceive what lurks on the other side of the dimensional wall.

Please feel free to contact me further. I haven't had an adventure in a long time, and you seem about to embark on a remarkable one. Now, there's a comfortable chair and a radio play that I must attend to.

My best,
Peter

––––––––

Gilliam and I emailed back and forth a number of times. He recommended additional materials, and I learned more about a subject on which I was completely ignorant.

And his comment about the radio play encouraged me to recommend *Video Palace*, and he indicated that he would listen to it. I felt gratified the old boy was getting something out of the deal.

I considered my experience with Casper Johnson in the context of my correspondence with Peter. Not only did I yearn to know where Casper Johnson went in his dreams, I wanted to know what he saw.

And who might have seen him.

TWO UNEXPLAINED DISAPPEARANCES IN SOUTH BRISBANE, RECALLED BY AN INNOCENT BYSTANDER

Merrin J. McCormick

Professor,

I wish I didn't have anything to tell you about the Eyeless Man. I wish I'd never read about him or dreamed about him. I can't erase what I know, so it's probably time I told someone about it. You seem to be a willing audience.

I read somewhere that memory is influenced by the act of recall. Ruminative thinking and repetitive storytelling create opportunities to misremember or embellish events. The second time you "remember" you're actually recalling the memory you created the last time you revisited an event. If that's true, you're in luck. I've never told this story to anyone or written about it before now.

To the average person this story wouldn't sound credible; I lived it, and I hardly believe it. I trust you're one of the few people still alive who will understand.

—Merrin J. McCormick

T HE FIRST DISAPPEARANCE.
Her name was Laura. I didn't know her well. This is
what I knew: she had a high-energy vibe, the type that attracts
people. I got to know her a bit when we both volunteered at the
Brisbane International Film Festival in our second year at uni.
She was particularly excited to meet Roger Corman, who had
a late-night retrospective at the festival. She liked to travel. She
could afford to travel. She seemed fearless. She went missing at
the beginning of the second semester in 2004, of our final year.

No one was particularly concerned when Laura didn't show
up to classes at the start of our final semester. Her friends assumed
she'd extended her trip to Turkey into a gap year. It's not normal
to start a gap year when you only have one semester left, so other
theories circulated. I heard that Laura had definitely done heroin, as if heroin alone makes women disappear. Flyers appeared
around campus—a photocopied picture of Laura grinning and
tear-off phone numbers at the bottom. The same posters appeared on telephone poles in South Brisbane, where she lived in a
sharehouse with three other students. Her home was surrounded
by halfway houses that looked after people with mental illnesses
and recovering drug addicts. It faced Musgrave Park, a grassy expanse with shady trees, park benches and a playground no children played on because the Parkies lived there (the park was a
remnant of the Kurilpa Aboriginal camping ground). When the
city hosted Expo 88 and the southern shoreline was refashioned
into a weird international Disneyland and renamed Southbank,

the Turrbal and Jagera people were displaced to make room for international tourists, but they couldn't be deterred from their home. Not for long.

Laura worked two blocks from her home at a bar called Rumpus Room. Out front there's a big goanna statue, though the six-foot lizards aren't native to the area. You'd be more likely to find a carpet snake curled up in the yard. Rumpus Room faces Boundary Street, the main drag that goes through West End and South Brisbane. It got its name because it was a literal boundary that Aboriginal people had to get on the other side of by 4:00 p.m. Monday to Saturday and all of Sunday. A rule that started in the 1850s. Musgrave Park is on the "wrong" side of Boundary Street (and the city is on the wrong side of history). Laura mostly worked afternoon shifts, sometimes the late shift, which started at 9:00 p.m. and could end at 3:00 or 4:00 a.m. Closing time depended on when the students and backpackers ran out of money. Of course, most of them took pills and drank water to save money. You could get off your chops on pingers much cheaper than you could get shit-faced on vodka. It was bad for business but good for the dance floor. The drug problem wasn't easily identifiable in South Brisbane because anyone who was walking the streets wired may have been schizophrenic or a manic-depressive on a mood swing. Walking down Boundary Street, you were likely to cross paths with someone high on drugs, looking for drugs or off the drugs they should've been on. All of this to say, the short walk between Laura's work and her home had its hazards. It was easy to conclude she'd been in the wrong place at the wrong time on many occasions. It's forgivable to go missing, but when women must be "perfect victims" to earn sympathy rather than judgment, it was unclear if Laura met that high standard.

The people living in South Brisbane and West End are different now. Gentrification slithered through, raising high-rises, raising rents, displacing locals and replacing the community with a "village vibe and convenient lifestyle" that developers sell to young professionals and investors looking to diversify their property portfolios with some inner-city rental apartments. Even in 2004 the streets were busy enough that there should've been witnesses. But the photocopied flyers faded on the telephone poles—no one tore off the phone number to supply information. Either no one had seen anything, or they knew better than to talk about it.

Lesson one: Don't walk alone at night, not even two blocks, past thirteen houses, from work to home. Not even if you know your neighbours.

The second disappearance.

I have more to say about the second disappearance. I didn't regularly hang out in South Brisbane, but circumstances brought me there halfway through that final semester (after we'd stopped expecting Laura to reappear). I'd missed a screening for American Film because of the flu (there's nothing worse than watching a movie in a full lecture theater while you're sick). Once the pseudoephedrine got my symptoms under control, I went back to uni and searched the library database. Both copies of *Eraserhead* were checked out. I emailed my tutor, and he suggested I try a few places: Blockbuster Video in Fortitude Valley, Civic Video in Paddington and Trash Video in West End. Trash Video was the easiest for me to get to. I would've chosen another option if I had my car, but inner-city parking was too expensive. The guy said he'd hold a copy until the end of the day.

I took one bus from the city to the Cultural Centre in South-bank, then had a twenty-minute walk to Trash Video. It took me past Musgrave Park, and Laura's sharehouse and Rumpus Room on Russell Street. I took a left at the goanna statue and passed the Greek and Vietnamese restaurants to where Boundary Street meets Vulture Street and South Brisbane meets West End. I'd worked up a sweat by the time I slid open the door to Trash Video. I'd expected the familiar cool hit of air-conditioning I'd been accustomed to at suburban video stores. Instead I was hit by more warm air and the buzzing of ineffective wall-mounted fans. The guy behind the counter casually apologized, "Sorry, air con's busted."

He was sweaty and red-faced with small blue eyes magnified by thick glasses. His name badge said his name was Andrew. I signed up for membership, and he inspected my driver's license.

"We usually restrict membership to locals. . . ."

"I study across the river."

"Media studies?"

"Yeah."

"I graduated 2002."

I nodded and forced a smile. I wondered if this was where my arts degree would take me—casual employment at a niche video store with no air-conditioning. A flash of existential panic triggered fresh sweat on my brow.

"Wanna look around? It's Two for Tuesday, so you might as well take another one."

I passed the "Filipino Dwarf Exploitation" and "Vintage Smut" shelves and found the "Auteur" section. I picked out Wes Craven's *The Last House on the Left*. I took it to the counter and stacked it on top of *Eraserhead*.

"If you're into horror, you might be disappointed. This is pure exploitation."

"I don't mind being disappointed." I handed over cash; he handed me back my change and a temporary membership card.

"If you're into horror, you might be interested in this." He slid over a photocopied flyer promoting his horror flash fiction group.

"I'm not much of a joiner." I feared I was already trapped in an awkward conversation that might never end. I was trying to get the balance right—don't be too nice, don't be too bitchy. Both are dangerous.

"We don't meet up. It's a text group. . . . We just write short stories to scare each other. I already have your mobile number. . . . I'll send you some stuff, and you can make up your mind. It's just a bit of fun."

I nodded. If you don't fuel the conversation with words, you can end it faster.

"It's anonymous. I'll be the only one who knows who you are."

I heard a mobile phone ring across the store as I shoved the videos in my backpack. The ringtone was distinctive. Rather than a clean sound, it was distorted by static, making it difficult to recognise the tune. But it was familiar.

"See you next Tuesday. . . ." He waved and didn't rush to

answer the phone. I felt vulnerable as I stepped into the sunshine. I felt a prickle on my skin and a desire to be invisible.

Lesson two: If they can't see you, they can't get you.

You're probably familiar with the Joseph Heller quote from *Catch-22*: "Just because you're paranoid doesn't mean they're not after you." Yes, I can be defensive and paranoid. That doesn't mean I'm imagining danger where none exists. Women's intuition is not mysterious or magical; it's a survival mechanism. With a quick analysis, a few things seemed dodgy about the encounter. The way he said, "I already have your mobile number," as if I didn't have a choice about the texts. "I'll be the only one who knows who you are," as if that would give me any comfort. Then the final phrase, "See you next Tuesday." The rentals were due back next Tuesday . . . but he may have surreptitiously called me a "c-u-n-t." Or maybe I was a paranoid bitch.

Lesson three: Don't give your phone number to strangers. (I hadn't. I'd added my details to a database to rent a video for my university education. Yet this stranger now had my number and knew where I lived. Every rule is a floor with a trapdoor; watch where you step.)

Later that afternoon I received a text from an unfamiliar number.

WELCOME TO THE GROUP. THE RULES ARE SIMPLE. U CAN TELL A STORY IN MORE THAN 160 CHARACTERS, IF U WANT TO SEND MORE THAN 1 TEXT MSG. JUST DON'T WRITE A NOVEL ;-)

USE "..." TO CONNECT TEXTS & USE "." WHEN THE STORY ENDS. PLAGIARISM WILL BE PUNISHED. NO CHAT. JUST SCARY SHIT. U SEND IT 2 ME. I SEND IT TO THE GROUP. ANY QS?

It seemed self-explanatory. The question I had for myself was, did I want to get involved? I texted "NO," so I guess my answer was "yes."

THIS FIRST STORY MIGHT INSPIRE YOU ...

Andrew sent me a series of messages that were inspired by a crime that shocked Brisbane in the late 1980s, the Lesbian Vampire Killing. A twenty-three-year-old woman stabbed a man to death and drank his blood. The story was sensationalised by the local press—it was a tabloid editor's dreams. The man was portrayed as an innocent victim, even though he was a "family man" lured away from a nightclub by a woman (who was almost half his age) under the pretences they'd have sex, and she was a monster, a "lesbian vampire." I'd been expecting a little less true crime and a little more fiction from the group; some people have trouble disguising their inspiration. On the spectrum of horror literature, I'm drawn to Edgar Allan Poe's gothic macabre rather than lesbian vampire killers. I'd even argue that Oscar Wilde's *The Picture of Dorian Gray* is a decent rival to Poe's "The Tell-Tale Heart."

That night I had a dream with the clarity of a premonition. I was walking through an old house with creaky floorboards and a narrow hallway. I was confused. I heard the familiar ringtone from Trash Video and followed the sound. My body and brain felt like gel, my feet melted into the wooden floors. I was becoming part of the house. I opened a door, and the room was a wall-to-wall mattress; there was a continuous mural of mangrove trees on the walls. It looked as if the banks of the Brisbane River had wrapped around the room. There were other people in the bed, curled up under blankets. They looked trapped, like flies wrapped in silk on a spider's web. Someone grabbed my hand, and I turned to see Andrew lick my arm from my pinkie finger to my elbow. I squeezed my eyes closed, seeking escape. When I opened them, there was a tattoo of musical notes on my skin where his tongue had been. I crawled onto the bed and wrapped myself in a blanket. I couldn't move my head, but my eyes scanned around. I saw Laura sleeping peacefully beside me. Her eyes were sewn shut. I heard the ringtone in stereo, like the phone was inside the mattress, inside the ceiling and trapped between the walls. The mural of the mangroves began to animate, and hundreds of spiders came down from the trees. As the spiders got closer to my face, I pulled the blanket over my head. I felt myself being sucked to the top of the bed, and I was swallowed by the walls. I had the feeling of mucus on my face. I woke up, soaked in sweat. Afraid to fall asleep again, I wrote about it in my dream diary, hoping to exorcise it from my mind. It didn't help.

Dreamers have the instinct to tell people about their memorable dreams, even tedious ones. In the morning I felt the need to share my nightmare, as if that might erase the mark it left on me. I just used it as inspiration, trying to change it into something I could control. In six texts, I told a story about a corrupt police officer who'd been paralysed by drugs and buried neck deep in mud by the mangrove trees. As the tide came in, the cop faced his wrongdoings, inch by inch, as he confessed his dirty deeds.

I watched *Eraserhead* seven times, hoping to unlock some secret. Other than superficial themes like fear of intimacy and adult responsibility, I couldn't find a deeper meaning. After enough viewings, I figured that movie would drown out any alternate nightmares. Dreaming in a film seemed like a safer option than whatever my brain had created the previous night. In contrast, *The Last House on the Left* did not require repeated viewings. It had made me feel grimy while I watched it, and I wanted to wash my eyeballs when it was over. The weirdest choice was the banjo soundtrack. It gave the violence and rape a comical distance, like it was happening behind glass in a museum. This film was an example of a rare thing that doesn't hold any intrinsic value. A rare fossilized dinosaur shit is still just a piece of shit. That's my review of *The Last House on the Left*. It was worse than disappointing.

Also disappointing ... the quality of stories I was getting from the text group. There were a few ghost stories, a generic haunted house, a little satanic sacrifice. Only one story held my interest in the first week. It was about a man with no eyes, he could never be seen completely, only sensed in peripheral vision, and he was drawn to people with obsessions.

Lesson four: Don't go down the rabbit hole. Alice's "wonderful" adventures were pretty terrifying.

The following nights I had the same dream on repeat with slightly different endings. The first night spiders came into the bed, just like the original dream (but instead of having eight eyes, they were blind). The second night giant water rats came down from the trees. Night three, snakes. Night four, goannas. Night five, I sensed distorted human shapes in the trees, but they just shifted their weight on the branches while I waited to be swallowed by the walls. When I woke up, there was a new story on my phone about the Eyeless Man. It was written like an eyewitness account, not like fiction. He'd been "seen" in West End by a resident of a halfway house. An unreliable witness. I prepared myself to go back to South Brisbane; the videos were due back.

Trash Video didn't have a returns chute outside the store. The guy behind the counter looked like a taller, skinnier version of Andrew. I dropped the videos into the returns hole cut into the counter, forced a smile and turned to leave.

"Nothing new this week? I could give you some recos."

"Nah, I've got heaps of assignments due this week. No distractions."

"Well, we're always glad to get a new member. I'm Andrew, the owner."

"Hey . . ." I did not introduce myself. This was my second socially awkward encounter with an Andrew at Trash Video. The next comment slipped out of my mouth before I thought it through. "You have a lot of Andrews working here?"

"Just me. . . ."

He must've understood my furrowed brow.

"Sometimes the casual staff forget their name tags and use mine."

My phone rang, which allowed me to end the conversation and get out of the store. It was my mum checking in on me the way that mothers do. Nothing to say, just needed to hear my voice.

Lesson five: Carry your mobile phone at all times. They're good for real emergencies and can help you avoid unwanted social contact. You can fake a phone call to avoid a conversation.

I was almost back at the Cultural Centre bus stop when my phone rang again. There was static on the line, but a man's voice was clear enough: "Told you I'd see you next Tuesday."

There was time for me to respond. I didn't.

"I'm going to send you the start of a story. I need you to finish it."

I didn't say anything or hang up the phone. I held my breath. The call disconnected. I got a text alert.

HE HAS NO EYES BUT SEES STRAIGHT THROUGH YOU, CLOSE YOUR EYES, YOU CAN SENSE YOUR WAY, OPEN YOUR EYES AND YOU'LL NEVER SEE ME AGAIN...

The tone was different than the other stories about the Eyeless Man. Even though the subject matter was familiar, this was written like a riddle, not a story. I wondered if a new writer had joined the group, someone inspired by the other stories. Late that evening another text message came through.

HELP ME?

I couldn't help. I didn't know how to build on the story. "You'll never see me again" sounded like a great way to end a narrative, not begin it, so instead I started something new. I switched up my voice to match the poetic cadence of the latest story.

EVER WONDER WHAT THE ABYSS LOOKS LIKE? IF YOU CAN SEE IT IN YOUR MIND'S EYE, YOU'RE ALREADY THERE.

An almost instant reply:

I SEE UR DREAMS...

It was followed by an MMS that loaded slowly on my mobile's screen—a pixelated photo of the goanna statue on Boundary Street. Then another MMS came through—an old house.

It could've been the one from my dream (which may have been the one Laura lived in). Another grainy photo followed—it was Laura's face, the same gleeful expression as she had on her "Missing" flyer. It could've been the same photo.

Then a text came through:

THIS IS A RORSCHACH TEST. WHAT DO YOU SEE?

An MMS began to load. The image did not look like an inkblot test. It was a sketch of Laura's face and my face overlapping.

THIS IS A TEST. WHAT DO U SEE?

Another MMS—a forearm with music notes on it, just like the markings left on my skin in the dreams.

WHAT DO U SEE?

A human face without any features, just a plain shape. The night's final message came through:

THIS IS A TEST.

I switched off my phone before any new images could start loading. It was late; I was tired and unlikely to make any progress on the Marxist analysis of *The Simpsons* that was due in two days. I closed my eyes, expecting the nightmare that came. It was the eyeless spiders again. This time, as they crawled down from the trees, their eight legs played a note from the ringtone. The tune was played in order and out of order, creating a cacophony. I sensed the Eyeless Man was up in the trees, listening to my screams. After the dream I stayed awake until the sun streamed in my window. I slept a little after that and postponed turning on my phone again until late afternoon. There was a "U UP?" from a (presumably) drunk ex-boyfriend, but I hadn't missed anything more frightening than that.

I tried to discount the previous night's texts and the nausea they triggered. The counterargument went something like this: How do images from my nightmares end up as text messages? I'd never mentioned the details to anyone. They weren't the standard nightmares of losing your teeth (a dream I'd had many times). These dreams were so specific. If I tried to explain that someone was texting me images from my nightmares, I'd sound insane. And if that made me sound crazy, maybe I *was* crazy. And did the difference between those two things even matter? Sanity isn't something you define for yourself—you have to ask other people to diagnose you. But if no one believed me, I would feel like I really was losing my mind. So, I kept it between me, myself and I.

Lesson six: Don't give anyone reason to doubt your sanity or sobriety.

I became obsessed with the ringtone I heard in Trash Video. When there was silence, it filled the void. I thought that if I knew why it was familiar, I could disarm it. I decided it must be the score to a horror film; that was why it sounded so creepy and familiar. I borrowed all the classic horror films from the university library (five at a time since there was a limit). I kept a list of what I'd watched. It wasn't from *The Exorcist, Psycho, Halloween, Friday the 13th*, or any of the *Nightmare on Elm Street*s. I binged horror films every night into the early morning, hoping they would transform my nightmares. But I had the same five dreams, alternating between spiders, rats, snakes, goannas and human shapes—I always felt the presence of the Eyeless Man, like a spectator to my horror. I was swallowed by the walls every night, sleeping through my alarms in the morning, constantly running late for uni and work. I was unable to find the ringtone in any movie and unable to stop searching for it. When I ran out of horror films at the university library, I went to the Blockbuster store in Fortitude Valley. I saw countless women chased, tortured and killed by men and monsters. I never heard the ringtone in a soundtrack and the Eyeless Man became a fixture of my nightmares; no alternate monster could claim his territory.

The next Tuesday I got another call from the number I associated with Fake Andrew and the text group. I didn't pick up. The caller left a voicemail. Then called again and left another. And then a third voicemail. I didn't listen to them, and I didn't delete them. I was down a rabbit hole, always in a nightmare, sometimes my eyes were open and sometimes they were closed. I flinched when the text alert came through.

THIS IS A TEST

An image loaded, revealing my face—my mouth and eyes were stitched closed, and I was curled up in bed under a blanket . . . like a fly cocooned in silk on a spider's web. Followed by two more texts:

UR FAILING

U WILL END UP LIKE ME

Over the next few days my brain battled with itself. I wasn't a perfect victim; I'd been stupid. I deserved bad things, and I felt them coming. If you decide to play along, you don't get to decide when the game ends. I wanted to switch off my phone so I could stay in control of the situation, but that would deprive me of information. What if the texts were clues that could help me? I wanted someone to know the answers and tell me what to do.

Lesson seven: What you don't know will hurt you. Ignorance is no defence.

That night there was a variation in my nightmare. When I saw Laura, her eyes were open, and she was free from the bed cocoon. I was trapped beneath the blanket as she carefully stitched my mouth closed with a needle and fishing line. My right eyelid was stitched closed next, then the left. I didn't know what came down from the mangroves to crawl over me. I felt the pressure of something shifting over my body before I was devoured by the house. When I turned on my phone the next morning there was a new text message.

I SEE UR DREAMS, IT'S THE ONLY THING I SEE.

That's when I had my first panic attack. I felt my pulse vibrating in my neck and reverberating in my stomach. I felt like I was dying. I took deep breaths to calm down but almost hyperventilated. I wanted to crawl out of my skin or scratch my way out. I had to keep moving. I went on long walks and thought about stepping in front of buses. I took long drives and thought about crossing the double line into oncoming traffic. I didn't want to die; I just needed a reset. I paced around the house on long phone calls to friends. I'd talk about their boyfriends, a recent personal drama—anything normal, anything to keep busy. I was thinking in circles. I rewatched all the horror movies I'd watched two weeks before. When my eyes did close, I was having dreams about nightmares. The dreams would begin with my waking up from a nightmare, screaming, jumping out of bed to turn on the lights, my heart racing, my hair wet with sweat. I felt the presence of the Eyeless Man but could never find him. I was searching for the source of the ringtone; I could never find it. When it sounded really close, almost within reach, I'd wake up and realise I'd had a nightmare within a dream. I wasn't close at all.

I had no appetite. I hadn't slept properly in almost a month. I wasn't answering my phone or making calls anymore. After watching so many horror films, I'd developed a phobia of phone calls. I questioned the safety of phones. What would happen if the girl in the horror movie never answered the phone? Would the man/monster go away? Was the phone call a way to check if a victim was at home, and if they didn't answer, would they just move on to a different phone number and a different victim? How personal was this? The victims often seemed random, except it was always the girl who answered the phone call. I only communicated through texts and email. My brother made a doctor's appointment on my behalf. I was diagnosed with generalised anxiety and panic disorder. I was going to argue the diagnosis, because my anxiety felt pretty specific, but I'd kept the details of my mind-fuck to myself. I'd just told the doctor about the insomnia, the nightmares, the panic attacks, the phone phobia and the fact that my brain was thinking in circles. She referred me to a psychiatrist, gave me scripts for Lexapro to help curb the panic attacks and Restavit to help me sleep. I think those things helped, but what really made the difference was a new phone number and a new ringtone.

It was a labor-intensive process to import my old contacts

and text them my new number. I anticipated a reduction in my social circle, as people would miss my message and continue to text my old number. I'd already experienced reduced social contact as a result of my anxiety. I didn't care what I lost, as long as I could feel sane again. All my old texts and voicemails were gone. When final exams came around, I was functional. Still having the same nightmares about the ringtone and the Eyeless Man, but they weren't sharp. They no longer felt like premonitions or recent memories; it was progress. I had other things to feel anxious about, like what the fuck I was going to do postgraduation. I'd been invited to apply for a year of honours, provided my GPA held steady. That was my backup plan.

I didn't feel safe all the time. I feared that getting out of the text group may have been too little, too late. I still wondered how those images from my nightmares came through to my phone. I decided to believe in coincidences. I decided to believe there was a logical rather than a magical explanation. I decided to doubt the feelings of fear that made me question my safety and my sanity. I decided to teach myself lucid dreaming and borrowed a book from the library. If I could control my dreams, I'd be okay. I made some progress, even had some flying dreams early in my sleep cycles (when my intention was strong). But later in the night, the ringtone and the Eyeless Man still found me.

Final exams came and went; it was time to celebrate the end of something and the beginning of whatever came next. I didn't like not knowing what was next. I'd planned to meet a small group of friends at Rumpus Room. It was early afternoon and hot as hell as I walked from the Cultural Centre bus stop, crossing South Brisbane, skirting Musgrave Park and passing by

Laura's old sharehouse. I noticed a photocopied flyer taped to a telephone pole. There was a grinning photo of the guy I'd been calling Fake Andrew. I recognised the phone number listed as the point of contact. My skin prickled. The poster listed the date he was last seen. It was the day he'd served me at Trash Video. My body tingled from my fingers and toes and moved toward my core. It was the familiar feeling of a panic attack taking over. I felt eyes on me. It could have been the Parkies, the neighbors, maybe the police. I didn't know who was looking.

I repeated my anti–panic attack mantra under my breath: "I have anxiety, so what? I have anxiety, so what?" It was a technique the psychiatrist taught me. I walked past the properties between Laura's home and her work. Two doors down from Rumpus Room I heard the ringtone. Not at a distance, but almost at my feet. The sound had never been this close, except in my dreams. I glanced toward the low hedge that bordered the property of 50 Russell Street. The call was for me. I knew it. I pushed aside branches and saw a metallic grey clamshell phone at the base of the bush. It was cradled in a shallow nest of leaves and had been placed there very carefully. The phone was marked with people's initials, roughly etched into the plastic. I recognised Laura's initials, and I recognized my own. There were a few others that weren't significant to me. The call rang out. The caller didn't leave a voicemail. They immediately redialed. I felt compelled to answer the call. Maybe that was the only way this would end?

Panic is often described as the "fight or flight" response. But it's not a duality; there's a third option: "freeze." Being very still and very quiet is the third survival instinct. It's often accompanied by disassociation—emotionally distancing yourself from the source of danger. I found a quiet place in my mind that the ringtone couldn't reach. It became a literal ringing in my ear, something I could walk away from. I don't remember walking away. I remember meeting my friends and switching off my mobile (to be safe) and ordering too many two-dollar drinks at Rumpus Room. I had a massive hangover the next day, but I survived.

It's been almost two decades since these incidents took place. I've spent most of those years trying to forget and only a few weeks trying to remember. I kept dream diaries during these events and managed to remember the bulk of those texts pretty accurately (I think). I acknowledge that memories don't form properly during panic attacks or periods of anxiety, but I haven't made anything up. I walked the blocks from Musgrave Park to Boundary Street, up to Vulture Street and back around. I counted the number of houses between Laura's home and her work. Walking the streets helped me remember everything I've told you. I spent an afternoon in the archives of the Queensland State Library, looking for news articles about Laura's disappearance and the subsequent disappearance of the guy from Trash Video (whose name wasn't Andrew). I didn't find any mention of young people going missing from the area. No police statements or warnings that women needed to take care or be vigilant. No hint of blame placed on Laura or a perpetrator—it was as if nothing had happened.

I can't recall how close my hand got to that phone in the hedge on Russell Street. I can see my hand reaching down to grab it; I don't remember making the decision to walk away. Maybe on the other end of the call there was someone who needed help. I could've been a lifeline. But there's a surf safety tip they teach kids in Brisbane: Don't drown yourself trying to save someone else. It comes to mind when I think about the missing people, the missed calls and the Eyeless Man.

DR. MAYNARD WILLS:
A FOREBODING RHYME

While I continued my email exchange with Peter Gilliam, I investigated several other threads, ones more obviously adjacent to legends and folklore. Like many researchers, I'm both an omniologist and compulsively scattered. It's a good thing I'm able to get by on little sleep, though I worry what this deprivation will cost me as I progress steadily through my senior years. Dreams, songs, religious texts, creation myths are just a handful of topics amid a legion of book piles and open browser tabs. But late last night I found myself lost in a different subject. One that, in all my years of study, I had not given much attention: nursery rhymes. Regionally specific nursery rhymes.

Nursery rhymes and children's stories, whether written down or shared orally, present an interesting map (or perhaps chart is the better metaphor) of values, religious belief, history, illness—most aspects of culture and civilization if you look through the right lens. Around one in the morning, I downloaded a collection of regional nursery rhymes collected by the researcher Carol Bernhardt in 1998. She hypothesized that even the more universally known ones would be slightly different due to their evolution within separate, contained communities. Of course, her study took place before YouTube codified content around the world.

Of note to our investigation is the following verse, unique, Bernhardt believed, to a small community in southern Louisiana, a grouping of about four towns, each with a population not over eight thousand. I've copied it on the following pages. My thoughts and a discovery of my own follow.

Eight o'clock and Mommy said,
Brush your teeth and get to bed,
So much TV kills your brain.
And drives little ones insane.

Nine o'clock and Mommy screams,
"Didn't I say to start your dreams?
And turn off that terrible set.
Don't make me come back with threats!"

Ten o'clock but they don't look.
They're downstairs reading their books.
We'll keep the sound really low
While we watch forbidden shows.

Eleven o'clock, eyes open wide
Then through the screen we see him glide.
Our mommy hasn't heard us, though
And she can't stop what she don't know.

Twelve o'clock, the midnight hour
And so we fall under his power.
Why would we ever wanna escape
When he has so many tapes?

One o'clock, it's like a dream
Inside his endless static stream.
We're not sure what we should do
Feels like we should travel through.

Two o'clock and he speaks back
Tells us more about the Stack.
Says we can go and join his legion
Far beyond this time and region.

Three o'clock we must choose.
But scared there's too much to lose.
From his gaping ebon maw
He speaks, "O Ta Keta."

There's no more time,
There're no more rhymes,
We ignored Mommy's plan
And now we serve the Eyeless Man.

Chilling, isn't it? I looked for more context, more connections. I found two of note. In the eighties and nineties, at the intersection of this Louisiana parish, there was a video store called Herm's Movie Hut. Like Video Palace, it burned.

I also discovered that this nursery rhyme was popular in one other area of the United States, a fact that eluded Ms. Bernhardt. I found it recorded on the defunct blog of a concerned first-grade teacher in Conway, Vermont. The town Mark Cambria and Tamra Wulff visited, where they stood over the ashes of Video Palace.

THE SATANIC SCHOOLGIRLS

Meirav Devash and Eddie McNamara

Professor Maynard Wills,

How about you do me a favor and stop bothering my wife with this Eyeless Man shit? As I've explained to you before, she's not interested in talking to you. I know she got into some fucked-up shit with her friends back in the early nineties and you're documenting firsthand accounts. I get it—that's what professors do. She's not about that life anymore, and that whole mess is in her rearview. I'd appreciate it if you'd stop trying to contact her.

Look, when I met Meirav on Halloween in 1999, she was fresh out of the cult or whatever the fuck that whole Satanic Schoolgirls thing was. She lived in New York's East Village and wore motorcycle boots and wasn't scared of anything, except for late at night, when she'd talk about this Eyeless Man as if he was a supernatural force. She's finally sleeping through the night for the first time since I've known her, so I'm keeping you as far away from her as I can.

—Eddie McNamara

Professor Maynard Wills,

Wow, my husband can be a real dick, right? Don't take it personally—he's just looking out for me. He's right. I don't want anything to do with you or the Eyeless Man. Here's what I'm going to do. Just before the turn of the millennium, I wrote this story in therapy and never did anything with it. I think I hoped I'd forget about it. Take it and do whatever you want with it. And never contact me or my family again.

—Meirav Devash

I WAS TWELVE YEARS old the year that the Satanic School-girl murders happened in my dinky little hometown, so they've had a pretty big impact on my life. I mean, I went to school there, and I actually became friends with Alizon, who people claim was the killer. At the time of the murders, I had this babysitter named Danielle. She was the coolest girl ever, with blue hair and a piercing just above her lip that made her look like Marilyn Monroe. (If Marilyn had been in an all-girl punk band with Kathleen Hanna.) I was obviously way too old for a babysitter, but my parents were strict and I wasn't great at following rules, so Danielle and I mostly shared cigarettes on the front stoop and talked about boys.

There was an unmarked VHS tape being passed around her high school—it was fuzzy footage made by somebody with a camcorder that a local kid subsequently recorded off late-night public access. By lunchtime, everyone at my middle school had caught wind of the story. Danielle told me we could watch the tape if I promised not to get scared and tell my parents.

As soon as the grainy found footage started, my stomach felt queasy. I wanted to close my eyes, but I kept watching.

Three high school boys hung from the big oak tree in front of the local school, their Nike Airs dangling just a few inches from the ground. There was a low hum, and then the soles of Alizon Nahash's Dr. Martens made a soft sucking sound in the mud. She quickly stepped backward.

Click

It hadn't rained the night before. The soil under her feet was sludgy with blood.

Click

Stripped from the waist down, the corpses were identifiable only by their varsity football jerseys. Below the hem of their jerseys was . . . nothing. Just darkness and wet. Castrated.

Click

Using an old-timey box camera she probably bought at a flea market, Alizon peered into the viewfinder. She photographed their pale bodies and the blood that glinted in the early-morning sunlight.

Click *Click*

First, she used a tripod at about eye level; then she lay on the grass, stomach down, propping up her elbows for a low-angle shot. She got each boy alone, then a grotesque group shot.

Click

Alizon went to the same school as the dead boys and Danielle, but they weren't friends. Ordinarily, she'd never get that close to those guys if she could help it—that's what Danielle told me—but on that morning she was discovered taking artsy photos of them for the cover of her occult fanzine, *Elemental*. And according to the burnout kid in town who hung out in front of AlJohn's Pizza, the one who always wore a Red Hot Chili Peppers T-shirt, they were "meathead jocks" who had bullied her for years. In elementary school, they made fun of her for being poor and getting free lunch in the cafeteria, and then they knocked over her lunch tray to make her cry. In middle school, they called her Elvira and left a dead bat in her locker.

By high school, she made herself as small as she could and tried not to attract too much attention. But she was kinda weird. It was hard not to notice her.

And you know how predators are with prey.

The next part of the tape was filmed from a closer vantage point with the camera still pointed at Alizon and the stately oak decorated with dead football players. A school security guard pointed a Taser at Alizon, the vein in his neck pulsing angrily. He looked like he might have a heart attack. The wind muffled the audio, but we could still make out the words.

"Get on the ground! Get on the goddamn ground, you witch bitch!" he said.

"I . . . I am on the ground," Alizon said.

"Show me your hands! Show your hands now!"

Alizon let go of the camera and pressed her palms into the ground to lift herself up. She raised her hands, stained with a mix of mud and blood, in the air. That's how the cops first spotted her—frozen like a deer in front of the local high school, with blood and grass stains on the thrift-store Catholic school uniform she wore as an ironic fashion statement (inspiring her future nickname, the Satanic Schoolgirl).

The quality was terrible—there was that rumble again—but Alizon's photos flashed across the screen one by one. Sure, they were eerie, but they were actually kind of beautiful, too. You know, if you're into chiaroscuro or whatever, there they hung: framed by a sliver of early-morning light, three swaying corpses heavy with muscle, vertical shadows long and rigid like . . . like dildos, to be honest, which it sounded like they were. Mark Hammersmith,

Tim McNulty, Jonny Bowers—in just a few years, their names would be forgotten and they'd just be the three dead dudes from the Satanic Schoolgirl case.

Serves them right.

Danielle paused the tape and pointed to a dark spot behind the bodies. Oh, my God. I didn't want to see any more.

"Look carefully," she said. "What do you see?"

That's when my stomach went from queasy to full-on cramping. I booked it to the bathroom and started dry heaving over the toilet, but nothing came up. Danielle was knocking on the door like she was the damn police, and it freaked me out.

"Did you see him? I know you saw him," she badgered me.

I wailed that I only saw three dead bodies.

"You couldn't see a shadowy figure in the background? Tall and blurry? You can't see him?"

"No!" I said. Hell no, I didn't, and I wasn't going to. Nausea rolled over me as my stomach twisted and blood rushed in my ears. "Please leave me alone. I promise I won't tell my parents. Just leave me alone!"

Danielle beat against the door loudly with her fists, whispering frantically through the keyhole, a bunch of guttural, ugly-sounding words strung together that I couldn't understand. I leaned in closer, putting my ear against the door, and suddenly all noise—the banging against the door, the cryptic whispers, the blood pounding in my head, the low rumble on the videotape I didn't even realize was there—stopped cold.

I must have fallen asleep on the couch and dreamed of being smothered by the shadowy male figure she tried to force me to see. My parents said I was mumbling in my sleep when they got home, and they were furious that Danielle had left me alone.

That night was the last time I saw Danielle.

Eventually, our local news media caught wind of the underground tape. They even played it on that UHF channel that came in all scrambled. The murder case was in the town paper every day back then, and it was really polarizing—"god-fearing" people like my parents, for example, thought Alizon was evil incarnate, while the smaller alt-girl community rallied around the gothy chick who was being unfairly accused of a triple homicide simply because she was creepy. I realized what happens to poor folks in the system—the ones who wear thrift-store dresses and qualify for free lunch. I saw, in real time, how outcasts and weirdos become scapegoats in small-minded towns. She was so insignificant that the national media didn't even report on the story. The word got out in the underground through networks of tape traders, indie zine and comic collectors, pen pals, touring metalheads, crust punk train hoppers, underground venues and anarchist squatters.

Nothing pissed off the powers-that-be more than Alizon's die-hard supporters. They called them the Satanic Schoolgirls and treated them like our generation's version of the Manson Girls. But unlike Charles Manson, Alizon Nahash wasn't some two-bit pimp eating garbage in the desert with teenage runaways. She was a destination. She was a revolution!

Everyone knows the smartest girls from every high school

in America go to New York for a career, the prettiest girls go to LA to get famous and the most boring girls go to DC and buy a bunch of blazers. Well, all the misfit girls made their pilgrimage to my little town to support Alizon, who was definitely one of their kind. I saw them from my bedroom window as they drove past my house in their beat-up Chevys and Jettas covered in bumper stickers. They came in droves from Oakland, Olympia and Burlington, where they played guitar in a punk band, or read tarot cards and practiced spells or wore too-short skirts and too much eyeliner. I wished I could leave my boring life and run away with this riot grrrl circus, so I blew off school and started hanging out on the periphery.

The cool girls all kept vigil at the courthouse. They drank Dunkin Donuts coffee, handed out informational flyers and fanzines and busked for spare change on the courthouse steps. They smoked clove cigarettes and chugged wine coolers out of brown paper bags. "That could be me in there," they told the news cameras, snuffing out their cigarette butts with their boots.

Sitting in the back of the courtroom, I documented each day's events in my journal. The element that was too hard to put in words was the specter of fear that bound the Satanic Schoolgirls. Alizon really could have been one of us. Nobody believed she was innocent, but the case against her made zero sense.

Granted, taking photos of your classmates' corpses looks really bad, but it was circumstantial evidence. Beyond that, the cops had nothing on Alizon. No tire tracks or disruptions in the surrounding grass. No drugs in the boys' systems, though they had a buzz going with blood alcohol contents between 0.04 and 0.06. No indications of blunt force trauma. No sign of a struggle. Even if all three guys spontaneously lost consciousness while standing right in front of that tree, how exactly was Alizon—underweight at five-foot-nothing—physically capable of tying three nooses, flinging them over a high branch of that massive oak and lifting two hundred pounds of deadweight by the neck? Three times, no less.

Alizon Nahash was being railroaded and everybody knew it, but no one was doing anything about it. Except the Schoolgirls. As the prosecution made its case against her, the Schoolgirls moved together as one. Shoulders back and heads held high with sneers etched in red lipstick, they wore Catholic school uniforms and ripped fishnet stockings. They pulled up their sleeves silently, each showing the ALIZON carved into their forearms with a razor blade—the *A* became an anarchy symbol, and the *O* housed a crude pentagram. One day, I used a red marker to scrawl Alizon's name on my arm. A Schoolgirl in an L7 T-shirt named Ivy finally noticed me and welcomed me to sit with them in the gallery. After that, they quickly became my second family.

We watched the judge ask Alizon point-blank if she worshipped Satan. She rolled her eyes and focused her gaze right on the TV cameras.

"Satan isn't real," she said. "And if he was, he'd be boring. You know what's evil? Mass media that incrementally erodes your daughter's confidence over years until she believes she's not good enough, just so they can sell lipstick and diet soda."

Predictably, the questioning devolved into asking if she "experimented with witchcraft." As if a teenage girl existed who hasn't lit a love potion candle or fondled a few crystals by the light of the moon.

"What are you so scared of anyway? God?!" she said, muttering under her breath. "It figures, for a bunch of dirty old men. Hypocritical poseurs!"

"You're out of order," the judge said.

"You are," she said, pointing at Judge Nowell, a ruddy-faced man in his late sixties. He looked like he was choking on words. "Your time is up. All of you. You're going to answer for this insatiable need to dominate, control and commodify everything that matters," she said.

The courtroom erupted. The judge clutched his throat and banged his gavel against his wood desk as she was dragged out, yelling, "No gods, no masters!"

I felt something burning inside me as I watched the scene play out. This wasn't just a girl crush. It sounds hyperbolic, but I was supernaturally drawn to Alizon. Like finding the Virgin Mary burned into a Pop-Tart. She was my awakening, and I knew my life was never going to be the same.

A local news clip of the wild courtroom scene spread as quickly as mono at a game of spin the bottle. It made our town's most-feared teenager into an icon for disaffected youth; a pinup for smirking atheists and science geeks; a paradigm for outcasts, weirdos and girls who aren't like other girls. It was the moment that ensured she'd get the death penalty, too. Her detractors acted like she was a sea hag who stole the judge's voice, and he was the Little Mermaid. Thanks to the local news and papers, the court of public opinion had already made its call.

Only one reporter hanging around seemed as though he was on Alizon's side. He took the train in from New York City to interview her about the case for *The Village Voice*, one of those alternative newspapers where you can find concert listings for the week. Somehow, she managed to alienate him. I heard that she called him a pimp and said the ads for 1-900 phone sex and escorts on the paper's back page sold women. He considered himself a feminist, so he didn't appreciate having his hypocrisies called out. He abandoned the story along with Alizon, and she abandoned any chance she had of getting a fair trial.

When the guilty verdict was read, I was sitting in my usual spot in the gallery with the Schoolgirls. I buzzed with an angry determination to do whatever I could to help Alizon and felt the same energy vibing off the Schoolgirls. I balled my hands into a fist, and my nails pierced the skin of my palms. This was the same kind of bullying she had to deal with from those jocks, but now instead of football jerseys, they were wearing suits and judicial robes. Who actually believed in the devil anymore? Sorry to break it to you, but no Satanic daycare centers ever served blood-tinged Kool-Aid to kids, Judas Priest didn't put subliminal messages on their records that drove kids to suicide and Alizon was *not* responsible for killing three future date rapists on March 21, 1992.

When the trial ended, I couldn't just leave her in there to rot. I thought to myself, *What would Alizon do?* and I started my own cheap, photocopied fanzine called *Strega Nona* and dedicated it to her. Not in a creepy, stalkerish way, but in a pursuit-of-justice way, like Rage Against the Machine and Leonard Peltier. I tried to get Ivy on board, but her phone was disconnected and no one knew where she was. Jessa, one of the other Schoolgirls, had a family T-shirt business, so we sold hundreds of "Free Alizon" shirts through the mail.

We used the money to send Alizon care packages and fill her prison commissary account so she could buy all the tampons and waterproof mascara she needed. Weird thing about prison: no CDs are allowed, since they can be broken and used as a weapon, and no mixtapes (bummer). We sent lots of zines, Poppy Z. Brite's new vampire book, meditation guides, stuff like that.

For the zine, I interviewed Alizon's recently released cellmate from county lockup. Her name was T (just the one letter), a former raver who got locked up for distributing a fuck-ton of Ecstasy. She would only talk to me if I bought her a carton of Marlboro Ultra Lights and $20 in scratch-off lotto tickets. She said Alizon mostly kept to herself and did a lot of meditating. Like, a lot.

"She ain't any kind of devil; she's a little meep-meep mouse," she said. "Bitch don't sleep. All she does is look at static on the day-room TV screen, acting like she's crazy. And get this shit—instead of getting snuffed, she's got girls sitting there with her looking up at nothing. They took over the communal TV. Can't even watch *Sally Jessy Raphael*."

I wrote letters and sent zines to Alizon once a week, but the guards probably threw them out before they got to her because it took 137 days for her to get back to me.

Thursday, August 6, 1993

Hi Meirav,

Good news! This dude Randy and some guys who own a bunch of video stores are going to make a documentary about all this. It's gonna be called Sympathy for the Devil

Girl. *Do you like that name? I'm finally going to get to tell my side of the story. The Schoolgirls said they made a bulletin board about me on the Internet. I never had a computer in my whole life, so I don't get it, but they say they're "reaching people."*

I can trust you, right? I know I can. I shouldn't admit it, but I'm scared. All I have is my TV in here. Help the Schoolgirls help me get out.

Thanks for the snacks and meditation stuff. It helps pass the time. I feel like I'm starting to unlock my inner potential. I wish I could unlock the door instead but, you know.

Alizon

When the documentary came out, it changed everything. People started to pay attention to what Alizon's supporters already knew—that this case wasn't about Satan at all. It was about a bumbling, small-town, small-brained police department dead set on nailing a weird-looking girl for a crime she clearly was incapable of committing. I was actually making a difference by spreading Alizon's story, and it felt amazing.

There was so much interest in her story, in fact, that none of us even noticed it was weird when a team of attractive people who looked like TV lawyers arrived to appeal her case for free. (I don't know who was footing the bill for it all, but the McLawyers brought a camera crew with them for a reality show. I have no idea if it ever ran.) Even the same people who hated Alizon seven years earlier were now obsessed with *Sympathy for the Devil Girl*, the splashy true crime documentary. Suddenly, there was a legit public outcry for a new and fair trial.

We were making things happen, and Alizon was psyched. By then, riot grrrl had come and gone, but the sisterhood of the Satanic Schoolgirls was still rock-solid. Since the documentary painted us in a positive light, I even got a little notoriety as the number one "pen pal"—the true believer DIY girl printing *Strega Nona* and distributing Alizon's sigil art. I also petitioned for her release, wrote feminist essays and printed "Missing" posters when one of our Schoolgirls disappeared (something we lived in constant fear of). Our street team plastered the "Missing" posters around concert venues, record stores, comic shops and college campuses. The Satanic Schoolgirls didn't have an official roster or anything, but we all sort of knew one another from our activism. Over the past seven years, at least eight of us had disappeared into thin air like Ivy, the girl who invited me into the coven. Nine if you count Danielle, which I definitely do.

I never met Randy or the video-store guys, but the documentary crew filmed everything we did, sunup to sundown. The footage of poor Alizon wasting away in prison was heartbreaking. Driven to madness by a cruel system, sitting in front of a television set tuned to snow. (Fun fact: They cut Alizon's *Poltergeist* scene short. One of the boom guys told me he felt creeped out filming because there were nine or ten other inmates sitting near her, their eyes also transfixed on the TV. He said it felt like walking into a viper's pit.)

Anyway, one constant in my life at the time was this: no matter where I was, I crossed my legs and sat for a meditation at exactly 7:00 a.m. I began every day with Alizon's freedom mantra, repeating, "May she be free, may she be free. Released is she who is released by will, with inner sight unbounded." In her cell on death row, Alizon also sat in meditation and chanted, "Ota Keta. Ota Keta. Ota Keta."

Miraculously, the lawyers managed to convince the judge to hear a habeas corpus appeal, which has nothing to do with dead bodies but would make an awesome band name. We pooled our money together and rented out a big, old movie theater that probably should have been condemned, and gathered to watch live closed-circuit coverage of the courtroom hearing. We chanted in unison and focused our collective consciousness on freeing Alizon until our will was done.

If you don't believe in magic, let me be the first to tell you you're wrong. Within weeks of the documentary's release, we got Alizon in front of the same awful, conservative Judge Nowell who had ruled against her. And after seven years, seven months and seven days of dutifully performing the freedom mantra, that asshole had some kind of revelation. Right there in his courtroom, he began to sputter, then spoke in tongues and overturned the verdict. We cried until our mascara ran down our faces. We fucking did it. We actually did it.

I felt such a wave of relief and pride. There's no such thing as black magic or white magic. There's just people, and when enough of us get together, we can do powerful things. Like manifesting Alizon Nahash's release from death row. That's the story the news channels went with, anyway, probably since the Spice Girls were everywhere. Girl Power and all that.

Hundreds of supporters and about as many protesters swarmed Alizon as she walked out the doors of the correctional facility to liberation. She looked exactly the same as she did when she went in. I mean, she looked like she hadn't aged a day. It was eerie. She still dressed like a teenager in her Catholic school uniform with cat-eye makeup and oxblood Dr. Martens, but on her it looked cool.

The rumor among the Schoolgirls was that Courtney Love, the guy from Pearl Jam or the heiress to the Slim Jim fortune (depending on who you asked) was a big-time Alizon supporter and invited her and her friends to use their house in California as a retreat center, where we could get away from the world. We vowed to create our own society, forged by and for women—a witchy, bitchy world full of punk rock and love where we could be ourselves, or maybe even better versions of ourselves. I was so stoked when we packed into a tour bus and rode with Alizon to Palm Desert.

A strange thing happened on the road. I was in a deep sleep, in the middle of the same nightmare I had every night—being slowly consumed by a shadowy man whose face I couldn't quite make out. This time, I was jolted from my nap by a bump on the highway. All around me, the Schoolgirls were slumped in their seats, whispering in unison as they slept, "Ota Keta. Ota Keta. Ota Keta."

In the center of the aisle, surrounded by their folded bodies, Alizon stood wide awake with her arms outstretched. With her hands curved like she was holding invisible oranges, she repeated the same mantra.

I'm not going to lie: waking up to that situation was creepy.

I tried to embrace the woo-woo and let their chanting lull me to sleep, but it didn't work. The yoga soundtrack from hell went on for hours. Alizon was completely in the zone. I tried coughing and dropping random stuff on the bus floor to get her attention— my Walkman, a can of Jolt Cola, a handful of change—but no response. A little bit of chanting is hardly the weirdest thing to happen around these girls, so I didn't make too much of it.

The following days in Palm Desert were the best ones of my life. It was all so perfect, it was hard to believe it was real. School-girls from around the world stopped by for a day or a week— it was hard to keep track, and it's not like we took attendance. Alizon suggested we try a raw foods diet—pineapples, hemp-seeds, almonds and little clementines were our staples. Some of the girls even took their steaks raw and bloody. Not my thing, but I don't judge. Our days were spent creating art, practicing yoga, sitting in meditation and in vodka- and weed-fueled lectures with Alizon. We were happy. We were beautiful. We were glowing. Every night was a sleepover party at Alizon's place— albeit one with a soundtrack of girls who spoke a dead language in their sleep. All but one girl. The whole time I was at the Palm Desert house, I never saw Alizon sleep.

During that time, one of those true crime shows (*Crimeline* or *72 Hours*, something like that) did a story called "The Lost Schoolgirls." By this point, our TV was always on but never on a channel. We all gathered our pillows and tuned in to the network, watching in stunned silence as our missing friends and sisters— the girls I wrote about, the girls we loved—were profiled on the show. But instead of being a call to action to find them, the story was about the dangers of goth and punk and witchcraft. Basically, they said, don't let your daughter become one of those girls. Alizon was pissed.

She stood up and addressed us matter-of-factly: "In case you were wondering, no one will look for you." She paced the room and pointed at Stacy, with her green hair and septum ring. Stacy stuck out her tongue and gave her the devil horns in return.

"Where's your graduation picture? The one where you look like an innocent, blond girl brimming with potential?" she asked.

"I didn't go to graduation," Stacy said, and the room started cracking up.

"Of course you didn't. Graduation's fucking lame," she said. "But now no one's going to look for Stacy. See, Stacy ran off with a boyfriend. Must have OD'd. You know how those Satanic Schoolgirls are." She was right, that was the sucky part.

Later that night, before we dragged our sleeping bags into the big room, Alizon pulled me aside, saying we had to do something. "And we have to do it ourselves, because if we don't take control of our girls, we're going to lose them," she said.

Alizon wanted to do a live interview with me that everyone who mattered could see. We linked up with a local public access television station, and within a few days of booking it, stations around the country agreed to broadcast us live. This was beyond exciting. Alizon was right about doing this our way. We didn't need corporate media—we could reach every teenage girl in the country ourselves.

Alizon started the show with a simple body scan meditation and encouraged viewers at home to follow along. Then came the chanting in unison with the Schoolgirls: "Ota Keta. Ota Keta. Ota Keta." She explained that those words helped everyone watching open their psychic channels and be receptive. I waited impatiently, looking off in the distance, as she and the girls mumbled for a few minutes. Then it was showtime.

I officially introduced Alizon, and the girls in the studio clapped. With images of the Lost Schoolgirls burned into my mind, I let her talk for a few minutes about how thankful she was for the missing girls who helped her when she really needed it. Then I asked for her thoughts about how the world treats misfit girls and what we can all do about it.

"Everyone overestimates what they can do," she said. "Here's what you can do: You can be blond. And white. If you can't do that, be pretty. If you can't be pretty, you can at least stage one wholesome photo that these ratings-chasing talking heads can show on the news, or no one is going to care."

Awkward silence. I started to feel dizzy, like I was about to have a panic attack. I tried to smooth it over by bringing things back to her struggles.

"I think I speak for most people when I say we were appalled when you were convicted of murder despite being totally innocent," I said.

"Innocent?" She cocked her head to the side. "What in the world makes you think I'm innocent? Everything they said about me is true."

I giggled, assuming that Alizon wasn't serious. But oh, my God, she was.

"Yes, I did spells. I practiced rituals for hours after school. I made blood sacrifices. I killed a rabbit, which was so fucking cute I still feel guilty about it," she said. "What a waste of time. It took me over a decade of ritualized practice to contact an interdimensional entity. I spent twenty-three hours a day in that cell in silent meditation. Years went by, and I was still scratching sigils into my flesh and drawing magical circles and triangles on the floor. For nothing!"

I realized that I was hearing that low buzzing noise I first heard on that underground videotape, the one Danielle had played for me years earlier. My stomach started feeling sick.

"And then one night I fell asleep, and woke up to static on the screen and the buzz of white noise, but I could hear it forming into words. His words," Alizon said. "He can piggyback on their signals, all of their signals. If you're watching a screen, you've already let him inside.

"When I was in prison, he showed me how to feed a monster and how to raise an army," Alizon continued. "No theatrical rituals and pentagrams. Just a little blood sacrifice now and then. All you really gotta do is be receptive."

She kept talking at the camera instead of to me.

"Did you know that some neurology experts believe that the brain doesn't actually bring about consciousness? It's really a receiver, a little radio tower tuning in to whatever's on the air," she said. "He wills it, and we receive it. He creates, and we consume. We're a garden, he's the sun. Resisting him is betraying the natural order."

Alizon sounded crazy. But she wasn't. I saw the Eyeless Man on that videotape with Danielle all those years ago. He was shrouded in shadow, shaped like a praying mantis—long, tall and spindly. When I tried to make out his face, there was nothing there.

He had no eyes, just holes of swirling darkness. He still haunts my dreams every night.

I shouldn't be surprised that Alizon disappeared soon after that TV special. There was a big push to find her (the irony!), but the search petered out after a while. I'm not sure what happened to the Satanic Schoolgirls—I no longer watch TV, read the paper or view any media anymore. It's not safe.

Believe what you want, but the monster is the medium. Jesus Christ, Moses, the Buddha—if they ever existed, they only spoke to a couple of thousand people in their lives. The Eyeless Man reaches billions, as long as people leave their psyches wide open. The body is a temple, right? People read nutrition labels like they're sacred texts. They're worried about taking in too much sugar or fat, but they'll give anything direct access to their minds.

Look, I'm lucky. I'm not missing. I escaped the Eyeless Man, and I'm not sure why. Probably because I only encountered him once, only for a moment. (I *may* have had my eyes shut most of the time.) Or maybe it's because the part I played was spreading the disease by printing zines, participating in the documentary and interviewing Alizon.

On the precipice of a new millennium, I see the new world rising as Alizon did, with no God and nowhere to hide. Soon every movie, song, TV show—all the audio and visuals ever created—will be available on the 'net in an instant. Imagine yourself linked to all the people on the rest of the planet? Like it or not, you'll invite the whole world in and they'll crawl inside, bringing their demons along in binary code.

Already, you can't tune out the news and propaganda, and you don't know which is which, but it doesn't really matter. That's entertainment, replacing prayer and outranking ritual.

Information is spoon-fed, digestible but twisted into half-truths. In this virtual world, reality is relative.

Consume or be consumed. You might not notice the Eyeless Man, but let me assure you he's there. You'll watch your three and a half hours of TV every day, and twice that long on a portable device you carry with you so you and him never have to be apart.

Consume and be consumed. Monsters need to eat. The white noise makes it hard to hear the real world. It's too late to open your eyes. Ota Keta. Ota Keta. Ota Keta. Repeat after me. Ota Keta. Ota Keta. Ota Keta. He's already in you. You're already gone.

DR. MAYNARD WILLS: THE VOYAGE OF PETER GILLIAM

Something terrible has happened. My enthusiasm for this material has transferred to another, and I worry I have destroyed a brilliant man. For weeks now, Dr. Gilliam and I have exchanged ideas over email. He was both fascinated and terrified by *Video Palace*. I even shared early drafts of the personal stories collected in these pages.

But ultimately, he couldn't heed his own advice. When he wrote to me, "I beg you to be cautious, though, as we really cannot conceive what lurks on the other side of the dimensional wall," the man was talking to himself as much as he was warning me.

At his advanced age, Peter feared he'd die before he'd solved the scientific mysteries that have spun around in his great mind for decades. After listening to *Video Palace* (on my recommendation), he wanted to understand what had really happened to Mark Cambria. And the only way to do that, Gilliam decided, was to replicate Cambria's experience. Though I warned him against it, my new friend searched for and found a wealthy collector of esoterica, who lives deep in the Hollywood Hills. The man claimed to possess a White Tape that originated in the late 1970s. He offered Peter the chance to own it for a tidy sum: $100,000. Unmarried and with no heirs, he took out a loan against his home and made this shadowy deal.

When he received the tape he was as exuberant as I was concerned, but his missives quickly shifted in tone. He became despondent. The White Tape did indeed seem authentic in both its age and its content, but it didn't have any effect on Peter. He watched it for hours and hours, making himself the subject of his own dangerous experiment. He recorded his sleep with the same app Mark Cambria used. Nothing. No Os. No Tas. No Ketas.

After a week of this, he seemed ready to crack. I spent hours on the phone with him, hypothesizing as to why some are susceptible to these tapes and others are not. We looked to Cambria's story. We looked to the stories we'd received for this book, and our best guess is that Dr. Peter Gilliam doesn't have any kind of compulsive, perverse, addictive or otherwise unhealthy relationship with media and its consumption. The man still listens to radio plays! We wondered, was it possible that this Eyeless Man myth was the result of some kind of shared neurobiological response to overstimulation? My interest at this time was still the origin story of the Eyeless Man, and I believed it was a worthy idea to pursue. Gilliam, however, was inconsolable. Our conversations deteriorated. The poor man wept incessantly. And then he stopped picking up the phone, and I stopped calling.

After our last conversation, he sent me an email with an attached audio file. The email and a transcription of the audio file are provided here:

Dear Maynard,

I know our friendship is new, but I want to express my appreciation for your patience and loyalty these last several weeks. And I'd like to apologize for my recent behavior. I also want to let you know that I DID IT. I had the breakthrough.

I FOUND THE EYELESS MAN. I wasn't sure it would work, but it did, it did! I knew there was a way to see him, and I did! Unfortunately, I have no memory of this experience, but I have audio, a recording that proves all! You see, I procured a sample of psilocybin from a former student who now works in the campus mycology lab and devised a contraption that would operate my VCR, playing, rewinding and replaying the White Tape. If the Eyeless Man would not come to me, I would come to him! Play the recording, and learn what my inner eye saw!

Best,
Peter

Here is a transcription of the audio file attached. I can confirm it is Peter's voice.

9:57 p.m.: [Indistinguishable grunts]

10:13 p.m.: I see a path, a way into his world.

10:42 p.m: A vessel. A vessel through the cosmos.

11:12 p.m.: Who are you, you at the helm? You are not him. Where are you taking me? What is the Stack? Is he there?

11:30 p.m.: I see so, so many. The suffering multitudes, glitching in and out of time, lost in a fog of static. The air burns like acid.

11:53 p.m.: He knows. He knows I'm not supposed to be here.

11:54 p.m.: Massive, expanding shadow. His eyeless face, like dripping tar over ancient bone.

12:04 a.m.: I flee. I flee back to the vessel. The being asks me, "Which realm?" Home! Home! Home!

I do not know what to think. I do not know what to feel. Either my new friend has been driven insane or the path this story has taken is beyond my area of expertise.

THE
INWARD EYE

John Skipp

Dear Professor Motherfucking Maynard Wills,

Wow! And WOOO-HOO-HOO!!! Thank you for your insanely synchronistic message of inquiry. I gotta admit, I haven't a clue as to how or why you plucked my name out of your mystery hat, given the gazillions of media freaks and conspiracy junkies out there to choose from. It's not like I've ever gone on the record with this shit.

But your timing couldn't be better, as the odds are 50/50 or worse that this may be my last goddamn night on earth. And given the nature of the topic at hand, I guess that's just par for the course.

The universe works in mysterious ways.

And that ain't but the half of it.

As it turns out, yeah, I have plenty to say about your "Eyeless Man," although (as you'll see) I might describe him somewhat differently. Let's just say I know him well. And he knows me, a whole lot better than I wish he did. Never more so than now.

The bulk of the enclosed, as fate would have it, is a piece I've been working on for the last several weeks, in between wrapping my last remaining deadlines, locking down my last will and testament, making a point of telling all the people I love how much I love them and fending off the itching in my brain with as much beer as I can swallow. Before the acid kicks in.

You wouldn't believe how hard it is to scratch the itch in your brain, once it gets started. Unless you already know. Which I pray that you don't.

Fingers can't reach it. There's a skull in the way.

But you do what you can. So I'm cutting and pasting the most pertinent bits in. As a researcher, I suspect that providing my case history might come in handy. At the very least, it provides context for the crazy-ass shit I'm about to say.

The question, of course, is: Am I crazy? And the answer is, well, of course! Ask anyone! I've been weird since well before the day I was born, whether you measure that in embryonic terms or presuppose (as I do) an endless litany of past lives, with an equally infinite litany of future lives to come.

This is what gives me hope, on my way through forever.

I hope to God, or whatever you wanna call it, that what I have to share is useful. And that it's not too late for you. Should you choose to publish it, I would think that was fucking great. But just in case, I'm cc'ing it to my family and most trusted friends. The last drip in my bucket list.

So STRAP IN, BABY! This is gonna take a while.

Here's hoping I make it all the way.

—John Skipp

I'm not sure precisely when I first became aware of the vibrational frequencies underlying all existence. I'm guessing as ripples through my mother's amniotic fluid, as I gradually took form, moving from zygote to meatwad to flipper-sprouting eyeballed thing full of nerve endings on their way to babyness.

I don't know if you've read Stanislav Grof's brilliant *Beyond the Brain* (1985). But if you haven't, you probably should. It's without a doubt the smartest, most comprehensible book I've ever read about the actual nature and evolution of consciousness itself. (Grof's one of the founders of transpersonal psychotherapy, as well as a serious psychedelic researcher. A contemporary of Terence McKenna, in the post-Leary years.) And it spends some serious time on the rigors of the pre-birth experience.

People tend to think of life beginning the second you pop out of the womb. But that's even dumber than thinking life begins or ends in high school. Fact is, we spend months taking shape before the nascent brain grows a single fissure. And yet we are—albeit at the most basic level—aware.

(And no, for the record: this is not a pro-life message. At that point, I was just another lump of meat struggling to be born, just like every other creature on this world or any other. *I made it! BALLOONS FOR ME!*)

But I know for a fact that my mother loved the music of Rose-mary Clooney and the laughter of studio audiences on radio talk and game shows. Not sure if TV existed in our home yet. (It was 1956 when I was "conceived.") My oldest sister was in love with rock 'n' roll. The sound of rebellion in that era. Elvis Presley in my DNA.

So it only makes sense that—as I grew ears, and a brain at functional minimum, and a heart that could beat by itself—I was receiving those signals. Not as loud as Mom's comforting heartbeat, which was huge. But they were already having their way with me.

Which means that advertisements were also sneaking in. With their own insidious vibrations.

More on that in a minute.

My earliest actual memory—recounted in various interviews over the years, and most specifically in the novel *The Cleanup*— is of the day the rats came down the walls.

I can't recall the specifics of my little boy bedroom. I can't tell you what was on the TV. (Which we had, at that point. It was 1960, and I was three-anna-half years old.) And I certainly didn't know that my experience was—as far as my parents and sisters were concerned—a hallucination.

All I knew was that the rats were pouring down the walls. Malformed. Spindle-legged. And sharp of teeth. Black pearl eyes glistening. They chittered, descending.

They came like torrential rain, sluicing the walls to either side. Not dropping on me from the ceiling—I have no memory of the ceiling—

but with an M. C. Escher–like pattern of infinite onslaught. Dozens unto hundreds of thousands. Not just pouring, but pooling underneath me. Like a maelstrom of hunger into which I would be swept.

And I remember screaming. Not just baby screams. Not "WAAAAH! My diaper is pooped!" Or "WAAAAH! You said no, and I don't like it!"

It was my first experience with genuine terror.

I remember my dad scooping me up and yelling words I didn't understand. But I knew he was scared, too. Our frequencies conjoining.

Then I was in the bathtub, and my mom and dad were there, pouring ice cubes upon me as the chilly water flowed. Burning off my fever. My delirium fever. As I screamed and screamed. Body engulfed in rising cold.

And this was the thing: *The second the rats hit the water, they vanished.* Not dissolving. Just ceasing to exist.

Then the fever broke, and they stopped coming.

It was a total *Jacob's Ladder* experience. And taught me, for the first time, the difference between my inner and outer experiences.

Some might say it's about the difference between delirium and fact.

Me, I might beg to differ.

In the childhood years that followed, I took in everything the world shot my way. Fell in love with cartoons, which brought me joy and fun and chaos. Cartoons were where *anything* could happen, and usually did. Bugs Bunny and Daffy Duck ruled my world. Old Max and Dave Fleischer *Popeye* shorts. Those vibrations were not lost on me. Are my lifeline, to this day.

The news, back then, had a gray stentorian tone. The "Voice of Authority." It was male. It was old. Wore a stupid suit and tie. Shot in black-and-white, but totally white in presentation. (That said—living in the West Allis suburb of Milwaukee, Wisconsin— I'd never met anyone who *wasn't* white, so I had no broader frame of reference.)

My main impressions were that a) I didn't understand a thing they said, and b) I found no comfort there. If this was the wider world, I wasn't sure I liked it. It didn't feel good, that much was for sure. It made me want to leave the room or beg my parents to turn back to cartoons.

But then—one Saturday afternoon, somewhere between *The Flintstones, The Jetsons,* and *Top Cat*—the terror frequency came back, in the form of a commercial for Dr. Cadaverino's *Nightmare Theatre.*

The monster in question was Frankenstein.

And, in my soul, the rats returned.

I didn't know who Boris Karloff was. But there was something in his flattened skull, his haunted eyes, his shambling gait, that took me straight to panic. A bandwidth I knew all too well and had all but forgotten, until that moment.

I shrieked and ran from the TV room to the dining room, howling desperately for my mom. The room was dim, the curtains pulled. And she was nowhere to be found.

When the footsteps started pounding up the creaking basement stairs, I hid under the table, quaking, until Mom dragged me out, consoled me and informed me that monster movies were strictly off-limits.

But of course, I had tasted the forbidden fruit.

The first scary movie I watched in its entirety—alone, at the ripe old age of six—was the 1953 science fiction classic *Invaders from Mars*. And, of course, it scared the living shit out of me. The notion that space creatures had landed in the field out back of this little kid's house, creating suckholes of cosmic quicksand that could drag you under and send you back alien and transformed—or, worse yet, *do that to your parents*—was purest nightmare fuel. And left me seriously questioning authority for the very first time.

Underneath all that, though, was the music. Music designed specifically to induce fear and dread. Up until then, the creepiest music I'd ever heard was "Dance of the Sugar Plum Fairy," in Music Appreciation (a class they actually used to teach in elementary school). Which I loved. But this was something else.

It was, I believe, my introduction to the theremin: the first pre-Moog electronic instrument. Its unearthly portamento sweeps and hovering vibratos sent chills from my skull down to my toenails. I knew this was something that changed the frequencies of *my* world. And suspected this was true of the world at large.

At which point, I was hooked.

From there, I watched every horror movie I could get my eyeballs on. And quickly drew the distinction between the ones that were genuinely scary and the ones that were just laughably stupid. But those were beautiful, too. They put the terror in perspective and allowed me to realize I didn't have to be scared. That they were, in their way, just as funny as cartoons.

And by the time the Beach Boys slapped a theremin on "Good Vibrations," as its signature feel-good sound, I felt pretty well integrated.

Then my family moved to Buenos Aires, Argentina, when my dad got a job with the State Department. And several life-altering things transpired.

1) I witnessed actual violence and death, mostly at the hands of an authoritarian regime where even the traffic cops carried machine guns. Saw people beaten to death in front of me. Saw rivers of blood flow down the steps of a *fútbol* stadium, after a riot over a 0–0 match between rival teams River and Boca that I'd hoped to attend on my birthday but mercifully missed. Thereby opening my deep well of sorrow.

Now I knew that death was real, because I could smell the blood and see the bullet holes. Horror wasn't just a fantasy. It was an actual fact. And it could happen to me, if I didn't watch my ass.

2) I discovered psychedelic music. First from purchasing my first-ever record album, *Sgt. Pepper's Lonely Hearts Club Band*, by my absolute favorite band, the Beatles. Between "Being for the Benefit of Mr. Kite!," "Within You, Without You," and "A Day in the Life," my world was sonically transformed by vibrations the world itself admitted had never been heard before.

Then I made friends with a kid named Donald Hunt, whose older brother was sending care packages from Berkeley, California, the heart of the hippie scene. Suddenly, I was deluged by Frank Zappa and the Mothers of Invention's "The Return of the Son of Monster Magnet," Grace Slick's witchy crooning on Jefferson Airplane's "White Rabbit" and "Lather" and—most of all—the unparalleled trippy delirium of Jimi Hendrix on guitar, ripping apart and recalibrating forever what six strings and a piece of wood could do.

3) This led to the purchase of my first electric guitar: a sunburst Stratocaster copy hanging in a music-store window, which I demanded my parents purchase for me. So I could follow that path myself.

And here's the hilarious thing. They bought it for me. I had never been more excited in my life. We took it home. Plugged it into a stereo amplifier.

But because the amp was running on 120 volts of US current, and the transformer adapting it ran on the Argentine 220 . . .

. . . *I was electrocuted, from the moment my fingers hit the strings. Frozen in place, as the maladapted voltage poured through me. Paralyzed. Juddering like Jell-O on a spring. As the world went white and shuddery and gone.*

In that moment—for the first time—I ceased to be myself. I was pure screaming energy. Mind erased. Body almost irrelevant.

My sister Reenie—the only one in the room—thought it was the funniest thing she had ever seen, right up until she realized I might be truly dying. At which point, she had the smarts to pull the plug out of the wall.

A sane person might have called it quits right there. But again, I have never claimed to be sane.

So we got a new amp that wouldn't kill me. And I taught myself how to play, by ear. Mimicking every bass note, every chord change, every riff of the music that captivated me. Song by song. Lick by lick. Melody by melody.

I couldn't touch the sonics of Jimi or Frank or the Beatles. I had no fuzz box, no Wah-Wah pedal, no Echoplex. But I understood that the music itself cast a spell, no matter what instrument you played it on. That songs told stories, carried direct experiences. And that music didn't need words to tell you how it felt, and make you feel it.

By the time my family was forced to flee Argentina—when the military overthrew President Onganía, and the tanks were in the streets (where some people I knew were about to disappear, only to be found thirty years later, in mass graves containing countless thousands of others)—I was ready to return to the U. S. of A. I wanted to be part of the counterculture that was brewing. I wanted to see the live bands weave their sonic magick onstage. I wanted to *be* in one of those bands, weaving magick of my own.

But almost most of all, I really wanted to do me some drugs.

I was thirteen years old. It was 1970. And at Stratford Junior High School in Arlington, Virginia, drugs were everywhere. It didn't take long to find the cool kids at the smoking corner, who loved the same music, grew their hair long, wore the closest to hippie clothes their parents would let them get away with. And a lot of them were holding.

Over the next several years, I tried every mind-bending chemical known to teenage humankind. Quickly found I hated heroin. Hated speed. Hated downers. Was not super fond of cocaine. Hated PCP (known as angel dust) with a passion: a drug so stupid that my body literally *forgot how to shit*, for several hours that seemed to last forever.

That said, I fell in love with weed, which has been my near-daily companion ever since. I consider it a benign and reliable entryway to fifth-dimensional experience. Attenuating my sensory apparatus. Colors sharper. Music deeper. That is my energetic comfort zone, and I ain't afraid to say it.

But the biggest game changer was LSD, be it a sugar cube or a microdot or a slip of blotter paper.

That was where my inner eye irrevocably opened at last.

Maynard, muh man? I really can't overstate the importance of psychedelic drugs, particularly as it pertains to your inquiry. Had I not dropped acid, I would never have had full waking access to the subconscious mind—the stomping ground of dreams—and the even deeper universal mind underlying all existence.

Cuz here's the thing. Peyote is great. If you want to talk with the Mushroom People from the Mushroom Dimension, right here on Earth, that's your big chance! They're out there (or in there, however you choose to frame it).

But LSD is the direct link between your central nervous system and the mind of God. All the doorways blown open. All the gates unlocked.

You wanna understand infinity as not just a concept but as a direct experience? Then I dare you to do what I used to do, on a regular basis, in those teenage years.

Drop some good clean acid, in a nice safe place. And as you start to hit the hallucinatory peak, FORCE YOURSELF TO KEEP YOUR EYES SHUT FOR THE NEXT TWO HOURS AT LEAST.

What unspools there—in profound Sensurround—is a relentless onslaught of fractal unfurlment, the likes of which computer imagery has barely cracked the code (though the Brit animator Cyriak comes super close). One electric glowing image after another, in replicating patterns both evocatively abstract and stunningly specific.

Shapes, yes. Shambling. Slithering. Soaring.

But mostly faces. Faces within faces. Faces morphing and mutating into and out of each other. So that something unspeakably beautiful decays into monstrous nightmare, turns cartoonishly comic, flows into ineffably gorgeous again.

All coming at me. Closing in. And blowing through me.

It was there that I saw that all things are truly One. That what we call life is a sliver of a fragment of a dream of the All-That-Is, as It envisions Itself in every possible configuration. A perpetual-motion machine, reinventing Itself by the microsecond. The push-me-pull-you that keeps infinity running forever. Boundlessly, inexhaustibly creative. As It explores all that It might be.

It was there that I first saw your Eyeless Man, over and over and over again. Wearing many faces, of various shapes. Some with teeth like stilettos. Some with no teeth at all, mouths as empty as the sockets of his eyes.

The thing that conjoined them was that empty space where the gaze had sucked back to nothingness. Peering into me, without seeing the real me at all. It was an absence of love and recognition.

But his hunger was very real.

I ain't gonna lie to you. That was terrifying shit. You think he's scary in sobriety? TRY HIM ON FUCKING ACID. It was all I could do not to open my eyes, escape from him into what passes for consensual reality.

What made it possible was the fact that he was only one of the endless forces underlying the deeper reality.

He represented the pit into which I could fall, if I let myself. A truly bottomless pit, where every landing I hit was a trapdoor opening up to an even deeper darkness. Plummeting farther and farther from the last stitch of light remaining. Until I was as lost as he.

For me, the saving grace was how quickly he transmuted, if I did not submit. His doorway was potent. But his doorway was fleeting. And I did not have to take it.

There were other options. Like light, for instance. Like love. Like joy. He was just another color on the palette. With so many more to choose from, in the vast sprawl of life.

This became clear when I finally joined, then formed, my own bands, getting the tools at last with which to unleash my own vibrations. I had a '65 Strat, and all manner of gizmos to unleash with, playing guitar at least five hours a day, every day. I was writing my own songs, shaping my sadness and hope into sonic vision. And I can't tell you how many hours I spent noodling around on synthesizers, even though I couldn't play keyboards for shit: exploring the filters, plumbing the frequencies, experimenting with soundscapes at every range, down to the subsonic. Where I felt, rather than heard, what was blowing back at me.

All of this dramatically changed how I perceived all other media. Not just music, where I could smell the insincerity of most pedestrian prefab radio pop. Now every commercial ad psychically reeked of naked greed I could not help but taste on my mind's tongue, and wanted to spit out as fast as possible. Almost all network television left me feeling the same way.

Little wonder I became an outlaw, at least in my own mind.

All of which came into sharp, profound focus when my past lives began to flash before me.

The first one hit in ninth-grade detention, where I was serving time for calling out a bullying math teacher on his abuse of one of the slower kids. ("Excuse me, Mr. Miller," I said. "I know it's easy to pick on poor ol' Butch. But how'd you like to try that shit on me?")

So there I was, doodling weird faces and shapes cartoonily into my notebook while the principal called my mom . . .

. . . and suddenly, I was on fire, tied to a stake in front of a leering crowd. I could smell my hair burn on either side of my face as the flames licked up. Smell my own meat crackling. Could feel the off-the-charts pain blaze through me . . .

. . . and in that moment, I knew I was a young woman, unjustly accused of being a witch . . .

. . . and I was soooooooo angry at being killed for this . . .

. . . and then the bell rang, dragging me back to the classroom. Where I sat, drenched in sweat. Wondering what the hell just happened to me.

But it wasn't the last time.

Over the next many years, I found myself spontaneously flashing back to other lives. A young Native pre-American brave, taking an arrow through the throat from a rival tribe, falling back into a stream, where I drowned as I bled out. Others too muzzy for me to recollect but sooooo vivid as they happened. Leaving marks upon my soul. Or perhaps just alerting me to the marks already there.

Were they past lives? Was it genetic memory, my DNA randomly squirting out its encoded history? Or was I just hallucinating, my brain playing tricks based on some kind of faulty wiring?

I had no way of knowing. My entire way of knowing had been thrown into question.

All I could say was that it felt real to me. Every bit as real as everything else.

So when I suddenly found myself getting glimpses of Heaven, the only frame of reference I had was my own experience.

That's when shit really started to get weird.

Suddenly, I was an angel. I knew that for a fact. I had ascended as far as I could go as a soul. Was experiencing unparalleled beauty and peace. The true fulfillment of all that I might be.

And yet, as I gazed down on all creation, I saw unspeakable suffering and torment. Staggering injustice. Wrong after wrong after wrong. Saw the terrestrial food chain tear itself apart and swallow itself, through every mouth ever opened. Felt the pain of every tooth and claw.

So I said to God, "What the fuck is this? I mean, here we are in perfection. You can clearly do anything. You can clearly do everything! So why is this allowed to happen?"

And God said, "That's just the way it is."

Needless to say, I was not satisfied with this answer. And I was not the only one. There were a bunch of angels who were right there with me. Including this guy named Lucifer—aka the Light-Bringer—who was the most beautiful and radiant one of all. Going, "Dude, this is totally not cool. We think you need to change this. Like, starting right now."

But God said, "No."

Just like that, there was war in Heaven. A small army of us, rising up, in an attempt to force the issue.

Unfortunately for us, God's faithful were stronger, and under the leadership of Generalissimo Archangel Michael, we thoroughly got our asses kicked in short order.

At which point we were vanquished to Hell. Where we languished for the next untold-trillion years, if time existed at all.

But while the newly renamed Lucifer—now Satan, or the Adversary—has been widely quoted as saying, "Better to rule in Hell than serve in Heaven," my personal experience was vastly different. For one thing, I wasn't ruling.

For another, they didn't call Hell "Hell" for nothin'.

It was the worst fucking place in God's creation. Specifically created by God in order to house and punish all the worst of the worst in one place. Deploying the deepest cruelty, the most punishing punishment, upon many of the biggest assholes ever unleashed on said creation, from any and every domain.

I'm not saying there weren't some really good parties. If there's one thing I can tell you, it's that evil knows how to party. And some might argue that truly horrible sex is better than no sex at all. (I am not one of them.)

What I mostly felt was a bottomless sorrow, a smothering sense of loss. To have been wrenched from such heights and thrown all the way down to this sulfurous soul-pit of ultimate degradation was the authentic goddamned definition of unbearable for me.

I had no aptitude or inclination toward torturing others. It was the last thing I'd ever have wanted to do. Making me complicit in the very thing I'd fought against was the worst punishment I could possibly have imagined.

Was I furious? Absolutely. Did I feel like I'd been wronged? Without a doubt. Did I blame myself? I wasn't sure. I still thought that we had been right.

But did I hate myself, for having screwed up so royally?

Oh, baby, more than you will ever know.

All I really knew was that I refused to be this fallen angel. This was not what I wanted. This was not who I was.

And even if it took for-fucking-ever, I had to get out of that place.

I don't know how I managed to escape. All I know is that I did. My eyes on the beacon at the heart of All-That-Is.

And so—for life after life after life—I gradually crawled my way back to and through the land of the living. Step by step. Incarnation by incarnation. Learning the lessons that might take me back to the place where I hoped I belonged.

Now, Professor, just to be clear: I'm not saying that all this personal vision represents any kind of certifiable fact. I mean, I'm not even a fucking Christian. But I went to some Catholic schools, read enough of the Bible to get the gist. So that whole mythic template was yet another set of symbols and wavelengths I'd attempted to integrate, on the infinite road to understanding.

All I can say is, those were the flashes that came to me unbidden. Sometimes tripping. Sometimes just walking down the street, or lying in bed or taking a leak.

And all of this has informed my perspective, all along this strange path.

Which brings us, at last, to the heart of your inquiry.

PART TWO: THE WHITE TAPE, AND ME

Flash-forward almost twenty years. My musical career never panned out, but I wound up on the *New York Times* bestseller list, writing outsider horror fiction that attempted to translate those trippy frequencies, nightmares and gnostic longings into prose.

Suddenly, I was semi-famous. The only kind of rock star I would ever be. Millions of people had bought my work, whether they liked it or not. And a lot of them did. For better or worse, they were surfing my wave.

This resulted in fan mail. And in the pre-Internet days, this came either through forwards from my publisher or people who tracked me down sideways. My listing in the phone book. A friend of a friend of a friend.

It was the era of VHS. And I was now devouring movies as hard as I'd once devoured albums or novels. Had hundreds in my collection. Some bought. Most taped off cable.

But every once in a while, somebody would send me a tape of rarified shit I was not liable to find in my local video store, or pretty much anywhere else.

There were three of particular note.

The first was autopsy footage of a drowning victim, from a local York County, Pennsylvania, coroner's office. She didn't look like a person anymore. She had been bloated and rubberized by death into something that more resembled a shabby special effect from a C-grade monster movie. At first, that's what I thought it was.

But the more they methodically peeled her apart, the clearer it became that this was all real.

"Thought you'd like this!" the coroner fan said.

I didn't. It hurt. Took me down the dark hole. I could smell the formaldehyde rot and deeply felt the indignity of this poor person, organ-splayed step by step before me. It was not something that was meant for me to see.

But it was real, and it was true. And I watched it all the way through. Did not feel like the person who sent it meant me harm. They just wanted me to know, in case I didn't.

I kept that tape in my collection for many years. Though I never watched it again.

The next (unlabeled, with no return address) was a compilation of bestiality scenes: women getting fucked by dogs, or sticking snakes up their vaginas. All shot on video, in trailer parks or shabby hotels. The women all tragically hot young junkies who rolled their eyes, not even bothering to fake it. Radiating narcotized despair and the hope beyond hopelessness that this next fix might somehow help wipe their memory clean.

I watched as much as I could stand. Then took the tape out back and beat it to death with a hammer, shredding the loops of tape that unspooled so that nobody else would ever have to suffer that shit on my account. Tossing it all in the trash, as I shook off the heartbreaking vibrations as best I could. Which took a while.

And then came the White Tape. Unlabeled as well, like the last one. No name on the return address (which turned out to be false). Just the initials I.C.U.

But on the white VHS was a Post-it in the center, with the words *YOU WANT TO KNOW WHAT REAL HORROR IS?* in a jagged scrawl that looked like the writer could barely keep the pen from shaking out of their hand.

That was my first warning sign. And after the last two surprise tapes, I was a little gun-shy, to say the fucking least.

So, I took the tape upstairs with me to my office, as I set into my day and night of writing. And only after my daughters and sweetheart were in bed and fast asleep did I venture back down to the living room. Grabbed a Rolling Rock from the kitchen. Fired up a bowl. And popped the tape in the VCR, then settled back on my couch to see what they claimed real horror was.

I will never forget the moment I picked up the remote and hit play.

It wasn't the image on the screen. I don't even remember the image on the screen. Have no idea whether I ever saw it or not.

It was the sound that hit me. More precisely, the sound beneath the sound. A susurrating roar of wrongness that vibrated in my bone marrow, forced the sweat from my pores in rivers.

The feeling was so intense, so instantaneous, that it felt like an acid flashback made of daggers. Stabbing every nerve ending I had with live wires, like the long-ago electric guitar that electrocuted me.

Once again, I left my body. But this time, the world was not shimmering white.

This time, all was black. A shimmering blacker-than-black.

And the Eyeless Man was there. No other faces. Only his.

"You think you know," he said, through a cavernous grin that threatened to swallow his features entirely. "You think you remember. You want to dance with the angels again. But there are no angels here."

It was true. In this black, crackling space, there was no room for light, or appetite for it. He didn't give a shit about my light.

It was my darkness he craved.

As he pulled me toward him.

"Come in," he said, black sockets blazing with the anti-heat of a trillion nullified suns. "Let me remind you how I see."

The next thing I knew, I was inside his skull, crawling up inside his brain. The fissures like rows upon rows of occupied seats in a coliseum so huge my own skull threatened to crack at the enormity.

And every seat was taken by a glowing eye, staring down on me.

That was when I learned he was not eyeless at all.

They were all on the inside. Aimed directly at me.

Calling me back to Hell.

I can only guess that it was my body, working in self-defense, that made my thumb hit the stop button on the remote. Dragged me back to my seat on the living room couch. As I crapped my pants and vomited onto the coffee table, my beer, my bowl of weed.

Like I couldn't get him out of me fast enough.

But, of course, it was too late.

PART THREE: WHERE IT GOES FROM HERE

It's been nearly thirty years since the events of that night. I'm sixty-two years old, as of this writing. Quite possibly the last writing that I will ever do. But we shall see.

I gotta admit, these last years have been largely great. I'm grateful to have lived this long, learned this many lessons. Wouldn't mind sticking around awhile longer. I dearly love life. Have dearly loved this life, in particular, which I feel has brought me closer back to Godhead than I've been in a billion trillion years.

What I learned was that I would have to lean into life and love harder, even as the darkness assailed me. Try as you might, you can't beat up evil or sweet-talk it into not being what it is. Played on its own terms, resistance is futile.

All you can do is try to be a better person. Help others whenever you can. Shine light on the darkness. Show it for what it is. Because it's never gonna go away. Nor should it. It is part of the design. An intrinsic and important part.

But that doesn't mean you fucking let it win.

Once I peeled off my shit-caked pants, put on new ones and cleaned the puke off the table, I was left with the question of the White Tape, still sitting in my VCR. I didn't even want to touch it. The thought occurred to me: *Should I just take the whole machine out? Maybe the shelf it sat on? Does the TV need to go? SHOULD I JUST BURN THE WHOLE HOUSE DOWN?*

Eventually, I grabbed an oven mitt and a can of lighter fluid. Popped the eject button. Grabbed the tape with the mitt as it slid out. Took it out past the back alley, into the field behind my house. Kicked a preexisting hole in the dirt to make it deeper.

Dropped the tape and the mitt. Doused them profusely. And burned it all to molten sludge.

Then I got a bag of rock salt from the toolshed. Poured it over the sludge and melted it, too.

Then I covered it with dirt and salted the goddamned earth five feet in every direction. So that nothing might ever grow there again.

Then, just to be safe, I tossed the VCR in the trash and bought a new one the next day.

As fate would have it, my TV was not possessed, and the walls of the house were not infected with the horror. My kids were fine. My lady was fine. We watched cartoons and scary movies, threw parties, loved each other and lived life there quite nicely through all the ups and downs for a couple more years, before moving to California. (Where we eventually broke up. But that's another story.)

The only one infected was me.

And the good news is, I guess, that it took this long to catch up with me. That I toughed it out this far, even as I've watched that dark vibration spread further and further into the mediascape. Yes, in ugly movies and music. Yes, in ugly TV. Yes, in advertisements. Yes, especially, in the news.

But mostly in social media, where the Eyeless Man is everywhere projecting its solipsistic inward gaze, then squirting it out, one trillion rage-tweets at a time, through every hapless soul who ever sucked the venom. Even at low doses, that shit adds up.

You might think I'm totally nuts at this point, and you're certainly right. Who wouldn't be? And more to the point, WHO ISN'T? All things being equal, I sincerely doubt I'm the craziest sonofabitch you reached out to. Especially if they watched a White Tape.

In terms of evidence trail, though:

A couple of weeks back, I had some brain scans done, because the itching inside my skull had finally become intolerable. And what they showed was not some big tumor but *hundreds of tiny little nodes*, draped in every cranial crevice like pebbles. Too small to see the almost infinitesimally minuscule irises and pupils that I know for a fact they contain.

I got the results tonight, half an hour before I got your email.

Now it's an hour-anna-half later. And though my very last hit of acid is kicking in hard, I've tried at least that hard to stay focused, so that I might share this with you. In the hope, as I said, that it's helpful. Because we need all the help we can get.

All I ask is that you share what I've just shared with you, unexpurgated. Cuz it's the best I've got.

In a couple of minutes, I'm going into the garage. My housemate Darren is a carpenter. He saws boards for a living. Is constructing a really sweet backyard awning, so we can sit on that porch in the Portland rain without getting drenched, as we party together. That's a thing I would dearly love to do.

But I always said that I would save my last LSD trip for my deathbed. Part going-away present. Part welcome-back present. Welcoming myself back to the All-That-Is.

Turns out there is no bed in there. But there is a big-ass table, with a big-ass power saw I've strategically placed at the end. Right where my forehead goes.

I also brought out a couple of synthesizers, preprogrammed to spin out my favorite frequencies. And an amp wired to some super-sweet effects pedals, so I can play my Fender Stratocaster to my heart's content as I lie down.

In a couple of minutes, I will play my heart and soul out, as I close my eyes and let infinity unleash upon me once again. The sweet and the sorrowful. The benign and the malign. The comic and the tragic. The pain and the gain.

And we shall see what we shall see.

If God tells me I'm not done, I will stick around as long as I can. As I was told long ago, and now finally get: *That's just the way it is.*

But if God agrees that I have ridden this particular roller coaster as far as it goes, then I will bring that whirling blade down on my forehead, hard. Sawing all the way through.

Cuz if that motherfucker doesn't scratch the itch, I frankly do not know what will.

My hope is that the light shines bright. As I dive into the infinite. Not for the last time. For the next.

But the fact is that the rats are back. Streaming down the walls. Pooling at my feet. And this time, they're biting. Wrenching psychic meat from cosmic bone, while the not-so-Eyeless Man presides.

They want me back. But I ain't going.

My own inner eye is clear.

DR. MAYNARD WILLS:
MY STATIC DREAM

Poor Carter. I arrived at my office this morning as Daniel prepared the day's lectures. I think I nearly gave him a heart attack! He was relieved to see me, but his face quickly reddened and he demanded an explanation. "In due time, I promise, Daniel." That's all I could tell him. He processed this and—thankfully—nodded in acceptance and trust. Soon, though, I'll need to enlighten my young friend. I am better for this time away following Peter's heightened experience.

But it was a dream, a dream I had last night, that has been most illuminating. And I am quite sure it is the product of my own subconscious. Despite Peter's repeated offers, I have resisted watching his White Tape. And no supernatural bogeyman has appeared at my door or under my bed.

I remember this dream more vividly than any I've ever had before. I often forget them instantly. The smells were vibrant, the light glinted in my eyes like the sun itself. Allow me to describe it for you:

I awoke in a city, in my apartment. But it wasn't my home, my waking domicile, yet I just *knew* that it was my apartment. And I saw that the walls were "on." The best way I can describe this is when you wake up in the middle of the night after falling asleep on your couch, and your television is filled with static, or some kind of late-night infomercial, because you'd left it on by accident. And so you think to yourself, *Oh, I left the TV on.* This was the exact same feeling, except it applied to my walls.

Because my walls—and indeed all the walls in this city—buzzed with life. They weren't covered in wallpaper, or made of bricks or masonry of any kind, but were instead made with the same kind of electrical fuzz that makes up white noise on a television. A cool, vibrating material that shifted endlessly, tiny white and black voids interchanging with one another, popping up at random intervals. They showed nothing at all and everything, if you looked deeply enough.

The hum of the electricity filled my head like a million bees, but it was, somehow, comforting. I could feel vibrations in my teeth and behind my eyes. I bathed in the feeling and in that sound and never wanted to leave the room.

But I realized that I had to go to work, and so I left the apartment and walked outside, where every building, street, bus stop—every piece of solid material—was composed of this same white noise. And people were walking in and out of the buildings themselves, instead of doorways. They'd suddenly manifest from the static like through some kind of stargate. They ignored me, but I could see that while they all looked human, their faces were obscured, made up of the same kind of static stuff. Perhaps they were looking at me, but I couldn't see them. I wondered if I looked the same as them, but I couldn't find a reflective surface to check.

And so, I walked to work. I don't know what this job was, but it seemed very important. My office was in an enormous, imposing building (made of the static stuff like the rest of the city). I walked through a wall and into this building. Because the hallway was so narrow and the floor, walls, were all static stuff, it felt more like floating than walking. It felt like I was stepping on mercury—a liquid so buoyant it can hold all your weight. And the pops and fizzes of the static stuff tickled my ankles like champagne.

And that glorious sound, that vibration, in my teeth and my eyes and my brain and my gut and my groin, it was so intense now. To be candid, it felt like an orgasm, or maybe like a sneeze, consistent and over my entire body, rolling and cascading as I floated through the material toward my office.

I was in my office, which was even smaller, no larger than a broom closet, and with nothing in it except the static stuff. I was standing, my hands pressed up against the wall, feeling the hum and the buzz and the champagne fizz, but also a new sensation, like a telephone call. A sort of vague, tinny voice that sounded as if it had traveled light-years to get to me, and instead of coming through my ear it came through my hands, up my arms, through my heart and into my brain. And it wasn't saying words, so much as emotions, and thoughts, and feelings and ideas.

I felt an immediate connection to every other person in the city and every building, too. Every wall, every floor, every plant, every-thing, was flowing in and out of me. And the feeling extended up, and out, into the sky, into space, into the void, and eventually to Earth, where I could sense billions of eyes, through which I could enter their minds and we would share everything.

And while I danced in their minds, I realized that I no longer had a body. I was now static stuff too, and I was no longer seeing but feeling, and simply being. And I melted into the other static stuff, and I was at once everywhere and nowhere.

In this body, in this place, I could do anything I wanted. Anything at all. And I remember feeling that all my base impulses, the things that we, as a functioning people in society, suppress, were no longer things to contain. None of that mattered. And learning of this place, I realized even life itself was an illusion. For this place existed beyond life and death. Beyond time.

I laughed then, a nonverbal gesture of wonder, happiness and omniscience. Because I was now beyond all those things too, and I was ready to experience everyone, every*thing*.

And then I woke up. It was the most incredible dream I've ever had. I longed to return to that place immediately, to live there forever.

To my astonishment, I saw that my bedside notepad was open, and in my hand I clutched a pen. I looked at the page and saw that I had written a kind of poem in my sleep, an invitation, maybe? I do not remember writing this:

> *Fly*
> *Amidst the stars*
> *Between endless aeons*
> *Come*
> *Through the Stack*
> *Eight Doorways*
> *Await the chosen*
> *A coin for the Ferryman*
> *And the cosmos is yours.*
> *Endless wonder*
> *Beyond death*
> *It is not madness*
> *To leave your void.*
> *You don't need eyes to see*
> *The one true path is to serve me.*

ECSTATICA

Ben Rock

Hello, Maynard, and thank you for your interest in my story about the Eyeless Man. I hope I don't disappoint, but I only recently encountered the idea of this cryptid/supernatural creature/whatever-it-is under that name. Anyone who knows me knows that I'm squarely ensconced in the so-called Skeptical movement, and I tend to scoff at ideas that present themselves as supernatural even as I find myself fascinated by them for folklore value. Things like the Mothman, Slender Man, Bigfoot, UFOs and sightings of the Virgin Mary are great windows into the human brain and our need to create an ordered universe out of the pile of chaos with which we've been given to work.

But as I looked into it, something about the Eyeless Man legend stirred an old memory of mine. One I tend to avoid dwelling on because it's surrounded with so much personal pain. It happened when I was a teenager. My parents, hippies who'd turned into yuppies and were facing middle age and a failing marriage, attended a series of seminars that were an outgrowth of the so-called Human Potential movement. Your request led me to dig up some old journals and reconstruct the events I witnessed and in which I unwittingly participated. I don't know if this is about the Eyeless Man (although some of what I recall does line up with stories about him), or if this represents something else entirely, but upon reflection I think it's about the most disturbing thing I can recall experiencing, and it might even explain why I have found science and skepticism to be as comforting as I do all these years later.

—Ben Rock

"WHO'S IT GOING to be this time?" I asked Scotty.

It was raining at monsoon levels that July night in the rented HoJo's ballroom as I waited for the evening to start. Rain thudded on the aluminum roofing, and I looked down at the gouges left in the carpet by the plastic room dividers that would be used if there were fewer people in attendance. The hotel's beaten-up AV cart was tucked behind the speakers, Radio Shack electronics loud enough to fill the room.

Scotty looked at me, a smirk caged in his braces, and pointed at a couple probably in their early thirties who'd isolated themselves in the crowd of twenty-five or so adults—all beaming with revelation—and a handful of kids like ourselves who were only there because our parents dragged us. The adults mingled, drank store-brand cola out of white Styrofoam cups and cried tears by the bucket while synthesized New Age music underscored their epiphanies and my boredom.

But Scotty fixed on those two.

Like everyone else in the room, tears glazed their reddened cheeks, and the man and woman clung to each other as if yearning to become one whole creature, miserable with the knowledge that they couldn't.

"Them," he said, referring to the couple we'd come to know as Frank and Melinda Ricci.

Frank, mousse working overtime to make his ginger hair fluff up and forward to cover his balding forehead, had just opened his own optometry practice. Melinda, whose diagnosis of infertility had caused her to self-medicate with Bartles & Jaymes wine coolers and store-bought doughnuts, raised money for nonprofit organizations. They embodied the ideal of the mid-1980s, and this past weekend was meant to help them both realize the true, optimistic future they held together if only they had the spiritual strength to keep it.

But Scotty saw a different destiny.

"They're doomed. They got the stink on 'em. I don't give them a month," Scotty said with a wink. The lights dimmed as a prerecorded audio intro began.

"Good evening, beings of light," a soothing British woman's voice said, and the adults gasped. If only for that night, whatever that meant, it felt true. *"Thank you for joining us this weekend, and thank you to everyone who came along to tonight's Culmination."*

"Culmination" instead of "graduation." At that point, I understood that part of the group's tactic was to get everyone to use different, more grandiose words that meant almost the same thing. Everything anyone did wasn't a "choice"; it was a "conclusion." Your body or identity were called your "being." Advice of any kind was prefaced with the phrase "I suggest," on and on. Jargon.

The linguistic assault was just the beginning of the changes to one's behavior instituted by the weekend-long, personal-growth seminar called *The Experience*, put on by an organization called the Center for Loving (CFL) but unofficially talked about by us kids as the New Age Divorce Factory—the thing to which Scotty was predicting the Riccis were about to fall victim.

The deal with *The Experience* was that it was only open to people eighteen years of age and older, meaning me and my friends were about three or four years too young to take it. Regardless, we had to hear about parts of it nonstop from our parents and all their friends who followed them into it. That knowing code they spoke in among one another, what they'd learned in "the courseroom," the inside jokes, the subtle changes in their language from which we were perpetually excluded.

If only that exclusion allowed me to stay home, but no luck there. My parents brought me to witness middle-age professionals clinging to one another after their weekend of feeling and growing, afterward crying and snotting on one another's expensive button-down polished cotton starched shirts or poly-blend shoulder-padded blouses. The only benefit was that I could avoid studying for the Geometry midterm I had coming up, one I knew I would fail.

From the moment I heard the voice fill the room, I prepared for the hour and twenty minutes I knew the night would take. There would be the canned intro; then the thrice-divorced Lead Guide named William Fairgrove (but everyone called him "Brother Bill") would talk about the significance of the weekend to the participants without ever divulging what was said or done in the room. Finally, each participant would come up and say a few words through their joyful tears. It was all stage-managed and predictable to those of us who were forced to witness it.

After the prerecorded intro, as always, I heard the piano riff that would kick off the night's festivities.

Most people associate the song "The Greatest Love of All" with the pop and gospel singer Whitney Houston, but her recording from the eighties was actually a very successful remake. The original sickly-sweet personal anthem about children needing to see their beauty and the unbelievable power of self-acceptance was originally recorded in the 1970s by George Benson, and that was the version of saccharine that was chiseled into our eardrums monthly.

When my parents first went through the seminar (really just a prelude to *The Experience*) two years earlier in a starter program called the *Gifted Parenting Workshop*, they'd left it with a renewed vigor for each other and us as a family. CFL had at first seemed like an amazing experience for them both. They'd come home with the exuberance of people who'd just run a marathon. They looked at each other—and me—differently. Our lives were going to improve; it was inevitable, even if everything they did was labeled as a "choice" or every direction given to me or each other was prefaced with the phrase "I suggest . . ." Lots of talk about karma and dharma and balanced chakras and intention.

Then the books piled up around their bed and in the living room. They couldn't wait to tell me about *Ramtha* or *A Course in Miracles*, or stuff with the word "Quantum" in it for no reason.

When I'd ask what they'd learned at *The Experience*, they shut down; I wasn't to know about it. When I asked who'd created *The Experience*, I learned that neither of them and nobody in the course or involved with it seemed to want to know the identity of the nameless character behind the scenes who monthly swam in suburbia's substantial enlightenment budget.

"It's not for children," my mother would say. Nobody under the age of eighteen could take the course, still three years away for me if I'd wanted to. And at that point, maybe just out of curiosity, I was interested.

And then there were the audio tapes.

A plastic shell that held eight tapes that I was strictly forbidden to listen to. I would see my parents listening to them sometimes, on the tile floor with their legs crossed, wearing headphones and zoned out. I was forbidden to discuss the tapes, more verboten than *The Experience* itself.

After each Culmination, a social hour began. In the same ballroom, the lights would come up to full and the adults would mingle and discuss their favorite esoteric topics: homeopathy, energy healing, astral projection, how if you held a crystal on a string and asked it questions it would pendulum-swing one way for "yes" and spin in a circle for "no."

The repeated refrain of how we were all *beings of light.*

Even though we lived five miles apart, Scotty and I didn't go to the same school, so Culminations were where we got to hang out the most. And our friend Julie's parents divorced after a few rounds of the Center for Loving, but they both returned separately every month to try to improve themselves even more, bringing Julie every time. During the discussions of crystal healing and spirit channels, the three of us would sequester ourselves away from the adults to mock what was happening—but I was afraid that my senses were betraying me and there was something *real* to all the crystal magic and invisible forces.

A couple of weeks after that Culmination ceremony, Scotty called me.

"I was right," he blurted.

"Right about what?" I said.

"They're over. That couple, Frank and Melinda. My mom

just got off the phone with Melinda. I could hear her crying over the phone from the next room." He giggled. "I mean, it is so predictable. Why is that?"

"Ask Julie's parents," I joked, and Scotty grew quiet, like we weren't supposed to talk about our friends' parents, only anonymous assholes whose marriage couldn't survive *The Experience*.

"Sorry . . . ," I said.

"It's okay," he said.

Making light of a friend's pain was probably the only way one could transgress against Scotty, and I'd done it.

I felt the sting of guilt, but all my friends' parents were getting divorced. Like the terms of a Faustian love bargain from the 1960s dictated that all affection would run out two decades later, and here we all were stuck with the check. I didn't understand why anyone would get married or divorced—I was still struggling with geometry; X, Y and Z space; and Pythagoras's goddamned theorem.

I was nursing a throbbing headache two weeks later, in August 1985, when Scotty picked up Julie and then me in his family's blue Volvo station wagon so we could meet all our parents at that month's Culmination. It was raining as usual, and the air smelled like a moldy shower. The three of us jammed out to our favorite band, an obscure heavy-metal act out of New York that Scotty had introduced us to called Höhlentroll, who'd only released one EP in 1977, and gossiped a little about Frank and Melinda while keeping an eye on Julie to make sure the divorce talk wasn't upsetting her.

But something else was on Scotty's mind as we drove through an industrial wasteland between the touristy hotel section of town by the airport and the places where people who weren't visiting had to live. He pulled the Volvo into a closed Phillips 66 parking lot and idled.

"Guys," he said.

"Why are we stopping here? Are we buying crack?" I said, looking at the soaking-wet raw concrete hole where the gas tanks had been ripped from the earth, rebar reaching to the sky like evangelicals at a revival.

Julie laughed. I rubbed my temples; my brain throbbed, a blob of pain threatening to leak out of my eye sockets.

"We're already late," she said. "We're gonna get in trouble."

"Fuck them. I gotta show you guys something," he said, pulling his backpack over the bench seat from the back. He unzipped it and pulled out a one-gallon plastic ziplock baggie filled with audiocassettes. I could barely read Scotty's shitty handwriting on each, but they seemed to be numbered.

"Guess what I copied today?"

The audio course. It could be nothing else. As much as I wanted to listen to them, the headache was beginning to overwhelm my abilities to pretend it wasn't happening.

"Holy shit," Julie said. I gasped.

"Have you listened to it?" she said.

"No, I wanted to do that with my two best friends!" he said.

I looked at the store-bought Memorex cassettes, thinking

about how the mysteries of life could have been distilled down to a rusty magnetic strip in those plastic cases.

"Wanna pop one of 'em in?" he said. I was afraid.

"Yeah," Julie said.

Scotty looked at me, the light catching on his metal-mouthed grin.

"Eh?" he said. My headache throbbed in my skull like someone hit a bass drum. *No way*, I thought.

Involuntarily, I nodded.

Sure.

Not just "sure," but *of course.* My body wanted it no matter what my brain thought.

Scotty hit eject and handed me the white Höhlentroll EP that spit out of the dashboard tape deck.

"We'll start at the beginning," Scotty said, grabbing the tape with his scribbled *1* on it and chucking it in with a thin plastic click.

He and Julie giggled when he hit play, and some early-1980s synth music started up and a deep reverberating noise seemed to pulse under it, pumping more bass than the Volvo's speakers ever had. Immediately I noticed something familiar to the music as well, less New Agey in its chord progression and maybe more like one of Höhlentroll's songs. I stopped thinking about the similarity when a familiar voice intruded.

"*The Center for Loving presents...,*" the same British woman's voice who introduced the Culmination ceremony said, "*Daily loving affirmations, Part One...*" Synthesized xylophone overtook the voice.

The volume on my headache turned up.

Everything became pain.

I wanted to scream but found that I couldn't—the muscles in my throat refused to participate. I squinted my eyes against the pain and looked up, assuming I was having a migraine.

I couldn't breathe, like my chest was locked between two metal plates that were being squeezed together. I needed to go to a hospital.

Am I dying?

With great effort, I opened my eyes. The world outside was like staring into a hundred eclipses, blinding and blue, and the light cut into my headache and through my skull.

Yes, I am dying.

I could still feel the music playing, or at least the bass chords progressing through the song pounding in my chest, as familiar as if I'd written it. Through the assault of light, I managed to see the laughing faces of Scotty and Julie go flat and expressionless, then wash out in that field of bluish-white.

The rain pelted the roof of the car like hail.

Or rocks.

Or bullets.

The voice came back, reverberating in my brain and bouncing painfully off every neuron.

"The Experience *was only the beginning. Now your journey moves on, into your life beyond* The Experience, *manifesting in every facet of your radiant life. Now—close your eyes. Imagine you're floating above yourself. You are a being of pure light. . . ."*

A gash bisected my field of view, and I felt a sensation like moving into it, but not all at once. Like each cell in my body, starting with my face, was being pulled off me, still connected to me, and each cell expired in ecstasy. The most pleasant way to obliterate.

Then the pitch of the voice bent downward, like it was slowing down and remaining the same speed all at once, harmonizing with itself. One voice that was two, one of them sounding like mine.

I heard a jumble of scratching sounds that came directly from my head—like something was trying to escape my skull. I tried to open my eyes but couldn't.

There was someone else there, not one of us. Inside the car. Outside the car looking in. Both at once.

A chitter-chitter sound, like a bird or a bug, but resonant like it came from a person.

A scrape-scrape-scrape inside my head and out.

The stranger, staring down at us. I could almost open my eyes. Almost see the stranger. The pain getting worse, worse than any pain I'd ever experienced.

I forced my eyes open, could almost make out the outline of a tall man whose face I couldn't see through the sensory overload. All I wanted was to know that face, understand something about the thing that understood me.

I could hear nothing else and see nothing at all until—

Blink.

I was at HoJo's again, at the Culmination, flanked by Julie and Scotty. I looked at Scotty, and for the first time he didn't look back. Just stared at the lectern on the raised stage. I'd missed the grown-adult snotfest and "The Greatest Love of All," and we were watching Brother Bill speak to the group.

I touched Scotty's shoulder, and his face turned toward mine and stared with no recognition, then returned to Brother Bill. At the time I thought Scotty was pranking me, pretending to be hypnotized.

Brother Bill's script unfolded the same way it always did:

"... And to the people who came in this weekend on a leap of faith that it might heal some secret wound you carried with you, I have bad news. The healing is now your job, your responsibility, your dharma." Brother Bill said this with deep sincerity like he'd said it every last Sunday of every month. Every inflection was the same, and I knew we had five more minutes before everything ended, people deflated back to normal and traded phone numbers of past-life regression therapists, the hotel ballroom emptied and we were at home. Somewhere in that, Julie and Scotty returned to themselves. I remember seeing Frank but not Melinda Ricci milling through the crowd, hugging and wiping tears out of his eyes, now permanently decoupled and desperate for the human connection he'd probably had before. I guess he got to keep us in the divorce.

Brother Bill finished with the quote from the unnamed founder of *The Experience*, and the full group of graduates said it with him. "You are a being of light," they all said. "The world will forever be lit by your spirit."

Great. Sure. Being of light.

My headache was gone, but I felt like puking.

I still had the Höhlentroll cassette in my pocket, so I listened to it on my Walkman in the back seat of my dad's beige Buick Regal all the way home, while my parents stared wordlessly at the road.

I could feel the tension between them. Like we all could breathe their divorce in the air, taste the pungency-to-come—it would explode our family, and we all knew it was there.

My headphones on, I fast-forwarded to the third song on the tape. The track was called "Animal Magnetism." As far as I could tell, the lyrics were about a scientist who'd figured out how to use spinning magnets to open a door to Hell or something. I hit fast-forward and skipped to the guitar solo.

Then I heard it—it might have been dressed in a heavy-metal costume, but it was the same music that introduced the audio course, and outside of the woman's voice, the music was the only thing I'd remembered. I rewound the tape, played it again. And again. It was the same.

Scotty called me the next day.

"Dude. We need to get together," he said.

"What's up?" I said.

"The tapes! We gotta finish the tapes!" he said.

"Can I be honest?" I asked.

"Yeah," he said.

"I don't really remember the one we listened to last night."

There was a pause.

"Me neither! Do you even remember driving to the hotel or getting to the Culmination?" he asked.

"Nope," I said. "I don't remember shit."

There was a sizable pause.

"Wanna do it again?" He laughed out loud. Scotty was the first of our friends to experiment with any new thing—drinking, smoking weed, getting laid, listening to new music from bands

like Höhlentroll that nobody had heard of. I was content to survive my teens, but he wanted to really *live* them. I admired his
adventurous spirit—wished I had it, too. I also had that Geometry midterm to study for, and my need for adventure balanced
poorly against my fear of impending failure.

"Why do you think we blacked out?" I said.

"I was thinking about it—that old gas station. Chemical
fumes from where the tanks were, I bet." It made as much sense
as the hypnotic power of an inspirational tape.

"Did you . . . Did you see *someone* there when it all happened?
Like a tall guy, something over his face?" I asked.

"I saw a homeless guy, is that who you're talking about?" he
said. It was a relief to think that was all it was—a horrible headache, a chemical high, a drifter staring at three kids tripping balls
in a blue Volvo.

I didn't want to do it, but one thing would still convince me.

"Is Julie going to listen as well?" I asked, hoping she'd said no.

"Yup."

The next night my father sat in our living room going through
his Rolodex, calling each person alphabetically in turn and recit-
ing the same pitch about an upcoming *Gifted Parenting Workshop*
that CFL was about to have at Frank Ricci's newly Melinda-free
house, while my mother lay in the next room reading a CFL book
and not talking to him. All I could think about were the tapes,
and I was terrified of them.

After I "went to bed," I opened my bedroom window and
stepped into the fresh mud outside. Silently I crossed to the other
side of the house where I'd stashed my bike and rode five miles

to Scotty's house. Scotty, a veteran of doing whatever he wanted without his parents noticing, had told me how to get away with sneaking out, and he had been right.

Scotty's parents lived in a two-story home they'd custom built five years earlier. His parents slept on the second floor and he was on the first, which gave him easy access to leave the house whenever he wanted. I could see the shadows of him and Julie playing on the curtain as I walked up and gently knocked on the glass.

The two of them fell silent. Scotty parted the curtains, as if expecting his parents or the police, but a smile burst out of his face when he saw me.

"You're late," he said. "We were about to give up on you."

Inside, next to his waterbed and a pile of surfing magazines, Scotty had set up his boom box with two headphone splitters coming out of it and three black-foam-padded headphones. We could all be there in the room, listening at the same time but making no noise to wake his parents.

Next to the boom box was that ziplock baggie full of cassettes.

He sat down and motioned for us all to put on our headphones, so we did. He sat at his desk, Julie lay on his bed, and I sat cross-legged on the floor.

"Before we start," I said, digging into my pocket for a tape of my own. "Can we listen to something else real quick?"

"What is it?" Julie said.

"It's this. Höhlentroll. The music they play on the CFL tape—it sounds a lot like one of their songs."

I'd ruined Scotty's flow, but he and Julie let me play it, and afterward they both stared at me blankly. They didn't hear the connection, but I was more convinced than ever that it was the identical chord progression we'd heard the night before.

"That's neat," Scotty said, ejecting my tape and handing it back to me. "Can we move on to the main course now?" He stuffed a tape into the boom box. He hit play. The same intro filled my ears:

"The Center for Loving presents . . . daily loving affirmations, Part Five."

Before the rolling synth vibes could kick in, I hit stop.

"You said we were going to do part two," I whispered.

"Does it matter?" Scotty said. "You don't remember part one, and neither do I. I just grabbed another tape."

"It's fine," Julie said, putting her hand on mine, her physical touch defusing any will I had.

"It's all the same," she said, looking deeply into my eyes, with so much intensity that I broke the gaze. I assumed she was right.

She took her hand away, and wordlessly I hit play.

Scotty smiled like the fucking devil.

The tape played on, the intro music sounding the same as what I'd just played them. Scotty hit stop.

"You're right, you're fucking right," he said. We all looked at one another, searching for how that could be. But there wasn't an Internet yet, and there was no way to know who Höhlentroll was or how the band could be connected to whoever had made these inspirational tapes.

"Now that we've acknowledged that," Scotty said in the jargon all our parents spoke in, "I'd like to hit play." Scotty pressed the button.

The same British woman's voice soothingly directed us: *"Now it's time to take the first four lessons and weave them together. Imagine you're floating above your body and look down. You're floating down, ever downward toward yourself, and when you intersect with yourself, you can look into your own eyes. What do you see?"*

This was having no effect. At Culmination ceremonies, I'd nodded emptily while trying to ignore the graduates discussing ideas like astral projection and visualization. Is this what they were talking about? I was already bored as the woman prattled on.

"Now we're going to move through your seven chakras, beginning with the root—" Rage coursed through me at the mention of chakras—I'd heard enough of that hippie bullshit from my parents before they found *The Experience*. To squash the anger, I forced a laugh, which ended in a tiny cough. At the tail end of the cough, in my throat, the pain exploded into all of me.

Next in the ears. Like static electricity arcing from the headphones to my eardrums, and I realized I could hear nothing.

My eyes shot open.

Julie and Scotty sat frozen like statues, their mouths agape, headphones on and eyes rolled back in their heads. Were they having a seizure? Were they in a trance?

I stood up, and my headphones pulled all the headphones out of the jack, and I could hear again as the tape boomed out of the speakers on the stereo.

"The universe is cradling your soul in a state of pure radiance. . . ." Scotty and Julie didn't move.

I hit stop on the boom box as quickly as I could, hoping it hadn't woken Scotty's parents.

In the silence, outside the window I heard something like

footsteps, and I turned off Scotty's blue light. The shadow of a figure hit the curtain from the outside. Instinctively I knew it was whoever had been with us in the car, and that it was no vagrant.

The shape was human, but the walk was not.

It stopped like a cockroach would when a light turns on; its head seemed to almost vibrate.

Then it *did* vibrate. So fast that its shadow on the curtain became a blur, then an insect-like sound.

Scotty and Julie still had not moved.

I took Julie by the shoulders and shook her, trying to be as quiet as I could. I grabbed her chin and twisted her head toward me.

Nothing.

"Julie! Julie! Wake the fuck up!" I whispered right into her ear.

The figure outside sounded closer, but whenever I trained my attention on it, movement ceased. Like it was tuned into whether I was watching it back. It felt like it was in the room with us. It felt like I could see it hanging in my peripheral vision but never fully there.

A hand landed on my shoulder.

My head snapped up, and I saw Scotty standing over me, his eyes still rolled back somnambulistically, and that guttural, insect-like sound that a human doesn't make came out of his mouth. I looked back down at Julie to make sure she was safe from whatever was going to happen next, and she glared up at me with the same expression and made the same sound.

The chatter was also coming from outside the house, from the silhouette that appeared to be pressed right up to the window.

Or was it inside with us?

Julie's hands clamped down on me. Scotty wordlessly plugged the headphones back in, slapped mine back on my head and hit play again.

The sound of whatever or whoever it was outside rose in my ears, and I knew I was about to black out. The British woman's voice still repeated in my ears:

"RADIANT STATE."

"RADIANT STATE."

The light flooding my eyes overwhelmed my sight and bled into all my senses.

I see Scotty and Julie on fire.

I see them fucking.

I see them skinned on the floor in a pond of blood.

I see them alive and crying through the waterfall of my own tears.

The figure outside moves through the window without touching the glass.

"RADIANT STATE."

The two words cycle in my head until they mean nothing. Just the syllables, individually meaningless. Then parts of syllables, like the idea of language devolving, slices of pieces of the building blocks of those words ripping apart like toilet paper in a hurricane, meaning itself obliterating.

"RA"

"DI"

"ANT"

Everything I can see, hear, smell, remember or imagine does the same.

All that was solid is insubstantial, all that was real is an illusion, a dream, a thought carried on a neuron that couldn't exist in the first place.

SILENCE.

Whatever I have been in the past is irrelevant. I don't acknowledge the idea of "past." This is all that ever would be. I see nothing, but I know. "Scotty" and "Julie" are lost ideas, ancient myths, but they are both here in me and I in them.

I am a point in infinite space staring out onto an equally infinite plane. Observation is all that I am, consciousness is all I have.

I am nothing, without mass or volume, but light falls off me, I can feel it; I just can't see it because there's nothing to reflect me.

I am a being of pure light.

Pure light.

Eyes snap open, in my room, totally safe, late for school, Geometry test that I hadn't studied for. My bike is locked in the garage where I have no memory of having returned it.

I exist again. But I don't know—is the life I am living just a dream that the empty point of light is having, or is that a dream I'm having?

Blink.

At school, staring at my locker, positive that it isn't a physical form and neither am I, so I should just be able to reach through the flimsy metal and grab the geometry textbook and pull it through in one piece. I time it perfectly, shoot my hand at the gunmetal green door and with a loud crunching clang I fail to reach through. My thumb bleeds.

Blink.

In my Geometry class taking a test I have no business passing, but as I answer the questions with lightning speed, I know that I will have a perfect score. There's blood from my hand on the paper; I don't do anything about it.

Blink.

Thoughtlessly two words pass through my consciousness: *Scotty* and *Julie.*

I felt myself pull back into my body.

The dream was a dream, this was reality and I had no idea what happened to my friends.

The six hours that passed before I could call Scotty felt like two weeks. I noticed my brain filling in gaps in perception that it had edited out over the years—the texture of the school's cinder-block walls with thirty years of paint, the tiny sprouts of gray in Mrs. Boutwell's hair. The way rain had dulled one side of the admin building but not the other. The world was a fuller, but more vacuous and meaningless, place than I'd remembered.

"Hello?" Scotty sounded normal as he picked up the phone.

"Scotty, it's me," I said.

"Oh, hi," he said, a distracted air in his voice.

"What the fuck happened last night?" I said.

"Now isn't a good time," he said.

But I *had to know.* "Can I come over tonight?"

In the pause that ensued, I heard my parents arguing about who would get custody of me if they separated. I was relieved when I heard him say, "Sure." He was distant, like I wanted something more than he wanted to give it. Like I'd showed up on his porch on Sunday morning holding a religious tract.

"Should I call Julie?" I asked.

"I wouldn't do that," he said.

Julie, it seems, had experienced something that night that she didn't want to revisit.

Same routine: "went to sleep," snuck out, biked to Scotty's house. Walking up to the window I saw the area where the figure had seemed to stand as I'd experienced sublime nonexistence the night before. There were no footprints in the loose dirt. Out of the corner of my eye I caught a shadowy movement, but when I turned to look, I saw it was a blackbird perched on a sycamore branch.

Julie wasn't there.

Scotty let me in, and we moved a pile of magazines out of the way and sat on his floor. There was a long silence, us looking at anything but each other. Usually Scotty would regale me with his latest adventure, but something in his eyes looked tired. It was unusual being there without Julie; she always broke up these moments. It was on me this time.

"Do you . . . Do you remember any of it?" I asked.

Long pause. "Yes. And no," he said.

"What do you remember?"

He looked deeply at me. "I don't know. A bunch of inspirational crap, you two blacked out, I tried to wake you up. . . ."

"Do you remember someone outside the window?" I asked. His face locked on mine. An hour passed in a second.

"Yeah," he said, as if trying not to cry. His gaze shifted; he didn't want to think about it. He went to his closet, opened the door.

I said, "That wasn't a homeless man at the gas station. It was . . . It was . . ." I couldn't name the faceless thing that had stepped through solid matter and led me to a place where nothing was real.

"Why do you think Julie isn't here?" he said.

"I don't know," I said. Another long pause.

"She's not okay. Whatever happened," he said, not looking at me. "She doesn't want to talk to us. I tried calling her five times, and she just hangs up. Can you do me a favor?"

"Sure," I said.

He grabbed the bag of copied tapes out of his closet, shoved them into my arms. "Take these. Burn them," he said, suppressing a desperation I never thought lived in him. "Piss on them. Hide them. Bury them in the ground and don't tell me where. I can't. I don't . . . I just can't."

"Scotty? Is someone in there with you?" His dad's voice boomed from the other side of his door.

"No!" he said, feigning being woken up. "I'm asleep!"

"Sorry!" his dad said. Scotty glared at me—time to go—and, as silently as possible, I snuck out his window with the tapes in hand.

It was my last conversation with Scotty.

That bag sat in the top drawer of my dresser, where I kept all my tapes, for the next three weeks. And then it was Sunday, and another Culmination. No rain this time as my parents wordlessly drove me to the hotel ballroom. I hadn't talked to Scotty or Julie, but I knew they would both be there. I brought my Walkman and grabbed the same Höhlentroll tape so I could sit in the corner and zone out when I saw Scotty and Julie. I assumed they wouldn't want to talk.

I was right. They were both there. Scotty sat in the front row away from his parents, and Julie was at the far right with her mother. And neither would look at me. The lights dimmed; everyone settled as Brother Bill took to the dais.

"Hello, friends!" he said like he always did. "Welcome to our latest Culmination." I stared at him, angry I'd gotten into the car and allowed myself to be driven to this miserable experience. I'd never felt so uncomfortable, and my only two friends in this situation wouldn't look at me.

My family sat in the third row, my parents on either side of me, simmering in contempt for each other, and I wanted to disappear. I grabbed my Walkman out of my coat jacket and loudly jammed in the tape I'd grabbed, threw on the headphones. I'd catch shit from my parents for this, but it was better than sitting through another fucking Culmination.

I hit play, but instead of Höhlentroll singing about the mix of occult and science that was their trademark, I heard treacle-smooth synth music and a familiar British voice:

"The Center for Loving presents . . . daily loving affirmations, Part Eight." The music swelled as always, and then her voice came back mid-sentence—a sentence I already knew.

". . . Time to say farewell to the person you have been your whole life, no matter if you're twenty-five or seventy-five. . . ." I guessed her next phrase, then the next. I'd heard it before multiple times. Her voice blended with the outside voice of Brother Bill, somehow

saying what he was saying with identical timing. I opened my eyes and saw him mouthing the words she said. I turned down the volume and could hear him in perfect sync with her.

"You've spent your whole lives up until now not living out of your best selves, not living out of the beings of light that you were meant to be. And some of you will continue on that path, but my hope is that each of you stays on this path with me from this moment forward," Brother Bill and the tape continued, mixing the two octaves of their voices.

I stared at Brother Bill, wondering how he was pulling off this magic trick and why I was the target of it. *"And to the people who came in this weekend on a leap of faith that it might heal some secret wound you carried with you, I have bad news. The healing is now your job, your responsibility. Your dharma."*

I could have transcribed it.

Then a pulse of intense static garbled through my headphones, and at the same instant the room blacked out. Dark except for light coming in from the open doors of the ballroom, and the adults laughed.

"Speaking of responsibility," Brother Bill said, "I think we need to talk about whoever pays the electric bills in this place." The tape did not say that in unison. Another laugh, and an intense pulse of noise hit my brain again. I hit stop on the Walkman and stood up. The lights flickered faster, and I saw Scotty and Julie, also standing and staring right at me each time the lights strobed back to life.

And when the lights went out, I saw the outline of the form from the car, from Scotty's window. Just a silhouette and the residue of the echo of that insect sound bouncing off the laminate faux marble when the lights came up.

Another deafening hit of the noise, now through the room's loudspeakers. The lights shot back on, brighter than any generic hotel ballroom fluorescents should ever be, like looking into a malfunctioning strobe. The crowd groaned with pain from the sound and shielded their eyes.

An assistant for the course ran up and turned off the amplifier, and the noise stopped but the lights kept going.

Brother Bill stood onstage, trying to hold it together when— FLASH—everything would go either too bright or too dark. It continued on and off with an audible pop each time.

"Heh, well this will be one Culmination to remember," he said with a raised voice, but nobody laughed. Every time the lights flickered, our persistence of vision gave our eyes a latent image standing behind Bill, the silhouette of the tall man who didn't seem to exist in the light. Like that night in the car, I tried to scream and couldn't. I looked around the room and saw the same look in everyone's eyes. They couldn't make a sound.

The intensity of the flashes increased as the intervals between shortened.

A void appeared—a portion of my vision had been blanked out like a magnet taken to a tape. Inside that void area, I saw into the world I'd experienced, a being of light.

As the lights flickered in and out, it seemed to grow and shrink away. I knew I could have it again, but it wouldn't be free. I was going to have to *earn* infinity. I looked at Scotty, who didn't look back, then at Julie, whose gaze seemed to flicker onto me for an instant, and I knew what I had to do.

I grabbed my Walkman and pushed through the two rows in front of me, shoving the stunned seekers out of my way.

I reached the hotel's AV cart, unplugged the one-eighth-inch jack the microphone was plugged into and plugged my Walkman into the speaker, turned on the amp and hit play.

The lights flickered faster. Faster.

I looked up and saw Scotty, Julie. They were both standing, trying to muscle their way through the crowd to me.

Scotty screamed at me, and Julie yelled, "No!" They ran at me.

Adrenaline coursed through me, the hairs on my arms stood up like I was standing in a Tesla coil and I felt it again, this time able to force myself to cross over without hallucinations like before. Without the pain, I walked through the people who were no longer solid, then fell through the equally insubstantial floor.

Silence.

I am in the void, a being of light. I can see nothing, but I feel the presence of everyone from that room, manifesting in our own nothingness. I can feel them in me and me in them, the family and community that they hunger for, the understanding and apotheosis I assumed would come later, except now there is no such thing as time. The group of us join consciousnesses together.

In this void, we are not able to be apart.

The Radiant State, collectively, for all time if we deserve it.

Eternity passes, stops, rewinds itself, shoots out into every direction.

I know every thought in the entire lifetime of everyone in that room, and they know mine.

Even though I can't see the light, I feel the light of every soul, every life-force. Our bodies, our senses, gone. No words, just wisdom. This for eternity, and eternity in an instant. Then time comes back, ugly. And I know whatever is disrupting us is here to unmake whatever we have become.

Something none of us perceives tears the infinite plane and, in so doing, makes it finite. First time, then space. The Radiant State shreds, remaking the old reality in its undoing. Then one piece of us, one atom in our larger invisible body, just *isn't*. Something that isn't us is here.

I hear real noise, real-world noise again, with my physical ears. The noise becomes a scream. The scream becomes many screams, and my eyes pop open to see people running, Brother Bill standing in the center of the dais, shrieking and covered with someone else's blood.

Blink.

In Radiance, none of us had seen a woman—Melinda Ricci—walk in through the open doors, find her estranged husband and stab him in both of his eyes with a hotel steak knife and then gut him while nobody (including him) reacted.

When the lights came back on and we all returned to the finite, Frank Ricci stained the light-brown room a deep red and Melinda screamed at the group of us: "What's wrong with you people! Wake up! You have to wake up!"

And as we reentered her world, she saw our eyes open and buried the knife into Brother Bill's temple on the stage in front of us. She pulled it out bent, his skull failing to hold on to the cheap metal, and then shrieked and jammed the bent knife into her throat sideways and pulled it forward and out toward us. For an instant she tried to speak but had destroyed her throat and the muscles holding her neck up, and her head dropped to the side under its own weight. Then the rest of her did the same.

She lay dead on the dais as that soothing voice still pumped through the speakers.

"... *beyond your fear, beyond your imagination, beyond your sense of self lies the true reservoir of pure consciousness, pure experience, pure exaltation.*"

We heard a deep gasp, and Frank Ricci stood up, screaming in pain, blinded, bleeding out with what was left of his intestines spilling out of his body. He would last six more hours.

While the tape's voice failed to soothe us, the lights flickered again, then faster. As my eyes tried to adjust to the light, the chitter-chitter rose in my brain, and I saw shadows of that figure in every pool of light in the room. Like he or she or it, whatever it was, was somehow everywhere in the room at the same time, and never there at all.

I remember the screams, desperate pleas to stand up, and seeing bodies falling around the room, tangling with metal folding chairs, twitching.

In that soothing chaos, twenty-seven friends, family or participants in the Center for Loving went into clonic seizures, and eight of them (including Julie) slipped into comas and died. My father grabbed my wrist so hard that he crushed one of my tendons, dragged me out of the building as we heard police sirens swarm. I looked back into the ballroom for the last time, and when I turned back around my father had collided with someone—the tall figure who'd somehow been a part of this, either pulling me in or stopping me from going further or summoned by the tapes or whatever he was. In layers of clothes, in a frame that had to be taller than six-five. I stood beneath him, my eyes maybe a foot lower than where his should have been, but I couldn't see any features at all. I tried to look into eyes that were not there.

Just the chitter-chitter.

With a final yank, my father dragged me out of the building and into his car. I knew that I'd never have to listen to "The Greatest Love of All" again.

Criminal investigations probed into CFL and what happened that night. My Walkman and the tape in it were seized as evidence. I did as Scotty asked and smashed all the other copies, spread them in separate dumpsters lest someone find and listen to them. The web of LLCs that owned and controlled the intellectual property of CFL would end up entangled in lawsuits and criminal trials for years, exposing the reclusive billionaire who'd profited so much off a wide array of seminars, books and recordings. He lived on a secluded plantation outside Bangalore, and without extradition he faced no criminal charges.

Scotty's parents got divorced and so did mine, and we never discussed what we'd done. Scotty struggled with drug addiction, taking his life years later after his own marriage failed.

I'd tried to track down the band Höhlentroll but had no luck. They'd cut the one EP, and other musicians from the time were creeped out by the lead singer, who'd sung under a pseudonym and had played all the instruments on the album I'd listened to so many times. While other heavy-metal bands of the time acted the part of devil-worshippers, Höhlentroll's lead singer had dedicated his life to an obscure scientist and occultist by the initials

VG, who had, in the 1950s, combined occultism with the princi-ples of physics, including magnetic recording media.

About ten years later, my mother died of cancer at the age of fifty-two. While going through her things, I found a shrink-wrapped new plastic tape holder with a pristine set of audio-cassettes of the course. My face flushed, like I'd seen an old girlfriend I'd broken up with decades earlier. When I was younger, I'd had the courage to listen to them, and then the resolve to destroy them. But now I just keep them—I don't even have a way to play them.

Sometimes when I'm feeling out of control of my life, or when I wish I could feel like more than I am, I'll pull them out of that box in my garage, run my fingers around the plastic casing and look deeply at the magnetic strip bound in those cases.

DR. MAYNARD WILLS: AMONG THE BELIEVERS

In the days following my dream, I fell into a deep depression. I stood at a precipice. I could continue on, talking with our contributors and looking for clues as to the origin of this myth, or I could take a bolder step and become what it is I study; I could engage the cryptic community of Eyeless Man acolytes. Consider the obviously depraved Randy Wane, a piano tuner who lured Mark Cambria to an unclear fate, and the mysterious Z from the TV auction. These men are not alone. I long to discuss this difficult decision with Dr. Peter Gilliam, but since his experiment, he's in a constant state of delirium and digests large quantities of psychedelic drugs, both organic and designer, in his frequent attempts to repeat his voyage. He speaks in gibberish, and I can no longer discern his truth from the delusions.

I will never forgive myself for what I have done to that man.

With or without him, I need to find my truth in this. And so I employed the help of another (who shall remain anonymous) to secure voyage into the nether regions of the Internet, what's known colloquially as the dark web. My caffeine-fueled days led to pep pill nights, scouring boards as I worked to infiltrate the many dark ministries dedicated to the Eyeless Man. It was clear to me that since the release of *Video Palace* these communities have experienced intense growth.

Most people just want to know what happened, to understand how and why Mark Cambria has vanished from our world. But a very, very small subset of lurkers, quieter people, seemed to have answers. They were not creepypasta enthusiasts, folklorists or goth LARPers. They're believers, and the Eyeless Man is their god. I've worked to gain access to their liturgy and their rituals, but this is a reticent group not quick to bring just anyone into their trust. When they do engage the occasional stranger, I do not understand their criteria, and I sense a predatory motivation.

There is one thread I wish to tug a bit harder. Among the slew of PDFs by theorists and ZIP folders filled with arcana, I saw a file with a name that stole my breath: *The Static City* by Valeray Gournay. The connection to my dream is apparent, and I'd seen this name, Gournay, mentioned among countless others.

I read through his hundreds of pages, a kind of memoir mixed with an experiment log. Living in California in the 1940s and '50s, this scientist conducted thought-control experiments for the military and spent his off-hours in his Pasadena garage laboratory. His myriad scribbles and diagrams suggested he discovered eight frequencies during his research that had strange and counterintuitive properties. From his text, he seems to have lost his job but never ceased work in his home, until his former employers shut him down. The last entry in the scanned pages implies he feared government prosecution, but had one final experiment to conduct. There is much to study in this tome, but nothing I can share with you now. Not until my own understanding is deeper.

I have to be honest with you, my readers. This quest was driven by curiosity, a desire to expand our understanding and help to make sense of our world. That is no longer my motivation. All I think about, all I pray for, is a return to that Static City.

DEEP FOCUS

Bob DeRosa

I only watched the tape once, but honestly, that was enough. Back in the early nineties, we didn't have the Internet to share video content. We could go to video stores to rent stuff, but the truly hard-to-find oddities were passed around by hand. This one was an unmarked VHS that my college roommate got from a guy he knew who made custom skateboards out of his garage. He called it "the truth," and after watching it, we realized that was the dumbest possible title for this particular piece of strangeness.

It appeared to be a recording of a student meeting held in a dimly lit university conference room. After some initial business, a young student rambled on strangely before playing a tape on an old box TV. Things got meta (long before the term was invented) when whoever was recording the meeting zoomed in on the television screen and locked off the camera. What it recorded was an assortment of indecipherable images accompanied by a strange soundtrack that included audio of people in great distress. And then it was over. We were uncertain what qualified this particular tape for pass-around status, but then again, we didn't smoke weed. It felt like it was meant to be real, but it was obviously fake, as if its makers were trying to invent something akin to the found-footage genre. But if that was their goal, they failed in at least making something entertaining.

I actually forgot about the tape until I worked at a film festival many years later. There I met a hardened film buff who had not only seen "the truth" but was fairly certain that it had been created at a state college only a couple of hours away. It turned out that his girlfriend's sister actually knew someone involved in the events surrounding the tape and, for a pair of screening tickets, would part with a phone number. The possibility of getting to the bottom of all this fascinated me. I made a phone call, which led to several others, and I finally spoke to a Cuban American woman about my age whom I'll call Miranda Velazquez. After hearing her first-person account, the story fell into place. And it wasn't at all what I was expecting. It wasn't a group of filmmakers trying to invent found footage or create the ultimate stoner pic. No, this all happened because a university student had a crush on a girl.

I decided to change the names of everyone involved, as well as the name of the school. But not the time. The time is crucial. I guess every story starts with time. And ends with it. Unless the story doesn't end. Unless it's something that remains to haunt us forever.

—Bob DeRosa

D ANNY WAS TWENTY-TWO years old, baby-faced with dark-framed glasses and a doughy physique from drinking cheap beer and watching too many movies. He was about to graduate in late 1990 with a bachelor's degree in telecommunications from Southern U, one of the largest schools in the state. Danny had no plans for after graduation. He'd gotten straight C's for the most part, mainly because he only sorta cared about telecom. What he wanted to be was a filmmaker.

Danny had grown up on a steady diet of Spielberg, Cameron and Carpenter. He saw the original *Evil Dead* on VHS during his sophomore year and was inspired enough to spend the next two years shooting and editing his own blood-drenched extravaganza that he lovingly called *Revenge of the Dead*. Southern U had no dedicated film program, and the telecom department provided no resources for outside projects, so when it came to making his own movie, he would've been on his own if it hadn't been for the Deep Focus Film and Video Club.

The school-funded organization was made up of students who met every other Monday to talk about movies and show original work. The club offered a Super-VHS camera package that was available to check out. Members could also reserve time in the Deep Focus editing suite, which was really just a tiny office space on the second floor of the student union. It was more like a closet with barely enough room for a tape-to-tape editing setup.

Danny finished his epic a few weeks before graduation and reserved a screening room in the student union. He put up flyers and invited everyone he knew, including all his senior telecom classmates. It was in the dark screening room, as blood flew across the screen, when Miranda Velazquez realized Danny wasn't like any of her other classmates. She was Cuban and had grown up in Miami with her family, who was very proud when she landed a scholarship at Southern U. She was a journalism major but really wanted to make documentaries. She talked her way into a senior-level telecom production class, figuring it would count as one of her electives. She got along well enough with her classmates, who were all working toward entry-level television jobs. But she and Danny had something in common: the dream of something more than just a basic job after graduation.

After the screening, Danny threw a party at his apartment for his cast and crew and friends. He ended up talking to Miranda for most of the night. She had a loud laugh that made her lean in, her dark hair falling into her face until she'd tuck it behind her ears.

"So what'd you really think?" Danny asked her.

"It was hilarious," she said with a smile.

"It wasn't meant to be a comedy."

"I know," she said. "But I loved those crazy camera moves and all the blood."

"It's just Karo syrup and red food coloring."

"And you're a really good editor."

"You think so?" he said.

"Yeah, I love the way you cut stuff to the music."

"Thanks," he said sheepishly, taking a gulp of his very cheap beer.

"I'd like to make a documentary one day soon."

"What about?" he asked.

"I don't know yet. You wanna help me?"

"You mean shoot it?"

She shrugged. "Or edit it. Maybe both. I'm going home for the holidays, but maybe next semester."

"I'm about to graduate," he said. "So I'm not sure I'll be around."

"Well, if you are, let me know," she said, smiling.

And that's why Danny graduated two weeks later and decided not to move back home. He figured he could keep his table-waiting job through the spring and maybe make a documentary with Miranda. It was a decent plan, and when he drove home for Christmas and told his parents, they didn't seem to mind. They were used to him being out of the house, and honestly, "documentary filmmaker" sounded more respectable than making schlock like *Revenge of the Dead*. What they didn't know was that Danny was about to make his masterpiece. Except this time, he wouldn't need fake blood.

Soon after classes started up in early January, Danny had lunch with Miranda to talk over ideas. She was most interested in doing something about the coming war. Iraq had invaded Kuwait the year before, and the UN Security Council had set a deadline for them to withdraw their troops. US armed forces were gathering in Saudi Arabia, and if Iraq did not withdraw by January 15, then war felt inevitable. Miranda had male cousins her age, and they were all concerned there might be a draft.

"That's a pretty big idea," Danny said nervously.

"What if we do something small?"

"Like what?"

"Can you get a video camera this weekend?"

"Probably," he said. "Why?"

"There's an antiwar rally happening outside the post office on Saturday, and a bunch of counterprotesters are going to be there, too. We can shoot some B-roll. Maybe do a few interviews."

"I can check out the Deep Focus package if no one's reserved it yet."

"You're the best," she said warmly, which was probably when Danny realized that sticking around Southern U was definitely better than some crappy camera job in Jacksonville.

Danny picked up Miranda early on Saturday morning. She was wearing a big floppy hat and sunglasses because she said she was expecting a sunny day, but Danny also wondered if it was because there was a photo of a documentary filmmaker dressed that way in *Premiere* magazine and he was almost certain she'd seen it, too.

They drove to the post office and had to park a couple of blocks away. Danny had checked out the Deep Focus package, which was a Super-VHS camera that had to be connected by cable to a separate deck. He nodded at the white notebook Miranda was carrying to take notes and said, "Hold that up. I have to white balance." She did, and he focused the camera on the cover.

When he was finished, Miranda eyed the sizable camera on his shoulder and the deck that was still sitting in the trunk of his car. "Can you carry all that?" she asked. Before he could answer, she picked up the deck by its plastic handle and said, "Let's go."

The police had blocked off the road with a cruiser and a

couple of orange cones. Outside the post office, the antiwar contingent was about fifty strong, mostly students. There were some local hippies mixed in, as well as some teachers.

Across the street were about thirty counterprotesters, the "pro-war" side. It was mostly men, many waving American flags. There were several bikers with long beards and worn denim vests. A young man in a wheelchair had a flag laid across his lap, which he would occasionally hoist above his head with both hands.

It was a strangely civil affair. The pro-war side would fire up a few rousing verses from "America the Beautiful," and the antiwar side would answer with a chant such as, "Hey, hey, Uncle Sam, we don't want no Vietnam." They were careful to pronounce "Vietnam" so that it rhymed with "Sam."

Danny turned on the camera and started with a long tracking shot along the antiwar side. He was the only one with a video camera, and as he passed, everyone directed their chants right to him. When he reached the end, he and Miranda crossed the street and then tracked along the pro-war side. They were a passionate bunch, flags waving, voices loud with song.

After they finished that side, Miranda pushed the pause button on the deck and said, "We should shoot some interviews."

Danny nodded, and they began.

A few days later, Danny and Miranda met at the Deep Focus editing closet in the student union. Miranda brought a medium pizza, and Danny brought the Super-VHS master, which was everything they'd shot at the rally. The plan was to copy the master in real time onto a regular VHS tape so they could watch it at Miranda's place and make what Danny called a "paper edit." Since the master was irreplaceable, Danny felt it was best to use it as little as possible.

Danny inserted the tapes and hit the record button. He and Miranda ate as they watched the footage for the first time. It wasn't bad. Danny's tracking shots of the two protest groups were effective. The interviews were nicely framed. The audio wasn't the greatest, as they had used the camera's built-in microphone, but it was good enough. The footage ended with Miranda speaking passionately to the camera with both sets of protesters visible behind her. Even though she was completely antiwar, she tried to make a point about meeting in the middle in order to better understand both sides. The final shot was Miranda walking away, the protesters getting smaller behind her. Danny suggested cutting to black after that shot and then maybe playing a Pixies song over the credits. Miranda liked that choice and made a note of it in her notebook.

By the time the copy was finished, they had demolished the pizza. Danny stuffed the greasy box into the wastebasket in the corner of the closet, packed up their tapes and turned off the system. They made a reservation at the front desk for another editing session a few days later, but by then, Chet Meyers, the president of the Deep Focus Film and Video Club, had found the pizza box in the trash. When Danny and Miranda showed up for their next session, they were informed that their reservation had been canceled.

Danny called Chet, and that was when he learned no food was

allowed in the editing closet and his right to use it was suspended for two months. Danny argued that he hadn't known the rule and that perhaps a warning was in order. But Chet insisted that the suspension had to stick so that none of the other Deep Focus members would think he was playing favorites.

Danny called Miranda and broke the news that they'd lost their free editing. The project was dead, or at least severely delayed.

"We'll find a way," Miranda said.

"Editing places are expensive. And we can't use any of the telecom studios; those are for classes only."

"We're making something important," Miranda said. "Someone will help us."

Danny didn't believe it would happen, but a week later, right after Operation Desert Storm commenced and US forces began dropping bombs on Iraq, Miranda set up a meeting for them at the local public access station. It was managed by a guy named Barry, but everyone called him Bear. He was barrel-chested with a graying mullet, and he always wore denim shorts with white sneakers. He had graduated from Southern U in the early seventies and spent more than a decade as a news cameraman for stations all over the East Coast before settling back near his alma mater.

He explained all of this to Danny and Miranda as he gave them a tour of the station's drafty halls. There was a no-frills studio with two Beta cameras on rolling tripods that was mostly used by private citizens making rudimentary talk shows. There was a Beta editing suite, but only Bear could use that. He showed them the rack room, which was filled with all the video decks and broadcasting equipment necessary to send the station's meager offerings out to local television antennas.

"This place is kinda empty," Danny said.

"Yeah," Bear said. "Philip's my tech guy, but he's only on part-time. It's usually just me."

"And there's enough going on to keep it open?"

"Your tax dollars at work," Bear said. "Or your parents' tax dollars, I guess."

They continued back to a second editing suite. Danny was expecting another closet but was pleasantly surprised when Bear opened the door. The suite was bigger than the closet, still narrow but much longer. There was a linear editing setup similar to the Deep Focus closet, but with larger tape decks, nicer monitors and a mixing board.

"You'll have to work in three-quarter, if that's okay."

Danny gave Miranda a nod, and she said, "It doesn't cost us anything to edit here, right?"

"You just have to let us air the finished product," Bear said, gesturing inward. They entered, and Danny gazed with curiosity at the mixing board.

"Power's back here," Bear said, reaching behind the board. He pointed at two faders on the far side marked A and B. "These are your two audio tracks. The rest is all bells and whistles; you don't wanna mess with that."

After he showed them the ins and outs of the editing system, Bear left them alone in the suite. Danny looked at Miranda, his mouth agape, and said, "This is incredible."

"I told you."

"I'll have to get the master copied over to three-quarter."

She nodded. "I couldn't do this without you."

Danny smiled shyly, and they shared an awkward moment of silence, punctuated by a soft, fuzzy hum.

"What's that?" Miranda said.

Danny brought up the board's faders. The hum intensified, echoing from the speakers mounted above the editing setup.

"Just the board," Danny said, and he turned off the power. The hum continued.

"Are you sure?" Miranda said.

Danny nodded, but his brow was furrowed. He turned the board back on and then off again, and the hum vanished.

"See?" Danny said.

"Uh-huh," Miranda said, an unsettled look on her face. They left the suite, shutting the door behind them, and set a schedule with Bear to edit every Monday, Wednesday and Friday afternoon. To maximize their time, they met over the weekend at Miranda's house to view the footage on VHS and create a paper edit.

As Danny coached Miranda on how to list and categorize each of the shots into a rough editing plan, she said, "How did you learn to do this?"

"I just kinda figured it out on my own."

"You're pretty smart, you know that?" she said, her eyes drifting to his.

Danny shrugged, and their eye contact lingered. If they were ever going to kiss, this would have been the moment. But they both hesitated, and for different reasons. Danny was scared of being rejected due to his socially difficult high school years, while Miranda was worried about confusing the chemistry of creative partnership with something more. After a few seconds, they turned back to the TV, and the moment was lost forever. She often wondered if things would have worked out differently if they had kissed that night, but unfortunately there was no way to ever know for sure.

They began editing the following Monday, and their first two sessions went according to plan. On Friday, Danny was setting up a shot from an interview with one of the antiwar protesters, a petite young student with a peace symbol on her T-shirt, when he paused the tape and looked vaguely displeased.

"What is it?" Miranda said, looking up from her notebook.

"I wish this guy wasn't behind her."

Miranda looked at the monitor. Behind the student's right shoulder was a balding hippie with a scraggly beard and a Neil Young shirt.

"Him?" Miranda asked.

"No. Him." He pointed over her left shoulder, at the glass front of the post office, which showed a distorted reflection of the protesters' backs.

"I don't see anything."

"He's reflected in the glass. Or maybe he's standing inside, I can't really tell. It's hard to make out."

Miranda leaned forward and squinted. "Really hard. What's wrong with him?"

"He's kinda tall and dressed too nicely. It's distracting."

Miranda searched the distorted reflection but couldn't find the offending figure. "You can see that?"

"Yeah, he's wearing a tie and a nice shirt and . . . that doesn't bother you?"

"I can't really see him."

"He just seems out of place with all these students and hippies."

"Can you cut him out?"

"Not really," Danny said. "He's behind her for the whole interview."

"I don't think anyone's gonna notice."

Danny stared at the monitor, his eyes narrowing. "I notice. Maybe we can cut the interview?"

"What? No, I think she's great. We use her three times in the paper edit."

"That's just a rough plan," he said. "Once you get into the footage, you have to figure out how to make it work."

He began to rewind in slow motion, eyeing the reflection behind the student, when Miranda reached out and touched his arm. "Danny. We need this shot. Please?"

Danny sighed and said, "Yeah, okay. It's fine."

"Thanks," Miranda said, as she glanced at her watch. "I have a study group at my place. You mind finishing up these next couple of cuts without me?"

"Sure," Danny said. "See you on Monday."

Miranda put her notebook in her backpack, squeezed his shoulder warmly and left. As she closed the door, she looked back at Danny. He was still watching the shot in slow motion, his eyes never leaving the reflection in the glass.

When Miranda returned to the suite for their Monday session, she found Danny already working with the master shot of the pro-war side up on the monitor. His eyes were bloodshot, and it looked like he hadn't shaved (or possibly slept?) all weekend.

"Hey," she said.

"Hey."

"You look wasted. Did you have to work this weekend?"

"I was here. Editing."

"Without me?" she said.

"I was just looking at the footage, trying to figure some stuff out."

"I thought they were closed on weekends."

"Bear gave me a key," he said.

She eyed the wastebasket in the corner. There were two pizza boxes and some empty soda cans.

"You should get that stuff out of here. We don't wanna lose another editing place."

"It'll be fine," he said. "You should look at this. I've been going through all the footage frame by frame."

"I thought you didn't want to put stress on the master?"

"It's not really the master; it's a copy, right? And anyway, it'll be fine."

"What are you looking for?"

"I saw that tall guy from the post office again. But this time, he's on the pro-war side." Danny rewound the footage, frame by frame, stopping on a biker as he held up an American flag. "There," he said, pointing to a group of people behind the undulating stars and stripes.

"I don't see him," she said.

"Watch closely," he said, moving the footage forward frame by frame. Standing at the right edge of the flag, there was someone tall, and Miranda wasn't sure, but it looked like he had a nice cuff to his sleeve. But just when it seemed like the flag was going to shift and reveal his features, the camera moved past him.

"Huh," Miranda said. "You think that's the same guy?"

"Absolutely," Danny said. "This was earlier, before we shot the interview with the girl, which means he must've crossed the street and snuck in behind the antiwar protesters. So that makes me wonder, which side is he on? Was he pro-war spying on the other side or vice versa? I'm starting to think that maybe he's our story."

"Danny," Miranda said softly. "We worked really hard on the paper edit."

"I know, but I told you. Once you get into the footage, things change. Sometimes there's another story wanting to be told, and you just have to go with the flow."

She looked at the monitor and shook her head. "You're talking about a guy I can't even see."

"He's there!" Danny said sharply.

Miranda held up her hands in a reassuring manner and said, "Okay, I believe you. But you know what else is there? Two groups of people who believe in opposite things who should meet in the middle but can't. I look at this footage, and that's the story I see. Don't you see it, too?"

Danny had a sour look on his face. "I guess so."

Miranda glanced at her watch. "Listen, I'm sorry to do this, but I have another thing I have to do today."

"Really? You just got here."

"I know, but I have this huge group project coming up in my mass-com class, and I have to be honest, it's going to take up a lot of my time. I was going to ask you if it was okay. . . ."

"You wanna quit," Danny said flatly.

"No, no. I just can't be here every time we edit."

Danny turned back to his work and said, "That's fine. I know what to do."

"Are you sure?" she said, glancing at the frozen image on the monitor.

"I've got your paper edit right here," he said, nudging a stapled stack of pages with Miranda's handwriting. "If I have any questions, I'll call you."

"Okay. Or I'm sure Bear or Philip could help."

Danny nodded, his attention fully on the monitor now.

"I'm going to go, then," she said as she stood and touched his shoulder. "Thank you, Danny. This project wouldn't be the same without you."

"I know," he said, gesturing at the open door. "Could you close that?"

She nodded and closed the door behind her, a worried look on her face. The long hallway leading through the station was empty and cold, a constant blast of AC flowing from the vents. She pulled her bag tight on her shoulder and moved slowly down the hallway. She passed the door to the rack room and saw someone she assumed must be Philip, since they had yet to actually meet. He was adjusting one of the broadcast decks, his back to her. She considered saying hi, but her encounter with Danny had left her shaken. She hurried down the chilly hallway and exited out into the warm day.

Miranda didn't return to the station until the following week. She was overwhelmed with balancing her course load and the group project, and she could barely find the time to even watch the evening news and hear the latest on the Gulf War. She felt this was exactly the right moment for the world to see their documentary, but carving out time to get into the station was proving harder and harder.

But then the phone calls started, and she knew she had to see Danny as soon as possible.

She entered the station on a Wednesday, midway through their allotted editing time. She passed the window with a view into the studio and saw Bear shooting a local talk show hosted by a white-haired man in a sweatshirt covered with American flags and eagles. She kept moving down the hallway to the editing suite, knocked once and then cracked the door open.

Danny was in his chair, head down on his crossed arms, quietly snoring. The suite was a total mess. There were empty Chinese takeout containers and potato chip bags piled in the corner, and the trash can was now reserved solely for empty Coke cans. It was warm outside, but Danny had a thick coat resting over the back of his chair. She was surprised to see the Deep Focus Super-VHS camera and deck connected to one of the suite's three-quarter decks.

Miranda pulled a full-size garbage bag out of her backpack, unfolded it and put the takeout containers and chip bags inside. When she got to the Coke cans, the sound of them dumping into the bag awakened Danny with a start.

"Hey, it's me," she said.

Danny looked back at her, his face dark with scruff. "What are you doing here?"

"I wanted to check on you. See how the project was going."

"It's going fine," he said.

"Can I see it?"

"It's not ready."

"I know, but can you show me what you've cut so far?"

"It's not going to make sense until it's all together."

"Okay," she said hesitantly. "What's with the Super-VHS setup?"

"Well, you wanted to use that interview with the student, so I figured out how to cut out that distracting guy with the nice clothes."

"Really?"

"Yeah, I just used the camera to shoot the girl's interview off the monitor, framed it tight so he's out of the shot and then I copied the new footage onto three-quarter tape."

"But won't that degrade the image?"

He put his hands in his lap, stared at her. "It's gonna look fine."

"But you're the one who was so militant about not copying the footage over and over and protecting the quality. Just shooting the image off the TV is—"

"It's a monitor," Danny said thickly. "The quality is much better than a TV. And I know how to use a camera, so maybe you should just trust me?"

"I do trust you, but—"

"But what?"

"When we started this, we wanted to make the same thing. And now, I'm not so sure."

"Don't worry," he said. "You'll still get director credit. No one will care who shot or edited the thing. It's like I don't even matter."

"That's not true."

"If you say so."

The suite was thick with the silence between them. Miranda picked her next words carefully. "Have you been calling me, Danny?"

"No. Why?"

"Someone's been calling my house. Two, three times a night. When I answer, there's no one on the other line. Just this hum."

"What kind of hum?" he asked.

She reached out, turned up the speakers as loud as they would go. Their incessant hum filled the suite. "Like this." She turned the volume back to normal.

Danny was silent for a moment. "Maybe you should call the police. They can tap your phone. Scare off whoever it is."

"I don't need the police to handle a crank caller. Especially if that crank caller is my film partner."

"Are we partners, Miranda?"

"Yes. Until this project is done, at least."

"And what about after that?"

"I'm graduating at the end of the semester," she said.

"That didn't stop me from sticking around to help make your movie."

"Let's just get through this. Then we can talk about what's next. But in the meantime, stop calling me."

"I'm not calling you, I swear. In fact, you wanna hear something really strange?"

"I guess."

Danny rewound the tape to the beginning of the interview with the pro-war man in the wheelchair. "This is the raw footage copied once to three-quarter." He hit play.

The man in the wheelchair was in the middle of an impassioned plea as to why they needed to go to war. "We have to take out Saddam IN-sane. Not Hussein, IN-sane." As his speech carried on, Danny reached for the sound mixer.

"Listen to this," he said, sliding down the A fader while keeping the B track at full volume, then switching them. "His audio is on both tracks, right? That's the way we recorded it, basic two-track audio."

"Yes," Miranda said, starting to lose her patience.

Danny stopped the interview. "Now this is the edited clip I made an hour ago." He hit play on the second deck, and they watched the edited clip that was just the man in the wheelchair saying again and again, "IN-sane, IN-sane."

Danny stopped the clip and rewound. He hit play and said, "Now listen again." He played the A track, and the man's voice sounded loud and clear. Then he played just the B track, but there was nothing except for the hum coming out of the speakers.

"I don't get it," Miranda said.

Danny paused the edit. "I copied original footage with two-track audio onto another tape, and one track is blank. So I tried copying it again, and no matter what, the second track is always blank."

"It must be a problem with the mixer."

"I thought of that. Bear came in before you got here, and we did a test edit with something he's working on, and the mixer worked fine. But when I copy this footage, one track vanishes and is replaced with this. Listen closely this time."

Danny played the edit, cranking the B track to maximum volume. The hum was intense, but there was something else inside it that sounded like static mixed with a looping, rhythmic noise.

"You get it?" Danny said.

Miranda picked up the garbage bag. "No, I don't. I'm sorry. That's just a tech thing. And all that matters to me is the truth of what we saw out there, which was two groups of people who hate each other."

"But it's only the truth until we edit it. Then it becomes something else. And we think we're the ones who are changing it, with our editing choices and montages and music and whatever. But maybe there's something else speaking to us through the thing we're making. And maybe it wants something beyond the truth."

"What's beyond the truth?" Miranda said.

Danny hit play and cranked up the volume again. The hum with the inner static bounced off the walls, and Danny said, "This."

Miranda looked at him sadly and said, "Don't call me until you have something I can watch." Then she left, closing the door behind her. She held back tears as she considered returning to ask Danny to let her finish the project herself, but was worried about what he'd do with the footage. She didn't even have the original Super-VHS master, which Danny had insisted on keeping at his place in a small fireproof box that he got at Target. She had never felt so helpless as she moved down the icy hallway with the trash bag. The talk show must've ended, as Bear was in the studio alone, coiling an orange extension cord around his elbow. He saw her pass the open door and asked if she was okay.

She looked at him, numb, and said, "Fine, I guess. Thanks for helping out with the sound today. And for lending Danny a key."

"Ah, that old mixer's on its last legs. Not to worry. What's this about a key?"

"Didn't you lend Danny a key?"

Bear shook his head. "That's against station policy."

Miranda took this in. "I'm worried about him. He's kind of obsessed with this project."

"That's what happens when you make something. You pour all your passion into it until there's nothing left over for real life."

"He's going to work by himself for a little while. Maybe you or Philip could check in on him from time to time?"

Bear put the cord aside and exited into the hallway. "Sure thing. But Philip hasn't been to work in two weeks. I think I gotta replace him."

"But I saw him last week. In the rack room."

Bear shook his head. "Must've been me."

Miranda nodded, her eyes haunted. She was sure that the man in the rack room wasn't Bear. The only problem was, if asked to describe the man she saw, she couldn't. Not if her life depended on it.

Miranda didn't come back to the station for several weeks. It was late February at this point, and the end of the Gulf War was in sight. Miranda was starting to wonder if their little documentary would have any relevance once the war was over. Finally, she got a call late on a Sunday night, and at first, all she heard was the speaker hum. But before she could hang up, Danny's voice cut through the noise and said, "Come tomorrow. It's done." And then he hung up.

The next day, Miranda entered the station for the last time. They'd been enjoying a rare cold front, and yet she was still shocked to discover that the hallway was colder than it had ever been. She pulled her coat tight, shivering as she moved past the Beta suite. Bear was in there editing, still in his ever-present denim shorts.

"Hi, Bear."

He looked back and said, "Hey, when you gonna finish up? I have someone that needs the three-quarter suite."

"Today, I think."

"Good. Make me a copy of your little show and I'll start airing it this weekend."

She nodded and kept walking. She reached for the suite door, but it opened before she could touch it. Danny stood there in his heavy coat with a wool cap pulled tight over his head. His beard had grown in patchy and rough, and there were dark rings under his eyes.

"You came," he said.

"Of course I did."

"You wanna see it?"

"That's why I'm here."

He stepped back, and she entered the suite to find it surprisingly clean. No more pizza boxes or soda cans, and the Super-VHS gear was gone. Danny shut the door and offered Miranda his chair, giving her a full view of the two monitors. The edited tape was sticking out of the playback deck. Scrawled on its label was just one word: *Truth.*

"You ready?" he asked.

"I guess. Do you wanna sit and watch it, too?"

"No, I've seen it. But I'll listen back here."

Danny nudged the tape with his finger, and the deck sucked it in. He hit play. There was no header, no opening titles. Just a few moments of static, and then it began.

The first thing Miranda noticed was the audio. It was like Danny had somehow isolated that strange sound deep in the hum and amplified it. She realized that the static was mixed with distorted voices. She couldn't make out any words at first, but it didn't matter as the images washed across her. The edited footage looked like nothing they had shot. It was distorted and granular, like someone had shrunk a camera and figured out how to record movement on the subatomic level. Miranda gradually began to recognize pieces of the imagery. Two lines crashing into each other were actually part of a star on an American flag. A dark cloud of rolling waves was an ultra close-up of a scraggly beard. Jagged white cliffs were gnashing teeth as the man in the wheelchair said, "IN-sane!"

Miranda realized that Danny had shot close-up images of the original footage with the Super-VHS camera and then shot close-ups of *those* images, again and again until everything on the screen was an ultra-magnified version of its original self. And those voices hidden in the hum? She now realized they were the protesters' interviews, woven together in a distorted aural pastiche that included something familiar that she couldn't quite place.

Miranda felt Danny pacing behind her. He wasn't watching the edit, but he was listening, letting the sound roll over him. Miranda wanted to look back, ask him, *What the fuck?* but she couldn't take her eyes off the granular images. They were intercutting now, in ways that were quick and strangely timed. It created a deep unease inside her, and suddenly she knew that something was very, very wrong.

She stood up and staggered for the door, but Danny grabbed her wrist and leaned in close, his breath hot in her face.

"We did it," he said.

"I have to go."

"No. You have to finish watching, or you won't know how the story ends."

"What story?" she said. "There's no story!"

"There is, you just have to look deeper. Into yourself. Don't you see? *We're* the story. The edit is just the lies we reflect back at ourselves."

"You're not making any sense," she said, looking back at the monitors. The images flashed by, blazing close-ups of eyes and teeth and clenched fists.

Danny caressed the side of her face. "He told me you'd say that."

"Who did?"

But Danny didn't answer. His hand moved from her face into her hair. His other hand cradled the back of her head, and she realized with mounting horror that he was forcing her face toward the monitors. She didn't think to close her eyes as she began seeing something else intercut into the footage, just a few frames at a time. It was that strange reflection in the post office glass, a figure with a face made unrecognizable by the process of repeat-edly shooting and enlarging it. And as the figure flashed across the screen, Miranda understood what else was inside the audio. It was her closing statement from the rally, amplified into a pitched, screeching shadow of herself.

A wave of nausea washed over her, mixed with raw panic, and she said, "Let me go, Danny." And when he didn't, she screamed, "*Let me go!*" and slammed her body back against him. Danny hit the wall and tumbled to the floor, and Miranda threw open the door and raced down a side hallway to the nearest bathroom. She crashed through the door and vomited into the toilet.

After she purged for a full minute, she sat on the floor and pressed her cheek to the toilet's frigid porcelain. She breathed in and out, her eyes closed, moaning softly. Hands grazed her shoul-ders, and she screamed, "*Don't touch me!*"

But when she looked up, it was Bear who stepped back through the doorway. "I'm sorry, I just wanted to see if you were okay."

"I'm not okay."

"What happened?" he asked.

"You can't show the tape."

"What do you mean? That's the deal."

"I don't care about the fucking deal. Danny's gone crazy. He made something horrible."

"Then let's go talk to him."

Miranda nodded reluctantly. She reached out a hand, and Bear helped her to her feet. They moved to the closed suite door, and Bear knocked. "Danny? We're gonna come in, okay?" There was no answer. Bear slowly opened the door.

But Danny was gone. The monitors showed nothing but cold static. Miranda pushed past Bear into the suite. "He was just here."

"Well, he's gone now," Bear said, a stern edge to his voice. "That little asshole."

Miranda followed his eyes and saw that one of the three-quarter decks was missing.

"What the hell's he gonna do with that?" he said.

But when he turned to her for an answer, Miranda was already racing down the hallway.

She was too late, of course. She didn't know that the bimonthly meeting of the Deep Focus Film and Video Club had moved to a conference room in the telecom building instead of its normal home on the second floor of the student union. By the time she figured it out and was running across campus, the air was thick with the sound of sirens.

It took two days before the police made a full statement about what happened. According to them, Danny had arrived at the Deep Focus meeting with the three-quarter deck under his arm, demanding to show his new project. Since no one was scheduled to screen that night, Chet allowed it. The conference room had a pull-down screen, but Danny insisted on hooking up the deck to a TV on a rolling cart. I would only remember later, from watching that strange, unmarked recording of this meeting, that in that moment, Danny had looked at his peers with a great sense of pride.

"You're my first real audience," he said. "And this is everything I know about telling the truth." He asked for the lights to be turned off and started the show.

It was a solid minute of watching Danny's video before a general sense of unease spread across the nine members in attendance. Someone asked for the lights to be turned back on, but apparently the switch wasn't working. Someone else tried to open the door, but it was stuck. While people argued in the dark, Danny's tape continued to play. The sound of retching and falling, convulsing bodies followed. Several members tried kicking in the door, but it held. A young woman said something about unplugging the TV, but she fell strangely silent after that.

Building security responded to a noise complaint and found the door locked. No one seemed to have the right key, but the screams from inside were loud and constant. By the time the fire department arrived, the screams had been replaced by the faint sound of weeping. Two firemen took the door off its hinges and entered. They found the light switch, and this time it worked fine. What they found was a TV playing white static and nine students who would never be the same again. Several were catatonic and would be hospitalized for weeks. Everyone had blood under their fingernails from scratching at their eyes and ears. The young woman had chewed off her tongue. The press had theories, from satanic hysteria to a gas leak in the building, but law enforcement suggested it was some sort of group seizure, and that was the theory that stuck.

Something that was left out of the police report was that a member always recorded the Deep Focus meetings. This particular recording was copied and passed around for years. Those sounds of distress we heard in the audio all those years ago? They were real. This wasn't someone's idea of a found-footage horror movie. This was actual found footage. I don't know why people decided to start calling it "the truth," but at least now I know where the name came from.

As that spring semester in '91 drew to a close, Miranda was ready to graduate and spend some time back in Miami with her family. She had some job leads, including a possible internship at the *Miami Herald*. The war was over, but she kept in contact with some of the activist friends she'd met at rallies she'd attended after shooting that first one with Danny. She still believed she would one day finish a documentary, just not the one she had originally set out to make.

The police questioned her about her working relationship with Danny, and when she called to follow up weeks later, she was told they would no longer need her help. She tried connecting with Chet, the former president of the Deep Focus Film and Video Club, and a week before graduation he finally agreed to see her.

Chet was freshly out of the hospital when he and Miranda sat on the porch outside his sister's house and drank iced tea on a warm spring day. He had longish hair and a goatee with a faded *Eraserhead* T-shirt that clung to his skinny frame. His memories of the incident were slowly coming back, but everything he told her was the same information she had already gleaned from police reports. If she wanted to get to the truth of it, she was going to have to dig deeper.

"Can I ask you a couple more questions?" she said.

Chet finished his iced tea. "I should go in soon. My doctor says not to push it."

"I know. I'll be quick."

He nodded.

"When the lights came on, where were you?"

"I was in the corner closest to the TV."

"Was Danny there?"

"I didn't see him."

"Did anyone?" she said. He looked at her strangely, and she added, "The door was locked until the fire department broke in. And when they turned on the lights, Danny wasn't there, was he?"

"I guess not."

"Was there any other way out of that room?"

Chet slowly shook his head.

"Danny hasn't been seen since that day. His parents haven't heard from him. The police think he's on the run, but from what?"

"From making us watch that sick fucking thing," Chet said, moving to stand.

"Wait, I'm sorry."

"I don't really care what happened to him. All I care about is that he's gone and I never have to watch that tape again. Now I gotta go."

He held out his hand, and Miranda handed him her half-full glass of iced tea. She stood up and said, "One more thing."

"What?"

"The police never got the tape."

"Yes they did," Chet said.

"According to them, it wasn't recovered."

"That's bullshit," Chet said. "A fireman was taking my vital signs when I saw a cop take the original tape out of the three-quarter deck."

"Was he wearing a uniform?"

"No, he was in nice clothes. Like a detective."

"What did he look like?" Miranda asked.

"I don't know," Chet said, opening the screen door and moving to enter.

Miranda took his arm gently and said, "Please tell me."

"I said, I don't know."

"You didn't get a good look at him?"

"Oh, I did," Chet said. "That's the crazy thing. He turned and looked right at me. And I swear to God, I have no idea what he looks like."

Miranda said nothing, like she wanted more but was afraid to ask.

Chet looked at her with haunted eyes. "You want me to describe his face, is that what you want? Well, I can't."

Miranda shivered in the warm day and said, "Why not?"

"Because I don't think he had a face," Chet said before he went inside, shut the door and never spoke to Miranda Velazquez again.

DANIEL CARTER: SICK WITH WORRY

Daniel Carter here again. I have included a journal entry I composed around the time Professor Wills delved into the dark web. I believe it speaks for itself.

> JOURNAL ENTRY: DANIEL CARTER
> MARCH 14, 2019
>
> I am very concerned about the professor. He is in and out of the office unreliably; he is completely disinterested in (and not likely capable of) teaching. When he is present, he mutters to himself and scribbles down incomprehensible notes.
>
> I have resigned myself to being a full-time instructor in his stead (despite my meager compensation) until the end of the semester. I have told the students that he is on an extended sabbatical, working on a research project. I'm covering for him with the university as best I can. I am growing increasingly tired of this burden, but of course I'll continue to protect my friend and mentor.

Two nights ago, I visited his office at the end of the school day to retrieve some papers to grade, and I took the opportunity to look through some of the newer materials generated by the professor.

I have never known the professor to be a creative writer.

Until now.

I counted over two hundred individual pieces. Notes, poems, sketches. Photo collages. Most only one page, or a part of a page, stacked on his desk in sloppy piles with no discernable order. I decided to stay late and xerox all of them. I am hopeful that this mania is temporary, but if I need to catalog his mental deterioration, I wanted to ensure I had this material for my records.

Here are a few of these pieces, provided to give you a sense of the professor's mind at the time he was writing the final entries chronicling his investigation.

That night, they showed me such sights
Beautiful and terrifying
So grateful
So happy, finally
You never know how blind you've been
Until the veil is lifted
Thank you, Z

Shepherd me, shepherd me
To my home, my Static City.
Tell me what gifts I must bring

And I shall arrive with glorious bounty
At the gates of your kingdom.

Three notes from the piper
Three notes for the famished
Let us satiate your craving
When we ring our bell.

One
  Two
    Three
      Four
        Five
          Six
           Seven
             Eight
Infinity

See me.

DREAMING IN LILAC ON A COOL EVENING

Rebekah McKendry
and David Ian McKendry

We came across this story on a subthread of a subthread on an LA message board, touting legends of the city. For the most part the comments section was filled with those claiming this story, by their own accounts, to be true. Some remembered a few of the details differently, but for most, this is how the story went.

—The McKendrys

G IDEON WAS ALMOST certain the light purple sheets were made from a high-quality Egyptian cotton. They had the woven texture of a finer softer thread. Definitely picked by hand. He would expect nothing less from a high-end luxury hotel. The wallpaper, on the other hand, was very confusing. A glossy black with incongruent accents of gold fleck, it was ten to fifteen years past being in style. According to Gideon's research, the hotel had undergone a full renovation five years ago. In his mind, this wallpaper should have been the first thing to go. Cecily's social media post was already two hours old by the time Gideon came to this conclusion.

The caption above Cecily's most recent post read, "Dreaming in Lilac on a Cool Evening." Gideon didn't give it much thought. Neither had the twenty-two thousand followers who had already liked it. Gideon figured Cecily's latest photo would hit a hundred thousand before leveling off; she still wasn't a major star in the influencer world. At the moment, she only had 151,000 followers. To Gideon, her low-level celebrity status brought with it intimacy and accessibility. However, her popularity was steadily rising, bringing in more followers and bigger promotions every week. It was only a matter of time before that intimacy and accessibility vanished. The thought of it twisted a knife in Gideon's gut.

With one more deep breath, the anxiety attack that drew his attention to the comforter and wallpaper had run its course. Gideon could now go back to studying Cecily's face. It was his favorite feature. Her face was perfectly arranged. Every contour and line was a display of flawless symmetry. It was a sight that brought tears to his eyes.

That was what made Gideon different. Most of Cecily's male followers spent their time ogling her body. They filled the comments section with rude and lascivious remarks. Gideon found their observations disgusting. The way they described in graphic detail the horrid sexual acts they would perform on her, it made Gideon want to vomit. Most of them were pulled down by the site's moderators almost immediately. Gideon made sure to jot down the usernames of repeat offenders, should the need for his intervention arise. Cecily didn't deserve to be hounded by that type of depravity.

Gideon found it hard to believe anyone could be as disgusting as those folks were. How could anyone look into Cecily's deep brown eyes and have such terrible thoughts? Gideon considered them a true brown that all other shades were born from, as though this honest hue only existed for Cecily. Her brown eyes were a truth she was kind enough to share with Gideon. The eyes shared with him both her joy and sadness. Her eyes exposed a loneliness in the way the light reflected off their moist surface. Even her thin smile couldn't belie the sadness. Her eyes never lied to Gideon.

A thousand reasons for her sadness crept through Gideon's mind, and with each one a solution only he could provide. Dwelling on those thoughts was enough to send Gideon into a panic attack. Gideon didn't handle panic attacks very well. Sometimes they made him act recklessly. He'd put a lot of effort and planning into the next few days. He couldn't let his emotions get the better of him. He couldn't let them ruin his plans. Taking a deep breath,

Gideon closed his eyes and cleared his mind as best he could. A small voice in the back of his head told him to look away, to just close his laptop and go to bed before he ruined everything, but Cecily's photo was making that too difficult to do. It was as though she was trying to distract him from his plan.

Maybe she was testing him.

In the photo, Cecily was lying on her side atop the light purple Egyptian cotton sheets. The hotel's complimentary bathrobe hung off her shoulder to reveal just the right portion of her left breast, just enough hidden to keep from violating the platform's policies regarding nudity. Gideon figured she was only a half centimeter from violating those policies. For a moment, he thought he could see the slightest bit of pink, but he knew Cecily was too careful to let that happen. She would never risk losing her sponsors or having her account taken down.

Gideon felt a sudden piercing pain behind his eyes. His mother always said a headache like this came from staring at filthy pictures on his computer for too long. Even now he could hear her voice and the way she would say that word. He couldn't even think of the word "filthy" without hearing her say it. Gideon knew this was just something that happened when he stared at one spot on his screen for too long. His retinas screamed for him to shift his focus and relieve the strain, but Gideon waited for the nausea to set in before moving his eyes to another part of his screen. Focusing on her long brown hair quelled the nausea, but the headache was only slightly abated.

Propped up on her elbow, the photo gave Cecily's hair the illusion of greater length. In reality, it went six inches past her shoulder, but in this position, traveling down her upper arm before pooling into gentle curls on the sheets, it looked much longer. Gideon wondered what those wisps of fine brown strands must have felt like against her soft, smooth skin. He wanted to know if her scent still lingered on those Egyptian cotton sheets. Gideon took another deep breath.

Studying the gentle contours of her body, he caught a glimpse of a small dark pattern affixed to the soft skin of her arm. His face inches from the screen, he could see the freshly scarred flesh, red and swollen. In the swelling, black vertical hash marks of varying length. The longest of the lines was no more than half an inch, the shortest measuring roughly an eighth. It was hard to see how many; they were too thin and too tightly packed together. A fresh tattoo, not more than a few days old.

Cecily didn't strike him as the type of person to get a tattoo. As far as he knew, this was her only one. Gideon wasn't really a huge fan of tattoos. He remembered the snide comments his mother used to make whenever she used to see someone with one, but she had a snide comment for nearly everyone she saw. There was never a shortage of styles, trends or quirks that bothered her. Gideon figured as long as Cecily was happy with her new tattoo, then he could be happy with it, too.

Through the large picture window behind her was the Los Angeles skyline at night. Her room was high enough to capture most of the city facing west toward the ocean. She had posted a similar photo of her room a couple of days ago. It made finding the hotel she was staying at so much easier. The floor number was a bit trickier to triangulate, but Gideon was confident she was staying on the twenty-first floor. Just to the right of center. He'd know the right room once he was up there.

Removing his glasses and placing them on the table next to his laptop, Gideon stood and stretched. Five hours of sitting on his motel room's thinly padded chair had done a number on his joints. They popped with each twist and pull. Gideon rubbed his eyes as he made his way over to the window. His view wasn't quite the same as Cecily's. His room was on the top floor of a cheap two-story motel, the view obstructed by an old three-story abandoned factory across the street. Gideon's room faced east toward Cecily's. From here, he was at least looking in her direction even if all he could see were broken windows and crumbling brick.

He took one last look at Cecily's photo before closing his laptop, then removing his underwear and sliding into bed. Lying on his back and looking up at the ceiling, he rehearsed conversations in his head about thousands of possible topics. All of them very real and plausible subjects that could come up in conversation at any time. This was his one shot at impressing her, at proving how perfect they were for each other. To practice, Gideon spoke at a low volume, just enough for him to get the inflections and tone just right. When the two of them finally spoke to each other, Gideon wanted every reply and inflection to be flawless.

Drifting out of practiced conversation, Gideon's mind wandered to her photo. It was burned into him, still there when his eyes were closed. As Cecily lay on her side, her stomach was smooth and flat. In its center, Cecily's belly button was a narrow slit delicately placed in the single vertical crease of her muscular abdomen. Not far below, the two halves of her bathrobe came together, united by a hastily tied bow. Gideon imagined the slightest bit of effort it would take to undo. Just beneath the bow, the robe separated once more, revealing a triangular shadow in their parting. Gideon's thoughts lingered here for a moment longer before drifting to the soft skin of her long, slender legs, which she had brazenly exposed to him. Looking up, he saw her face as it hovered above him, framed by her beautiful silken hair. It brushed delicately across his cheeks. Cecily's deep brown eyes gazing down at him before succumbing to the pleasure of having him inside her. Her eyes closed, her mouth an open expression of ecstasy.

Gideon's body convulsed for a brief second before his stomach quickly seized with guilt. Gideon cursed his base desires and his disgusting lack of control. Cecily deserved better. She deserved someone who wasn't so filthy. Gideon winced as he rolled onto his side. Curling into a ball, he pulled his knees to his chest, wishing he could squeeze the remorse from his body. Staring out the window in the direction of her hotel room, Gideon could only see the building across the street. Maybe she was looking out her window too, staring out in his direction. Taking in a few more deep breaths, he relaxed his grip on his knees as he straightened out his body. After tomorrow, everything would be right. Tomorrow they'd be together.

The sun topped the building across the street and cut a harsh light through Gideon's motel window. On the sidewalks below, junkies slept in interrupted intervals as the morning withdrawal set in. Their irate slurred curses and desperate tears echoed off the concrete labyrinth of buildings all around them. A few blocks away, a car blared its horn, initiating a symphony from an ensemble of vehicles behind him. The thin motel windows did little to dampen the cacophony of morning in Downtown Los Angeles.

Gideon did his best to shut out the din. He had problems with loud noises, which triggered his anxiety. Sometimes it got so bad Gideon would nearly black out. His doctor said it was a type of misophonia, an extreme sensitivity to loud noises. He told Gideon to take deep breaths and focus on something specific when it got really bad. His mother told Gideon it was because he was just a big coward. Gideon laughed to himself, wondering what his doctor would have said if he knew his mother's voice was his biggest trigger. Gideon now practiced his breathing as he brushed his teeth. The noise would barely reach Cecily's lofty room. Her hotel windows were probably a lot thicker.

His hair was still wet from the shower, and Gideon wondered if it was cut too short. He had only seen a couple of men in Cecily's photos. They were traditionally handsome with strong jaws and muscular physiques, but they dressed poorly, with hairstyles that were purposely messy. They were what Gideon's mother would refer to as "slovenly."

Those relationships never lasted very long. They made it into one or two photos at the most. With Cecily, looks could take them only so far. That's what made Gideon different. His face was rounder, his jaw weaker, his body softer, but there was more to Gideon than just his looks. Cecily would see that. She'd know. Besides, Cecily promoted a lot of health products, and several of her posts were dedicated to her exercise routine. Her healthy lifestyle was bound to rub off on Gideon. He'd probably be reluctant at first—there were a lot of bad habits Gideon would need help with—but he'd eventually come around.

A familiar sound from Gideon's phone drew his attention to the device, which was resting next to the sink. It was an alert, a special tone he had set to inform him whenever Cecily posted something new. On instinct, Gideon had his phone in hand, checking to see what had just gone up. Entering his security code with nervous anticipation reminded Gideon how much he preferred the simplicity of using his laptop. Getting his phone open and scrolling to the right app with all this nervous anticipation was incredibly difficult on such a small device. Gideon's brawny fingers didn't make it any easier either, even in the best of circumstances.

Cecily's latest post already had five likes. Gideon cursed his fat fingers for making it take so long. He always tried to be the first like to go up. After she posted something new, there was a better chance that she was still on her computer with the app open. Being one of the first likes gave him a greater chance of being noticed. Gideon figured after about five or ten likes Cecily would lose interest in the minutiae of the post, checking in later just to see its overall success. He liked knowing she saw his name first.

After at least making sure he was the sixth person to press the like button, Gideon took a deep calming breath before feasting on Cecily's latest photo. She must have woken up around the same time as Gideon. Her towel was tightly wrapped around her freshly showered body like a form-fitting minidress. Cecily's breasts were modest in size. Gideon thought of them as pleasant, but then, Gideon didn't possess a large vocabulary when it came to describing a woman's chest. In this photo, their size was striking. The towel compressing them to such a degree, threatening to push them out and over the top, that it made Gideon dizzy. At the same time, the bottom proved to be barely long enough to cover what Gideon's mother would call "a woman's sin."

Cecily's hair was soaking wet, hanging in damp clumps down the side of her face. Her arms and legs still had a sheen of moisture to them. She stood by her hotel room window, holding a croissant in her hand. The sun rising on the opposite side of the building gave just enough light to the city skyline behind her. The caption read, "Morning Vibes." Her new tattoo was slightly more visible in this photo. He could now see that the lines that composed it occupied about three inches of horizontal space on Cecily's upper arm. The lines formed a pattern that reminded Gideon of the sound waves on his doctor's laptop. The sound waves his doctor would play to test Gideon's auditory condition.

Gideon put down his phone. He didn't have time to get wrapped up in that right now. He was about to see her in person, and there would always be time to look at it later. He looked at his hair one more time. It wasn't too short, Gideon assured himself as he slicked his hair to the side with the palm of his hand. Gideon tossed his dark gray jacket over his shoulder as he stepped out of his room with a confident stride to his step.

The bus ride over to Cecily's hotel made his stomach twist up in knots. When he formulated this plan, he had imagined that he'd find a seat on the bus. He hadn't anticipated the morning rush hour. Breathing deeply, Gideon clung tightly to the overhead rail, trying to convince himself it was just a tiny inconvenience, but he could feel his fellow passengers' eyes on him. He tried ignoring their beady-eyed glares, but he could still feel each one of them burrowing into his brain. How many were already reading his mind? How many of them knew already? Gideon hoped his counterfeit security badge would avert most of their eyes. He hoped it would be a shield against their piercing looks, but it didn't seem to be working. Keeping up his breathing, Gideon repeatedly told himself not to dwell. It was only a ten-minute bus ride to her hotel, but if they hit traffic, Gideon was sure he was going to collapse into a screaming heap on the floor.

Just eleven minutes after stepping onto the Eastbound 31 Local, Gideon found himself standing on the sidewalk a block from Cecily's hotel. Getting off the bus was a blur compounded by the sounds of the busy city street. Enclosed by elegant high-rises and beautifully refurbished historic buildings that seemed to bounce the noise and confusion back and forth in every direction, Gideon's head gyrated. He struggled for air, his vision narrowing into a tightly packed tunnel. An intense wave of confusion fell over him. The city assaulting every sense, Gideon stumbled as his legs failed to keep him upright.

Purpose escaping him, he wanted nothing more than to be on the ground begging for mercy, seeing himself lying on the filthy pavement while annoyed commuters stepped over his bloated nuisance of a body. Crying like a baby for his mother to save him. His head continued to spin in uncontrollable circles, each one overlapping the other, sending him further into confusion. His stomach churning, Gideon knew it was only a matter of time before he was a heaping vomitous mess on the sidewalk. He heard his mother's venomous words echoing through him. Her raspy voice hurling its insults and obscenities at him.

Suddenly, he felt something hard, round and metallic in his

grasp. He squeezed it tightly, willing his other hand to take hold as well, his knuckles turning white in his unrelenting grasp. His eyes began to focus; he could see the metal signpost in his hand. A mercy his subconscious brain managed to cling to. Squeezing it filled Gideon with comfort; the feeling was familiar.

It had been two days since he thought he had silenced her. But here on this downtown street he could still hear Mother.

When he stupidly told her where he was going, she laughed in his face. She laughed at his plans to be with Cecily. She threatened to call the doctor. Here she was tormenting him all over again. He remembered her feeling much softer in his hand than the metal signpost, her face turning red, before turning a deep purple. Her eyes bulging out of their sockets yet still somehow stabbing him with a deep hateful glare, right up until their final moments.

Tightening his grip on the unrelenting metal pole, he continued squeezing as his mother's voice grew quieter. Mother's miserable, bitter voice, struggling for air yet still capable of spewing poisonous vitriol at him. She never wanted Gideon to be happy. Squeezing even tighter, Gideon anticipated that same sharp crack of bone he remembered hearing two days ago, a sound that the signpost refused to make.

The sudden jolt of a car horn snapped Gideon back to reality. Next to him, a car stopped at the intersection; the confused driver watched Gideon squeezing the life from a stop sign. Enthralled by the scene Gideon was making, the driver refused to continue onward until compelled by the horn of the irritated vehicle behind him. Thankful to be once more in control, Gideon released his grip on the metal pole. His hands were stiff and sore.

He opened and closed them several times, getting the blood to return to his knuckles. Once the color had come back, Gideon straightened his suit jacket before continuing on toward Cecily's hotel. It was his worst attack so far, but somehow, he had made it through.

This was Gideon's third trip to the hotel. The first two times he went to familiarize himself with its modern open layout. Standing in the doorway, he already knew the path to the elevators that offered the least exposure. Everything from the location of the front desk to the patterns repeated throughout the marble flooring were burned into his memory. He had expected more people circulating about at this hour, maybe a few more people checking in, something that would have made the front desk too busy to notice him. The only people he saw were two men seated in postmodern chairs buried in their phones and a young woman working behind the counter. She was speaking to an older woman standing across from her. Thankfully she was currently occupied. That would make getting to the elevators easier.

Walking slowly yet with purpose, Gideon kept the clerk in the corner of his eye. She was still speaking to the older woman. Passing closer to the counter, he caught brief snippets of their conversation. He wasn't paying attention to the words, but he could tell by the old woman's tone that she was upset about something. Gideon recognized that tone; it was his mother's tone. Gideon made it three-quarters of the way to the elevator; the hardest part was almost over.

"Hey." The words coming from the front desk hit him like a bullet.

There was no mistaking that they were directed at Gideon. There was no denying that he'd have to stop.

"Excuse me." The tone demanded acknowledgment.

Gideon turned to her, trying to force a smile. The best he could muster was a pitifully confused look. The young woman made no attempt to hide her aggravation. The older woman had a scowl that made Gideon's stomach churn, but he was thankful she only sounded like Mother.

"Can you please let Ms. Marsh into room 812? There's a problem with the lock."

"Third time since we checked in," the older woman added, not even trying to hide her hatefulness.

Gideon noticed the younger woman holding her arm out toward him. Gideon thought she might be pointing an accusing finger at him. Looking closer, he saw a keycard in her hand.

"Okay," Gideon managed to get out.

She held the keycard in a manner that suggested she would have thrown it at him if she could have. Commanding himself to move forward, Gideon took the card from her hand. Turning to the older woman, Gideon made a polite motion for her to come with him. She thankfully did so without Gideon having to verbalize the request.

"Wait." He had only gotten a few steps away when the young woman's voice stopped him. "Take the master key just in case."

Turning back to her, he saw that she was holding a second keycard. The master keycard. Gideon couldn't believe his luck. He knew in his heart that the universe was aligning with him. There was no denying that he and Cecily were meant to be. His good fortune was proof of that. Gideon happily took the key from her hand, and with an added injection of confidence, he escorted Ms. Marsh to the elevator.

Rigidly standing in the middle of the elevator, Gideon towered over the older woman. Her arm occasionally brushing against him, she made it clear she had no intention of moving to any other part of the elevator. She had staked her claim to this spot, and she wasn't giving it up for anyone. Gideon thought that she was nearly the same age as his mother. There they stood in silence, neither of them willing to surrender ground to the other. Gideon kind of admired her mettle. Her attitude may have been different had she known what he was capable of.

"I've had nothing but problems since check-in!" she spat out angrily.

Her tone snarled Gideon's stomach. As physically intimidating as he was, Gideon folded at her odious tone. It so closely resembled his mother's that it ate away at his abdomen in much the same way. She only spoke that one bitter sentence, but already Gideon was nauseous to the point of retching all over the elevator. He imagined himself doing so. Gideon wondered what her reaction to that would be. The thought of it amused him, which helped with the nausea slightly.

"I will be speaking with the hotel manager about all of this." Her words were filled with virulence. They pierced Gideon's flesh and worked their way into his veins. She was making it harder for him to fight the urge to react.

"This is the last time I will stay here; I promise you that."

Gideon tried his best to tune her out. He clenched his already sore fists until the color drained from them, the pain preventing him from doing that for too long. He barely heard the ding of the elevator doors opening.

His vision narrowed to a small tunnel as they walked toward her room. Gideon pondered silencing her. By now her voice was just angry background noise, but still it had its effect on him, even if he wasn't paying attention to the words. Gideon wondered if he could do it as quickly as he had to his mother. Ms. Marsh looked a little frailer than Mother; it probably wouldn't take as long. Maybe it was easier the second time.

The door closed in Gideon's face with a heavy thud. Gideon had lost time. He had tuned out the old woman and now couldn't remember letting her into her room. He began to worry. Had he blacked out? Was she on the other side of this door, lying on the bathroom floor with giant red handprints around her neck?

Maybe it was easier to kill the second time. Gideon's breathing was strained. What if the cleaning lady found her before he was able to follow through with his plan? He'd never be with Cecily if the hotel was suddenly locked down until the police arrived. He thought about going in and checking to see if he hid the body well enough to buy him some time.

But then what if he hadn't actually killed her? He'd have to come up with an excuse for why he let himself back inside. If she didn't believe him, then he'd have to kill her. He thought about knocking, maybe throwing her an apology or making something up about her breakfast being free. That would work.

He raised his fist to knock and then realized that he wasn't standing in front of 812 anymore. Gideon was standing in front of room 2110. It was Cecily's room, he was certain of that. Despite his panic and despite his wandering mind, his body had managed to carry him to her room. Somehow, he had willed himself here. Gideon's destiny was just behind this door.

"I'm so sorry. The computer said this room was unoccupied. Hey, aren't you Cecily Rogers? I follow you online!" He said it over and over again under his breath. All he needed now was her reply so he'd know where to take the conversation next.

Gideon slid the master key into the lock. After a few flashes of yellow, a lock clicked and a green light lit. Pressing down on the handle, Gideon opened the door with ease.

The smooth gray walls were the first thing Gideon noticed. Everything else looked just as it had in the picture. The Egyptian cotton duvet, the imitation down comforter and that view. It was the exact same view from the photo. Missing was the black wall-paper with its gold accents. Just then the dull clang of the house-keeper's cart caught his attention. Turning around and looking out into the hallway, he saw the cleaning lady keying into the room across the hall.

"Excuse me." Gideon's need for an answer overpowered his anxiety.

"That's been empty all week," she answered, after flipping through a clipboard attached to her cart.

Gideon stepped back into what was supposed to be Cecily's room. Walking up to the window, he looked out at the view. Could he have gotten it wrong? It looked exactly as it had in the photo. But maybe . . . Gideon thought for a moment. Crossing to the other side of the bed, Gideon lined himself up to where Ceci-ly's camera would have been. Stepping from side to side, varying his angle, he wondered just how off he could have been. He knew none of the rooms in this building matched the one in the photo.

Was it possible that he was in the wrong building? Gideon's chest felt like someone had stabbed a knife in his heart. He started to feel dizzy. His forehead pressed against the window, he looked down at the street beneath him. He saw himself falling forward through the window and down onto the pavement below. He said a silent prayer that the glass would give way, that he could feel the rush of air pushing against his body, and then the hard slap of concrete that would end his suffering. He could hear his mother's thick, horrid and raspy laugh.

"Are you all right?" the housekeeper asked from the hallway.

Gideon placed a hand on the window to steady himself. Without saying a word, he turned around and stormed out of the room.

Before he knew it, Gideon was back on the sidewalk. He couldn't remember if anyone had said anything to him in the lobby. He couldn't even remember if he had used the elevator or just somehow appeared downstairs. Whatever brought him down here was a forgotten blur that would never reveal itself to him.

Standing there in the dizzying blur of the city once more, Gideon looked up at the wall of buildings towering over him. His head flung back, Gideon walked about blindly, with no control over where his movements took him. Seconds later a sharp, violent agony ripped through him, his head throbbing in pain. Gideon pressed the palms of his hands to his ears, but it did nothing to stop the pain. Its assault was relentlessly brutal. The origin was somewhere out beyond his tightly shut eyes. Frozen in fear, he couldn't bring himself to see the cause but knew it wouldn't stop until he opened his eyes and saw its source.

When he opened his eyes, the city revealed itself to him. Gideon was no longer standing on the sidewalk. In front of him a car furiously blared its horn. The woman behind the wheel un-relenting as she pressed against the center of her steering wheel with both hands. On her face a look of unyielding refusal. She would not stop until he moved. Inside Gideon a rage grew, an intense desire to pull her from her car and beat her head against the hard concrete until there was nothing left of it.

Before he could act on that impulse, salvation appeared out of the corner of his eye. There, across the street from the hotel, a fresh carving into the facade. It wasn't very big, just enough to catch his attention. Gideon gave up on his thoughts of murdering this angry commuter as he walked across the street, drawn by this oddly familiar carving.

In front of Gideon was a building a few stories shorter than the one he had just left. His glance passing back and forth, he saw now how easy it would have been to mistake these two mam-moth structures. The other being a hotel made it the obvious choice. He wasn't sure what occupied this building. A much older construction, it looked almost forgotten, an old high-rise ready to be removed so that a newer one could take its place.

The carving that had caught Gideon's eyes was freshly etched into the brick. Roughly three feet wide and a foot and a half at its tallest point, the design was perfectly carved into one of the building's large gray blocks. It was Cecily's tattoo. Gideon excit-edly searched for the door, fate once again moving in his favor.

The large wooden doors, their window inserts covered over in a thick layer of old newspapers hung with a thick layer of glue and aged by the sun, were unlocked. Stepping inside, Gideon marveled at the condition of the lobby: a clear, unadorned, dimly lit chasm of concrete covered in a layer of dust that danced in the rays of what little light made its way through the newspaper-covered windows. The building felt empty of any life. Gideon had expected a make-shift shelter filled with the discarded belongings of homeless inhabitants. Either the homeless didn't know this building was open, or they were afraid to enter. It didn't even look like rats had set foot in here.

The lobby left very few options as to where Gideon could go next. There were only two doors, the one he'd come through and a pair of wooden art-deco sliding doors he assumed hid an eleva-tor behind them.

Crossing over to the doors, he saw to the left of them a single button. Above them a needle indicating that the elevator was at rest on the lobby floor. Gideon pressed the button. A bell imme-diately dinged as the elevator doors slid open. Before he stepped through the doorway a second sound hit Gideon's ears. It came from his phone. A new post from Cecily. Quickly and excitedly fumbling for his phone, Gideon managed to be the first like.

Cecily stood once more in front of the window, a window Gideon assumed was now just twenty floors above him. Hold-ing in her hand a single purple flower, she wore a bright yellow blouse that hung softly off her right shoulder. Her hair falling like a smooth, velvety blanket gave brief glimpses of the skin under-neath. Her makeup was subtle, a tinge of yellow eye shadow and the faintest bit of blush. The caption read, "I am yours in eternal splendor." Not taking his eyes from his phone, Gideon moved as if in a dream as he entered the elevator. The doors sliding closed behind him, Gideon forced himself to look away from his phone. Pressing the only button on the control panel, the elevator sprung to life and lifted him toward her.

Gideon's knees jerked as the elevator came to a stop with a slight jolt. Breathing deep, he wondered if the rush of anticipation might stop his heart. The doors slowly slid open, putrid air rushing into the elevator to greet him. His stomach churned. Gideon grabbed hold of the sides of the elevator, pulling himself across the threshold. The intensity of the stench was like pushing through a thick fog. As he stepped out onto the floor, Gideon immediately dropped to his knees.

Had he not skipped breakfast because of his nerves, his retching might have been more productive. Instead, he found himself choking on the sweet bile from his stomach, accompanied by bouts of dry heaving. Pulling himself up off the concrete floor, Gideon looked around in awe at the fabricated reality that surrounded him. It was all strangely familiar yet alien. This wide-open room had been sectioned off into a different truth. Constructed from wooden flats, individual backdrops made up Cecily's online world. All around him were memories of Cecily's former posts. In this one space Gideon saw Cecily's bedroom. It was nothing more than three thin walls held upright by A-frames and sandbags. In another corner, a single window flat with a round metal table and chair set in front of it. On the other side of that flat, the illusion of a garden terrace; really an enlarged photograph anchored to a metal frame. This was the café Cecily liked to go to when she needed to be alone with her thoughts. Everywhere he looked, Gideon saw all of Cecily's most frequent posts. Around him nothing but lies.

A sudden burst of white noise grabbed Gideon's attention. Anchored high up on a concrete wall was an old television. A thirteen-inch screen housed in a black and white plastic console, it sat upon an unfinished plank of wood hastily anchored to the wall with a few cheap metal brackets. Looking down from the TV, Gideon saw a lone figure sitting in a chair facing away from him. It was Cecily. Her back was to him, but he knew it was her. What was this game she was playing at? Whatever it was, he was in no mood for it. As he slowly walked toward her, the smell of decay in the air, his only thought was of her lies. All he wanted now was to punish her.

His hands out inches from her neck, Gideon paused. Something was wrong. He could feel the very tips of his fingers touching a single strand of her hair, yet Cecily didn't move an inch. That was when he saw her. That was when he realized the source of the decay.

Her head tilted to the side, matted hair draped across her face. Gideon fought the urge to pull back that curtain of hair and see what remained of Cecily's face. He wanted to touch her skin but knew the dead flesh that now hung from her bones wouldn't feel like it had in his imagination. Her skin now crawled and undulated underneath. The long slits that ran up her wrists made an opening for the thousands of insects that now devoured Cecily from the inside. Dark brown stains of dried blood ran down the arm of the chair, surrounding it in a bloodstained circle. On the floor, carelessly dropped at her feet, a knife filthy with Cecily's dried blood.

Looking away from the horrific remains of his love, Gideon turned toward a wall, which had written across it, in smears of dark reddish brown, a prayer:

"I have become one with the Eyeless Man. I will live on as part of him."

On a small stand placed deliberately in front of the wall was Cecily's laptop, an Internet browser opened to her account. Lying across the keys, that same purple flower she held in her hand. Now dead and decaying, just as she was.

Desperate to preserve her memory, Gideon quickly turned away. He looked at the sets that Cecily used to create a life that never existed. Eventually his eyes landed on the one that brought him here.

Crossing over to the bed, he saw that familiar Egyptian cotton duvet cover. Placing his hand on it, Gideon confirmed that it was a four-hundred thread count. He still couldn't tell if the comforter inside was real or imitation down.

Gideon placed a hand on the wallpaper. Textured gold flecks jutted out to meet his touch. Looking closer and deeper into them, he saw a pattern form. It wasn't random, as he had previously thought. Each fleck of gold came together to create the soft petals of a flower. A golden lilac repeating itself. Gideon's mind slipped into a trance as it glided from one flower to the next, a black nebula separating them.

Just then his phone sounded an alert. It was impossible. It was all impossible. Yet his phone was telling him the impossible was true: there was a new post. A flash out of the corner of his eye drew his attention back to her laptop. On the screen he saw Cecily's posts. From where he stood he could see there was, in fact, a new photo displayed on the screen.

He feared the laptop but had to see for himself what it was showing him. Moving in a haze, Gideon brought himself to the screen. As he got closer, an image began to form. It wasn't a photograph. They were words formed from a delicate calligraphy. Single lines gently flowing across the screen. Gentle and beautiful, they formed two sentences that Gideon found himself compelled to read aloud.

"I surrender to you as we merge into one. Where once there were many, there is only the Eyeless Man." With the final word the screen went black.

"What the hell?"

A whistle of feedback filled the room. Gideon covered his ears to no avail. He looked up at the TV on the shelf as the sound burst from its speakers, and through the snow on the screen the faint outline of a faceless figure looked down at him. Just then the whistling died down, replaced by a soft, gentle voice.

"I'm so happy you're here to share eternity with me, Gideon." The voice was Cecily's. If he had heard it any other time, it would have filled him with joy, but now it only brought him terror. "And he is, too."

Her words drew Gideon's attention to the wall above him and that name, the Eyeless Man. As he grasped for understanding, the sharp, piercing sound of feedback filled the room once more. The intensity dropped Gideon to his knees. He covered his ears with his hands, but it did nothing to deafen the sound. It was coming from inside his head now.

As he cried out in pain, something else started making its way through the feedback. It was a voice, hard to hear but slowly coming in clearer. He refused to believe it at first. How could that voice be here? He felt her neck collapse in his hands. He heard the snap of it breaking in his grasp. It was soon unmistakable and clear. The piercing whine of feedback accompanied by his mother's hateful, raspy voice. Every taunt she had ever hurled at him was echoing through his brain.

He looked up to Cecily for mercy but saw only her lifeless corpse looking down at him. For a moment he thought he could see her smiling at him. Following her arm as it hung by her side, he saw what she was seemingly pointing at. It was the knife. The one that ended her life and now lay at her feet. Now it was offering Gideon relief.

Crawling toward it, the intense hate of his mother's voice was now joined by the cruel laughter of a young woman he now knew was Cecily. All he wanted was her love, but all she would give him was endless torment. Eyes filled with tears, Gideon stretched out his arm and grabbed hold of the knife. With one final look at his love's desiccated body, Gideon grasped the handle tightly.

A final scream as he forced the blade through his ear. Gideon pushed and pushed with all the strength remaining in his body, the bones of his skull cracking as metal pushed by muscle made its way through. The blade passed quickly through the soft tissue within, but Gideon still heard the voices, the high-pitched whine and now his own pained screams. Once more halted by bone. Gideon paused as he filled his lungs with air. One last push, one last crack of bone, the bloody tip of the knife now visible above his other ear.

Gideon's body convulsed one last time before going completely still.

He was on the floor in a lifeless, bloated heap, his face a blank mask of death. Inside his brain, far from any living being's comprehension, the voices continued.

It had been two full weeks since Cecily had posted any new content. Some of her followers had started leaving concerned comments under older posts, while others had sent direct messages wondering what had happened to her. Cecily's absence hadn't hurt her popularity. In fact, her followers had inexplicably doubled during her two-week hiatus. Her last post had actually three times the number of likes Gideon had originally projected. It had gotten so much attention that Cecily's inbox was filled with offers to promote a wide array of products.

Not many people wondered what became of Gideon. He had been replaced at work after not showing up for two days in a row. Most of what he left in his hotel room had been tossed in the dumpster after it sat in a main office for a week. All but the laptop. That ended up at the night manager's apartment before making its way to a used computer store.

It sat on a shelf in the back room of the shop for another week before an employee decided to give it a look on her lunch break. It took only a matter of minutes for Lisa to get past Gideon's low-level security code. Lisa never considered herself a thief. Sure, she hadn't paid to see a film in years, and she knew the best sites for torrenting games and software. But she had never swiped anything she considered to have real value. That was until Gideon's laptop finally booted up, revealing to Lisa the last website he had ever visited.

Instantly seduced by the first post she saw, Lisa found herself compelled to slip the laptop into her messenger bag and take it home. That had been two weeks ago. Since then, no one, not even her boss or her roommates, had seen her.

Locked away in her room, she waited every day in eager anticipation for a new post to go up so that she would see him again. Lisa didn't even mind if she was in the picture with him. She was, after all, a beautiful young woman with dark silken hair and deep, soulful brown eyes. In her latest post, Lisa couldn't help but notice how mesmerizing her smile was. It seemed to reveal a pure joy and bliss, the likes of which she had never seen before. In the photo, her head leaned to one side, resting on his shoulder.

He was lean and handsome, with dirty-blond hair. His body was chiseled beneath an expensive, tight-fitting shirt. It wasn't Gideon's body, but those were unmistakably Gideon's eyes. Lisa was helplessly trapped in his eyes. There was something expressed in them that didn't fit with the rest of the photograph, she thought. She couldn't help but notice that they did not express the same joy as Cecily's did. There was no smile, just pain and a captivating sadness. A young stunning couple, together in an extravagant hotel room, with a perfect view of the Eiffel Tower, but she saw the pain in his eyes. They tore at Lisa and made her heart ache. She could see all the pain echoing through him. The screams and taunts that continued to haunt him. An eternity of suffering all reflected in his eyes. He needed her help.

The caption above the posted photograph read, "Two Souls, Intertwined."

DANIEL CARTER:
MISSIVE OF MADNESS

EDITOR'S NOTE: This entry was not typed, as the others, but was found written in Maynard Wills's handwriting on pieces of parchment paper. The handwriting was analyzed by a forensic expert and was concluded to have been written in a rushed manner. We have left all spelling and grammatical mistakes as found.

Before I go, I need to share at least a bit of what I've learned.

I will take you through it, quickly. I have an appointment, a very important appointment to keep.

FACTS:

1. There are infinite worlds, but we are bound to this one by our limited imaginations and an inability to influence our own bodies. At the quantum level, our particles visit these places every nanosecond of

every day while always coming to the same utterly insipid conclusion: that we belong here. But there are paths to other realms for the chosen and the awakened.

2. Those who prove their worth in life receive a gift: they can hear his whispers in their dreams. A long-distance call through space and time.

3. It is difficult to understand what makes one worthy in his eyeless gaze. Through the tales in this book, he seems drawn to subjects with a wanton lust or unbridled relationship with broadcast and digital media, but I have not yet discerned a deeper pattern.

4. The eight TV screens in the Video Palace basement; doors to eight realms. Does he control all of these? Does he control some? And what of realms beyond? Is The Stack his purview or is The Stack everything? I cannot know. Nor do others, unless they see me unfit for this information.

5. I must tell you the truth. A regrettable omission. I re-contacted Z sometime after Peter Gilliam's experiment. Z has taught me so much. Not just an acolyte, a herald for the eyeless one. Without his guidance my traverses through the dark web would not have yielded such ripe fruit.

6. Though details vary as is the nature of legend even when steeped in truth the stories in this collection have the same protagonist; the same entity leading people home; whether in the 70s or today, Australia, Scotland and everywhere in between. He does his good work.

7. The truth is and it saddens me deeply-I am not to his liking. I cannot fake what I do not have; my relationships with media and material do not excite him. I must find a different purpose to serve. And perhaps, in grace, I will receive my passage upon the ferry. I must earn my coin.

8. I am leaving my home and the
   university. I know where to find
   the piano tuner. This is my destiny
   now.

I am sorry, Daniel, to leave you
like this. Since I began teaching, I can
hear colleagues snicker. I can feel their
stares. But not you, Daniel. You care.
You've always cared. But I don't mind
the laughter any longer. I am beyond this
place.
   I entered academia because I wanted to
know. I wanted to understand the world.
I wanted to unravel the great mysteries.
And now I can become part of one. I am
no longer a student of this world. I serve
a greater purpose in another.

A
CONVERSATION
WITH TAMRA

Mary Phillips-Sandy

As a freelance writer and occasional podcaster, I've conducted hundreds of interviews. This assignment, however, was different: I had to interview my close friend, Tamra Wulff, about the strangest, most painful event of her life.

When Professor Wills began work on this book, he asked Tamra if she'd agree to speak with him on the record. For reasons you're about to discover, Tamra is wary of strangers who express interest in her story. It has become difficult to distinguish harmless crackpots from stalkers and opportunists. The vast majority of what has been written about her and her boyfriend, Mark Cambria, consists of errors, flat-out lies and preposterous assumptions. The truth is definitely not out there.

Because I've known Tamra for almost a decade, and because I've spent the past year and a half working with her to solve the mystery of the White Tapes, she told Prof. Wills that she'd consent to an interview—as long as it was with me.

There are two things I want you to understand about Tamra. First, if you have only encountered her through the *Video Palace* podcast, you might have the idea that she's a supporting character, a sidekick to Mark's protagonist. Anyone who knows her in real life could tell you that was nothing more than a trick of narrative. Tamra is one of the most capable, self-assured, brilliant people I know. That's exactly why Mark fell for her, and he knew how lucky he was.

Which brings me to my second point: Mark and Tamra are a team, in every sense of the word. They're different in many ways—he's impulsive, she considers her choices; he can cook elaborate meals, she can open Seamless; he's a sci-fi nerd, she's an art house nerd. But they are two halves of a whole, and since Mark left, Tamra's singular focus has been finding him. What happened that day at Randy Wane's piano shop? What did Mark see when he went down to the basement? What did we really hear in his last phone call? We have a jumble of clues and scraps of information, but as of yet, no conclusions.

As for me, I didn't mean to get so involved in this, but Tamra was traumatized after the events documented in the podcast. I went out of my way to spend time with her, making sure she ate, keeping her company while she slept, that kind of thing. All she could talk about was what happened. What happened? How? Why? Why Mark?

I've never been able to resist an unanswered question. I love nothing more than patching fragments of information into a story with a beginning, middle and end. (This is why, over the years, people have hired me to research their books and fact-check their publications.) The more Tamra told me, the more I wanted to know. And without Mark, she needed someone who not only believed in her but was willing to push forward to find answers.

So here, for the first time, is Tamra in her own words, on her own terms. We spoke one Thursday evening in her studio apartment in northern Manhattan. I apologize that our conversation ended abruptly.

—Mary Phillips-Sandy

Mary Phillips-Sandy: Okay, we're recording. Let me know if you want to stop or take a break at any point, there's no rush. By the way, I'm proud of you for doing this. I know it wasn't an easy decision. It takes a lot of courage to share your story with a world full of strangers who may or may not believe a word you say.

Tamra Wulff: I appreciate that. I wish I felt courageous. I don't, though.

MPS: No? How do you feel?

TW: Like I have nothing left to lose.

MPS: Well, on that note, let's start at the beginning, or the middle, I guess, the inflection point. Fall of 2018, when you last saw your boyfriend, Mark Cambria. He left under unusual circumstances, and not voluntarily. Something happened to him in the basement of Randy Wane's piano shop—as most people would say, he disappeared. You don't use that word. How come?

TW: "Disappeared" means he was erased. Like he doesn't exist anymore. Which isn't true. He left, he's gone away, he's not here, but I believe he is somewhere, and he can come back.

MPS: He'd gone to the shop alone because he was convinced it had something to do with the White Tapes he'd found. The tapes that made him sick every time he watched them.

TW: Initially, I thought those tapes would just be another one of Mark's projects. He'd always wanted to start a podcast, and here was this topic that seemed interesting, at least to a certain audience. It struck me as— Maybe I shouldn't say this.

MPS: No, now you have to say it.

TW: It struck me as childish. The whole thing, the tapes, the rumors, these weird people he was talking to on the phone. Like, come on, you're a rational adult human! It's one thing to enjoy ghost stories. It's another thing to start acting them out.

MPS: You guys argued about that.

TW: Oh, constantly. From the beginning. You heard the arguments that were in the podcast? Believe me, there were a lot more that didn't make it in.

MPS: But eventually you decided to help Mark with—

TW: Wait, can I say one more thing? I wasn't the henpecking girlfriend. You know, that awful girl who's in every bro comedy ever made. "Don't go out! Stop wearing that T-shirt! I hate your friends! The thing you love is stupid! If you walk out that door, you're never coming back!" It's obvious from the minute she walks on-screen that she sucks, and as soon as her boyfriend dumps her, his life will be awesome.

MPS: Good lord, no, that's not who you are. Your relationship never worked that way.

TW: *You* know that. I want everyone else to know, too. Mark always led with his heart, or his gut. When he cares about something, no matter how trivial it seems to anyone else, he goes all in. That's part of what made me fall in love with him in the first place. I wouldn't say I'm overly cautious, but I am analytical. I want to assess the situation and see if it stands up to scrutiny.

MPS: There's value in both approaches.

TW: I agree. So, me being me, I wanted to stay out of it, mostly because I knew that if I got involved, we'd both get frustrated. The problem was, there were all these things happening that I, a rational adult human, couldn't explain. Mark's sleep-talking. Whatever, lots of people talk in their sleep. But do they sound like that? There were the sounds outside our door. The message from Thurman Mueller saying he was going to give a tape to Mark Cambria, even though the message had been recorded over twenty years ago, long before Mark knew Mueller existed. I kept thinking there had to be a logical explanation, but there never was. I just wanted to make it all make sense.

MPS: So you decided to help Mark pursue the answers, at least for a while. Eventually you asked him to stop.

TW: Of course I did! Someone broke into our apartment. Everything related to the White Tapes project was stolen, but nothing else. Who did it? Why? Nobody knows! That same day, our friend Cat, who'd been working with us, was nearly killed in a brutal car accident. Could be coincidence. People get in car accidents. But somehow Cat was the only one who got hurt? I didn't know what was happening, and I didn't care. We were in danger. We had to stop.

MPS: Mark disagreed with you. He wanted to keep going.

TW: He *had* to keep going. He was compelled. That's what I've been telling myself, anyway, because otherwise I go down dark holes of thinking, *I should have said this, I should have done that.*

MPS: There's nothing you could have said that would have changed his mind.

TW: No, probably not. He snuck out while I was sleeping and went to the piano shop by himself. From the recording, I know Randy Wane was there. And some others. I don't know what they were doing or what they did to Mark. I just know he screamed, "Ota Keta," the same weird thing he'd been saying in his sleep—and then the recording stopped.

MPS: The next day, you had a package at your door: a new White Tape.

TW: I should've thrown it away, or pretended I didn't see it. At the time, I just wanted to know where Mark was, and I thought maybe the tape would tell me.

MPS: You watched it, you even managed to isolate a voice—

TW: It sounded like Mark, saying that phrase: "Ota Keta."

MPS: You think it was him.

TW: I *know* it was him. That's when, I guess, my perspective changed a little. At an intellectual level, I still had a lot of trouble believing things I'd seen with my own eyes. Then I realized that skepticism wasn't going to help me or Mark. I had to find out what all of this meant, even if I had to do it myself.

MPS: I want to talk about those first few weeks he was gone. For me, as your friend, it was terrifying. You were barely functioning. I've known you a long time, and I'd never seen you so upset. You kept talking about evil, something was evil, "they" took Mark. Nobody understood who you meant by "they." Many of our friends were under the impression that the podcast was a *War of the Worlds* thing. But Mark was really, in reality, gone. You tried to explain—

TW: At first I thought it was important to tell people everything. I knew how unbelievable it sounded. But as I've learned, things can be both unbelievable and very, very real.

MPS: To be clear, you believe in the White Tapes.

TW: Yeah. I guess I do.

MPS: What exactly do you believe?

TW: *[long pause]* I believe the White Tapes are a system of some kind. Individual elements, and together they add up to something. What that is, I'm not sure. That's what you and I have been trying to figure out. I believe it involves— It's weird to say this out loud.

MPS: I know.

TW: I believe the White Tapes are connected to something that isn't part of this world. God, I sound crazy.

MPS: No, you don't. That's what I believe, too.

TW: It's something evil, something that's capable of destroying people. I think that's what it wants. Mark put some of the pieces together, so either he had to be taken away because he was a threat, or—

MPS: Or what?

TW: Or he was one of the pieces, too.

MPS: Right.

TW: You were one of the only people who didn't think I had lost my mind.

MPS: Well, no offense, you're not a great liar. You played me the recordings you guys made, even the stuff that didn't make it in the podcast. For me, even as a fellow skeptic, that was all the proof I needed. And, bottom line, Mark isn't here. We've gone over every plausible explanation. That leaves the implausible explanations.

TW: I've lost friends over this. People drifted away. . . . I knew they were saying things about me.

MPS: They didn't know how to process it. There's no con-text for this. Humans tend to shut down when we can't make sense of things.

TW: Remember that grief counselor I saw? After our first session, she said I had PTSD. A week later, she said, no, I was experiencing a break with reality. I screamed at her: "I *told* you the reality! You won't accept it. *You're* the one who's not in touch with reality." I didn't go back after that. I started keeping more to myself. I'm grateful you stuck with me—and Cat, of course.

MPS: We should give an update here about Cat. When the podcast ended, she was just starting to recover from that massive car accident.

TW: Yeah. God, she's been so strong. Becca, too. Thank goodness Becca's job has health insurance; they would've gone bankrupt otherwise. Cat's doing better, but it's been a long road. Traumatic brain injuries can leave you with symptoms for the rest of your life. She gets dizzy spells, headaches. It affected her hearing. She can't use head-phones, or listen to anything above a certain volume, or tolerate certain frequencies. If she's in a restaurant that's playing music, she has trouble isolating conversations—same with loud soundtracks and movie dialogue. It all blurs together.

MPS: Which would suck for anybody, but for Cat, it meant giving up her career as a composer.

TW: Everything she'd worked for. Her whole future was taken away, just like that. She's collecting disability now, which she needs financially, but it's been hard for her to accept.

MPS: She's started volunteering at that senior care center, which seems like a healthy step. It gets her out of the apartment, gives her something to feel good about.

TW: The old folks love her. It's quiet there. They tell her all their stories; they like having someone who listens to them. You know Cat: she always does things for other people. Even before she got home from the hospital, she was apologizing to me for not being able to help with the tapes. It was impossible, given her hearing issues, and it broke her heart.

MPS: Speaking of not being able to help . . . the police?

TW: What an infuriating experience. There was one officer who went to the piano shop with me, the day after I last saw Mark. The basement was totally empty. He was nice, but I think he was like, "You're wasting my time, lady." A few days later, you and I went to my local precinct and asked to speak with a detective. They took down Mark's information: date of birth, what he looked like, where he worked, what he'd been wearing. Did he have health problems, did he take any medication? Did he drink or use drugs? Even before I had a chance to explain *how* he'd gone missing, I could tell the detective didn't think this was particularly urgent. So instead of giving all the details, I just said Mark had gone to visit someone on Staten Island, he uploaded a recording of himself in distress and then he hadn't come home.

MPS: I said we suspected a crime. It can't be a lie if you don't know the truth, right? I've watched enough *Law & Order* to know that unless a missing person is very old, very young, suffering from mental or physical conditions or a crime victim, the police won't bother starting an investigation.

TW: He asked more than once if Mark had "some type of mental problems."

MPS: You could've said he'd been experiencing delusions, hearing voices, seeing things that weren't there. Everything would make sense that way, right? "He made up this story about a piano shop on Staten Island, a cult, weird voices, these white videotapes. He was fixated. He genuinely thought it was real."

TW: I know. Trust me, I've thought about that. If I had chalked it up to mental illness, maybe they would've prioritized his case.

MPS: Why didn't you?

TW: Because it's not true. Even if I can't do anything else, Mark would want me to tell the truth. That's the one thing I know for sure. I owe him that much. . . . I'm sorry.

MPS: Do you want to take a break?

TW: Sorry. I just— Yeah, let's take a break.

MPS: All right. We're back. When we left off, we were talking about the police investigation, or lack thereof. I was determined not to let the case get lost in the system.

TW: You kept after them. I was in no shape to make calls and take down notes about how many messages we'd left, who called back, who didn't.

MPS: About a week after we filed the initial report, the detective assigned to the case got transferred to a different precinct. So the file got passed to someone else. The new guy had a huge backlog of cases already. I left so many messages. Eventually he called back and talked to you for, what, fifteen minutes?

TW: Something like that. I knew it was a lost cause. Before I'd even finished what I was saying, he cut me off and said it sounded like Mark had ghosted. That's the exact word he used.

MPS: Because you mentioned you'd had an argument.

TW: He was like, "Well, guys do that, if you put too much pressure on them." What was I supposed to say?

MPS: I thought of some things I wanted to say. I was furious. I tried contacting his commanding officer, but he never called back.

TW: We made one last call to the detective, and he said he'd closed the file. And that was that.

MPS: We knew we were on our own. I think that's the way

it's supposed to be. So the next thing I want to talk about is the podcast.

TW: He was so excited about selling it to Shudder. Mark isn't the most—He doesn't always give himself enough credit. But he was proud of that deal, and he wanted the podcast to be a hit. It deserved to be.

MPS: It's got a niche, which is really the only way to stand out in this world of a million podcasts. I mean, fourteen new podcasts have launched in the time we've been talking. And true crime is one of the most popular genres there is.

TW: I used to listen to true crime podcasts myself, although I haven't been in the mood for them lately. They can be downright addictive. If that's what you're into, you always want more, and there's a whole community of people who feel the same way. There are people who go out and try to solve cold cases on their own. Conspiracy theorists. It can go far, far beyond the podcast itself.

MPS: You might even say that some people become obsessed.

TW: Yes. That's the part I hadn't expected. Maybe I should have. I didn't anticipate the level of interest that started to build up in certain corners of the Internet. Initially, it seemed like a positive thing. Maybe someone would hear the podcast and come forward with information. Mark spoke to all those people who knew about the White Tapes, right? Surely there are more people out there. I thought one of them might find us and be able to help.

MPS: Except that didn't happen.

TW: No. No. I'm trying to think of a polite way to say this. There were plenty of normal—not normal, just—people who listened and thought it was interesting enough to discuss online. "Normal" isn't the right word; I don't want to offend anyone.

MPS: What you're getting at is the subset of people who took it too far.

TW: You found those reddit posts.

MPS: There was a whole subreddit about the podcast. Several Facebook groups. And long threads on conspiracy forums, some truly weird ones.

TW: I couldn't believe the stories people came up with. There was a theory about Mark working for the NSA. Someone posted photos from his Facebook account next to photos of another man, saying they were the same person, but Mark had gotten a nose job to disguise himself. They said the White Tapes were part of a government experiment to link people's minds to surveillance satellites. There were thousands of comments about that. They figured out that someone Mark went to college with worked for an intelligence contractor and had top secret security clearance. They got this poor man's address and phone number; they called his house. He had no idea what was going on.

MPS: There was the one with the newspaper story.

TW: Oh, that was ridiculous. It turns out there are several Randy Wanes in the world. One of them lives outside Chicago, and in the 1980s he owned a VCR repair business. He was interviewed for a *Tribune* story about small business owners, and they ran a photo of him in his office. He's leaning against a desk with a window behind him, looking out on the store. There was a vertical shadow barely visible against the back wall, half obscured by Randy's shoulder. Some people said it looked like Mark in profile. Other people said it was the Eyeless Man reaching toward the window.

MPS: I'm pretty sure it was a coatrack.

TW: The worst one, though, was the story about Mark being a serial killer. They said he'd killed the Klims in 1998. How could he do that? He was in high school. But that was the idea, that he started young and used different identities, and then he made the podcast as a way of luring more victims. They said he killed Thurman Mueller and Jacob Manders and a woman who worked at a horror film festival in Atlanta. And he faked his disappearance so he could escape his crimes and resurface later as someone else. Some of them even said he'd killed *me*.

MPS: Can I confirm that you are alive?

TW: Yes, I am. That's an exclusive.

MPS: Mark's classmate wasn't the only one who got doxxed. People tracked you down, too.

TW: You read about these kinds of things. I didn't understand until it happened to me. I started getting mail—letters, packages, big envelopes. I was scared to open any of it. But what if there was a clue? What if someone found something useful? We opened everything together.

MPS: Wearing gloves and face masks.

TW: It seemed safer that way. Who knows? It was the same garbage I saw online, just taking up space in my apartment. People sent blank videotapes, tapes of themselves ranting. I made you watch. I couldn't bring myself to do it.

MPS: There were a few fake White Tapes made by people who'd obviously never seen a real one.

TW: I got phone calls, too. I had to change my number. I don't know how they found the new number, but they did, so I changed it again. The calls were worse than the mail. I never picked up if it wasn't someone from my contacts. Most of the messages were dumb, like, "Hey, Tamra, uhh, I got your number." But sometimes there'd be creepy voices saying, you know, "Tamra, you're next. I'm watching you." Heavy breathing. One guy called and pretended to be Mark. Who would do something so cruel?

MPS: The final straw was when they started showing up at your apartment.

TW: It was surreal. I'd find notes under my door. Or people would knock and run away. One time I left my building and there was a tall guy standing at the end of the block. He was wearing a long coat with layers underneath; he had scarves wrapped around his face and head. He started coming toward me. I wanted to run, but I couldn't; my whole body went cold and wouldn't move. I heard myself scream. Luckily a neighbor walked by with her dog and yelled at him to leave me alone. The dog barked up a storm. The guy took off, and when he turned around, he dropped one of the scarves, so I got a look at his face.

MPS: It wasn't the Eyeless Man.

TW: Not even close. He had eyes. Also a nose ring and a stupid goatee. But he sure was trying to make me think he was the Eyeless Man.

MPS: You decided to move. We'd discussed it for a while; you just didn't want to leave.

TW: I loved that apartment so much. We'd been there for two and a half years. Moving into a studio by myself was like, oh, okay. I *am* alone. My biggest worry was that Mark would manage to find his way home and I wouldn't be there. I still think about that.

MPS: It was the right thing to do. You had to put your safety first.

TW: I know. And I really couldn't afford to stay there anyway. I figure if—when—Mark gets back, we'll find another place. Bigger. Maybe I'll finally convince him to get a dog.

MPS: When I look around here, I see a lot of his stuff. Those shelves are all his books. Those posters. You have his sweaters in the closet.

TW: I didn't have room for everything. Mark was an ... avid collector, if you will. Some things had to go to a storage unit. The rest, what was I going to do? Throw it away?

MPS: It's a strange kind of purgatory you're in. At least when people die, when you know they've died, that's the end. All you have to do is accept it—which, I'm not saying that's easy, but there's clarity. You don't have that.

TW: None whatsoever. That's why I spend almost every waking moment thinking about where he might be. It's the last thought I have before I fall asleep; it's the first thing I think when I wake up.

MPS: I want to ask you a hard question, and you don't have to answer if you don't want to. We've never really talked about this. Is there any part of you, any at all, that thinks he is dead?

TW: No.

MPS: No?

TW: If I thought that, I wouldn't be able to do the work we've been doing. How many hours have we spent—you, me, both of us together?

MPS: I can't even guess. Hundreds. Many hundreds.

TW: I'm happiest when we're working. Staying up late, researching noise colors and frequencies. Going through Mark's recordings again, looking for clues online. It's the only thing that makes me feel human. The rest of the time, I don't know what I am.

MPS: We took a couple of field trips to Staten Island, which turned out to be pointless. The Internet gave us more to go on.

TW: I found a post on a message board from the early aughts where people wrote amateur movie reviews. Someone made a post with the address of Randy Wane's piano shop. Just the address, nothing else. The poster deleted their account, so their profile was gone, and the post replies had been removed, too. When I tried to contact the board admins, my emails bounced. It seems like a minor thing, but why would someone post a random address in Staten Island on a movie review board? That's no coincidence. It has to be connected.

MPS: Connected to—

TW: To Randy. To the White Tapes. I don't think Randy made the White Tapes, but I do think he's part of whatever they're trying to accomplish.

MPS: What about Thurman Mueller? Let's talk about that little adventure.

TW: Well, I worked up my chutzpah and called his wife, Bets. She almost hung up on me when I mentioned Mark's name, but then I told her, no, no, he's gone. I think she felt sorry for me—after all, she'd been through the same thing. Losing the person she loved, not knowing what happened. I said something like, "I lie awake every night wondering where he is," and she said, "I know, dear, I did the same thing until Thurman came home."

MPS: Record scratch!

TW: Yeah. I was not expecting that. I asked if we could visit, if we could meet him. She wasn't into it. She kept saying he wasn't well, he wasn't himself. I promised we wouldn't stay long. I was dying to know all the details, what he'd told her, what she meant when she said he wasn't well, how he came back. But I knew if I kept asking questions, she'd never say yes. Finally she agreed to let us visit, on one condition: no recording of any kind. It seemed like a pretty good deal. She told us to drive up on a Saturday when Shane, their son, wouldn't be around. She said he didn't like people coming around to bother his dad.

MPS: What were you thinking when we pulled into that driveway?

TW: I was thinking that Mark had described the place perfectly. I'd never been there, but it felt familiar because I'd heard him talk about it. There was the porch, the screen door; we could hear the dog barking when we got out of the car. Going up the front steps, it hit me: Mark had been here. He'd stood on this doorstep without me, waiting for Bets Mueller. And there I was on the doorstep, without him.

MPS: I was expecting Bets to be more wary and the house to be more cluttered inside. That was a surprise. She didn't seem thrilled to see us, exactly, but she was very polite.

TW: They must've cleaned things up since Mark was there. I remember him telling me the living room was piled with old newspapers, cardboard boxes, all kinds of junk. It looked tidy to me. Run-down but well kept. And you're right, Bets was being a good hostess. She offered us coffee. We chit-chatted about the drive. I was getting antsy. Enough small talk, let's meet your mysterious husband!

MPS: Honestly, I got the sense that she was enjoying having someone to talk to.

TW: Right? I thought that as well. Then you said something about not wanting to take up too much of their time, and she seemed to remember why we were there.

MPS: She led us down the hall to the den. Which, again, was exactly the way Mark had described it, although it looked better, the top of the desk was clean, everything had been dusted.

TW: The whole movie collection was there. Floor-to-ceiling shelves, completely full. I was so distracted, I almost didn't notice Thurman asleep in the recliner. He seemed small and frail, curled up under a blanket.

MPS: Bets woke him up very gently. She said, "Some friends are here to see you."

TW: He jerked his head around, all disoriented. His eyes were clouded with thick cataracts, and there was a weird strip of skin over his eyes, or something. I don't know. I didn't want to stare.

MPS: It looked like the pink bits at the inner corners of his eyes had grown up and over the white part of his eyeballs.

TW: Bets had warned us that he was basically blind and had lost the ability to speak. She said they'd gone to the hospital at Dartmouth, but none of the specialists could decide what had caused all this damage. The consensus was that he had suffered various traumas, and the damage was permanent, so there wasn't much to be done except keep him comfortable.

MPS: He turned toward us when you introduced yourself, so his hearing was okay. He kind of grunted.

TW: Bets said, "That's his way of saying hello!"

MPS: She was trying very, very hard to keep the tone light.

TW: I asked if I could talk with him about his movie collection, about some movies he'd seen, and he groaned. Bets was like, "He says that's fine! He loves movies! You do love movies, don't you, dear?" He pulled himself up in the chair and groaned louder, like he was trying to tell her something.

MPS: She said he had just reminded her to take her blood pressure medication.

TW: Who knows, maybe he had.

MPS: So Bets left. You were just about to ask Thurman another question when he leaned forward and stared at you. I thought, well, he must be able to see shapes or shadows. It was like he really wanted to get a good look at you.

TW: I came closer because I thought that would help him. He was shaking a little. He sort of squinted and strained his eyes, and they rolled back in his head, like he was having a seizure.

MPS: I was just about to run down the hall and find Bets when he grabbed your arm. He was looking right at you, and he must've seen you too, because the membrane over his eye had slipped away. The only thing I can compare it to is when I wake up my cat and she's still half asleep. Cats have that little inner eyelid that retracts.

TW: I was too startled to move. I didn't think he was strong enough to hold on to anything, but there we were. He tugged at my wrist, and his lips were moving, so I leaned down.

MPS: And what did he say?

TW: He said, "He's not all gone yet." Then he collapsed into the chair and closed his eyes. Bets came back a second later, and when she called his name, he looked toward her voice, and his eyes were all clouded over again.

MPS: We spent about fifteen minutes with them after that, awkwardly asking Thurman about his movies while he lay there and ignored us.

TW: There was no point in staying. Bets said he was getting tired, which was our cue to leave. Besides, I wanted to get back in the car and talk about that crazy thing he did when we were alone.

MPS: "He's not all gone yet." How do you interpret that?

TW: Well, call me an optimist, but it has to be a good thing, right?

MPS: I hope so. We got back to New York and tried researching the Muellers some more, but we didn't find anything. And when I called again, they didn't pick up.

TW: So, fine, forget them. Thurman told us all he could. I realize this sounds woo-woo. I just have a sense, a very strong sense, that when we hit a dead end, it's because we're not going in the right direction. Maybe I'm delusional. I don't know. I think everything we need will find us eventually, as long as we keep looking for it.

MPS: Well, and that leads us to our latest clue, or what we assume is a clue. Last week, my friend Jessica posted a photo on Instagram. She's from Maine, where I grew up, and she's a librarian, like you. She recently started a job at the Portland Public Library, and this photo was taken at the library's off-site storage building. It was a pile of old videotapes, hashtag LibraryLife, hashtag ArchiveFinds. I almost scrolled by until I noticed a white case sticking out from the bottom of the pile. There was no title on the spine. So I DM'd and asked if she could send a close-up of that one white tape and tell me where it came from.

Turns out, the tapes in the picture were from the Videoport collection. You know it takes a lot to make me cry, but I get choked up thinking about that place. Videoport was a Portland institution for almost thirty years. They had the best selection of movies I've ever seen—new, old, obscure, weird, really weird. The people who worked there were opinionated in the best way. I missed it when I moved to New York, and I was heartbroken when I heard it was shutting down. I assumed rent hikes were to blame—that part of town gets bougie-er by the day—but the owner said streaming services did him in.

TW: Makes sense. They can't compete, there's no way.

MPS: I know. And I'm part of the problem. Watching Netflix is so easy, you hardly notice you're doing it. When I stop and think, though, like when I remember running my fingertips along a shelf of staff picks, or leaning on the counter arguing about whether or not Lars von Trier is overrated, I do feel a little guilty.

TW: Now that you mention it, I guess I do, too. And he is overrated.

MPS: Correct answer! Anyway, after Videoport closed in August 2015, its entire collection—some eighteen thousand titles—was donated to the Portland library. Jessica explained that a selection of the most popular movies went into regular circulation. Everything else was put in storage. She was working to inventory the off-site titles, checking their condition and prioritizing preservation needs. Then she sent a second message with a photo of the tape in the white case, and my heart almost stopped. It had a hand-written label on the front. *Sans L'Oeil*. Which is French for "Without the Eye."

TW: You forwarded it to me, and I was like, that's it. We're going to Portland. Whatever this is, we need to see it ourselves.

MPS: We headed up a couple days later. I should mention that I'd noticed something else about the *Sans L'Oeil* tape. It was bigger than a normal VHS. I'd gone down a rabbit hole over the summer, so I recognized it right away. It was a U-matic, the first video format that stored tape in cassettes. Before that came along, tape was on open reels. Jessica hadn't been able to watch it because the library didn't have a U-matic machine.

Luckily, I knew someone who could help: my friend Rich is obsessed with old electronics. You name it, he's bought it from eBay. His house is full of tube TVs, video game hardware, broken printers, homemade effects pedals, Frankensteined circuit boards. . . . He tinkers around and makes cool blippy music with it. He had a U-matic video player circa 1974 in his basement, because of course he did. He agreed to meet us at the library's storage facility.

TW: You played some of his music on the way up. It's surprisingly catchy.

MPS: I have to say, though, that drive felt like forever. I was running on pure adrenaline. By the time we crossed the bridge from Portsmouth to Kittery, I couldn't tell whether I wanted the U-matic to be part of the puzzle or not. What about you? How were you feeling?

TW: *[long pause]* Hopeful.

MPS: Not nervous? Or scared?

TW: The only thing I was afraid of was that we'd get there and find out it was just a student film or an old TV show.

MPS: You wanted it to be part of whatever the White Tapes are.

TW: I did.

MPS: Even though the White Tapes are directly connected to whatever or whoever it was that took Mark.

TW: Look, the White Tapes frighten me. The more we learn, the more frightening they become, but nothing is as terrifying as not knowing what happened to Mark.

MPS: Talk me through what we did when we got to Portland.

TW: Well, we met Jessica at the storage facility a little after five p.m. It's a warehouse in the middle of nowhere, behind some office parks. Everyone else had left for the day. Rich showed up a few minutes later with the U-matic player, this clunky metal box with a separate power unit. It must've weighed forty pounds. We lugged it inside to an office where the archivists work. You hadn't told your friends the real reason we were so interested in this old tape.

MPS: I said it was for a story I was writing. It seemed easier that way.

TW: Rich hooked up the player to a TV/VCR combo while you and I examined the tape. There were no markings, nothing; the tape itself wasn't even labeled. Just the label on the front of the case, old-fashioned cursive handwriting on yellowish paper. We put in the tape and pressed play. At first there was nothing but static. No sound.

MPS: I had a sinking feeling that the tape was damaged.

TW: The static went on for a few minutes. We were just about to stop it when an image came on the screen.

MPS: Describe what we saw next.

TW: The picture was a little fuzzy, but not too bad. Black-and-white. There was a young woman sitting on a chair in front of a television set. The room was otherwise empty. No doors, no windows, at least not in the frame. She was wearing a cardigan, and her hair was curled, very 1950s style. The way it was shot, we could see her face and torso and the back of the TV, but we couldn't see the TV screen. She looked . . . I don't know, out of it. Dazed. She just sat there blinking at the screen in front of her.

MPS: Rich was like, "Is this a movie? Is she acting?" We couldn't tell.

TW: After a few moments there were footsteps off camera. A door opening and closing—someone entering the room. Then we heard a man's voice: "Begin."

The TV came on. You could tell because light flickered across her face. She focused on the screen. She raised one arm over her head, then her other arm. She wiggled her fingers, threw her head back, laughed hysterically, then stopped. She tapped each elbow four times. It seemed like she was mirroring whatever she was watching.

All of a sudden, she sat bolt upright and pulled a pair of scissors from her skirt pocket. Just like that, she cut off a chunk of her hair, a good five inches, right in front. And then she froze. The vacant stare broke for a second, she had this look—I've never seen anyone look like that.

MPS: Like an animal. Sheer terror.

TW: She was struggling to stay in her chair. And then— fuck. I haven't been able to get the image of this out of my mind. Her arm flew up. She jabbed the scissors into her right eye. Over and over and over. No hesitation. In complete silence.

I looked away when I heard you stumble against the wall. Right before Rich turned off the TV, I heard a laugh, a little chuckle. It was the man off camera.

MPS: For the record, I didn't faint, but I came close. If I hadn't sat on the floor, I would have blacked out for sure. I can't handle sharp objects and bodies. I have to take Xanax just to get a flu shot. Real life, TV, it doesn't matter. And this came out of nowhere. It was so shocking—worse than that scene in *Pulp Fiction*.

TW: You passed out then, too.

MPS: I did. And then there was an awkward moment. Jessica and Rich wanted to know how this awful tape was going to help me with a story.

TW: We ended up telling them everything, or almost everything. I was expecting them to be confused, or weirded out, but no. They both offered to help.

MPS: I have this theory that growing up in Maine makes you more predisposed to accept certain ideas. We've all seen things in the woods, or heard things. My dad's office building is a hundred and sixty years old; there's at least one ghost that I know of. I always say Stephen King is eighty-five percent fiction, fifteen percent just driving around Maine.

TW: And that is why I live in New York. Anyway, Rich volunteered to take the tape home with him and transfer it to a digital format. We went to Jessica's place and talked some more over dinner. That U-matic tape was nothing like the White Tapes. Was it related to them? I thought it must be. But how? We stayed up until almost two in the morning. I had trouble falling asleep, even though I was exhausted.

MPS: Me, too.

TW: We got up early to drive home. You drove the first leg so I could sleep, we switched in Worcester, you dozed off. And then—I don't know how this happened. You tell this part.

MPS: When I woke up, we were back in the city, but not here, where you live now. You'd driven to your block on the Upper West Side and parked in front of your old building.

TW: I don't know what I was doing. I guess I was on auto-pilot.

MPS: Old habits die hard. Plus, you were operating on two hours of sleep.

TW: Yeah. We laughed it off. What else could we do?

MPS: And that was two days ago, so we're all caught up, at least for the purposes of this conversation.

TW: I'm going to sound like a broken record, but I really wish Mark were here.

MPS: I know.

TW: He'd be so excited about that U-matic thing. He'd take it apart frame by frame. It still feels weird doing this without him. Life in general feels weird without him, but this especially. I do the dumbest things. Have I told you this? Every night I watch a video of him on my phone. I went through my camera roll, years and years of pictures and videos, and I put them in a folder so I can look at them whenever I want. Here. See? This is us at the Jersey Shore a couple summers ago. Remember I forgot to wear sunscreen?

MPS: Oh, my God, yes.

TW: Mark looked up all the ways you can treat sunburn, so every night he'd cover me with aloe gel and cold tea bags. Wait, go back, that's a good video.

MPS: This one?

TW: Yeah. From his birthday in 2016. It's him doing his karaoke song—

MPS: "Heaven Knows I'm Miserable Now."

TW: Let's watch.

[Faint sound of a man's voice singing, horribly off-key.]

MPS: Please, I can't take it anymore. Make it stop.

TW: I also have pictures from our— Hold on.

MPS: What?

TW: Rich just emailed. Do you want me to read it out loud? For the interview, in case it's helpful?

MPS: Sure, go ahead.

TW: Okay. *[pause]* He says that, based on the signal loss and sync issues, the U-matic tape is from the early 1970s. And it's a copy of a sixteen-millimeter original that was probably a few decades old by the time it was duplicated.

MPS: That puts us in the 1950s, or thereabouts.

TW: He sent a link to the digital version. He says it won't look the same as the tape, it's degraded, but at least we have it for reference. We should check to make sure it plays properly.

[The distant sound of static, for nearly two minutes, followed by a muffled voice saying, "Begin."]

TW: It works. We don't have to watch the whole thing right now.

MPS: We can do it tomorrow. I promise I won't faint! Hey, we've been talking since five o'clock; I have enough for the interview. Is there anything else you'd like to add?

TW: No, I've said what I wanted to say. It felt good to get it all out, actually.

MPS: I'm glad. You did great. I'll pack up my recording stuff in a minute, I just have to pee.

[Pause]

TW: Hey, Mary? Did you move anything around in my phone?

MPS: Just a sec, I can't hear you. I'll be right there.

[Pause]

TW: When you were looking at my phone. Did you change anything? Or rename the album I showed you?

MPS: No, why?

TW: Look.

MPS: What?

TW: My photos app. See the list of albums? It's gone. The album we were looking at just now was called Mark Favorites. It had all my pictures of him. All the videos. It's gone.

MPS: Did you delete it? Scroll down, there's a recently deleted folder. Open that.

TW: It's not there!

MPS: You must've tapped something by mistake. Don't worry. Deleting an album doesn't delete the photos. Here. Go to all photos. Actually—jump to 2016. Scroll down. The birthday videos will show up in April.

TW: No. They're gone.

MPS: Are you sure?

TW: Yes! See? April, April, April, and then nothing until May. How could this happen?

MPS: I don't know. You back up your data somewhere, don't you?

TW: Yes! Oh, my God, I almost forgot. My camera roll backs up to my cloud storage account automatically.

MPS: So you can use that to restore the photos and re-create the album.

TW: Hold on, hold on, here it is—camera uploads. This is a mess, it's every photo and video I've ever taken, I never bothered to organize it. . . . There should be . . . oh, no. No no no—

MPS: Is the—

TW: This can't be. No. They're not here. The pictures we saw five minutes ago.

MPS: Do you have another uploads folder?

TW: Mary, listen to me, they're gone. All my photos and videos of Mark are gone. They're not on my phone. They're not in my cloud backup. They don't exist anymore. What the fuck? That's not an accident, right? It can't be an accident.

MPS: Okay, okay, let's think. . . . Wait, I'm just turning this off.

TW: *Fuck.*

Postscript: I'm doing a final edit of this transcript two weeks after Tamra and I spoke. Prof. Wills suggested I add an update about the lost photos. Update: they're still lost. Tamra took her phone and computer to a repair shop, but they weren't able to recover anything. Luckily, she has some framed photos of Mark that she's hanging on to. And I had a couple of cute photos of the two of them together on my phone, so I printed them out and made a little collage. We know that whatever happened to Tamra's photos is another piece of the key that unlocks this whole mystery. We're still trying to put it together. I suspect we'll be trying for a long time.

I want to add one last thing. I haven't told Tamra this yet, and part of me thinks I'm being paranoid, but an even greater part of me wants to write this down in case—well, just in case. I came home this evening and found a small package outside my apartment door. I knew what it was. I didn't even need to pick it up and see that there was no return address. I knew from the weight and the shape of it. Just under seven ounces, four inches wide and about seven and a half inches long. I could have ignored it. Nothing made me pick it up and bring it inside, yet that's exactly what I did. I put it on my desk, where I'm writing this now. For the past half hour I've been sitting here thinking about choices—why we choose one action over another, why we regret the things we haven't done, why we think we know what our choices even are.

There's still time to get rid of this package. To toss it down the garbage chute and pretend I never saw it. But you know I can't do that, right? You understand.

DANIEL CARTER: THE END OF THE BEGINNING

Carter here.

Several weeks passed with no word from the professor. Sad but not unexpected, given his last missive. I continued teaching his classes and covering for him when the faculty asked questions. (I also dispelled the rumors they circulated. None stranger than the truth.)

Then one day I received this email:

To: Carter, Daniel
From: Wills, Maynard T.

Dearest Daniel,

I will not be returning. I have made arrangements such that you will be taking on my teaching duties, at compensation equal to your talents. I am embarking on a quest of unknown length, and of unknown end, and so I want to say—should I not return—that I have always valued our friendship and that you will make an excellent teacher. A better one than I.

As one final favor to an old man: promise me that you'll finish my book and work with the fine people at Tiller Press. The wonderful friends who shared their stories deserve to have them heard. And the world should have a sense of the powers that lay beyond our understanding.

Goodbye, Daniel. And thank you.

Maynard

I emailed back, I called him, I ransacked his office (which is where I discovered the parchment paper and list in the previous chapter interlude). Finally, I decided to go to his house. The key was where I'd expected it to be, but what I found inside was not. Maynard was living in his own Static City.

The living room was absolutely full of televisions. All of them were on, humming as white snow illuminated all. The sound was like a rolling wave in my ears, like the sound you hear when you put your ear to a conch shell, times a thousand. Some sort of feedback loop in my head.

I walked into the kitchen, where a number of radios were all playing, also static, but some of them would occasionally allow a voice or a piece of music to come through, phantom bits of media flying through the air, getting picked up at random and funneled into this room. The sound in there was different from that of the televisions, but it had the same unnerving DNA.

I went room to room and in each I found more devices: vinyl record players, projectors and screens, smartphones, iPads, laptop computers, video games old and new. All were on and unattended. The sound and the feeling of all these devices just on and running sent chills up my spine, as if I could feel the electrons bouncing around like some kind of energetic radiation passing through my body.

At last I came to the professor's bedroom, which only contained a single television in it. This one also projected static, but here vague shadows danced in the chaos. Sounds ebbed and flowed from the speakers, and I found I was unable to tear myself away.

It was beautiful.

I lost my sense of time. I only abandoned the room after hours of staring into the static. I left all the screens on. I thought to turn it all off, but I couldn't. It felt like kicking over a sculpture. I had to let it live. To let it breathe.

My head was clearer the next morning. I called the police and filed a missing persons report. Maynard Wills hasn't been seen since. At the time of this final update, eight months have passed since the professor disappeared.

I have been interviewed numerous times by the police, the faculty; even the student newspaper asked my opinion on what happened to Professor Wills. I obviously can only speculate, but the best I can think is that he met up with this Z person, and perhaps Z's friends or colleagues, and they held some kind of a ritual in the professor's home. At that point, either they killed the professor for some reason, or they all went together to some other location. Perhaps a commune of some kind? Again, I can only speculate.

But one bit of speculation does keep floating through my head: What if the professor really did discover a gateway, a door like he talked about in his entries? What if he was right? Or what if he joined with the likes of Randy Wane, in search of, well, for lack of a better term, sacrifices?

I have resigned from the university and have dedicated my life to pursuing the truth of this mystery. Not only to find the professor, if he is still alive, but to unravel the thread that he began over a year ago.

I will begin traveling the world with the release of this book, seeking out more stories of the Eyeless Man and piecing together what the professor could not. There are answers to be had and I'm going to find them.

I have set up an email address: EyelessManSearch@gmail.com, where readers can submit their own stories and encounters with the Eyeless Man. Think of it as crowdsourcing evidence. Please send me your tales. I will also send you information about book signings and other appearances that I'll be making in the future, where you can come and meet me in person.

I want to meet all of you. I want to hear all your stories. We need your voices. Voices to cut through the static.

—Daniel Carter

CONTRIBUTORS

Bob DeRosa believes that nice guys finish first. His screenwriting credits include *Killers*, *The Air I Breathe*, *White Collar* and the award-winning horror/comedy web series *20 Seconds to Live*. His short story "Listening" was recently featured on the sci-fi podcast magazine *Escape Pod*. Bob cowrote *Video Palace* (along with frequent collaborator Ben Rock), and they are currently cowriting a horror audio drama for Audible Originals. When he's not writing, Bob studies Kenpo karate and keeps his Little Free Library stocked with good stuff. He lives in Los Angeles with his wife, Jen, and their delightful cats.

Meirav Devash is a writer who has reported on everything from eyeball tattoos to sustainable skincare to goth fitness. Formerly an editor at *Allure* magazine, she has contributed to *The New York Times*, *The New York Observer*, *Vogue*, *Goop*, *CNN Travel*, *Ocean Drive*, and more. She is an inexhaustible wellspring of knowledge about red lipstick and heavy metal. She lives in New York City with her husband, Eddie McNamara.

Owl Goingback has been writing professionally for over thirty years and is the author of numerous novels, children's books, screenplays, magazine articles, short stories and comics. He is a Bram Stoker Lifetime Achievement Award recipient, a Stoker Awards winner for best novel and best first novel and a Nebula Award nominee. His books include *Crota, Darker Than Night, Evil Whispers, Breed, Shaman Moon, Coyote Rage, Eagle Feathers, The Gift*, and *Tribal Screams*. In addition to writing under his own name, Owl has ghostwritten several books for Hollywood celebrities. He is a member of the Authors Guild, Science Fiction & Fantasy Writers of America and the Horror Writers Association.

Brea Grant is a writer, director and actor. She wrote and directed the film *Best Friends Forever* in 2013 and wrote and created the series *The Real Housewives of Horror* the following year. In 2019, she wrote and directed the film *12 Hour Shift*, which premiered at Tribeca in 2020, and three weeks later, she wrote and starred in the film *Lucky*, which premiered at SXSW in 2020. Grant has also written a number of comics, including a horror series set in the 1920s, *We Will Bury You*, and her upcoming series, *Mary*, about a distant relative of Mary Shelley. She also directs television, including the series *EastSiders* and CW's *Pandora*. You probably recognize her from *Heroes* or *Dexter*, and she is okay with that.

Merrin J. McCormick is a writer and creative director whose advertising campaigns have been recognized at international award shows. She lives and works in Chicago but was born and raised in Brisbane, Australia. When not using words as tools of persuasion, Merrin writes prose, poetry and pithy Instagram captions.

David Ian McKendry is a screenwriter and director residing in Los Angeles, California. He is a contributing writer for Fangoria Entertainment and the host of *Penning Terror* on the Fangoria Podcast Network. His fiction and nonfiction writings have been featured on Blumhouse.com and in *Fangoria* magazine, as well as in Clive Barker's *Hellraiser Anthology*, Volumes One and Two. David is a voice actor on the podcast *Fear Initiative*, holds an MFA in Screenwriting from California State University, Northridge, and is the father of two little monsters.

Rebekah McKendry is an award-winning director, writer and producer with a strong focus in the horror and science fiction genres. She has a doctorate in Media Studies focused on the horror genre from Virginia Commonwealth University, an MA in Film Studies from City University of New York, and a second MA from Virginia Tech in Arts Education. Rebekah previously worked as the editor in chief at Blumhouse Productions and as the director of marketing for Fangoria Entertainment. She is also a cohost of Blumhouse's award-winning *Shock Waves* podcast and the host of Fangoria's *Nightmare University* podcast.

Eddie McNamara is the author of *Toss Your Own Salad: The Meatless Cookbook* (St. Martin's Griffin). His crime fiction has been published in *J Journal, Thuglit, Shotgun Honey* and more. Formerly, he was a police officer, 9/11 first responder and *Penthouse* dating columnist. He writes about panic disorder and anxiety at *HealthCentral.com*. He lives in New York City with his wife, Meirav Devash.

Mary Phillips-Sandy is a writer and producer from central Maine, now living in New York. She is the creator and host of *Let's Talk About Cats*, a podcast that Digital Trends called "an emotional gut punch" (it is also funny, and about cats). She has written for/worked with Comedy Central, Hello Sunshine, Getty Images, *The New York Times*, *The Awl* (RIP), Quartz Creative, *The Mash-Up Americans*, Part and Sum and many more.

Ben Rock is a genre obsessive with extensive credits in features, TV, web, audio and live theater. As the production designer for *The Blair Witch Project*, he designed the iconic "Stickman," created much of the mythology for the franchise and wrote and/or directed multiple *Blair Witch* spin-offs for Syfy and Showtime. He's directed cutting-edge content to promote properties including *Hellboy*, *The 4400*, and *True Blood*, as well as the award-winning Warner Brothers/Raw Feed horror/sci-fi movie *Alien Raiders*. Most recently, he cocreated and directed the international award-winning horror/comedy web series *20 Seconds to Live* and cowrote (with Bob DeRosa) and directed *Video Palace*.

John Skipp is a Saturn Award–winning filmmaker (*Tales of Halloween*), Stoker Award–winning anthologist (*Demons*, *Mondo Zombie*) and *New York Times* bestselling author (*The Light at the End of the Tunnel*, *The Scream*) whose books have sold millions of copies in a dozen languages worldwide. In 1989, his first anthology, *Book of the Dead*, laid the foundation for modern zombie literature. He's also editor in chief of Fungasm Press, championing genre-melting authors like Laura Lee Bahr, Autumn Christian, Danger Slater, Cody Goodfellow, Jennifer Robin, S. G. Murphy and John Boden. From splatterpunk founding father to bizarro elder statesman, Skipp has influenced a generation of horror and counterculture artists around the world. His latest screenplay (with Dori Miller) is "Times Is Tough in Musky Holler," for Shudder's *Creepshow* series. His most recent book (with Heather Drain) is *The Bizarro Encyclopedia of Film, Volume 1.*

Graham Skipper is an actor, writer and director, best known for acting in films such as *Almost Human, Beyond the Gates, The Mind's Eye, Bliss* and *VFW*, as well as originating the role of Herbert West in Stuart Gordon's stage production of *Re-Animator: The Musical*. Graham's directorial debut, *Sequence Break*, is now available on Shudder. Graham is also the cofounder of the Rated R Speakeasy, based in Los Angeles. Graham lives in Los Angeles with his circus performer wife, Jordann, and their dog, Mufasa.

Gordon B. White has lived in North Carolina, New York and the Pacific Northwest. He is the author of the collection *As Summer's Mask Slips and Other Disruptions* (Trepidatio Publishing, 2020). A graduate of the Clarion West Writers Workshop, Gordon has written stories that have appeared in dozens of venues, including *The Best Horror of the Year, Volume 12* and the Bram Stoker Award–winning anthology *Borderlands 6*. He also contributes reviews and interviews to outlets including Nightmare, Lightspeed, Hellnotes, and *The Outer Dark* podcast. You can find him online at www.gordonbwhite.com.

ACKNOWLEDGMENTS

O N BEHALF OF Professor Maynard Wills, I, Daniel Carter, would like to thank the New School staff, for their patience and support.

For his interest, passion and friendship, Maynard is indebted to the great Dr. Peter Gilliam. He was also grateful for Carol Bernhardt's scholarship in the areas of nursery rhymes, folklore and the literature of children.

Maynard was very fond of his remaining friends in Old Town, Maine, and surrounding areas.

Gratitude is owed to all of Maynard's friends and colleagues who contributed stories to this book. Special thanks to Tamra Wulff, for her agreement to an interview, despite all that *Video Palace* and the Eyeless Man, whether myth or something more, have taken from her.

Maynard's cat, Baba Yaga, is safe and in my custody. He deeply misses his dear friend.

Personally, I would like to thank Nick Braccia and Mike Monello, the creators and producers of *Video Palace*, for their help organizing and completing this volume.

I'd also like to thank my parents, Anderson and Mildred

Carter, for their undying support, despite their understandable trepidation as this enterprise turned ever stranger.

Nick Braccia and Michael Monello would like to thank:

All the wonderful people at Tiller Press, especially editor Anja Schmidt, publisher Theresa DiMasi, the amazing art director Patrick Sullivan, Samantha Lubash, Sam Ford and Michael Andersen.

Our friends at Shudder and AMC, who have believed in the Eyeless Man and supported *Video Palace* from the beginning. Thank you, Nick Lazo, Andrea Glanz, Sean Redlitz, Madhu Goel Southworth, Trudie Eppich and Craig Engler.

Owen Shiflett, who, along with Nick Lazo, shepherded the podcast from its infancy.

Gary Adelman and the team at Adelman Matz.

The entire cast and crew of the *Video Palace* podcast.

Our Campfire friends, especially Steve Coulson and Mike Knowlton.

All *Video Palace* fans, listeners and readers. The Eyeless Man waits for you.

Nick Braccia would like to thank:

His partner, Amanda, and daughter, Evie Blue, for their support.

The late Dallas Mayr, aka Jack Ketchum, for inspiration, guidance and mentorship provided during a 2013 writing course.

Michael Monello would like to thank:

His wife, Julie, and his daughters, Ava and Lila, for their love, support and encouragement.

His parents, Joe and Olga, and his brother, Mark, for always being there.

Those friends who lent an ear, gave an encouraging word or offered a valuable piece of advice.

ABOUT THE AUTHORS

Dr. Maynard Wills is Associate Professor of Folklore at the New School in New York City. He's spent years studying and publishing urban legends, both domestically and globally. He consults in the entertainment industry and frequently gives talks on popular myths. He's had a career-long fascination with the entity he believes to be the Eyeless Man and was inspired by Shudder's *Video Palace* podcast to publish aspects of his work for a mass audience. At the time of publication, Dr. Wills is missing.

Nick Braccia is the author of *Off the Back of a Truck: Unofficial Contraband for the Sopranos Fan.* In 2018, he cocreated and co–executive produced *Video Palace* for AMC's streaming service Shudder. While working at the marketing agency Campfire, he developed award-winning immersive, narrative experiences for TV shows like *Outcast, Sense8, Watchmen, The Man in the High Castle, Westworld* and *The Purge.* Braccia is a member of the Producers Guild of America and lives in Manhattan with his partner, Amanda, and daughter, Evie Blue.

Michael Monello is a pioneer in immersive storytelling. In the late 1990s, Monello and his partners at Haxan Films created *The*

Blair Witch Project, a story told across multiple media that became a pop-culture touchstone. In 2006, Monello cofounded Campfire, which creates groundbreaking participatory stories and experiences for TV shows such as *True Blood, Game of Thrones, The Purge, The Man in the High Castle, Westworld, Hunters* and more. He cocreated and co–executive produced *Video Palace,* a scripted fiction horror podcast for Shudder. Monello lives in Brooklyn with his wife, Julie, and daughters, Ava and Lila.